Praise for
SO LET THEM BURN

"By turns hopeful and devastating, *So Let Them Burn* is a masterful debut with a blazing heart. I was captivated from beginning to end."

—**Chelsea Abdullah**, author of *The Stardust Thief*

"Set my soul on fire in the best way possible! Cole weaves an enthralling tale by way of an authentic and complex sibling relationship that swallowed me whole from the first page."

—**Terry J. Benton-Walker**, bestselling author of *Blood Debts*

"Gods, dragons, and mechanoids all war against one another in a deeply imaginative and fantastical twist on colonization and island history."

—**Namina Forna**, *New York Times* bestselling author of The Gilded Ones trilogy

"Clever and utterly fresh, *So Let Them Burn* takes the fantasy genre and soars into brilliant new heights, subverting expectations and hitting every mark."

—**Chloe Gong**, #1 *New York Times* bestselling author of *These Violent Delights*

"Cole weaves a powerful narrative full of captivating lore, meddling gods, and young women willing to do whatever it takes. A heart-pounding delight."

—**M. K. Lobb**, author of *Seven Faceless Saints*

"*So Let Them Burn* elevates the game, asking hard questions about the power and agency of a chosen one whose destiny has been seemingly fulfilled. By the time you see the claws, they're already around your throat."

—**Margaret Owen**, *New York Times* bestselling author of *Little Thieves* and *The Merciful Crow*

"A riveting adventure, a deft exploration of colonialism, and a deeply moving tale of a fierce and complex sisterly bond."

—**Ava Reid**, award-winning and internationally bestselling author of *A Study in Drowning*

"Kamilah Cole has crafted a captivating story.... With deft prose and stellar worldbuilding, this is an excellent new addition to YA fantasy."

—**Tara Sim**, author of *The City of Dusk*

"A thrilling epic about family, strength, and the real costs of war.... Truly DAZZLING. I am OBSESSED."

—**Aiden Thomas**, *New York Times* bestselling author of *Cemetery Boys*

"With characters who will grip you by the throat, a skillful commentary on colonialism, and an immersive world filled with dragons, danger, and deception, *So Let Them Burn* is a remarkable addition to the fantasy canon, establishing Cole as a powerful new voice in the genre."

—**Adrienne Tooley**, author of *Sweet & Bitter Magic* and *The Third Daughter*

"Tender, witty, and with a plot that will keep you glued to the page, *So Let Them Burn* is a beautiful exploration of what happens after becoming the chosen one—and how even when the legend ends, the story doesn't."

—**Hannah F. Whitten**, author of The Wilderwood duology

SO
LET
THEM
BURN

KAMILAH COLE

LITTLE, BROWN AND COMPANY
New York Boston

Copyright © 2024 by Kamilah Cole
Map illustration copyright © 2024 by Virginia Allyn
Flame pattern © Dana Bogatyreva/Shutterstock.com

Cover art copyright © 2024 by Taj Francis. Cover design by Jenny Kimura.
Cover copyright © 2024 by Hachette Book Group, Inc.
Interior design by Jenny Kimura.

Little, Brown and Company
Hachette Book Group
1290 Avenue of the Americas, New York, NY 10104
Visit us at LBYR.com

First Edition: January 2024

Little, Brown and Company is a division of Hachette Book Group, Inc. The Little, Brown name and logo are trademarks of Hachette Book Group, Inc.

The publisher is not responsible for websites (or their content) that are not owned by the publisher.

Little, Brown and Company books may be purchased in bulk for business, educational, or promotional use. For information, please contact your local bookseller or the Hachette Book Group Special Markets Department at special.markets@hbgusa.com.

Library of Congress Cataloging-in-Publication Data
Names: Cole, Kamilah, author.
Title: So let them burn / Kamilah Cole.
Description: First edition. | New York : Little, Brown and Company, 2024. | Series:
    Sisterbound | Summary: After her sister Elara forms an unbreakable bond with an
    enemy dragon, seventeen-year-old Faron, who once wielded the magic of the gods
    to save her island from those same dragon-riding colonizers, must find a way to
    save her sister and the fate of their world in the face of impossible odds.
Identifiers: LCCN 2023012901 | ISBN 9780316534635 (hardcover) |
    ISBN 9780316534840 (ebook)
Subjects: CYAC: Fantasy. | Sisters—Fiction. | Dragons—Fiction. |
    LCGFT: Fantasy fiction. | Novels.
Classification: LCC PZ7.1.C64285 So 2024 | DDC [Fic]—dc23
LC record available at https://lccn.loc.gov/2023012901

ISBNs: 978-0-316-53463-5 (hardcover); 978-0-316-53484-0 (ebook)

Printed in the United States of America

LSC-C

Printing 1, 2023

To Lauren:
Without you, this novel would still be a scribble
in the back of my math notebook.
And to Max:
Your memory will never be forgotten.

N

W   E

S

CINDER CIRCLE

ISALINA

EMBER SEA

LUNA

SAN IRIE

MARIÉN

ARGENT MOUNTAINS
HIGHFORT
SEAVIEW   DEADEGG
PORT SOL
KAÉRE   GUIRLAND
PEARL BAY
SAN OBIE   SAN·MALA

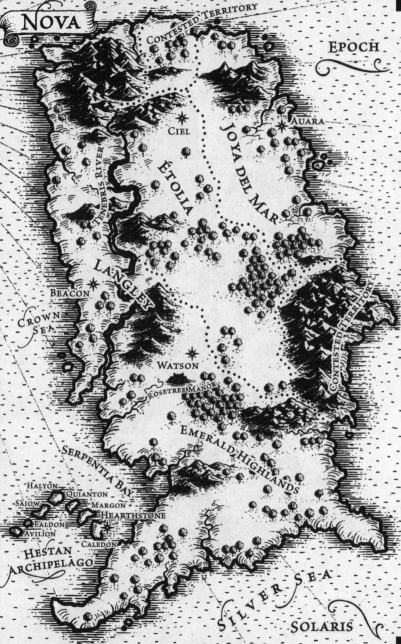

PART I

SEEKER

CHAPTER ONE

FARON

FARON VINCENT HAD BEEN A LIAR FOR LONGER THAN SHE'D BEEN A saint.

She'd learned from a young age that lies were a form of currency. They could buy freedom and earn forgiveness. They could alter reality faster than any kind of magic. A lie well told was itself magical, and Faron was nothing if not convincing.

She'd told three lies since this morning, and they'd each felt like a spell. She'd told her teacher that she'd try harder to bring up her grades before the end of the year. She'd promised her sister that she would go straight home after classes were over. And she'd sworn that she wouldn't use summoning to beat Jordan Simmons in this race.

Was it her fault they always believed her?

To be fair, Faron didn't always know she was lying in the moment. She'd intended to keep at least two of those promises— maybe all three, if she felt like acting particularly respectable. Then someone had spread around the schoolyard that she would be missing class to attend the Summit, and trouble had found her in the form of Jordan Simmons.

While the adults across the island of San Irie considered Faron a holy child, the same could not be said of her schoolmates. Jordan had approached her outside the gates, where she'd been standing in line to buy bag juice. The weather was the kind of hot that made her sorry to even be *alive*, and rolling up the sleeves of her shirtwaist had offered no relief. Faron had been watching the frost clouds curling from the vendor's open cart with such longing that she hadn't noticed Jordan until he was inches away from her.

"Missing school again, Vincent?" he'd sneered, flanked by two other fifth-form boys. Their horselike snickers had been a discordant note in her otherwise harmonious day. To anyone else, this might have signaled danger ahead. Faron, on the other hand, had only been bored. "Being the Empyrean is quite the con, isn't it?"

"If it were a *good* con," Faron had said without turning around, "then I wouldn't still be smelling the dung that comes out of your mouth."

She hadn't bothered to mention the reality of war or the lingering nightmares or the heavy expectations that came with being the Childe Empyrean. Five years ago, when the gods had first given her that title and the unique ability to summon their infinite magic, she had only been thinking of protecting San Irie. She hadn't realized what she was signing up for—or what she was signing away.

But even if she'd wanted to get into all of that with anyone, Jordan and his gang would have only used it against her. No one wanted to hear that being chosen by the gods to save the world was a curse rather than a blessing. She was a symbol, and symbols didn't complain.

Instead, Faron had traded a handful of silver coins for a

pineapple bag juice. While biting a hole in the corner of the bag to drink from, she'd eyed Jordan's calculating expression. He was the kind of bully who was too strategic to lose his temper. He thought about the best way to hobble his victims and *then* he struck to kill. So it had come as no surprise when he'd tried to hit her where it hurt: her pride.

"If you're so brilliant, then race me after school," he'd said. "No gods and no magic. The war is over. It's time to prove you're no better than any of us."

And Faron had never met trouble that she didn't want to get into. She'd extended her free hand with a smirk. "Thirty rayes if I win?"

"It's a deal."

With a handshake, Jordan Simmons had sealed his fate. Or so she'd thought then.

Now they were halfway through the agreed-upon track, surrounded by a screaming crowd of neighborhood kids, and Faron was losing.

Loose braids slapped her back and neck where they'd escaped from her head wrap. Palm trees waved in the wind. Her skirts were tied around her waist, allowing her nimble feet to dance over tan dirt and smooth stones. But here she was *losing* the footrace that would end at the fossilized dragon egg in the town square.

On this stretch of road, there were no shortcuts to take or obstacles to throw in her opponent's way. There was only a straight sprint to the egg and too much space between her and the boy in first place. Deal or no deal, that was unacceptable.

Faron held what little breath was still in her lungs and called on the gods.

Time slowed to a crawl, a second stretching into an eternity. The world took on a liquid haze, as if she'd plunged into the crystal-clear Ember Sea that surrounded the island. Her soul swelled into a beacon that screamed *come to me, come to me, come to me....*

And, like always, it was the gods who answered her call.

Irie appeared in a flash of light, her golden crown piercing the sky like a blade. She wore a hoodless robe, wide sleeved and embroidered with gold thread, over a white high-necked dress that fell to her calves. Her full gold-painted lips twisted into a frown. Even with her pupilless eyes shining amber, the sun goddess Irie, ruler of the daytime and patron goddess of the island, looked as if she should be going to see a play in Port Sol, not making house calls to a seventeen-year-old in the landlocked Iryan town of Deadegg.

But that was *her* problem. Faron had called. Irie had answered. Five years, and that hadn't changed.

Lend me your strength.

Faron gasped as she felt Irie's power flood her body. At first, it was almost too much. Summoners trained for years to hold the magic of just *one* of their ancestral spirits, known as astrals, without dying. Even the most advanced santi—summoners who had dedicated their lives to the temples—didn't dare channel more than five astrals at a time. But there wasn't a single summoner on the island of San Irie who could call upon a god.

Except for her.

Faron felt as if she were on fire for a second, a minute, an hour, a lifetime. Her nerves crawled as if she were being shaken from the inside out, as if Irie were shoving against Faron's ill-fitting skin in an attempt to make room for more magic than her body could hold. Her vision whited out. Her ears rang. Her heart pounded so fast that she thought it would stop.

Then it was over. Irie was within her, but Faron was in control. And she had a race to win.

A bead of sweat rolled down Faron's cheek as she blinked into the present. The riotous jeers of the crowd flowed back in. The dragon egg peeked out from over the top of the corner store in the distance. Jordan was still in front of her.

But not for long.

Faron called on the divine magic now at her fingertips and willed it to push her body beyond its limits. In the five years she'd spent with the gods, she'd found more creative uses for Irie's powers than roasting breadfruit. The sun was fire, energy, *power*. She directed that power into her lagging muscles and wheezing lungs, feeling Irie's magic leak past the goddess's obvious disapproval.

One minute, Faron was trying not to faint before she crossed the finish line. The next, she was eating up the distance between her and Jordan until she was close enough to count his locs.

He frowned at her. "Hey, Vincent! That's not fair!"

"Take it up with my patron," she sang back. "You can find a statue of her in any temple!"

Jordan cursed so colorfully that Faron laughed as she skipped past, leaving him to choke on the cloud of dust her feet kicked up.

The town square yawned open before her, surrounded by squat wooden storefronts too low to block out the sun. Her hand slapped the short brick wall that surrounded the egg a moment later. Technically, this was where the race ended, but adrenaline pulsed through her, twining with her borrowed magic. She jumped the wall and kept running until she hit the egg, then reached up to grab one of the massive scales that made up its sickly gray shell. The wall had been built to keep people from doing exactly what Faron was doing right now, but she wasn't the first Deadegg teenager to make this climb and she wouldn't be the last. The egg predated the town, probably predated the island based on the petrified stone that coated the scales, and Faron had come to find it comforting.

Sure, dragons hatched from living eggs this size—eggs of gorgeous color hiding terrifying young monsters within—but *this* one was a monument. It was part of her home. More than that, it was proof that dragons couldn't just be born and cruel and dangerous; they could be killed and defeated and forgotten.

Faron had survived the decades-long war against the Langlish Empire, a world power to the east of San Irie that used dragons as fire-breathing weapons to conquer land that was never theirs to own. By now, she knew the monsters' weaknesses better than almost anyone. But it was nice to have more than memories. More than nightmares.

She perched on top of the egg, her skirts spilling back down to her ankles, and grinned as she waited for Jordan to catch up. The constant scent of brimstone wafted from the base, but Faron ignored it. Magic still hummed under her skin, waiting for further direction, and she didn't want to let it go yet. She wasn't ready for the crushing emptiness and dizzying exhaustion that would follow.

This is a poor use of my abilities, Empyrean, a smoky voice grumbled at the back of her mind. *Must you always be so childish?*

Of the three gods, Irie was always the one most devoted to making Faron feel like a toddler. Obie, the god of the moon and the lord of the night, spoke so rarely that Faron could ignore his disapproval most of the time. Mala, the goddess of the stars and the keeper of the astrals, was the most likely to encourage Faron's stupidity. But Irie took her role as the supreme goddess very seriously—so seriously that Faron often wondered if she regretted giving their power to Faron in the first place.

Even though it had been five years since Faron had completed her calling as the Childe Empyrean and freed the island from Langlish occupation.

Even though the gods were the ones who had decided, for some reason, to stick around after the empire's retreat.

Even though she deserved to live her own life now. A peaceful life. With or without Irie's approval.

Empyrean, Irie snapped when she didn't answer. *Ignoring me does not undo your immaturity.*

I'm seventeen, she reminded the goddess. *And my name is Faron.*

You are the Childe Empyrean. These insipid stunts cannot change the truth.

Faron forced herself not to respond. There was nothing she could say that wouldn't sound ridiculous anyway. The war was over, Langley's colonial hold on San Irie shattered and their remaining dragons subdued, but the iconography of the Childe Empyrean was still spread across the island. Santi commanded respect and reverence for devoting their lives to gods that may or may not answer their prayers, but Faron was a thing of legend. A living saint. Tangible proof that the Iryan gods not only existed... but they were listening.

If she entered the corner store that Jordan was currently jogging past, she would see her own face, five years younger, smiling in miniature from hand-carved statues. Every year, people across the island made pilgrimages to her house, hoping to catch a glimpse of her, begging her to intercede between them and the gods. Blaming *her* if their wishes didn't come true.

Even still, she didn't hold that against them. The war with the Langlish had taken something from everyone, including those who hadn't fought. Faron understood better than anyone how bleak helplessness could lead people to ask someone more powerful for help. She just wished she could tell those hopeful crowds that they wouldn't necessarily like the answer they'd be given.

"Cheater," Jordan complained as he approached, pulling her from her dark thoughts. "I didn't use any summoning to win the race."

"That's hardly my concern." Faron lifted her eyebrows in a picture of innocence. "And you *didn't* win the race."

"We said no powers."

"You said no powers. I don't remember agreeing with you."

Jordan scowled. "You always do this."

"And yet you always make bets with me."

"I can start ignoring you outright if you prefer. It would certainly make *my* life easier."

Faron waved away the comment with a lazy hand. It didn't matter how many times she lied or cheated. The people's memories for her heroic actions during the war were long, but those same memories were short when it came to any of her less-than-heroic actions since. Even Jordan was repeating the same things he'd said during their last footrace, and it hadn't stopped him from challenging her to this one. At this point, there didn't seem to be anything that Faron could do that would have real consequences.

Or maybe the problem was that she already lived those

consequences. Enemies and admirers were the closest that Faron had gotten to having friends since she'd come home alive but haunted, reeking of smoke and ash. She spoke to the gods more than she spoke to people her own age. She had her sister, Elara, but Elara also had Reeve and her sixth-form friends. Faron hated school enough that she already knew she would fail the exam for sixth form, if she didn't fail this year entirely, and school was the only chance she had to mix with her peers.

Maybe *that* was the real price she paid for being the patron saint of lies. There was no Faron Vincent. Only the Childe Empyrean.

"Give me my rayes and take the lesson," said Faron, forcing those thoughts away, too. "If you keep trying to use your track talent against me, expect me to use my powers against you."

Jordan's scowl deepened, but he dug through the pockets of his khaki trousers for the money. Faron shifted on the uncomfortable rounded tip of the egg as she waited, surveying the sprawling view she had of the town. Behind the businesses were rows of houses with thatched roofs, yards separated from one another by fences or cacti. Chicken coops pockmarked the grounds, and goats grazed in the open fields. She couldn't see her own house from here, but she knew which direction it was in; if she squinted, she might be able to spot the splashes of forest greens and cypress browns that made up her father's garden.

There was none of that right now, though. In fact, the farther she looked, the more the edges of Deadegg seemed to be smudged by fog.

Fog that seemed to be *moving*.

Within the cloudy puffs, she could see a shape—no, *shapes*. Shapes that were dark and large and worryingly familiar. *Horses.*

And not just horses, but an entire horse-drawn coach. It was an unusual sight, both because mules and donkeys were more common in rural Deadegg and because she didn't know anyone in town who could afford a coach of any kind. The longer she stared, the more she was able to make out the ocean blue of the carriage, the grass green of the drawn curtains, the golden detailing catching the sunlight. Her heart stopped, and in that long, silent space between beats, she noticed a flag in all three colors waving from the rooftop. The Iryan flag was the last confirmation she needed.

For the first time all day, Faron felt true fear.

The queen was here.

CHAPTER TWO

ELARA

ELARA VINCENT HAD BEEN A SURVIVOR LONG BEFORE SHE'D GONE to war.

It was a mandatory trait for an eldest daughter, the experimental first child whose personality was a diamond formed under the extreme pressure of her parents' expectations. Growing up, it had manifested in fervent peacekeeping and anxious respectfulness, especially after her sister was born. Faron, in all her glorious chaos, teased Elara endlessly for being docile. Nonconfrontational. Prewar Elara didn't believe in going to bed angry or being needlessly impolite—even to old Miss Johnson from down the street, who took the briefest pause as an invitation to tell you how each of her nine kids were doing.

But being gentle on a battlefield was a good way to get killed, and Elara hadn't survived the war against Langley at thirteen to shed the lessons that had kept her alive.

The first and most important one was simple: It was her or them.

Now eighteen years old, Elara sized up her ex-girlfriend Cherry McKay for a weakness to exploit, confident before they even began that she would win this fight in three moves.

Two, if Cherry made the same mistake.

The gods had blessed Iryans with the ability to summon ancestral spirits, and that gift was wielded in three general ways. For most, it was commonplace, taught in schools and mainly used for communication. For some, it was a religious calling, a talent to be dedicated to the gods at one of the temples across the island. For the rest, it was a weapon to be wielded in service of the nation, a means of protecting the Iryan people from their enemies.

Combat summoning was so heavily associated with the Iryan Military Forces that most civilians didn't bother learning it, but Elara was not most civilians. Before the war, she'd practiced her forms and tested her limits. During and after the war, she'd built on those skills and perfected them. Combat summoning required discipline: the knowledge of how to call an astral, contain an astral, and safeguard your own strength. The longer she channeled an ancestral spirit, the more her own soul eroded until her body shut down to save what was left—and that was a hard thing to remember with enemies raining down their own magic upon her.

But there had been no margin for error then, and there was no margin for error now. By the end of this week, she might be a soldier. *Officially*, this time. She just had to defeat Cherry first.

"And," Aisha Harlow shouted, "summon your astrals!"

Only Elara could see the ancestral spirits who answered her call. They were *her* relatives, after all, summoned by her to support her in this fight. For most, the astrals who came to them were the spirits of family recently deceased, though she'd heard stories of summoners who could call any dead relative to whom they'd had the strongest emotional connection. Luckily, for Elara, those ancestors were one and the same.

The astrals of her maternal aunts, each one killed during the war, surrounded her now: Vittoria Durand, the youngest, with her hair up in twists and a mischievous smile on her face; Mahalet Durand, the oldest, thick with muscle carved from years of swimming and running track; and Gabourey Durand, the middle sister and the most violent, whose love for the bottle was only equal to her love for the fight. Elara reached for Aunt Vittoria, her skin warming as the extra soul settled beneath it.

On a hot day like today, it felt like torture to summon. But Elara already felt stronger, powerful, more dangerous.

Across the grass, Cherry smirked at her. Elara smirked back.

"Ready?" Aisha's burgundy braids fluttered as she dived out of the way. "FIGHT!"

Lightning crackled across the field. Cherry's fingertips sparked white-hot, wielding the electricity her astral helped her conjure like a whip. Elara met her with a simple shield—*first move*—that swallowed the bolt, enhancing her own magic. The shield shrank to a ball of energy that hovered between her palms. Lightning shot across the surface of it, making it glow almost as bright as the sun.

Sweat gathered on Elara's skin. Her body felt as if it were on fire.

Finish her, niece, Aunt Vittoria crooned inside her head.

Not yet, Elara replied. If she attacked now, Cherry would just throw up a shield of her own. Her ex had quick instincts, but she was bad at multitasking; she could block an attack, but she'd leave herself open to a counterattack. In that time, Elara could take her down, a fight won in three moves. But she knew she could do it in two. She could do better, and wasn't that the goal? To be the *best*?

She wouldn't get into the Iryan Military Forces—into the aerial branch called the Sky Battalion—if she wasn't.

Beneath her feet, the ground shook as if an earthquake were hitting Deadegg, but Elara remembered this feeling too well to look away. Cherry had no such focus; she never did. As she'd done every time before, she allowed herself to get distracted by what was happening on the street.

And *that* was when Elara attacked.

She swung the ball of energy like a cricket bat. Cherry was blasted off her feet. Elara drew on Aunt Vittoria's magic one last time to soften the ground, saving Cherry from a painful landing. Then she purged the astral from her body and gasped like a drowning man rising above the waves.

Victory in only two moves. She was improving.

"Every time," Cherry complained as Elara joined everyone in gathering around her. "That one wasn't even my fault!"

"Nice job, El," Wayne Pryor said as Aisha helped Cherry sit up. "Did you catch the commotion, though? The queen has arrived."

Elara had ridden in enough of Queen Aveline's fancy coaches to know what it sounded like when the horses cantered over the intermittently paved Deadegg streets. It had been impressive the first couple of times, but now she just associated the rumbling sound with at least a full day of her sister, Faron, being in a bad mood.

"Do you guys have to leave?" Aisha asked. Her eyes flicked over Elara's shoulder to where Reeve Warwick was sitting in the shade of a guinep tree, buried between the pages of his latest book. As if he could sense the sudden attention, he glanced up, but whatever he saw in their expressions apparently wasn't more interesting than what he was reading.

This field, with its overgrown grass, wilted wooden fence, and fallen barbed wire, had once been part of a farm. But many of the farms in Deadegg had gone under, leaving fields like this as their graveyards. As sad as they looked, these lots were better off than the blackened patches of land that had been ravaged by dragonfire, charred soil that could never again yield new life, livelihoods that had been destroyed in an instant. At least here she could still dream that, in a few more years, this field would transform into something new.

Besides, Elara liked to spar here because it was only about a ten-minute walk from her house, so she could get home quickly when she needed to. Today, she didn't need to. She may have fought every battle alongside her sister, a soldier in theory though never in rank, but Elara was not the Childe Empyrean. The queen was never in Deadegg for her.

"No," she answered, and left it at that. "Cherry, are you all right?"

"I'm fine. *Humiliated*, but fine."

Cherry was on her feet now, her plump lower lip curled into an exaggerated pout. A year ago, Elara would have taken this as an invitation to sway forward and nibble at that lip, to wrap an arm around that narrow waist and pull their bodies together, to press a kiss to the little freckle on Cherry's throat until she forgot to be upset by her defeat. She didn't miss Cherry, but she missed that playful closeness. It had been a nice distraction from the doubts forever screaming in her head.

"Let's take a break," Elara suggested. "Who wants to go get us some juice?"

One quick hand game of sun moon stars later, Wayne was jumping the fence and jogging down the sidewalk to find a cart. Elara headed over to Reeve, who paused to hold his place in the book with a blade of grass before he set it aside. Her smile widened when he pulled a bottle of water from his bag.

"I love you the *most*," she told him after she'd downed half of it.

"We both know that's not true," he drawled, "but I'll take it."

Reeve was the picture of relaxation here, his back resting against the curved bark and his legs crossed at the ankles. It was a side of him that Elara hadn't always had access to. She had met him when he'd stumbled into the Iryan war camp at thirteen years old, and even that almost hadn't happened; the soldiers had been ready to kill him for somehow evading the scouts *and* the perimeter guard. He'd been shaking then, rolled papers stolen from his father's war room gathered to his chest as he'd gasped in broken patois, "I need—I need to talk to the queen!"

But he was Langlish, and the son of Commander Gavriel Warwick, the leader of the Langlish Empire. Reeve was now allowed, by royal decree, to live in San Irie, but it was only so he wouldn't be murdered for treason by his own people. As far as friends went, he had her, and by extension he had her neighbors Aisha, Cherry, and Wayne. As far as family went, he'd been taken in by the otherwise childless Hanlons, and they seemed to treat him well enough.

Everyone *else* in and out of the town line took one look at Reeve's silver dragon's-eye pendant or heard him speak patois with his persistent Langlish accent, and they held him personally responsible for everything the Langlish Empire had done to their island. Elara was glad to see him this loose, this open, this calm, but it made her sad, too.

Reeve had betrayed everything he'd known to be an enemy of two countries.

She dropped down next to him in the shade, wiping sweat from her brow with the back of her hand. "It's *hot*!"

"Is it?" Reeve asked with faux surprise. "On an island in the middle of the Ember Sea?"

Elara jabbed him with her elbow as the rest of the group made their way over. Instead of juice boxes, they were each holding a different flavor of freeze pop; Elara was handed a pineapple one and Reeve received the last cream soda. Because she was a good friend, she didn't complain.

"Can you believe that by this time next week at least one of us might be in the Sky Battalion?" Wayne asked, sitting in front of them. He shoved his dark curls away from his forehead, but they immediately tumbled back over his damp skin. Cherry's head rested on his shoulder, her eyes half-lidded, her skirts lifted to bare her shins to the mild breeze. "Or, even better, we could be chosen to pilot Valor."

"*I* can't believe they commissioned a new drake at all," said Aisha, using her freeze pop to cool the back of her neck. "It's been years. Not since—which one was it?"

"Nobility," Elara answered around a yawn. "The last one built before the war, and the one that now acts as the queen's personal transport."

Drakes—the giant flying metal war machines made from a textured material called scalestone—were semisentient; they were built by summoners channeling astrals to mold the scalestone into the size and shape of dragons. Iryan magic could affect any metal as easily as it affected the world around it, but scalestone was impervious to dragonfire, and it amplified Iryan magic until it could rival the war beasts in power. That made it San Irie's greatest resource, especially since it could *only* be found in San Irie.

Years of experimentation had revealed that using astrals to build the drakes left a faint trace of their lives behind in the particles of the metal. Those traces made it impossible to predict what the resulting drake would look for in a pilot, and three pilots were needed just to get it off the ground. But no one made the leap from regular soldier to Sky Battalion pilot without there being an open drake to fly.

Thankfully, Queen Aveline had decided to have a fifth one built leading up to the San Irie International Peace Summit, a drake she had named Valor. Political vultures from empires across the continent of Nova—Étolia, Joya del Mar, and, of course, Langley—would be arriving in the Iryan capital of Port Sol in just a few days. The queen wanted to establish San Irie as an independent island nation on an international scale. To *force* the countries of the closest continent to negotiate with San Irie as an equal, not as a temporarily freed Langlish colony. Though the announcement of the Summit had proven controversial, even with her own parents, Elara had barely registered the enemies who would soon be on their shores.

No pilots had been chosen for Valor yet. Recruitment was tomorrow. And Elara was old enough to enlist. Her dream had been rekindled. Better still, it was actually in reach.

So what if she hadn't gotten around to telling her family? She was *ready*.

She didn't have to be the Childe Empyrean to do something incredible.

As soon as she sucked the first piece of her freeze pop into her mouth, a ball of light swirled into view.

An astral call.

Elara squinted into the light, cool pineapple juice melting on her tongue as the astral resolved itself into her grandfather Winston. Her father's father looked exactly like his son, except his goatee was fully gray while her father's was gray*ing* and his head was shaved whereas her father had grown locs halfway down his back.

A message for you, said Pa Winston, flickering at the edges.

Elara already felt as if she could sleep for at least three hours, but if she didn't give her ancestor permission to share her body, then she wouldn't get the message. And if she ignored her father's message, then she'd be in for it when she got home.

She sighed. *Yes, okay.*

Pa Winston settled inside of her, his presence like a thick blanket around her soul. It would have been soothing if it wasn't so unforgivably hot today. But she breathed around the flare of heat and opened her eyes, allowing him to feel the breeze, to smell the earthy scent of grass and dirt, to hear the quiet conversation her friends were having. To feel alive again.

In return, he spoke in a voice identical to her father's: *Elara, you and Reeve need to come home as soon as possible. Dinner is ready . . . and Queen Aveline needs to speak to you.*

As soon as the message was delivered, Pa Winston faded away. Elara sagged against Reeve's side, her eyelids like weights. She had never gotten formal magical training after learning the basics at school; everything she could do was self-taught, especially without a local temple where she might have found a teacher. Impressive displays of summoning, like the ability to channel multiple astrals back-to-back without passing out, were few and far between outside the major cities. Most of the particularly gifted summoners joined the Iryan army.

Just as her aunts had. Just as Elara was going to.

"My father wants us at my house," she yawned into Reeve's shoulder. "Apparently, the queen wants to talk to us."

"She wants to talk to *us*?" Reeve asked. "You *and* me? Is he sure?"

"More likely he just wants us both there to present a united front for Faron. But there's dinner."

Reeve picked up his book, brushing grass off the cover. He lowered his voice when he spoke, but that didn't stop his words from piercing Elara's heart. "Are you going to tell them over dinner?"

Elara tried to imagine it. Her mother always went out of her way to cook as much food as possible when the queen came to visit. She conjured an image of market-fresh lobster, bright red on a bed of green vegetables and shining with a thin coat of butter, next to bright yellow pieces of chewy curry goat. They would all sit down to eat, and Elara would make sure to clear at least one plate before she brought up her plan to leave in the morning to enlist at the nearest base in Highfort.

Instantly, the fantasy cracked apart. Her mother would scream the same way she'd screamed when she'd gotten those condolence letters, one for each aunt, that now sat in her drawer at home gathering dust. Her father would go cold, his expression like the gray-purple clouds that gathered before a thunderstorm. And Faron...Faron hadn't even gone to war without Elara at her side. She'd be hurt. Furious.

Betrayed.

Elara's throat closed up. "Maybe I should save the announcement for if I even get in?"

"*If*?" said Wayne. "You're the best of all of us, Elara. If they don't take you, the rest of us won't even be considered."

"*You* taught *me* how to combat summon without burning out," said Aisha. "And I'm still not as good as you."

"I'm not going to inflate your ego," said Cherry, lifting her head long enough to stretch. "But I agree with them."

Reeve arched his eyebrows in a silent signal that he was well aware Elara was just making up excuses. But she knew her family well enough to know that they would take this dream from her before it even had a chance to blossom into anything real. They had already lost too much and too many to the military. Vittoria. Mahalet. Gabourey. Even Elara and Faron had only brought half of themselves back from the battlefield.

She'd spent five years rebuilding the trust her parents had in her. Five years of waking in the middle of the night to find one or both of them looking in to make sure she was still safe in her bed. Five years of being the responsible to Faron's reckless. Five years of ensuring that her parents looked at her with pride instead of fear.

If it were any other dream, they would support her. But they would never support this.

After she got in, after she hopefully became a drake pilot, maybe they would see her accomplishments and come around. But when it was just an idea, just a flame of aspiration she kept close to her heart, it was too easy for someone to blow out.

"I'll tell them," she mumbled to Reeve. "Not at dinner, but— after the queen leaves tonight. I'll tell them." Then she raised her voice, finding a smile for her friends. "And thanks, everyone. But we're *all* going to get in. Maybe the gods will smile down on us, and the three next pilots of Valor are sitting right here, right now."

Elara ignored the heavy gaze she could feel on the side of her face. Because if she looked at Reeve, she would have to acknowledge that she was lying to both of them.

CHAPTER THREE

FARON

THE ONLY LIE FARON HATED HAVING TO TELL WAS WHEN SHE PRE-tended the queen wasn't the absolute worst.

Dinner had been served. Usually, her parents would wait for the whole family to be home before even setting the table, but not when *she* was here. When Aveline Renard Castell, the gods-blessed ruler of the island nation of San Irie, arrived in Deadegg to visit the Vincent family, they brought out the good plates and their best manners. Which was annoying, because she was, well, the *absolute worst*.

And yet Faron was the only one who seemed to know that.

Four members of the Queenshield stood at ease in crisp, navy uniforms behind the chair where Aveline perched like a snake in a ball gown. Her deep blue quadrille dress was decorated with an off-the-shoulder lace bodice, complimenting her light brown skin, and her indigo head wrap sparkled with tiny stars that merged into the gold diadem that crowned her temples. At twenty-two, Aveline had gained some of the grace and sophistication she'd been lacking when Faron had met her six years ago, but all the poise in the world couldn't undo everything that had happened since then.

"Dinner is wonderful, Mrs. Vincent," said Aveline with a winsome smile. "I love salted cod."

Salted cod instead of saltfish. It was small and petty of her, but Faron *hated* the pretentious way that Aveline had started talking since she'd ascended the throne. The girl she'd met years ago had spoken the almost incomprehensible dialect of patois that was common in the countryside and had known curses that would make even the rudest soldier stare at her in awe. She'd been a hero to Faron, almost like another sister.

Now she was this: formal and official, so snobby that it was as if she constructed her sentences to send the implicit message of being better than everyone around her.

Faron stuffed a huge piece of curry goat into her mouth to keep herself quiet.

"For the hundredth time, Your Majesty, please call me Nida."

It was all Faron could do not to snort. As if nicknames and familiarity weren't off the table for the queen, too.

"It would hardly be proper," Aveline confirmed a moment later. "But I appreciate the offer."

Faron's mother smiled—only slightly frayed at the edges. Mama was forever torn between her maternal fondness for Aveline and her resignation that Aveline's appearances rarely meant anything good for them. She'd made a pot of steaming curry goat and fluffy white rice. On the side was ackee and saltfish, blended together into a buttery, peppery, savory stew. The adults, Aveline included, were having light beer; Faron had been given pineapple juice, which she used to wash down her bitterness.

It didn't work.

"All right," Faron said once her mouth was clear, "you didn't come here for dinner. Let's be honest with each other, shall we?"

Aveline's smile dropped like an anchor through the ocean. Her eyes were barren of warmth as they met Faron's over the table. "It would not kill you to have even a modicum of respect for your elders, Empyrean."

"And when have my elders ever respected me?"

"You think I don't *respect* you?" Aveline reined in her brief flash of human emotion. When she spoke again, her tone was smoothed of all edges. "Of course I respect you."

"You *use* me."

The queen laughed, and it was a cold sound. "You, of all people, do *not* get to accuse me of that."

Faron opened her mouth to argue but thought better of it. They'd been having the same disagreements for years, and she could see everyone else in the kitchen shifting awkwardly as they prepared to have it out again.

"Just," she said wearily, "tell me why you came, and get it over with."

Not even a flicker of remorse passed through Aveline's hard black eyes—but Faron hadn't expected any. Their stories were parallel legends of too-large burdens placed on too-young shoulders, and Faron knew Aveline's myth as well as she knew her own. Queen Aveline Renard Castell had been raised on a farm under the name Ava Stone, unaware that she was the heir to the throne, unaware that the people she thought were her parents were Queenshield soldiers, unaware that her life was a lie meant to protect her from a war that seemed endless. After the queens had been murdered by dragons in one of the lowest points of the revolution, the gods had sent Faron to retrieve Aveline, for San Irie could not win their freedom without the rightful heir to reclaim the throne.

But myths were lies by nature, transforming humans into symbols. The books didn't mention the way Aveline's cold expression had only grown colder when Faron had told her that it was the will of the gods that Aveline be crowned in Port Sol. That the Renard Castell bloodline continue its unbroken reign. That Aveline lead a shattered country through an unprecedented war at only sixteen.

They'd spent a year together, a year during which Faron had looked to the child queen for any guidance the gods could not provide. A year of defeats and victories, of fights and fire-forged bonds, of mistakes and machinations. And once the war had been won and Aveline had been crowned, Faron had gotten to go home to Deadegg. Her nightmare had ended, but Queen Aveline's had just begun.

Aveline had never stopped resenting her for it.

The books didn't mention that, either.

Faron had once hoped that if she apologized enough, she and Aveline could talk, *really* talk, about all that the gods had given them and all that the gods had taken away. She'd been disappointed every time, and by this point she knew to expect nothing better than to be used as a weapon or a trophy.

All she wanted to know now was which it would be.

"I need you, your sister, and the Warwick boy to come to Port Sol today," Aveline admitted, "and stay through the Summit."

Faron cursed, forgetting that her parents were even here until Mama smacked her in the side. But no stern comment followed. Her parents were equally stunned by this change in plans. They'd objected to the San Irie International Peace Summit as much as

Faron had, if not more, but Aveline had still convinced them to let her go. In their eyes, Aveline had brought their runaway daughters safely home from war. There was little they wouldn't do for her, even now.

San Irie had rebuilt a lot in five years, thanks to the summoners and the scalestone, but Faron thought it was far too soon to invite the empires here to discuss treaties and trade. When a burglar broke into a house and tried to steal the deed, no one in their right mind invited them back to see the new security improvements. But Faron was an overvalued guardian. Aveline was the ruler. If she said there was to be a Summit, Faron didn't get a say in that.

This, however, she deserved a say in.

"I'm not supposed to come until the weekend. And for *one night*," she snapped. "I was promised—"

"Things have changed." The queen's tone was even, a calculated move to make Faron feel as if she were being irrational. Worse, it was working. "We are moving the demonstration up to the beginning."

"The beginning isn't for another *two days*. And why do we have to stay the whole time after that?"

"The Langlish have arrived on Iryan land."

Mama placed a shaking hand over Faron's. Aveline had said *the Langlish,* but it was obvious what she really meant.

Their dragons.

"They are landing over on the nearby islet of San Mala as prearranged, but our people are starting to get nervous. We have not had this many dragons near the island since...well, you remember." Aveline's jaw tightened into a stubborn line. "We have drakes on standby at the airfield, but I believe—or, rather, I *know*—that

28

everyone would feel better if the Empyrean was there as well. In case there are any incidents."

Faron clutched Mama's hand tightly, the way she'd used to when she was younger. Before her prayer, before her direct line to the gods, before she'd gone to war, she had been a scared girl from a fading farming town in a flyover zone at the base of the Argent Mountains. Dragons would often burst over the peaks flame-first, killing the land with their blazing breath and blowing wooden shacks across the plains with their wings. Every morning, she had woken up wondering if today would be the day she would die, a fear that had done nothing but calcify over the years, overlooked but never completely forgotten.

With so much out of her control, she'd prayed. She had prayed and prayed and prayed to Irie to end this war. She'd never expected that she would be that ending.

Even now, it was still surreal to hear Aveline talk about her as if she were the only hope of a bunch of strangers. They should be praying to the gods, not pinning all their faith on her. She barely had any of that left for herself.

"How many dragons?" she heard herself ask.

"So far, three."

"*Three.*"

Faron felt as if she were an astral and the person sitting there between her parents was a different girl with the weight of the world on her shoulders. She just couldn't seem to fit herself into this scene, where the queen of her country could tell her that the only thing that would make her people feel safe from the presence of three dragons was one seventeen-year-old girl.

"—students from their training academy, Hearthstone," Aveline was saying when Faron snapped back into her body. "Apparently, they are here to 'observe,' not to participate. That is something that I did not think to ban." She brushed imaginary dust from the bodice of her dress. "I assure you I will *not* make that mistake twice."

"Will we need to have a peace summit more than once, Your Majesty?" Papa asked, his politeness just shy of reproachful. "I thought the point was to make a show of our strength. Won't that message lose effect if you have to repeat it?"

"Well—"

Faron heard keys in the lock and ran to meet Elara at the front door.

Her sister was sweaty but smiling, her waist-length braids twisted up into a half bun on top of her head. She was wearing a casual black riding habit with matching trousers, which meant she'd been out running with her friends again, and she sagged into Faron's hug, which meant she'd been out *summoning* with her friends again.

Faron had to laugh. "Overdid it today?"

"Don't you start."

"All right, all right. But I'd like to remind you that you're supposed to be the responsible one."

Whatever retort Elara muttered was lost when Faron caught sight of who she'd brought home with her: Reeve Warwick. It was always a bit of a shock, the sight of this white boy on an island of people whose skin tones ranged from fallow light to umber dark. Faron knew that the Langlish Empire had consumed too many countries for pale skin and pale eyes to be the only Langlish identifiers, but Reeve stuck out in other important ways. Almost a foot taller than Faron, milk skinned and ice eyed with oiled-up hair the color of reddish mud, he looked exactly like a younger version of his father, with the accent to match.

Considering his father was the current ruler of the Langlish Empire, being around him was awful even before he opened his condescending mouth.

Faron scowled at him. He smirked back.

"Racing again?" Reeve asked.

"*Faron*," Elara groaned. "You promised you'd go right home after school."

Her cheeks flamed. She glared at Reeve. "How could you *possibly* know that?"

"Your ankles. They're dusty. So not only were you racing, but you haven't bathed."

"Are you implying that I smell badly?"

"I'm merely answering your question."

"Please," Elara yawned. Whatever scolding she'd been working up to had been submerged beneath her exhaustion. She was resting on Faron now, using her as a standing pillow. "Truce while we have company."

"I can agree to that." Reeve shrugged, adjusting his grip on the book he was carrying under one arm. "Truce, Faron?"

"Ass."

The smirk widened. "They really should write more books about your charm."

An acidic reply formed on Faron's tongue, but Elara gave her one last squeeze and straightened.

"Your Majesty," she greeted, nudging Faron out of her way with a hip. "Welcome back to Deadegg. I hope you had a *noble* flight. You know, because you flew over in Nobility?"

In the silence that followed, Faron rolled her eyes fondly then hated herself for it when she saw Reeve do the same thing. She didn't storm back to the kitchen, but it was a near thing.

Elara greeted every Queenshield soldier by name before she and Reeve sat in the remaining chairs. She piled food onto two plates, her eyes intent on her task as if that would help everyone forget her bad joke. Reeve said something to Elara that made the corner of her mouth tip up, and Faron swallowed past a wave of resentment. She wanted to believe it was all focused on Reeve, but, after the day she'd had, her sister's ability to be friends with *anyone* stung. Faron couldn't even get the queen to like her, and they had the most shared life experience.

"Now that we are all here, shall we continue?" asked Aveline. "I believe there is strength in numbers. I am the queen. The Childe Empyrean is an internationally recognizable symbol of divine retribution. Elara Vincent is the picture of familial loyalty, and Reeve Warwick betrayed all he was raised to believe in for justice and equality. Langley is trying to intimidate us by bringing more dragons than I ever would have sanctioned, so I want to remind them who won this war and how. I want all of you to return to Port Sol with me tonight. Will you?"

"Port Sol?" Elara asked with wide eyes. "Wait, *tonight*? Why do ...? That's not ... I mean ..."

Elara seemed to have forgotten how to speak, and Faron didn't blame her. It had been years, and Faron still had trouble thinking back on those days. She couldn't imagine how bad it was for her sister, who hadn't even had the protection of the gods. Elara had been thirteen to Faron's twelve when Faron had snuck out to go to war. Her summoning had been basic and her self-defense skills nonexistent, but her bravery? Immeasurable. Because everywhere Faron had gone, no matter how dangerous, Elara had been right there beside her.

Doubtless neither of them was eager to revisit those days, but Faron was at least relieved that they would be flying back into these bad memories together for the first time since the war had ended.

"Of course they'll go," Papa said. "But not tonight. The Summit begins the day after tomorrow, so let them have tonight to pack and say proper goodbyes. You're welcome to stay in one of the guest rooms, Your Majesty."

It was a compromise but not a question. Aveline nodded. After Faron and Elara had come home from the war, they'd discovered Mama and Papa seemed to have aged decades while they'd been gone, silver newly threading through their hair and bags thick beneath their eyes. There'd been screaming and crying, then more crying and *more* screaming, but five years of peace—and Elara moderating Faron's behavior—had allowed them all time to breathe. These days, her parents considered Aveline keeping them informed a better option than their children sneaking out in the middle of the night.

"I'll let the school know you'll both be absent for the rest of the week." Mama sounded so very drained. "Reeve, do you want to tell the Hanlons in person or should I astral call them?"

"I can tell them when I go home to pack," he said slowly. "But Elara can't—"

"Wait for the Summit. It's a once-in-a-lifetime event," Elara finished. Her fingers fumbled her spoon, which clattered off the table to the floor. "What am I going to *wear*?"

Aveline smiled, and it was the first time all day that it looked

33

genuine. Elara tended to have that effect on people. "We have had formal dress designed for you all by local tailors."

"Excellent. That's just excellent. I can't wait!"

Elara ducked under the table to rescue her spoon. Her laugh was squeaky. Reeve watched Elara as if he'd missed a step in a private waltz, but that only confirmed what Faron already suspected.

Elara was lying.

Her sister's palms began to sweat if she even suspected she was in trouble, and she'd once cried at the thought of failing an assignment. She'd never learned to lie as easily as Faron did, but she was lying now. About what? And why?

Elara sat up, her knuckles white from how hard she clenched that spoon. Faron frowned at her, wishing the gods could give her the power to see inside people's heads. She couldn't think of anything important enough that Perfect Elara would lie to her, to the queen, to their *parents*. And it cut deeply to think that perhaps she didn't know her sister—her best friend—as well as she thought.

Conversation flowed over dinner, topics and tones only slightly forced. Elara avoided Faron's every attempt to catch her gaze. Somewhere between emptying her plate and helping Mama wash up, Faron made her fourth and final promise of the day. One she knew she would keep.

Whatever Elara was hiding, she *would* find out.

And soon.

CHAPTER FOUR

ELARA

THAT NIGHT, ELARA SNUCK OUT OF HER HOUSE FOR THE SECOND time in her life.

As she landed hard in her father's garden, nearly rolling her ankle in the process, she wished she weren't such a coward. The wind felt too cold on her skin. Her heart was beating too quickly. Somewhere in the neighborhood, a stray dog howled, and it sounded like a warning.

Elara was not this person. She was not the one who rebelled. Rebellion gave her anxiety. *Faron* had been blessed by the gods, channeled their magic, saved the world. *Elara* had gotten in trouble for not stopping her, for following her without divine protection of her own, for forcing her parents to confront the fear of losing both daughters at once. While Faron had grown into a defiant teen, Elara stayed apologetically within the lines their parents had drawn. Thrived within them, really.

Given her good reputation, maybe if she crawled back inside now, they might forgive her in five years instead of fifty.

But if she crawled back inside now, she would only ever be a hero inside these walls. The rest of the world would make her a footnote in the books written about her sister, if she were ever mentioned at all. And maybe she shouldn't care about that, but she *did*. She wanted to matter, too. Sometimes it felt as if she were drowning so deep in Faron's shadow, no one could hear her screams.

She turned and had to clap a hand over her mouth to stifle a shriek.

Faron stood beneath the cherry tree, crowned in moonlight. She was still wearing her nightgown, a simple white cotton dress embroidered with her initials. It had been a gift from Miss Johnson, an elderly neighbor from down the road who saw the whole town as her family.

Faron spat a cherry pit into the bed of poinsettias to her left. Her eyebrows lifted.

"Who told you?" Elara demanded. "Was it Reeve?"

"If Reeve Warwick told me it was raining outside, I wouldn't believe him until I was drenched." Faron folded her arms. "*You* told me the second you tried to lie. You aren't good at it. Where are you going?"

Elara considered her options and immediately gave in. "I'm going to join the Sky Battalion. Enlistment opens tomorrow."

Faron sucked her teeth. "This? You lie to me for *this*?"

"I thought—I thought you'd be mad."

"I *am* mad. What was your plan here? If Mama and Papa wake up and your bed is empty, they're not just going to call the local police. They're going to have Aveline's whole military looking for you. For Irie's sake, Aveline would send the military herself!"

"I—"

"*No*," said Faron, holding up a hand. "You don't have to tell me you didn't think this through. I know you didn't. I'm the liar, Elara, not you. I know you hoped to be chosen as a drake pilot before anyone came looking, and I'm telling you that's not what's going to happen."

Elara's body went cold. "You don't think I'll be chosen as a drake pilot?"

"Of course you'll be chosen as a drake pilot." And the way her sister said that, as though it was such an undeniable fact that it wasn't worth debating, made some of the tension slide from Elara's shoulders. "Everybody loves you. Why wouldn't a drake?"

There was something surreal about this moment, standing with her sister in the starlit garden beneath her bedroom window, trampling her father's thyme and listening to the gods-chosen Childe Empyrean tell Elara that everyone loved *her*. If it weren't for the anxiety pulsing under her skin, she would have thought she was still asleep.

"What I'm saying," Faron continued, "is that if you leave like this, Mama and Papa and the queen and her guards will drag you home by your braids before you ever get the chance to try. It'll take you over half a day to make it all the way up to Highfort."

Her sister stood between her and freedom. And she was right, damn her. Elara led Faron away from the still-open window and back into the shadows of the cherry tree. "What do you suggest, then?"

"I can cover for you, make up a story about you wanting to go to the nearest temple and pray for your friends. Something to buy you some time to sign up."

"The Summit is being held in Port Sol, and they have a temple," Elara said dubiously. "Why wouldn't I just pray there?"

"With the Empyrean in town? You'd never get inside before your friends enlisted."

"I don't know…"

"*Trust me*, would you? I've been lying to Mama and Papa since I could speak. I'll handle it."

Elara kindly did not point out that this was, in fact, a good reason not to trust Faron. Because while Faron told lies large and small, she didn't usually lie to Elara. Not about something that mattered. Elara trusted her sister more than anyone in the world, and if Faron said she would handle it, then she would handle it.

Most of all, she knew that Elara could do this, and she was willing to help her. Even after Elara's lies.

"I love you," Elara finally said. "You know that, right?"

"I love *you*," Faron said without hesitation. "And I'll always be on your side. Okay?" If Elara hugged her more tightly than usual, Faron didn't comment. Instead, her sister glanced up at the star-flecked sky and added, "You should go. Mama gets up around three in the morning to use the bathroom, and she'll check our beds if I don't distract her."

Elara stared at her. "What in the…How often are you still sneaking in and out of the house at night?"

Faron winked.

Night faded into dawn, dawn into late afternoon, in the time it took Elara to arrive in Highfort and complete registration. Whether she was chosen as a pilot or not, she needed to be physically and mentally competent to enter the Iryan Military Forces. She'd always known that. But the forms and routine physical gave her too much time to think. To worry. To doubt.

By the time she was following the other hopeful cadets, the sun a white-hot globe in the clear blue sky, she had to clench her fists at her sides to keep them from shaking.

It had been five years since Elara had been this close to a drake. Five years, and her first sight of Valor in the center of the Highfort military base was enough to take her breath away. She was mere yards from a drake that had yet to pick its pilots—from a drake that could choose *her*. All her dreaming, all her praying, all her hard work: It had brought her here. She hoped that Valor could sense her yearning.

That, somehow, the machine yearned for her, too.

She didn't think she'd ever stop being awed by drakes. At this point, the Sky Battalion had five of them that Elara could name off the top of her head: Liberty, Justice, Mercy, Nobility, and, of course, Valor. The newest commissioned drake had been assigned a butter-yellow color that glittered in the afternoon light. Prominently displayed in the center of its flank was a white sun crowned by a sword that was pointing toward the sky, the symbol of the Renard Castell royal family. Though they had yet to let her and the other potential pilots inside the drake, she'd spent enough time in Nobility to know the layout of the interior by heart.

There was an open room inside every drake's torso, with an oval cockpit in the middle for one pilot. On either side of the cockpit were stairs, one set that led down to a cargo hold and one set that led up to suites and another cockpit for the second pilot. Though she couldn't see them from the outside, she knew that there were hidden windows lining the eastern and western sides of the flank for passengers to look through. Finally, north doors fed into the head, which contained a cockpit for the final pilot.

From here, drakes simply looked like a midsize scalestone

dragon, with eyes that lit up like spotlights and a mouth that could open to blast magic flame. But they represented San Irie's long history of taking the pain they'd been dealt and crafting it into victory. Drake pilots were treated the same as the gods and the Childe Empyrean: revered and celebrated. If Valor chose Elara as a pilot, she and Faron would finally be equals.

She was clenching her fists so hard that half-moon divots marked her palms. Elara loosened her hands. Took a breath. *Please, Irie, please.*

"You're being quiet back here," said Wayne, slowing down to keep pace with her.

"I just can't believe this is happening," Elara whispered. "I've dreamed about this for years and now..."

"It's here, and it's terrifying." Wayne touched her shoulder comfortingly. "But you're *going* to be chosen. You know, half the time, you're just this quiet girl who lives down the street from me. And then you spend time with us, and you turn into this...*incredible* summoner. I'd say you have an advantage since you've already fought in a war, but my father's certainly not doing *better* from having made it back alive." His hand fell to his side, and a shadow passed over his face. "I think *we're* the lucky ones, enlisting in peacetime."

Elara discarded three potential responses to that before they gathered in front of a stone-faced sergeant. Silently, she nudged Wayne's arm, and he gave her a small smile in return. Then she took a deep breath, smoothed back her braids, and tried to calm the rapid-fire beating of her heart.

The sergeant was a tall, balding man with honey skin, close-cropped hair, and a tag on his right breast that read OWENS. "Hello, potential cadets. We're very excited to have the next generation of soldiers in front of us here today. As I'm sure you all know, the queen commissioned a new drake for the Sky Battalion, and that drake, Valor, is in need of pilots. Before we prep you for basic, we need to evaluate if you are a match. Any pilots found will require additional training."

Elara could barely hear him over her rising panic. This was the part that was impossible to prepare for, because no article or book had ever revealed the military secret of *how* drake pilots were chosen. But Wayne was on her left. Aisha was on her right. Cherry was somewhere behind her. She was not alone in her hope. That made it a little easier to breathe.

"One by one, you'll enter Valor and sit in the flank cockpit," said Owens. The fabric of his uniform rippled in the wind as Valor's stomach door lowered onto the ramp that led up into the main chamber. "No matter what happens in there, don't be discouraged. There are many ways to serve queen and country in the Iryan Military Forces. That said," he continued as his dark eyes scanned them, "who wants to go first?"

Elara's hand shot up, but the sergeant called on a girl with her hair braided back into thick cornrows. She watched the girl disappear into that circle of darkness and waited for...what? That still wasn't clear. But seconds ticked by in an uneasy silence, occasionally broken by the sound of foot soldiers running drills or drake mechanics carrying tools. *Twenty-five seconds. Thirty seconds. Forty-five...*

One minute passed.

Sergeant Owens escorted the devastated girl out of the drake, handing her off to another military official. There were still three spots left open, which was good, but the odds that even one pilot was among them had just gone down, which was bad.

Gods, she prayed again, *please, please, please.*

Aisha was called next. Elara's fingers curled and loosened at her sides, again and again, for lack of anything to do but wait for *what—*

That.

The dark hole into which Aisha had marched was no longer dark. A golden glow raced halfway down the ramp, blinding in its sudden beauty, as if Valor were lit from the inside out. And it disappeared slowly, like the lingering details of a dream in the light of morning.

"There we go," Sergeant Owens said, impressed. "I honestly didn't think we'd find a pilot this early in the week."

Aisha stumbled out of the drake a moment later. Owens hurried to help her, but she waved him away. The glow lived within her now, making her look different. Stronger. She reached the end of the ramp and ran her fingers over the line of it, a fond expression on her face. Valor seemed to sparkle in response.

Two spots left open.

Unlikely that Valor would choose another pilot from Deadegg.

Unlikely but not impossible.

Elara hoped her smile held steady as Aisha walked past her. She wasn't sure that she was properly in control of her body anymore. *Two spots* was flashing behind her eyelids every time she blinked.

And then she was called.

Her blood rushed in her ears.

Her feet clanked on the ramp.

The darkness swallowed her whole.

Elara's eyes adjusted quickly. She was in the large inner room, surrounded by the metal that made up the drake's flank. It looked exactly like the one in Nobility, but this one was so large that it made her feel insignificant.

The door to the flank cockpit was open, beckoning her closer. She stepped inside, trying to keep her breathing steady. There was a cushioned chair in front of a flat panel with a dark screen. There were no buttons, no levers, nothing but a double-strap seat belt looping over the chair and a neck pillow built into the headrest. This was technological advancement beyond anything she'd ever seen in Deadegg, where mule-drawn carts rolled in place of stagecoaches and electrical lighting had yet to be installed in half the homes. But she refused to let that make her feel inadequate. This was where she belonged.

Elara sat down. She placed her hands on the panel.

Nothing happened.

Her palms flattened on the screen. She searched for the drake's heartbeat, even though it was made of scalestone and residual magic and had no heart to speak of. *Valor? Valor, I'm here. Please choose me. I'm choosing you, so choose me back.*

And nothing happened.

Elara was about to try channeling an astral through the machinery when Sergeant Owens appeared in the doorway.

"It's been a minute," he said. "If you'll follow me, I'll take you to your—"

"No, wait." The words burst out of Elara before she had even made the decision to speak, high-pitched and childish. "Just. Just let me try summoning. I didn't get to—"

"You don't need to do that for Valor to indicate you're a pilot—"

"But I didn't even—"

"Cadet Vincent." Irie help her, his voice was so gentle that it was *humiliating*. As if he had seen the core of her and found her weak. "There are plenty of other roles in the military. If serving your country is what you truly came here to do, don't let this discourage you."

A dream. Maybe this was all just a bad dream.

Elara stared down at the still-dark panel, wishing with every blink that she would wake up at home in Deadegg. "Yes, sir."

CHAPTER FIVE

FARON

PORT SOL WAS BEAUTIFUL WHEN IT WASN'T ON FIRE. THOUGH FARON had visited a handful of times since, she couldn't separate the capital from the destruction that still played behind her eyes.

During the ember days of the San Irie Revolution, Commander Gavriel Warwick and his family—his wife, Mireya, and his son, Reeve—had occupied Pearl Bay Palace on behalf of the Langlish Empire. The commander's dragon, Irontooth, had spent his time sitting on the rooftop of the stone manor house, spewing fire into the sky in smug satisfaction. But Port Sol had only been the most valuable jewel in Warwick's shrinking crown. One by one, the other Iryan cities had been reclaimed by Aveline's growing power and loyal army. One by one, Faron had channeled the magic of the gods to turn the tide of battles that seemed unwinnable.

Even choking under the violence of Langlish occupation, the islanders had secretly added drakes to their army to launch the revolution, hiding deep in the impenetrable Argent Mountains at the center of San Irie. But for the plan to march on Port Sol—to end this war once and for all—they'd had only four resources, if you could even call them that: a twelve-year-old girl with a direct line to the gods, her thirteen-year-old sister with beginner's summoning magic, an army led by a newly turned seventeen-year-old queen without a throne, and Nobility.

Just Nobility. The other three drakes had been busy keeping the rest of the island from being conquered again.

They should have died in that final battle. No one had said it, but she was sure everyone had been thinking it. Even now, as Nobility coasted to a landing on the runway of Pearl Bay Airfield, Faron could never forget that they almost did.

There was a circle of Queenshield waiting for them, but that wasn't what made Faron pause. Behind them was a small crowd of people wearing scowls and waving signs. STOP THE SUMMIT. NO NEGOTIATING WITH NOVANS. ONE PEOPLE, DECOLONIZED. As soon as the exit ramp opened, they began to chant. "No mercy to imperialists! End the Summit now! No mercy to imperialists! End the Summit now!"

Aveline looked out at her people with a lost expression. And then it was gone behind her queenly mask, curtained by distant politeness. Faron shifted so that she was standing half behind Aveline, happier than ever that she did not have to be a queen. "People of San Irie, I understand your outrage. But the Summit is important, and I promise you that I would not invite our enemies back without just cause. I ask that you trust me for now, and, once the Summit is complete, I will hold a public forum where all your concerns will be addressed—"

"We *did* trust you," someone snarled from the crowd, "and you organized a welcome for the very people who tried to kill us!"

"My daughters are *dead*," another one shouted. "They died to protect us from the empires, and you invite them here as allies?"

"They will *never* be our allies," exclaimed a third. "They will *never* again be welcome on our island. NO MERCY TO IMPERIALISTS!"

The chanting rose to new heights. The mob tried to surge forward. A line of Queenshield threw out their hands, which glowed with summoning magic that formed a barrier between Nobility and the angry throng. As the soldiers moved forward, so did the barrier, corralling the people backward like dogs herding sheep from the pasture. Faron saw Aveline's throat bob as she swallowed, but the queen's face remained placid until the protesters were gone. Only then did Aveline glide down the exit ramp, where her remaining guards swept her toward the safety of the palace.

Royal servants appeared next, dressed in cotton shirts and trousers of deep gold. They carried everyone's bags up the hill, leaving Faron alone on the tarmac with adrenaline pounding through her veins.

Well, almost alone.

"How did they get on the airfield?" Reeve asked, staring in the direction the crowd had gone. "I assumed there would be some outcry, but this close to the palace... That's dangerous."

"As long as Queenshield are present to keep things under control, Aveline opens the airfield to the public." It was a stupid idea, but Faron understood the politics of it. Aveline had taken the throne as a teenager, after all, and people wouldn't allow for her to rule in the shadows. If her every action would be scrutinized, why not allow that scrutiny on her own terms? "I didn't think it would be this bad."

The island must have been in true danger for Aveline to risk all this. Chosen queen from a blessed bloodline or not, she ruled only by the grace of her people. If they stormed the castle to dethrone her, Faron doubted the gods would intervene.

"That wasn't here five years ago," Reeve added when it was clear Faron had said her piece.

He nodded his head toward the greenery in the distance, greenery she had forgotten he'd never seen. While she had occasionally been called to the capital for one political reason or another, Elara and Reeve hadn't been back since the war. Faron had seen the city rebuild in leaps and bounds, scalestone and summoning magic re-creating what the Langlish had tried to destroy. Victory Garden, as it had been named, now cupped the palace grounds with lush palms, giving the ivory manor house the appearance of bursting proudly from a wreath of trees and flowers. Faron tried to muster up some of the awe she had felt when she'd seen it for the first time, but, as the adrenaline of her anxiety drained, there was nothing left inside her but exhaustion.

Elara should be here. She would have known how to comfort Aveline. She might even have had the right words to quell the dissenters. But if Elara became a drake pilot, Faron would almost never see her.

At least her parents had accepted the lie that Elara had gotten up early to take a stagecoach to the nearest temple. Her sister was a saint to them; of course they'd believe that she would pray for her friends out of the goodness of her golden heart. Then Reeve had promised to keep an eye on Faron in Elara's absence, and that had been that.

"I don't actually need you to watch out for me, you know," said Faron, the memory leaving a bad taste in her mouth. "In fact, I think this week will go by faster if we don't talk to each other at all."

Reeve stared at her. His hair rippled in the breeze as Nobility's hatch closed and the drake ferried down the runway toward the hangar opposite the palace. He'd cut it before they'd left, or the Hanlons had, so the wind did little more than tousle the dark strands into something that looked deliberately stylish.

Noticing that made Faron even more annoyed than his silence did.

"Well?" Faron asked. "Do we have a deal?"

No response but a gentle tilt of his head. Sunlight stretched through a break in the clouds, making his blue eyes glow and the red highlights in his hair shine like flame.

She scowled. "What, do you want to shake hands on it or something?"

More silence. But then she caught sight of the mischievous glint in those eyes, the way his mouth twitched as if he were trying not to smile, and she realized what he was doing.

"For Irie's sake, *why* are you so annoying?"

Reeve snickered. "I was doing exactly what you told me to. There's just no winning with you."

Faron turned toward the palace but didn't leave. As much as she wanted to, she knew the second she set foot into that building, she would be expected to perform the role of the Childe Empyrean. She'd be expected to act as pious and otherworldly as the adults across the island believed she was. The idea exhausted her more than staying out here being mocked by the enemy. Though it was odd to think of Reeve Warwick as the enemy right now when there were so many more of them flying in to see her.

"Sorry, but I'm not Elara," she said. Normally, reminders that she was nothing like her sister could ruin her mood, but she wanted to dig her way under his skin the way her anxieties lived under hers. "I don't make friends with spies."

Reeve snorted, but he didn't argue with her. He never did, not about her suspicions. Faron would love to have the freedom to believe that a thirteen-year-old Reeve had run across no-man's-land with Commander Warwick's battle plans, turning the tide of the war at the last possible moment, because he was a genuinely good person. But Faron was the Childe Empyrean, and war had taught her to be cautious. Reeve's father wouldn't have risen to become the leader of the Langlish Empire without knowing his way around a contingency plan.

And when Reeve turned on them at the end of his long con, it wouldn't be because Faron had let her guard down around him. The protesters weren't the only ones who refused to negotiate with Novans.

"I don't know how to feel about being back here," he said instead, his brow furrowed as he stared at Pearl Bay Palace. The white stone glistened in the midday sun, so bright it was almost hard to look at, but the deep windows were shadowed, hiding the dangers within. "My whole life changed here. One night, one moment, one decision, and my life was divided into a *before* and an *after*."

"Yeah." Faron sighed, relating to that more than she would ever admit.

"I know you think I'm a spy," he continued. "Other people have called me a hostage, as if the queen only keeps me here as insurance to stop Langley from invading again. I've even heard that I'm a target, here to be blamed for my family's crimes." Faron had no idea what he saw on her face when he looked at her, but it was enough to make him smile faintly. "I'm whatever you guys need me to be. I don't get a choice. But if you want to know what I think—"

"I admit that I'm curious to hear that as well."

The delicate moment frayed and dissipated. They turned as one to see Commander Gavriel Warwick approaching them from the direction of the side lawn. The clipped grass looped around the edges of the airfield and filled the space between it and a carved marble wall that blocked the ocean. On the other side of that wall, water seeped onto the shore, and one of the two islets off the coast of San Irie—San Mala or San Obie, both uninhabited but still part of Aveline's domain—was just visible on the horizon.

Faron would have noticed if he'd flown his dragon overhead, but he could have just been dropped off on the beach, or he could have been taking a walk, and she hadn't noticed until it was too late, and here he was mere feet away from her, and *she was trapped*—

Only Reeve's hand on her shoulder kept her from spiraling at the sight of this figure who had haunted her mind for half a decade. The commander was a tall man with skin the color of old glue, a close-cut beard the deep silver of a blade, and a smile that stretched his square face out to cartoonish proportions. A Langlish starburst pin decorated the right breast pocket of his black military uniform. He looked like someone's doting uncle, the kind who put sweets alongside the money in children's birthday cards.

It was hard to believe that he had given the order to burn San Irie's temples to the ground.

That he'd been planning to burn the rest of the island along with them.

The last time Faron had seen the commander was when Aveline's army had retaken the palace. He had surrendered in the throne room, his arms around his wife, his heavy gaze on his son, Reeve, standing defiantly among the Iryans. It had been too easy, so easy, as if the commander had known something that they didn't.

But as he stopped before them now, Faron began to doubt for the first time that his secret weapon was Reeve. Reeve had relaxed beside her, but it was a forced kind of relaxation. Even she could see it was off from how unruffled he usually was.

"Hello, Father," Reeve deadpanned. "Shouldn't you be inside with the rest of the dignitaries?"

"I wanted to make sure the Hearthstone Academy students were settled." The commander examined the hand Reeve still had on Faron's shoulder. She took a step to the side so it dropped away, but that drew the commander's predatory attention to her. "Childe Empyrean, it's an honor."

Is it? Faron barely managed to hold back. She didn't want to start an international incident just because she couldn't play nice as well as Elara could. She forced a smile that almost hurt. "Welcome, Commander. I hope you have time this week to take in more of the sights."

And she meant it, if only out of spite. She *wanted* him to see how well they had managed to rebuild, how much they had grown when they were not trapped beneath the claws of Langley's war beasts. Through centuries of colonization, the Novan empires had destroyed so much of what San Irie could have been, and Iryan culture was a hodgepodge of theirs. Their city names were a mix of languages from the countries that had occupied them. Many of their dishes originated from the parts of animals they were allowed to eat during enslavement. And while newer buildings were crafted in part or in whole with scalestone, older neighborhoods were built from metals and stones that weren't even native to the island.

But for these five years, they'd been free. They had flourished when no one had believed they would. They had come together under Aveline's rule, grown strong enough that there *were* sights to be seen. Faron wanted to rub it in Commander Warwick's face: *You have no power here, and you never will again.*

For the first time, she understood why Aveline had planned the Summit. She *felt* it.

Like his son, however, Commander Warwick smoothly avoided rising to her bait. His smile, when he looked back at Reeve, was a drawn sword waiting to strike. "You speak patois almost like a native. How quickly you adapt to the blood on your hands." He nodded in Faron's direction. "See you tomorrow, Empyrean."

Faron watched him stride toward the palace with the straight-backed posture of a soldier, and, as soon as he disappeared up the hill, she shuddered as if a lizard had crawled down her spine. Something about the commander's presence sucked all the air out of the area, making her feel as if she were suffocating under his influence. Reeve was silent beside her, his jaw clenched as if he'd lost something he hadn't expected to.

The look on his face... She'd never seen it before. For the hundredth time that day, Faron wished that Elara were here. Elara would know what to say, what to do, to stop Reeve from looking like an open wound that not even Faron wanted to throw salt in. She hated remembering that he was just an eighteen-year-old boy who was more acquainted with loss than she wanted to acknowledge. His countrymen had died because of his choices. The boy he'd been before that night had died, too.

Faron shoved those thoughts away. She couldn't stand any reminder that Reeve Warwick was human. It weakened her resolve.

"Adaptable, huh," she said, and if it lacked the usual amount of venom, then she refused to acknowledge that, either. "What an interesting skill. Useful for a spy."

That jolted Reeve out of his stupor. He rolled his eyes. "We should go find our rooms."

"Is that your polite way of saying you want to get away from me?"

"As much as I love letting you accuse me of things I didn't do, I figured you might want to take a bath and call your sister."

"How thoughtful of you," Faron said, mostly to hide the fact that it *was* thoughtful and she *did* want to call her sister. "Fine. I'll see you later, then. Or I won't. I don't care."

Reeve's slow smile almost reached his eyes. "Of course not."

CHAPTER SIX

ELARA

Unrest spilled through the streets of Port Sol, making Elara nervous as her squad rode into the capital. Faron had told her stories of the reconstruction—buildings restored, houses reoccupied, flowers replanted—but it was still hard to look at everything without seeing flame and ash every time she closed her eyes. People clogged the roadways, many of them holding signs that made their anti-Novan sentiments clear, and, though she didn't see evidence of the riot that had called them here, she could see why the officers had been worried.

Port Sol was a powder keg. It would only take an ember for it to erupt.

Reeve had encouraged her before they'd parted, without even mentioning that she'd been clinging to him as if he were the last buoy in a turbulent sea. "This is your dream," he'd said. "This is *yours*. Don't let them take it from you."

It was only his support that had kept Elara from quitting the Iryan Military Forces the second she failed to become a drake pilot, from returning to Deadegg with her tail between her legs to pack for Port Sol. Ending up here anyway, after the Queenshield astral called for extra security in the city, was the kind of irony that only the gods could conjure. Apparently, security detail was a job for green cadets, not experienced soldiers or newly chosen drake pilots.

Everything looked different from horseback, and not just because Elara so rarely rode horses. She could see above the brown-skinned crowds in the streets to the buildings that blocked her view of the crystal ocean, buildings that had been razed to the ground the last time she had been here. Cement and scalestone, iron gates and shuttered windows, thatched roofs and verandas shaded by palm trees. Overlooking it all was Pearl Bay Palace, sitting atop a short rise generously described as a hill, built in the style of the great houses the Joyan nobility had left like fingerprints across the Iryan countryside: a stone base and plastered upper stories, balconies that wrapped around the second floor, a double flight of stone steps that led to the front doors, panoramic views of the sea.

Faron and Reeve were somewhere inside, preparing for the first night of the Summit. Elara wondered if they could sense her closeness.

"You could be in there." Cherry, another drake pilot reject, pulled up her horse alongside Elara's, her chestnut hair styled into side-pinned coils. "And instead, you're out here with us. I'll never understand you, Vincent."

"That's the real reason we're no longer together," Elara said, because enough time had passed that it was mostly funny. "I don't want to benefit from my sister's status for the rest of my life. I want—"

"To make your own mark on the world, I know." Cherry rolled her eyes. "I just think that, with your talents, mind, and heart, there are so many other ways to make that mark. Why would you want to go back to war?"

Elara opened her mouth, but nothing came out. Cherry was an only child; she didn't understand the twin pillars of love and resentment that made up a sibling bond. Elara didn't *want* to go back to war, but when her sister's reputation loomed so large that it spanned the world, she couldn't match that with a quiet life as a teacher or a santi.

Unwilling to have this argument again, she turned in time to catch a glimpse of Port Sol Temple, a massive, one-story structure with an understated elegance compared to the ostentatious palace, glass sunrooms on either end reflecting the light in rainbow prisms. Commander Gavriel Warwick had burned it to cinders during the war, but it was another thing that had since been restored. If she got closer, however, she was sure she'd see nothing but blackened soil around it, lifeless earth like the patches all over San Irie, killed by dragonfire.

They rounded a corner onto a path that fed into the city center, an intersection of various streets and shop-lined sidewalks that met at a square packed with market stalls. A vendor with a machete chopped the top off a bright green coconut before handing it to a little girl. Bunches of yellow and green bananas spilled out of someone's cart, next to a cart with cherries, next to another cart offering bags of fresh-caught shrimp. Port Sol Temple overlooked it all, an attentive lover of the colorful minutiae of Iryan life.

"Get out of here, you Langlish whelp!"

Commotion in front of one of the corner shops made Elara draw her horse up short. A scrawny man, tan skinned and gray haired, was shoving a boy to the ground in front of the store.

The boy clutched something close to his chest, barely managing to hang onto it as he hit the pavement. His red-brown hair was haloed by sunlight as the Iryan man stood over him, but, even from only the back of his head, Elara would recognize this boy anywhere.

Reeve.

Elara's heart climbed into her throat as other shoppers began to turn. She clambered down from her horse and elbowed her way through the throng, ignoring their curses, the surprised cries of her squad behind her—anything and everything but the boy she could no longer see. Unbidden, her mind flashed back to the last time she'd found Reeve in a circle of people, in the schoolyard, his dragon relic hanging useless beneath his shirt. The relics, crafted from the remains of dead dragons, allowed their wielders to do some form of magic, weaker than that of a dragon Rider and limited by how much power was left behind by the beast it was made from. But, instead of using the weapon he wore around his neck, Reeve had allowed himself to be shoved around by Iryan students who'd needed an outlet for their rage and grief.

She knew part of him thought he deserved things like this. She knew he didn't regret his choices during the war, but he still saw the ghosts of his dead countrymen every time he closed his eyes. His nightmares, his guilt, his trauma were different, but she had connected with the sorrow in his eyes that matched her own.

But those were angry kids in a schoolyard. This was an angry adult, provoked by the Novans who slept mere miles away. She saw Reeve as he must appear through this man's pained eyes: a Novan child walking these streets as if they were his home, seemingly indifferent to the damage his people had caused theirs. And not just any Novan, but a *Warwick*, whose family had destroyed parts of the very city he now strolled through.

A wrathful cloud hung over the island as the Summit began. Anything could happen.

And as she shoved at someone who shoved her back, nearly sending her off her feet, Elara realized that she would never reach Reeve in time. Not without magic.

She drew on her summoning, and the astrals of her aunts cut through the crowd like a hot knife through butter, ready to help. As always, when they appeared, she had two options: use the power, the raw energy, of their souls to craft whatever her mind could come up with, or send them to accomplish a task for her in exchange for a subsequent ride in her body. Most summoners used the latter for astral calls, but Elara reached for Vittoria and begged, *Protect Reeve.*

Her other two aunts disappeared, and Vittoria soared over the throng like a blinding bird of prey only Elara could see.

By the time Elara made it to the shop, her aunt had created a shield between Reeve and the man, one that had stopped him short. This close, she could see that the man's eyes were lined with silver. A tear ran down his cheek and disappeared into his beard, which he wiped away impatiently. Like the man, Reeve could not see the astral who stood sentry above him, but, for once, it wasn't just because of the nature of Iryan magic. Reeve was staring at the pavement, his legs drawn up to his chest as if to make himself as small as possible. This vulnerable display only made the man angrier.

"It's too damn much," the man grumbled, harsh voice thick with more tears unshed. "We *just* attained our independence, and now they're all back, swarming like mosquitoes hungry for blood. I don't want his money. His very *existence* is an insult. Look at him." The man gestured down at Reeve. "Playing the victim after everything they did to us. My wife would turn in her grave if she knew I'd sold to this—this *spy*."

"Reeve Warwick is a *child* under the protection of the crown," Elara told him gently as Aunt Vittoria withdrew her shield and disappeared to let Elara handle this.

She understood; she really did. Elara knew from her friendship with Reeve that Iryans did not feel grief the same way as the rest of the world, but they *did* feel it. Astrals were impressions of the people who had died, incorporeal memories. Summoning her aunts for magic could not replace the feel of a hand ruffling Elara's hair, the nudge of a hip to move her out of the way in the kitchen, the warmth of a midday hug. For all its benefits, summoning was also a reminder of all the things they'd never have again, thanks to the war, and so of course she understood the bitter edge of this man's despair.

But Reeve had not caused these wounds. No one had to thank Reeve for doing the right thing five years ago, but they didn't have to hurt him, either.

"I know you're angry. I'm angry, too," she continued. "I wouldn't dare tell any of you how to process that pain when I'm still trying to myself. But this—attacking him just because he's here—is something you would regret. That's not who we are. That's who they are."

The man stared at her as another tear spilled down his face. Then he spat at Reeve and stormed back into the shop.

Slowly, the sounds of market life swooped back in, vendors

calling for people to come over, buyers arguing the price of fruits and vegetables, horse-drawn carts clopping along with packs of people inside. Despite the unrest, most seemed content to ignore the Langlish boy in their midst rather than pick a fight. One man broke away from the crowd and offered Reeve a cloth handkerchief to wipe his damp face. Reeve murmured his thanks, but the man just tipped his hat and moved along. A woman offered Reeve a cup of water, and she blended into the throng without a backward glance when he shyly refused. In her place, Cherry and the rest of the squad rode in.

But they were too late. Reeve was all right. For now, everything was okay.

Elara whirled on him, and he winced. "I'm sor—"

"Why are you here right now?" she snapped, punching him in the shoulder. Behind her, Cherry had dismounted from her horse, but thankfully, she didn't dare approach. "What are you doing outside Pearl Bay, let alone without the Queenshield? You don't exactly blend in here."

"You enlisted," he groused. "I wanted to send you a gift."

He opened his arms enough for her to see that what he had been carrying was a bag full of ripe mangoes. Her favorite fruit. She could only get them when they were in season and only when out-of-town vendors set up in Deadegg Square on market day. And he had risked his life just to send her an entire bag of them, freely available in the capital.

"Oh," Elara said. "You complete ass."

"You're starting to sound like your sister," Reeve said with a smile in his voice. Then he ran a hand through his hair, the smile dropping. "I really am sorry. I know that everyone is hurting now more than ever with the Summit going on. I should have sent someone else to buy them or something. This is a safe place for this community, and I invaded it, no matter my intentions. I'm sorry for putting you in this position."

"Are things that bad? In the palace?"

His next smile was a brittle thing. "Let's just say I was only thinking of how the walk to the market would clear my head. But I missed you."

"I missed you, too."

They met in a hug. Reeve's arms around her, his heartbeat steady in her ears, was a comfort she hadn't even realized she'd needed. He was her best friend, the one who knew all the parts of her that she hid even from herself, and he'd believed in her before anyone else. She started shaking, seconds away from crying over Valor's rejection, and she could feel him shaking, too, as if he craved this simple affection.

And then she heard her name.

"Elara."

She didn't recognize the voice, deep and yet clearly female, but it formed her name again as if it were something to be honored. And then it spoke:

"Don't cry, little one."

Elara yanked back from Reeve to look around the square.

No one was paying attention to her. No one was close enough to have spoken to her, no one but Reeve, who was watching her in confusion. And yet she was sure that she'd heard . . .

Elara Vincent. A ball of light appeared before her, speaking in Queen Aveline's voice. An astral call, though she was unable to see *which* relative of Aveline's was delivering the message. *It has come*

*to my attention that you have arrived in Port Sol. Please come to Pearl
Bay immediately. I will notify your superior officer.*

As quickly as the light had appeared, it was gone. Elara could
not channel someone else's ancestor, so it had gone to collect its
taste of life from Aveline. Aveline, who had already discovered she
was in the capital. Aveline, who had somehow discovered she'd
enlisted.

Aveline, who would probably kill her when they saw each other.

Now it was Elara's turn to wince. "Can I have one of those mangoes? It might be the last thing I ever eat...."

Reeve and Faron were not allowed to come with her, though not
for lack of trying.

When Faron was pried from Elara's side, she informed Aveline
that she would be waiting right outside the audience chamber
and glared until the twin doors closed. The queen weathered this
without comment or expression, but Elara could tell that she was
annoyed. She had spent her thirteenth year surviving the impossible with this woman. Under those conditions, it had been difficult
for Elara to ignore that she felt about women the way Aveline felt
about men or the way her sister felt about no one at all. Queen
Aveline had been Elara's first love, and though she was long over it
now, she had spent enough time studying every line and angle of
the queen's face to be able to read her.

Those dark eyes traveled to meet hers, and Elara blurted, "How
did you find out I'd enlisted?"

"I am the queen of this island," said Aveline incredulously. "Did
you think you could enlist in my army and I would not be notified?

I expect this sort of behavior from Faron, but I was under the impression that you were more mature."

Only five years ago, she would have given anything to hear those words. Now that she was eighteen, and Aveline was twenty-two, it felt like disappointing an older sister. "Your Majesty, this was always my dream. You had to have known that."

The queen sighed, and it was a familiar kind of sigh. The kind of sigh made by those who had been exhausted for so long that it had become part of their personality. The kind of sigh that had only gotten deeper and longer over the years as tiredness built in San Irie's young queen.

And even standing on the dais, her hands clasped before her, Aveline looked so *young*. Her smooth skin, the color of black milk tea, her big black eyes shaped like walnuts, her thick curly hair that fell down her back and framed her oval-shaped face—all of it gave her a childlike quality, but there was no color on her full lips, no jewelry decorating her round, pierced ears. She wore a diadem, a silver one that circled her broad forehead and disappeared into the shadows of her hair, but that was her only adornment. Elara could blink and see Aveline as a seventeen-year-old again. She seemed to be drowning under the weight of that crown.

"What's going on?" Elara asked. "Faron alone can't make you sigh like that."

Aveline laughed, though it was more a puff of air. "If I may be frank—"

"Please."

"—it is the dragons." Aveline lifted the front of her golden dress, which hugged her curves and fanned out around her legs, and descended the dais stairs. "The Langlish, yes, but the *dragons*.

I thought I was clear that each guest was allowed a small retinue, including guards. I thought there would be only one dragon, the commander's dragon. Instead, I am trapped in the position of seeming weak for not preparing for this loophole to be exploited, or cruel for sanctioning this so soon after the war. Every time I think I have a handle on ruling, I am proven laughably wrong." She paused at the bottom, taking a deep breath. "Sorry to—"

"No, it's all right," said Elara quickly. "I can—I'm happy to listen."

There was such a long silence that Elara could practically *feel* Aveline worrying that she'd said too much to the wrong person. But her need to vent eventually outweighed her need to keep everyone at a distance.

"The Summit hasn't even begun, and I've already been asked twice if I'm willing to loan out the Empyrean for independent contracts like a mercenary. I've been promised a trade agreement only if I agree to a marriage. He brought a ring with him already, so confident was he that I would accept and cancel any other negotiation. And I've been reminded *countless times* that I'm at least fifteen years younger than any other ruler in this building or in Nova. I'm irritated, I'm tired, and I'm playing political games with people who were born studying the rule book." Her eyes were flaming coals as they bored into Elara. "The last thing I need is any more *surprises* from you or your sister. Everything has to go perfectly, Elara. I need to know that you're going to be where you say you are. That you're going to be who I think you are. At least until the end of this week."

Guilt flared to life in her stomach. "Aveline, I didn't mean to—"

"I know you didn't." Aveline's hands came to rest on Elara's shoulders. "If you want to stay enlisted in the Iryan Military Forces, I support you. Please don't mistake this for disapproval. I think you are more than capable of doing anything you put your mind to, and I'm well aware that it is selfish of me to ask you to pause that dream for me and your sister. But if you want to serve this country, to serve me, then here is where you're most needed."

Elara was silent, tears gathering from the simple belief in Aveline's eyes. Would she still have that faith if she knew that Elara had wanted to become a drake pilot and failed? Would she still think Elara capable if she said no, turned around, and returned to her squad in the city?

Watching her sister, taking care of her sister, protecting her sister, protecting people *from* her sister... maybe it wasn't a paying job or the calling that she would have chosen. But she was good at it, and people depended on her to be that person. The mature one. The reliable one.

Maybe she could pause her dreams for a little bit longer.

Elara reached up to place a hand on Aveline's wrist with a reassuring smile. "Whatever you need."

"Thank you. *Thank you*," Aveline said, practically sinking with relief. She was an inch taller than Elara, but in that moment, they felt like equals. After all, who else could reassure the queen of an entire country just by existing? "The Queenshield outside will show you to your room. I'll have your clothing sent up." Aveline took a step back, her hands once again clasped before her, and raised her chin without a trace of emotion left behind. "I will see you tonight, Miss Vincent."

Elara dipped into a bow. "Yes, Your Majesty."

CHAPTER SEVEN

FARON

EVEN WITH ELARA RESTORED TO HER SIDE, FARON WISHED SHE hadn't come to the Summit. Donning the costume of the Childe Empyrean was harder now in peacetime, and she wondered how long it would take someone to realize she always felt like a fraud.

Aveline had her in a floor-length chain mail–like dress that evoked the armor she wore in every depiction of her across the island. Her shoulders were covered by a studded silver bevor, a thin collar at the base of her neck that expanded outward in an inverted half circle to cover the top of her chest. The pauldron extended in four lames down her arms and ended in shimmering silver sleeves that looked as if they could be a part of her dress. Palace servants had woven her box braids into a side ponytail to complete the look, but they had mercifully allowed Faron to do her own makeup.

Even so, she felt more like an ornament than a person, and the stares from the surrounding crowd were not helping.

Calm down, she told herself as another servant nearly twisted their neck to keep their eyes on her as they passed with a tray of white rum in crystal tumblers. *It's just one week, and then you can go home. Think of something else. Anything else.*

Behind her was a line of windows carrying the twin scents of seaweed and ocean salt on the breeze. The eggshell curtains brushed her arm with each exhale of the wind, as gentle as a mother's touch. *Her* mother was probably pacing the floors back in Deadegg, worrying the way she always did when Faron and Elara were out of her sight. There weren't enough astral messages in the world that could take that look out of her eyes now. That look saying, *This might be the last time I see you alive, and I want to memorize every moment.*

No. She couldn't think about that.

Instead, Faron inhaled the scent of the food that lined the tables to her left and right. Oh, the *food.* She could smell steamed red snapper stuffed with seasoned callaloo and cocooned by white rice. She could smell chicken glittering with dark jerk sauce. She could even smell braised oxtail pieces that swam in a black pepper sauce she longed to taste. Reeve and Elara were by those tables, her sister a sight in a bronze dress with flared sleeves and black buttons, both of them laughing over their full plates. Faron longed to join them, if only to use their bodies as shields against the endless stares.

But the Summit would not be ignored. Everywhere, she could hear conversations that could make or break her floundering new nation.

The banquet hall was filled with diplomats from the eastern continent of Nova, where the now-defunct countries there had been divvied up among three world powers: Langley, Joya del Mar, and Étolia. The few autonomous states in Nova were paying dues to the nearest empire to retain that autonomy. San Irie had fought for decades for its independence from Langley, the latest of the empires to steal the island's resources. And now the Langlish had come to shake hands with and pay respect to a nation that, five years ago, they had considered a neighborhood of their own.

Faron knew nothing of diplomacy, but she knew more than she wanted to about war. Every dignitary in this room was a predator sniffing their island prey for any sign of weakness. She refused to be that weakness, not here and not now, but *she wanted to take this godsdamned outfit off.*

No sooner had she reached up to adjust the collar than Reeve Warwick melted out of the crowd. He'd been stuffed into clothes that were more practical for the occasion: a newly tailored navy pinstripe suit with a silver tie that brought out lighter flecks in his bizarre blue eyes. His dark hair was slicked back, a single comma of a curl loose by his side part.

He looked mature and confident, someone to be taken seriously. She just looked like a child playing dress-up.

"What do you want?" Faron grumbled.

"To present a united front, of course."

"No, seriously, what do you want?"

"You seem about ready to jump out the window," Reeve admitted. "Elara sent me to stop you."

"She sent *you* to stop me?" Faron's eyebrows lifted. "Do you actually think you can?"

A smile tugged at the corner of his mouth. "I think I can distract you, at least."

"For that, I'd have to be interested in anything you have to say."

It wasn't lost on Faron that they were both now standing as far away from the Langlish delegation as was possible without leaving the banquet hall. But, right, he'd come over *just* to distract her. She tugged at her bevor again. Gods, it was so *hot* in here.

Reeve tilted his head toward a Joyan woman in a night-blue ball gown. "That's Rey Christóbal's favorite cousin, Pilar Montserrat. I heard she was in consideration for the Joyan throne until she set a potential suitor's hairpiece on fire during dinner."

Faron was surprised into laughing. "You're lying."

"It was in all their papers."

"Why were you reading papers from Joya del Mar?"

"I like to know things," Reeve said simply. "Now, that man over there—that's the tournesol from Étolia, Guienne Lumiére, surrounded by his musketeers. He's only sixteen years old, but he's already notorious for that thing with the wolf...."

And so it went. Reeve was full of funny anecdotes about the dignitaries, stories that reduced them from carnivorous monsters eager for their slice of San Irie to flawed humans with public shadows they couldn't even hide from their own people. Against her will, Faron found herself smiling, though her skin continued to prickle from the invasive sense that she was being watched. Even that was less grating with Reeve at her side. It was equally likely that everyone was staring at *him*.

After all, he was wanted for treason in the Langlish Empire, and his own parents had signed the warrant for his arrest. That had made *international* news.

The crowd shifted, giving Faron a clear view of a familiar figure across the room. Her mirth curled up and died. "Do you know any trivia about your dear father? You know, while you're still pretending that you're not working for him."

Reeve's smile, already as narrow as a waning moon, fractured into nothing. He stared across the banquet hall so intensely that Faron nearly wanted to take the words back. Then, as always, he decided that silence was his best defense against her.

He grabbed a tumbler of white rum off the tray of a passing servant and cut a path back to Elara's side. She saw the pinch between Elara's eyebrows when she noticed the glass but turned away before her sister could wield those disappointed doe eyes against her.

She ignored her flash of guilt. Whether Faron wanted to admit it, this was the second time that Reeve had stopped her from spiraling in public since they'd landed in Port Sol. But whether *he* wanted to admit it, she had more to lose by trusting him than she did by keeping her distance—especially with his father on the island. She was being careful, not cruel.

Wasn't she?

"Um. Um, hi," said a new voice. "Empyrean?"

Faron's nerves were strung so tightly that it took her an entire minute to realize the voice had not been in her head. She turned to see a servant staring at her with reverence.

"Hello," Faron said, drawing on the reservoir of politeness instilled by her parents. She didn't draw on it often, but it was always there, waiting for her to dive in. "How can I help you?"

"The queen would like to see you, Empyrean. When you're ready."

Faron held in a sigh. "Thank you."

The servant scurried away. For a moment, Faron longed to be her, to have nothing more to do for the night than hide among the rest of the staff. Then she sent a quick prayer to Irie for patience and went to find Aveline.

The second she stumbled into the crowd, Faron was accosted by hands to shake and names to forget. She locked her nerves in a box at the back of her mind as she made small talk and volleyed compliments and smiled until her cheeks snidely advised her to stop. Gossip followed Faron's every step, snatches of sentences piercing her forced calm.

"Did you see the Childe Empyrean with the Warwick boy?" an Étolian woman whispered as she passed. "I didn't even know he was still alive. In Étolia, he would have been put to the noose."

"All this power, all these resources, a direct line to their supposed gods," her companion whispered back, "and it's wasted on the Iryans. They barely knew how to—"

The crowd swallowed the pair before she could hear what else they had to say. Thank Irie. Rage bubbled under Faron's skin at how brazenly they spoke of the very kingdom that had welcomed them here. She thought of the protesters and their signs, of Commander Warwick and his sneering words, and she had to fight the urge to scream.

When Faron finally caught sight of Aveline, the queen was in a crescent of cleared floor space, flanked outside this polite distance by several dignitaries. Behind her were six members of the Queenshield, their scalestone swords visible and glittering at their sides. This time, Aveline's dress was emerald green with golden suns embroidered at the cinched waist and on the puffed sleeves. Her hair was twisted up into knots that looked like a crown, even without considering the bronze diadem that bisected her high forehead.

"Ah, Empyrean," said Aveline, her black eyes glinting like a blade in the dark as Faron took her place beside her. "We were just speaking of you. This is Commander Warwick."

"It's nice to see you again, Empyrean."

Commander Gavriel Warwick's bland tone made it impossible for an outsider to tell that they had spoken just yesterday. She hadn't even noticed him standing there, though that *did* explain the queen's poisonous smile. Unsure what game he was playing, she gave him a polite half smile and nothing more. The Iryans called him a monster, but he was dangerously human to her.

If she'd learned nothing else from battle, it was that *everyone* had a shadow. War just had a way of making some of them darker.

"The commander was telling me about the latest advancements in the Dragon Legion and the Hearthstone Academy," the queen said. "Apparently, they have added diplomacy classes to their training of Riders to emphasize their commitment to peace."

"And classes on public service," he added. "For Riders who want to become involved in local government. But all classes include mentorship, with the former group having the opportunity to learn from me and the latter group having the opportunity to learn from my wife."

"Did you bring your wife with you?" asked Aveline.

"Ah, no. There have been some minor issues recently, and, as the prison director, she just didn't feel comfortable leaving the Mausoleum in other hands."

For a moment, Faron felt a howling absence of emotion. The Mausoleum was the federal prison of the Langlish Empire; it was where they would take Reeve if he ever dared return to Langley and where they would gleefully have locked up Faron if they'd managed to capture her during the war. The casual way that the commander had invoked it, as if he didn't care about its reputation but knew that she did, made her wonder if he was trying to intimidate her on purpose.

That flame of anger roared back to life, licking up her arms. How dare any Warwick try to make *her* feel small? It was she who had made a fool of *him* half a decade ago.

"How interesting," Faron managed through gritted teeth. "She sounds very dedicated."

The commander noticed nothing amiss, but Aveline had a special sense for when Faron was seconds away from causing trouble. She raised an eyebrow. *Are you okay?*

And Faron knew what the queen was really asking: *Can you do this? Are you ready?*

She also knew that the answer to all those questions wasn't yes. At best, the answer was maybe. But the fact that Aveline would doubt her, after everything, rankled. If she could blast a dragon out of the air with her menstrual cramps making her feel faint, then she could do a simple magic demonstration with nothing but anger humming beneath her skin.

She gave the queen a thin smile in response. *I'm ready.*

"I think that now is a good time to proceed," Aveline said with a clap. The Queenshield corralled the crowd of diplomats back until the empty circle of floor had increased to a rectangle. "Our visitors came for a different kind of demonstration. Empyrean, if you will. Give them something worth talking about."

"Yes," the commander said, as if he deserved the last word. As if he were entitled to it, even here, even now. "Show us something legendary."

Oh, Faron thought with a fury so bitter that she nearly choked on it. *I will.*

CHAPTER EIGHT

ELARA

ELARA TRIED TO BE DISCREET ABOUT WATCHING THE COMMANDER, but it was hard to be discreet when she wanted to punch him in the head. Reeve was on his second glass of rum, and he was looking everywhere but at the father who was ignoring him. He'd recounted their brief interaction, as well as Faron's "pedestrian" insults, but he was hurting. Elara could tell he was hurting. It was hard, she imagined, longing for his father's forgiveness while hating everything his father continued to stand for.

But all Reeve said was, "He's not my father anymore. And he never will be again, because I don't think he'll ever change."

"It's okay that you still love him, you know," Elara reminded him. "No one expects you to just extinguish years of familial affection."

"He's killed so many people, destroyed so many cultures. He was going to end the war by burning every inch of San Irie to the ground." Reeve wiped a hand over his face. He left a trail of grease by his temple from the plantain she'd convinced him to eat. "How can I love someone like that? How could anyone?"

"It's complicated," Elara said, taking a cloth napkin and reaching up to wipe it away. "That's all I'm saying. It's a complicated situation for you, and I don't judge you for—"

"Look," Reeve interrupted in an obvious attempt to move on, "I think that's one of the Hearthstone students."

She followed his line of sight toward the windows. A girl stood with her back to the room, though from her side profile she looked to be around Elara's age. Her skin was a shade of bronze darker than any Langlish woman Elara had ever seen, and her ink-black hair was styled into fluffy waves. She was dressed in a candy apple–red gown that did nothing to hide the lines of her athletic body, and her lips were painted the same color as her dress.

In short, she was beautiful.

And Langlish.

Elara dragged her eyes away. "Is she the only one here?"

"The only one I've seen so far, but not the only one he brought." Reeve's eyes met hers, dark and wry. "According to the rumors, there are two more."

"Shouldn't it be four of them, altogether? I thought Riders came in pairs."

"She doesn't have a co-Rider yet."

"Hmm."

Reeve set down his glass, a grin spreading across his face. "You think she's pretty."

"I'm just going to go and be diplomatic. Do you want to come?"

"Ah, no. I don't think that would be . . . No. No, I'll just go and watch Faron's demonstration."

Reeve left before Elara could apologize for the misstep. She considered going after him, but he would have hated that. She could apologize later.

The girl turned as Elara approached, revealing a face as beautiful up close as it had been from across the room, all high cheekbones and glossy skin. Elara expected to see her eyes widen or her lips part in surprise at being sought out by an Iryan, but no emotion flickered across that perfect face.

"Welcome to San Irie," Elara said in greeting. "I'm Elara Vincent, the sister of the Childe Empyrean."

"Signey Soto," the girl said in flawless, if formal, patois. "To what do I owe the honor?"

Elara made her smile as bright as her voice. "I'm just doing a circle of the room. Getting to know people."

"Your circle looked more like a straight line to me." Signey tilted her head, and a hint of a smile crossed her face. It was a nice smile, but not a kind one. "You're not a very good liar, are you, Elara Vincent?"

Elara had no defense against that. Especially not when Signey Soto was looking at her as if she were an annoyance.

"I understand why she's here," she drawled, tilting her head in the direction of Faron and the lights that made up her demonstration. "I even understand why he's here, as much as I wish he weren't." Signey's head shifted a different way, in the direction that Reeve had gone. Expertly sculpted eyebrows inched toward Signey's widow's peak. "But why are *you* here? I doubt the Empyrean needs company in the royal palace."

"I'm just here for decoration," Elara said.

Signey laughed, and she looked as surprised about it as Elara did.

"*That's* your humor?" said Elara, delighted. People so rarely laughed at her bad jokes. "Your standards must be low."

"I'm laughing at how *bad* that statement was."

"You think I'm funny!"

"You're something, all right."

The smile that Signey's laughter had left behind softened her face. Before, she had looked distant, perhaps even a little feral. Now she looked open. Attainable. Elara shook that last word out of her mind before it could take root, swiftly moving on to the reason she had come over in the first place.

"So, you're a Rider, right? Where are the others?"

Signey seemed to weigh the potential consequences of releasing that information and then shrugged. "They decided to remain in San Mala, that little strip of land your queen has repurposed into a place for our dragons to roost. I'm taking diplomacy classes at Hearthstone, though, so getting to attend this Summit is the entire reason I came."

"I know what San Mala is. They do teach us about our own country here," said Elara. "What I *didn't* know was that Hearthstone Academy had diplomacy classes. I thought Riders were in it for the flying part." *And the destruction of other cultures part*, she didn't add.

"I do love flying, but being a Rider comes with certain responsibilities and expectations. Some people are in it to be soldiers, but those of us who have a choice..." Signey sighed. "There are many ways to help people."

"I can understand that better than you think. I actually just enlisted in San Irie's Sky Battalion because I thought it was the best way to help people, but now I wonder if...if maybe I did it for the wrong reasons."

Signey's smile was tinged with bitterness. "If you have to wonder, the answer is obvious."

The words cut through Elara's very soul. The reasons to become a soldier always seemed good enough at the time. Her aunts had taught her that. But she'd been enlisted for only a day and she couldn't stop doubting herself. On the other hand, Riders like Signey were chosen by their beasts before they were ever forced into the Dragon Legion. Elara knew that much from Reeve. But Signey stood before her now, claiming that, when given a choice, she was pursuing diplomacy. Elara had lost her passion for the Sky Battalion the moment that Valor hadn't chosen her, but she *did* still want to help people, even if she didn't know how.

She just knew now that she had chosen the wrong way.

"Maybe you're right. Maybe I..." Elara realized that Signey's eyes now caught on something over her shoulder. She turned to see that they were getting looks, not just from dignitaries but from a handful of the Iryan servants carrying trays around the room.

Elara imagined what they saw: the sister of the Childe Empyrean, laughing with a Langlish dragon Rider. Even though it was meant to be a peace summit, not many people wanted peace—unless peace meant being left alone.

Her own smile faded. "Well...I just wanted to say hi. Welcome you to the Summit. Um."

The way Signey was watching her now—as if she were a trap—made their brief connection feel like a dream that Elara had been having. She cleared her throat and awkwardly wandered off before she could do any more damage to Faron's reputation.

Or San Irie's.

Elara was contemplating a second plate of roasted breadfruit when the wind breathed her name.

"Elara..."

She looked around, but no one appeared to be paying her any attention. Faron was at the queen's side, surrounded by a crescent moon of Queenshield and a small pack of dignitaries. That had left all three tables of refreshments clear for Elara to put together a plate for her sister, who would want it once she was free of the demonstration. But now Elara set down the plate next to her own empty one, her skin tingling with awareness. The nearby curtains fluttered in the breeze, and the low rasp of her name seemed to ride those same currents, settling in her abdomen.

"Elara..."

She knew that voice. She'd heard it before, only a few hours ago.

"Elara...Elara..."

It felt as if she were the one being summoned. Was this how astrals felt when they were called?

A tugging sensation urged her forward, like a hook around her heart. But it wasn't unpleasant. Instead, she felt buoyed by a purpose she had yet to define, drifting through the banquet hall on light feet. For once, the fact that no one ever looked at her worked to her advantage. No one stopped her as she slipped out. Even the Queenshield on either side of the double doors gave her nothing more than a nod of acknowledgment. She wasn't needed in here.

But someone needed her out there. She just had to figure out where *there* was.

Her body carried her to the eastern courtyard, lit by the flickering glow of the windows that gazed upon it from above. Like the other sides of the palace, it was home to bushes and palm trees, to flowers and cacti; unlike the other sides of the palace, it was also home to the main part of the Victory Garden. Beyond the garden was a cliffstone wall, and beyond that wall was the open ocean, held back by a private beach only the queen could access. Elara followed her calling into the trees, pushing branches and broad, flat leaves out of her way until she emerged into a clearing.

She bit back a scream.

Perched in the center of the clearing was a dragon.

The dragon was at least fifteen feet tall and as broad as a building even with her wings folded against her spiked back. She was a forest-green color that blended in with the plants. Her eyes were golden, bisected by catlike black pupils. Her snout curved up toward the sky over sharp ivory teeth the size of Elara's forearm. Scales in a lighter spring green lined the dragon's stomach.

Currently, her neck was bent toward the ground, her triangular head parallel to the grass. And standing in front of her was a girl.

No, not just any girl. It was Signey Soto.

Her hand rested on the snout of the monster as if this dragon were her pet. It probably *was*, but that didn't change the fact that the queen had decreed that all dragons were to remain on San Mala while the Summit was taking place to avoid the exact level of panic that pulsed through Elara's body now. Whether Signey had called her dragon here, or she had flown over on her own, they were spitting in the face of Aveline's rule—and it was only a matter of time before *someone* saw them from the windows.

Aveline would be a laughingstock. She'd have to launch a show of force, to prove that ignoring her words had consequences. It would be an international nightmare.

Elara had to handle this quietly.

She stepped back, but a twig snapped beneath her feet. Both Signey and the dragon turned to face her as one, a puff of smoke escaping the dragon's nostrils. Elara froze there, her heart pounding in her ears. Maybe if she held perfectly still, the dragon wouldn't be able to see her. Or maybe she had to play dead? Her mind had emptied of everything Reeve had ever told her, everything she had ever learned on the battlefield, everything she had ever read in a book.

"Go back inside," Signey said in a waspish tone. "This doesn't concern you."

It took Elara a moment to realize that she understood her, even though the shape of her lips didn't match the words that Elara was hearing. She wasn't speaking patois anymore, but Elara still understood her, and she had no idea how that was even possible. Elara *had* been taught some Langlish in school growing up, but Aunt Mahalet had refused to let her practice at home. Her grades had suffered, her chance at fluency slipping away, until one day Elara had thrown a rare fit.

"Why do you *want* me to fail school, Auntie?" she'd whined. "Don't you want me to learn?"

Mahalet had kneeled down until she and Elara were at eye level, as solemn as a temple ceremony.

"Being forced to learn the language of your oppressors is an oppression of the mind. They rewrite your history when you're too young to know what you're giving away, and before you know it, it's too late to reclaim what you've lost," she had said. "Patois is your island's tongue, Elara. It's your *heritage*. It is the true expression of your heart. Don't give it away."

Elara now knew a few Langlish phrases, thanks to Reeve, but she wasn't conversational, let alone fluent. Faron had failed the class entirely. And, after the war, Langlish had been removed from their curriculum.

But Signey was speaking it now. And Elara understood her perfectly.

"Hello?" Signey jolted her back to the matter at hand, to the darkened garden dappled by silver moonlight and the war beast in the center of it. "I said that you can go back inside. Everything is under control here."

"*Under control?*" Elara found her voice to ask in patois. "Why isn't this dragon in San Mala with the other two?"

"An excellent question. One I came out here to get an answer to. I'd be able to get one more easily without you squawking at me."

Heat rushed to Elara's cheeks. *Squawking?* She'd been perfectly calm, considering the circumstances. No other Iryan would be so calm this close to a dragon. The last time she'd seen one up close, it had been trying to murder her sister.

But Signey didn't seem interested in any retort she could cobble together. She'd already turned back to the dragon and was running her hand up and down her snout and speaking to her gently. "I know you've been restless all day. I've felt it. But you can't just show up here like this. You have to go back before someone else sees you, or worse, before—"

"*I cannot return there yet,*" said a voice. That voice. "*Not until I have my Wingleader.*"

The dragon lifted her head to stare directly at Elara, and, though her mouth hadn't moved, Elara knew without question that the voice echoing in her head—now, inside, and in the city center—had come from the dragon. And she knew without question that she shouldn't have been able to understand her at all, no matter what language the beast was speaking.

What was *happening* to her?

What was *happening*?

"*She's here,*" the dragon said. "*It's her.*"

"*Her?*" Signey asked as though Elara were a disease she'd just been diagnosed with. Her downturned red-painted lips looked like an open wound. "But she's Iryan."

"*These borders you've erected between your countries don't matter to the bond. It's her. At long last.*"

Something about the dragon's eyes made the tugging sensation in Elara's stomach erupt back into being. Before she knew it, she was stepping forward, any fear she felt at the sight of a creature so otherworldly and enormous dissolving on the wind. Though the dragon's face didn't support expressions the way Elara traditionally understood them, her eyes seemed to be sparkling with happiness. Her joy was contagious.

Elara reached a hand toward her snout, but her wrist was snatched out of the air.

"What are you doing?" Signey snapped. "You can't just touch another person's dragon."

This is my *dragon,* Elara almost snapped back, but the thought paralyzed her. She couldn't have a dragon. She didn't even *want* a dragon. She had only wanted to answer this call, and, if it was leading her to a dragon, then she wanted to be set free. Signey's fingers were tight but warm against her skin, distracting her enough to gather her thoughts.

What had she been about to do?

"Signey," said the dragon. "*You know what must be done.*"

"There must be some mistake." Now Signey sounded frustrated, her grip on Elara loosening. "This isn't what... She's *Iryan.* We can't have an Iryan Rider!"

"Rider? I'm not a *Rider*. I don't want this," Elara said. Now she *was* squawking, her voice several octaves higher than usual, her words shaking on their way out, in time with her racing heart. "I don't—*I don't*. What's going on? I don't want this, either! Whatever 'this' is, I don't *want* it!"

Zephyra sighed, another column of smoke winding out of her nostrils into the open air. Fear lanced through Elara, not at the sight but at the name that had appeared in her mind as if it had always been there. She *knew* with startling certainty that the dragon's name was Zephyra, but how could she? What was happening to her? *"Come."*

Elara went. Against every urge in her body, she went, her feet moving with none of the hesitancies or doubts that always screamed within her mind. This time, Signey didn't stop her as she reached out to press her palm against Zephyra's scaly hide.

Fire raced through her body, fierce and blistering. A scream cut through the silence of the night, and it wasn't until Elara's jaw began to ache that she realized it was coming from her. She had assumed that joining the Sky Battalion would mean that she would one day die by dragonfire, but she hadn't expected it to happen so soon. Or like this.

This was *excruciating*.

"Breathe!" Signey shouted. "Reach out to her! Assert your control!"

Control over what? Elara wanted to ask, but her mouth was no longer her own.

Images flashed before her eyes, memories that didn't belong to her. She saw endless fields of flames and lava, mountains belching smoke into an ashy sky. She saw a dark-haired older woman who looked remarkably like Signey, pressing a young Signey's hand against the scaled egg of a dragon. She saw herself hurtling through the clouds, the sky little more than a blanket for her to roll in and gravity a suggestion that she could ignore. She felt rage. She felt ecstasy. She felt despair. She felt a keen desire to prove herself.

She felt everything and nothing, everywhere and nowhere.

She felt shattered and whole.

Her knees hit the ground, pain radiating through her legs and dragging her mind above the onslaught. *Assert your control. Reach out to her.*

Breathe.

She inhaled the scent of brimstone and ash.

Her chest caught fire.

"No." Signey's voice suddenly ricocheted through the garden, drenched in dismay. "Saints, not now. Please, not right now—"

Elara gasped out a breath, tipped her head back, and roared.

CHAPTER NINE

FARON

FARON STEPPED INTO THE SPACE THAT HAD BEEN CLEARED FOR HER. More dignitaries were drawn to her like moths to candlelight, presumably realizing that something incredible was about to happen. She could feel their eyes weighing her down, could hear their whispers clawing at her skin.

The Childe Empyrean. The chosen one, who is able to summon the spirits of the gods themselves.

A miracle.

A wonder.

A saint.

Faron closed her eyes and reached out for the gods. Anger pulsed through her blood, and she used it to help her concentrate on exactly what she wanted from this showing of power. Aveline had given her a list of ideas and warnings. "Do just enough to make them respect you, but not enough to make them fear you," she'd said. "We want them to believe we can handle any threats that come our way, but not that we are a threat they need to ally against."

The queen's lips had pursed as if she'd sucked on a lemon when

Faron had insisted on ignoring all her suggestions. She was the Empyrean, not a pet. Either Aveline learned to trust her, or the only demonstration she'd have was a demonstration of her inability to get the Empyrean to come when she called.

Now Faron summoned Mala, the goddess of the stars, the keeper of the astrals, the ruler of dawn and dusk. Mala appeared before her like a giant among ants. Her blush-pink gown rippled out from her trim waist in a waterfall of fabric, topped by a fitted bodice that brought out the red undertones of her leather-colored skin. Her waist-length curls were surrounded by a glowing halo of tiny silver stars winking in and out of view, a crown of the cosmos. Pupilless eyes gleamed silver as she collided with Faron, filling her with magic.

Power hummed within Faron until it felt as if she were made of the cosmos, too.

My dear Empyrean, Mala's girlish voice echoed from inside her mind. *Let's have some fun.*

Faron grinned in reply.

The lights flickered. The colors dimmed. The sounds hushed.

Make them see what I tell them to see.

Their magic sang in reply.

"Oh," the queen breathed, sounding, for a moment, like the gangly girl she'd been when Faron had first met her. "Empyrean..."

The hall had fallen away. In its place was a beach, white sand glittering beneath an imaginary sun with cool, clear water ebbing and flowing over the shore. The scent of salt and seaweed clung to the invented breeze that brushed over her skin. Faron had been to the beach twice in her life—only once for fun—but it was the kind of sight you never forgot: how the water seemed to go on forever, how it kissed the sky at the distant horizon, how the colorful fish twisted out of sight beneath the waves and gorgeous seashells clustered against the briny ocean floor. She put every bit of that memory into this living daydream.

But you can do more, Mala whispered in the back of her mind.

Any santi with imagination could make a crowd this size experience a beach, and that wasn't Faron's goal to begin with. She drew on more of Mala's magic and the sky darkened, shadows smothering the beach until the sand looked gray. A dragon flew above them, so large, its body was like a second sky. The heat of the day turned oppressive as the dragon spat flame across the endless blue.

She heard the gasps, the worried murmurs, and her anger returned tenfold. This was nothing but a conjuring, but it represented something that had been her life for *years*. These Novan dignitaries were just tourists to her trauma. They would return home to their continent, safe and snug in their beds, this memory tucked away somewhere to be forgotten. As if they weren't the reason this and many other moments formed the basis of her nightmares.

Faron released another wave of power, and a second shadow joined the first. A drake took to the air, its scalestone skin glowing. She had no idea which one it was—she wasn't Elara, able to name every drake and its color and its pilots by heart—but it aimed with single-minded focus for the dragon, then released a fiery blast of its own. It wasn't the natural flame that dragons held inside of them; instead, drake pilots channeled the magic of their astrals through the scalestone into an artificial fire that could burn a Langlish dragon's hide. The beautiful column lit up the beach, dispelling the shadows for a moment before the two figures collided.

The sun returned as their fight began in earnest, giving everyone a clear view of the battle. Faron didn't need to look since she'd lived it, but she did wave her fingers with a final pull of magic to change the ending. Instead of the drake tearing the wing off the dragon, sending it and its Riders tumbling into the water below, the dragon hung in the air in front of the drake before nuzzling its scaled head against the drake's metal one. A display of affection. An olive branch of peace. A moment that had never happened but contained the kind of symbolic resonance that these people would eat up.

"Amazing," someone gasped. Faron's body felt as if it were on fire, so she couldn't identify who had spoken, but their sentiment seemed to be passing around the room. Her job was done, thank the gods. She had to release Mala before she collapsed in front of them all.

Then a masculine voice resounded from everywhere and nowhere, as dark and seductive as eating the last slice of rum cake in the middle of the night.

It's begun.

The voice laughed, the deep sound so jarring that Faron's concentration snapped.

The beach scene dissolved around her.

And that was when she heard the screams.

Everyone turned toward the windows and doors, their awed murmurs turning to confused gasps and shocked calls. *Something is wrong*, Faron thought inanely.

The Queenshield who weren't closing around Aveline streamed toward the exit. Faron raced after them before anyone could stop her. Something was *wrong*, and where was Elara? Her sister would have forced her way through this crowd to be at her side right now, but she wasn't, and there was screaming somewhere outside. She knew that if her sister wasn't with her, then she would be running toward the danger in her eagerness to help. And she would never let Elara run into danger alone.

Faron's shoes slapped against the marble floor of the palace as she pushed her body as fast as it would go. But it didn't take long to find the source of the shouts. It took her longer to believe what she was seeing.

The Victory Garden had descended into chaos. There was a green dragon soaring low above the trees, a Rider clinging to its back. On the ground beneath them, her eyes ablaze, was Elara. Faron watched in open-mouthed horror as Elara threw a palm-size ball of fire at an approaching Queenshield soldier, knocking his scalestone sword from his hand and blasting him backward off his feet. The soldier's uniform, like many of the clothes made in San Irie in the wake of the war, was flame-resistant, but as he hit a nearby palm tree hard enough to crack the trunk, Faron winced in sympathy.

Being flame-resistant didn't save you from the threat of a broken back.

"What's going on?" Reeve gasped from behind her. The queen appeared seconds later, her fingers gripping her skirts so that she could run faster. Only Faron's battle-honed reflexes kept her from jumping at the unexpected sight of them, her mind already counting them as tools in her arsenal. "Is that—?"

"That Rider's clearly done something to her," Faron said. It didn't matter what she was seeing. It was *impossible* that Elara would do this if she were feeling like herself. "We need to contain the situation before it gets any bigger."

Aveline blinked. "The Queenshield are—"

"Making it worse." Faron turned to face them. She could see the rise in Reeve's button-down where his dragon relic was concealed, and she reached out to place a hand over it. She couldn't feel any of the Langlish magic it supposedly held, but it was warm beneath her fingers from its constant contact with his body. "Help me, and I won't complain about you for a week."

"That's a lie," he said, catching her wrist. There was a smile on his face as he drew her hand away. "But you don't need to convince me to save my best friend. What should I do?"

"I'm right here," said Aveline, and that was Aveline the soldier Faron had fought alongside. Gone were her pretension and her queenly mask. Here was her fear and determination on display, ready to act. "I'll help. What should *we* do?"

"Stop Elara. I'll take the dragon."

Reeve and Aveline disappeared into the garden without another word.

Faron's eyes locked on the beast, watching it bank over the ocean beyond the garden wall and turn to fly toward them. Suddenly, she was back on the battlefield, wearing armor that was too large for her small frame. She'd seen enough dragons spewing flame across the land to know what it looked like right before a storm of fire rained down. This dragon, a dark green that nearly blended in with the darker sky, had drawn itself upright in the air, its wings spread as wide as they could go, its head thrown back. Its stomach glowed a dull red, like an ember in a dying fireplace.

If Faron didn't bring it down, it was going to raze the palace grounds, and they would be back at war again. Faron couldn't deal with another war.

She needed a god. She needed Obie.

When the twelve-foot dark-skinned man with faintly glowing white eye sockets flickered into view, Faron paused to take him in since she called him so rarely. He was dressed in a milk-white suit under a matching robe, the hood drawn so that only his bearded jaw was visible. His trousers and the lapels of his robe were embroidered with gold, each phase of the moon set vertically on the fabric in silver thread. Against the darkness, Obie, the god of the moon and the lord of the night, shimmered like the pale face of his celestial body above. A king as beatific as his realm.

He merged with her, his power becoming her power, his strength becoming her strength. She stretched a hand toward the dragon, and magic raced through her body, radiating outward in an invisible wave. Irie was perfect for displays of raw power and burning flame. Mala could fool the senses, could consolidate the power of nearby astrals for stronger spells. But Obie's powers allowed her to manipulate the shadows.

Faron's will directed Obie's energy, and, as one, they sank into the broad shadow of the dragon; it surged up from the surface of the water and transformed into midnight chain links. These restraints looped around the dragon's body, and, as Faron closed her fist, they began to constrict. She saw the dragon twist its head in confusion for a second before her power yanked it downward, burying it in a watery grave. Her hand shook as she held onto it, and she could feel it fighting the grip of her chains. Would the queen be angry if she actually killed this dragon? Would that paint San Irie as the aggressor, or would it be considered self-defense? What if—

"FARON!"

She blinked out of the prison of her own thoughts, searching the garden until she found Reeve. The top buttons of his crisp white shirt were undone, and dangling from a black leather rope around his neck was a silver wire-wrapped dragon's-eye suspended in glass. A bulbous sapphire iris with a catlike pupil seemed to stare right at her, glowing like a beacon against the darkness as Reeve used the magic in his dragon relic to make a cloud of water hover in the air. His raised hand trembled as if the liquid was fighting him.

She was holding a *dragon* down with her powers, and his stupid relic couldn't even keep water in the air? No wonder she'd never seen him use it.

More details swirled into focus the longer she stared at him. He was kneeling on the ground, his free hand wrapped around a struggling figure—a figure she now realized was Elara. Her sister was wide-eyed and open-mouthed, coughing up water that rose in bubbles to join the rest over her head. Her sweat-soaked skin was losing color, and her hands were clenched around her own throat. Kneeling next to her was Aveline, her hands bright with summoning magic, ropes of pure energy keeping Elara from thrashing around and hurting herself or others.

"Faron, she's drowning," Reeve shouted. "Whatever you're doing to the dragon, you have to stop. It's happening to Elara, too!"

Faron released her spell immediately. The dragon burst out of the ocean, avoiding the orbs of summoned energy that the Queenshield threw toward it. Elara coughed up one more spurt of water before her eyes caught fire again. She blasted Reeve off his feet with a wave of flame that poured from between her lips. Aveline caught Faron's eye and nodded, a silent acknowledgment that they would switch roles. Her ropes of energy released

Elara, merged, and expanded until the queen had a glowing shield before her, taller than the castle. She pointed her fingers toward the dragon and jagged pieces of the shield broke off, slapping the creature back and forth like a toy.

With her last shard of magic, Aveline drew a trail of blood across its face—and it was Elara who Faron saw bleed. A scar wept crimson down her cheek as she threw fireball after fireball at Reeve's weaker shield. Elara brought a hand up to touch the blood and roared.

Like a dragon.

Like *the* dragon.

If Faron didn't take it down quickly, painlessly, a drake would mobilize to kill it—if Aveline didn't kill it first. Either way, it seemed that Elara would die, too.

Her heart pounded against her rib cage as she strained for some idea, some strategy, that could save her sister. Her thoughts turned to dust no matter how hard she tried to grab one. Tears stung her eyes.

Summon the dragon.

That voice, that voice from inside the banquet hall, had returned.

Faron wiped her damp eyes and looked around, but there was no one close enough to have said the words. Her fear for her sister's safety had pushed the voice to the back of her mind, but she knew now that it wasn't Obie nor anyone she had heard before. When a god spoke to her while she was channeling their power, it was not a whisper, sly and subtle, but a cutting command that overwhelmed all else. This voice didn't order; it beckoned. *Who are you?* Faron wondered.

Your salvation. Now summon the dragon.

Warmth suffused Faron's body, almost as if she'd stepped into a dream. Night had fallen, and she should have felt a chill wind made chillier by the nearby ocean. But this voice felt like stepping into an alluring darkness, a controlled danger, a level of comfortable thrill that she would have found strange in any other circumstances. It dulled all her other senses until there was nothing left but her sense of responsibility.

Her sister's life was on the line, so she listened to the voice.

Faron pushed Obie out of her body and, with the last dregs of her strength, flung her soul toward the dragon. Her knees buckled as her soul soared across the sky in search of a connection. This was idiotic. This was desperate. This was *impossible*. No one could summon a living soul, not even her. It went against everything she'd ever learned about summoning.

Still, she skimmed the contours of the dragon's soul, and it felt as if she'd leashed herself to a comet.

A rage like nothing she'd ever felt before pulled at her, nearly dragging her off her feet. It was like the first time she'd felt Irie's fire, but different because this wrathful power didn't burn. It consumed. It swallowed. But it didn't burn. She was like a pebble colliding with a mountain, a twig hitting a mighty oak. This was a soul as cosmic as the stars with a well of magic as deep as the oceans, and it didn't even laugh at her attempt to control it. She was too insignificant for it to acknowledge.

Take control, the voice said.

Control, control, control. The word echoed through her mind, strengthening her spine and forcing her forward.

Faron was tired; she was so very tired, but at the edges of her consciousness, she could hear shouts. Somewhere was Elara, poor

Elara, who only wanted to help people, Elara who could die—*would* die—if Faron let this creature overwhelm her.

No, she screamed, pushing more of herself into this connection with the dragon. *Listen to me. Obey me. Stand down.*

She felt the soul howl back, defiant but listening.

Stand down. I said, STAND. DOWN.

Against all odds, the dragon listened.

Now *she* was the comet, consuming the rage and the power and the will of a monster.

Faron forced it out of the air, forced it to land in a gentle arc upon the white sand beach. She forced its emotions to calm, its eyes to close. The Rider clinging to its back slid into unconsciousness with it, and Faron didn't need to open her eyes to guess that Elara had passed out, as well.

And then Faron couldn't open her eyes at all.

CHAPTER TEN

ELARA

CROCODILES WERE STOMPING AROUND ELARA'S SKULL.

She groaned back into awareness, every inch of her body alight with pain. Even her *eyelids* were hurting. For the love of Irie, what had happened to her? She poked at the gaping chasm where her memories should be, slowly piecing together a picture from what little she remembered. The call. The dragon. Signey Soto. The rush of power and the memories and the screaming, so much screaming. But no matter how hard she tried, she couldn't remember what had happened after that.

Her cheek was pressed to something soft, perhaps a pillow. From the gentle feel of the cotton fabric covering her, she was in a bed. She could smell herbs and antiseptic, which meant she was probably in a bed in the infirmary—assuming she was even still at Pearl Bay Palace. The ache that throbbed throughout her body with every heartbeat was distracting, but none of the pain seemed to come from an actual wound. At worst, she was just bruised.

Carefully, she opened her eyes.

Elara had spent a week in the palace infirmary after the final battle of the war, released after the first day but staying for the remaining six to stand guard over Faron's unconscious body. She recognized the mural on the ivory ceiling, which depicted the three gods—Irie, Mala, and Obie—surrounded by Aveline's ancestors going back generations. Closest to the gods were Aveline's mothers, the late queens Nerissa Renard and Kimona Castell, with scalestone swords in hand to protect their deities. This mural was just an approximation of what the gods looked like, based on Faron's childhood interviews with the santi, who had used her to fill in the gaps in their own spiritual knowledge, but Elara found it comforting all the same.

No matter how weak and confused she felt right now, gods and queens were watching over her. Irie was watching over her.

Elara tried to reach out toward them, but her hand was trapped. For the first time, she noticed that Faron was asleep in a chair by her bed, her head tipped back and her mouth wide open. She clutched Elara's hand as if someone might snatch her sister away in the night. Faron was still wearing the same dress from the Summit banquet, her braids loose and her baby hairs frizzing. Either no more than a day had passed, or Faron hadn't left this room since Elara had been brought to it. Or both.

Elara smiled, lacing their fingers together. Faron surged awake at once.

"Waa gwaan?" she gasped, blinking sleep from her eyes. She squeezed Elara's hand a moment later. "You're awake! I was worried about you. How are you feeling?"

"Confused." Elara's dry throat rasped out the words. "What happened?"

"We bonded," said Signey Soto. "You're now co-Rider to my sage dragon, Zephyra."

There were a lot of words in those sentences that Elara didn't understand. Even the ones that she *did* understand didn't make any sense. Signey was lying in a bed two rows over from Elara's, silver bracelets around her left and right wrists. A closer look revealed that they weren't bracelets; she was shackled to the bed frame. Elara didn't need to squint to know that the shackles were made of the same scalestone as the Queenshield's weapons and the Iryan drakes. Signey Soto was a Rider, after all, and the only thing capable of holding her would be scalestone chains.

Despite the name, scalestone was neither made of scales nor stone; it was the ridges in the metal, so similar to dragon scales, that had made the name feel appropriate. Found solely in the heart of the Argent Mountains, it was the reason the island had been colonized, prisoners shipped down from Étolia to work in those dangerous mines by the droves. Then the Joyans had come, ousting the Étolian militia and turning San Irie from a prison island to an enslavement colony. There was a seemingly endless supply of scalestone to mine and not enough crime to justify the free labor of prisoners alone. The Joyans had soon discovered that scalestone could nullify Langlish dragon magic and slice through impenetrable Langlish dragonhide, but it was the Langlish who had discovered the metal could also amplify Iryan summoning magic.

For an island new to having a national identity at all, it had seemed like a gift for the Langlish to help them craft the first two drakes in order to drive the Joyans out.

They'd been too desperate to ask what Langley might want in return.

"What did you say?" Faron asked, pulling Elara out of her thoughts. No matter how many facts she clung to or how much it comforted her to recite them to herself, her skin still crawled with the unpleasant awareness that Signey had upended her entire state of being. "Neither of us speaks Langlish."

Elara's heart stopped. She had forgotten her strange new ability to understand Signey no matter what language she spoke in. She hadn't even noticed the change this time. What was *happening*?

"I'm good with languages," said another voice, this one inside her head, the deep, feminine tone of Zephyra. *"But then, all sage dragons are. As long as we are connected, no form of language will be unknown to you."*

Signey smirked but didn't bother to translate for Faron. Her point had been made so well that Elara's world cracked in two. Bonded. She was bonded to a dragon. She had a co-Rider.

She . . . This . . . Oh, *gods.*

"That's Signey Soto. She said that Elara's her co-Rider and bonded to her dragon, Zephyra," Reeve said. Elara hadn't noticed him standing by the door, too disoriented to count all the people in the room. He, too, was still dressed in his clothes from the Summit, and his expression was pinched, as if he wished there weren't this many people in here so that he and Elara could have a frank conversation. Elara was abruptly glad to have that talk postponed. She couldn't process any of this, let alone talk about it. Not yet. "The queen and my—and the commander have been waiting for you to wake up. Are you ready to see them?"

"She *just* opened her eyes," Faron grumbled. "Can't they send a medical summoner in first to make sure she's healed?"

"You're fine," Elara heard Signey say clear as day, though the girl was leaning back against her pillow with her eyes and mouth closed. *"You're a Rider now. We're near invulnerable."*

"I'm fine, Faron," Elara parroted, numbness spreading through her entire body. "Send them in."

Commander Gavriel Warwick and Queen Aveline Renard Castell appeared shoulder to shoulder in the doorway of the infirmary. Queenshield stood in the hallway behind them, their faces solemn, their hands hovering by their swords.

A faint memory of attacking Queenshield soldiers flickered to life at the back of Elara's mind. Irie help her. They might be here to arrest her. They might be here to execute her. Surely, there were *some* things that being the sister of the Empyrean couldn't save her from.

But the queen closed the door on her guards as if they were no more than wall decorations. The commander observed the way that Signey was chained up without expression. Reeve had shuffled almost to the corner of the room, but he was close enough that the resemblance between him and his father was unsettling. They had the same paper-white skin, the same light eyes, the same thick brows, the same sharp jaws. They even stood at a similar height, towering over the women in the room, and carried themselves in a similar way, as if it were their right to occupy so much space.

It wasn't that Elara ever forgot where Reeve had been raised. But it was the first time in a long time that the sight of him sent a chill down her spine.

She dropped her gaze to the sterile sheets. "Is...everyone okay?"

"We managed to fix the damage in the garden," said the queen. "And the soldiers you fought are no worse for the wear. But perhaps the commander can fill in some blanks as to why we are even having this conversation?"

Commander Warwick swept past her to Signey's bed, tugging on one of her chains to test its give. Elara felt the odd sensation that he was stalling, but she had no basis for that assumption. If anything, he was being protective of a student he had inadvertently put in harm's way. "Perhaps we can have this conversation as a group of equals? I promise that Miss Soto is of no danger to anyone in this room."

"She and her dragon tried to set fire to the palace," Faron pointed out.

"An explanation for that will come in time. But for now, please trust me when I say that we really are as dedicated to maintaining peace between our countries as you are, and what happened tonight was not Miss Soto's fault."

"Technically last night," said Zephyra. *"It is long after midnight."*

Elara ignored her. It was hard enough trying to keep up with what was going on around her. Reeve was as still as a statue in the corner of the room, observing. Signey still hadn't opened her eyes. The commander and Aveline stood stubbornly near Signey's bed, as if waiting for the other to relent first. And then there was Elara, still holding hands with her sister and ignoring the signs that her life as she knew it was over. Maybe Commander Warwick wasn't the one stalling. Maybe it was just Elara who wished this moment would last forever so she wouldn't have to deal with the consequences.

But Faron clearly had no such reservations. She stared down the commander of the Langlish Empire as if he were a tree she wanted to fell. "Why would we trust you when you say anything at all?"

"Empyrean," Aveline said around an exasperated sigh, her silent confrontation with the commander coming to a tense end. "Enough."

Faron scowled as the queen knocked on the door and spoke to the Queenshield who opened it to attend to her. A soldier crossed to the bed, channeling the power of an astral into the chains. They snapped open and slithered down the mattress like garden snakes, curling up in a pile at the foot of the bed. Signey sat up, her back against the brass headboard. From that position, she could see everyone in the room.

"Commander Warwick," said the queen with barely enough diplomacy to keep the words from slicing. "Before anything else, please explain why a feral dragon was loose outside the Summit when all your dragons were supposed to be stationed at San Mala."

The commander traced the bed frame absently. Scalestone shackles were still attached to it, found by his curious fingers. "What I am about to tell you cannot leave this room. This is a matter of national security for the Langlish Empire, and I would hate for it to be wielded as a weapon against us when we have come to you in peace."

"One of your dragons tried to 'peacefully' burn down our Victory Garden," said Faron. Elara squeezed her hand lightly and she settled, tucking her head against Elara's shoulder.

"Shortly after the insurrection—or, rather, your revolution—our dragons began to act strangely. Feral." As he spoke, the commander's fingers danced over the shackles, back and forth, back and forth. "One dragon set fire to a small fishing village off the Emerald Highlands. Another attacked a professor at Hearthstone, who was then forced to retire. Yet another left the capital of Beacon under the cover of night and attacked a military base. We had our leading dracologists study this phenomenon, and they coined the term 'the Fury.'"

"You needed a researcher to tell you that dragons are feral?" Faron said. "Any Iryan could have told you that."

"They're not, normally," said Signey, her tone icy. "The bond between dragons and Riders is meant to, in part, temper the dragon's natural aggressive instincts with the human's empathy and logic. Once a bond is formed, a dragon should be no more or less feral than their Riders are."

"Indeed. But, instead, the Fury seems to drive the dragon into a state of rage that infects their Riders, as well. At first, it will last a few minutes. Then, a few hours. Then..." The commander finally lifted his restless hands, his jaw tightening. "Then it becomes permanent for both dragon and Riders."

Faron sat up so suddenly that she nearly collided with Elara's skull. "Wait, so what happened to Elara in the courtyard—?"

"Was merely the first step in a downward cycle."

Elara's pulse raced, and her throat felt as if it had sealed itself up. She still barely remembered what had happened in the garden. The idea that it was just the start of something worse was more than she could deal with right now. Faron's hand in hers was the only thing that kept her from drowning in her own panic.

"So how do we stop it?" Faron asked. "Have your dracologists found a cure?"

"If they had, I assure you that this incident would never have happened. Whatever you did in that garden was the first time we've *ever* seen an episode end without having to harm either the dragon or its Riders. So why don't *you* tell us what you did so we can replicate it?"

Faron's hand trembled. "I...I don't..."

Commander Warwick approached them both, his hands in his

pockets. In his midnight-black suit and tie, he looked like a living shadow. But his face was open. Genuine. If, of course, this man was ever truly genuine.

"Empyrean, it appears as though you're our only hope. I come to you on behalf of my country and my people. Please—help save us from the Fury." Something in his eyes hardened. "Or I'm sorry to say that your sister will be its next victim."

CHAPTER ELEVEN

FARON

Faron lied to the leader of the Langlish Empire without blinking.

"I don't know how to help you," she said. "I don't know *what* I did. I just saw my sister in danger, and... and the gods did the rest. I don't know if I can do it again, and I certainly can't tell you what happened."

His expression didn't change, but Faron had spent a lifetime hiding her own tells. If she could lie to the High Santi at a temple without an uptick in her heart rate, she could lie to Commander Gavriel Warwick. Besides, it wasn't entirely untrue. She had no idea what had happened out there, or how she'd done what she had done, or who owned the voice that had coached her through it. And until she had the answer to those questions, the commander didn't need to know she was asking them.

Besides, Iryan summoning was inaccessible to Novans, their astrals invisible to those without Iryan blood and their gods unseen to anyone but her. As far as she knew, every empire had unlocked their own form of magic, worshipped their own gods, and guarded their own cultural secrets. But even when people like

Warwick scorned Iryan magic or scoffed at Iryan gods, they still coveted their lands and their powers. They hated that Iryans had something they didn't.

The gods did the rest was tantamount to telling the commander that he would never, could never, understand the cure he sought, and she took petty pleasure in that.

"So what happens now?" Elara asked into the taut silence. "Is there any way to—to reject this bond?"

"A bond, once formed, can't be broken," said Signey Soto, still sitting straight-backed in the bed across the room as if her spine were a steel rod. "It lasts until death."

"I don't want to cast blame here," the commander said in the tone of one who was eager to cast blame, "but it's possible that the incident was caused, in part, by your newness to the bond. Signey is one of the best Firstriders in the Dragon Legion, and she's managed to keep Zephyra's moods tempered by herself all this time. Miss Vincent, you'll need to receive the same level of training and control, or you'll continue to be overwhelmed by your dragon. And that will only accelerate the Fury for all three of you."

"Spoken like someone who already has a plan, so why won't you just tell us what it is, Father?"

Another taut silence ignited as father and son met each other's gaze for the first time since the commander had entered the room. Reeve's expression was one of mild curiosity, but there was a coldness in his eyes that he couldn't quite hide. The commander studied him the way one would a rat seconds before trapping it. It was another riveting performance of hostility, but Faron had no patience for it.

"What *are* you suggesting, Commander?" she asked, drawing his attention back to her.

"I'm suggesting that Miss Vincent would be best served by the instructors at Hearthstone Academy in Langley—"

"You're not leaving the country with my sister. I absolutely won't allow it."

"Empyrean," the queen snapped, "please show the commander some respect."

"Not for this! Didn't you hear him? He's trying to take Elara away!"

"For good reason. Not as a personal attack against you."

Faron's cheeks burned. Leave it to Aveline to make her sound like a child again. "It's not that—"

"Is there any other option?" Elara murmured. "Can the instructors come here, for example?"

"They certainly could, but I don't think your people would appreciate your dragon being here, let alone more than one. Especially after tonight. Unless Her Majesty thinks otherwise . . . ?"

Faron wanted to slap his sardonic smile right off his face. She turned her head toward the wall to hide her scowl. It just seemed so ridiculous that a single night had dissolved into something that had changed her world forever. She and Elara had never been apart for the last seventeen years, and now her sister had to leave the country entirely? To train to be the very thing that Faron had become the Childe Empyrean to fight?

It wasn't fair.

It wasn't *fair.*

"Regardless of the number of dragons, we cannot have what happened in the garden repeated," said Aveline, but she was looking at Faron. If the clipped words were meant to be an explanation in lieu of an apology, then they were falling flat. Nothing could justify this. Not this. "If Elara needs training at Hearthstone to keep this under control, then she will have it." Now her gaze shifted to Elara. "How soon can you be ready?"

It was a long time before Elara actually spoke. "I don't know if I'm on leave since you—"

Aveline's eyes were pitying. "We cannot have a dragon Rider in the Iryan Military Forces, Elara. I *am* sorry, and I know I said otherwise, but it is true...."

Faron glanced at her sister, who sat curled in her infirmary bedsheets like a baby bird with broken wings. She didn't look surprised or even hurt by this. She just looked exhausted, as if the worst had already happened and there was nothing that she could do now but bear it. That was what Vincents did when they were hurt too deeply. They shut down. Faron would have done anything to take that look off her face, to share this burden with her, but she couldn't.

All her divine power, and she couldn't help her sister now when she needed it most.

"Please concentrate on healing," said the queen. "Commander Warwick and I will discuss the details of this training after we all get some rest. A medical summoner will be by to check on you both in the morning."

It was close to dawn. Moonlight peeked into the infirmary from behind the curtains that covered the windows on the other side of the room. The reminder hit Faron square in the chest, and weariness radiated outward from there until her body felt as if it could sink through the concrete floor. Even Elara was hiding a yawn behind the back of her hand, and she'd been unconscious for hours longer than Faron had.

Commander Warwick and the queen filed out, speaking quietly to each other. As soon as the door clicked shut behind them, Reeve crossed the room. "Do you want some water?"

"Please," said Elara, settling back against the pillows.

"And you?"

When Signey Soto realized that she was being spoken to, her lips thinned. "Not from you, traitor."

Reeve let the barb pass unchallenged and went to get Elara water.

"Don't worry, okay?" Faron said, taking her sister's hand again. "I'll talk to the gods, see if there's a way to get you out of this bond. If anyone can fix this, it's them. And if anyone can bring you home, it's me."

"You heard Signey," Elara said miserably. "The bond is permanent. This is *permanent*. I don't—"

"Langley has never understood or respected San Irie's magic or its gods. They can't do it, so they don't take it seriously. You can't believe a word she says when they're probably over there teaching everyone that we're primitive upstarts who are going to drive our fledgling country into the ground."

Across the room, Signey snorted. "I just want to point out that you're currently the one showing a lack of respect for Langley's magic and our gods." She shot a glare over at Elara. "And could you please put up at least rudimentary walls between your thoughts and mine? I can hear everything you're thinking, and it's loud and sad."

For the first time since she'd woken up, Elara looked more annoyed than scared. "I'm not exactly used to having to guard my thoughts. If it bothers you so much, put your own wall up."

In response, Signey turned her back to them. Her hair spilled across the pillow like a wavy wall of its own.

Elara muttered a word that made Faron giggle. "You know what? All right. It wouldn't hurt to at least ask the gods what they think."

"Exactly," said Faron as Reeve reentered the room with a cup of cool, clear water. If he noticed any tension between them and the other Langlish person in the room, he didn't bother to comment on it. "I'll talk to them. They'll break the bond. You'll be at Hearthstone for a week, maybe a month at most. Everything will be okay, I promise."

It wasn't the first time that Faron had lied to her sister, and it certainly wouldn't be the last. But as she watched Elara drain the cup as if she'd been denied liquids for days, Faron couldn't help feeling that she'd started lying to herself, too.

CHAPTER TWELVE

ELARA

ELARA BIT INTO ONE OF THE SWEET, RIPE MANGOES THAT REEVE had bought her as she stared out over the city of Port Sol for the last time.

She barely saw it. In her mind, she was back in Deadegg, a place surrounded by cities and villages and a mountain range shrouded in mist. Before the war, she'd never left her small town. Parts of her still hadn't. It took no effort at all to remember silver-haired Miss Johnson from up the street, a lonely old woman whose children had all moved on to bigger cities as soon as they could, and her glowing stories about all their accomplishments. She blinked and suddenly she was back in Blind Alley, a narrow gap between a restaurant and a clothing store that was nearly invisible until you were standing at the mouth of it, a popular location for neighborhood children playing hide-and-seek. The sticky mango juice on her fingers reminded her of the garden behind her house, of the bright green leaves of the cherry trees and skeletal blue mahoes, the rapidly spreading scarlet hibiscus flowers and deep indigo lignum vitae blossoms unfurling in the sun.

As far as towns went, Deadegg was a decimal point at the base of the Argent Mountains that wasn't even identified on most maps. But, gods, Elara was going to miss it.

Sea air on the breeze eased her out of her memories. The scent of salt and brine could never be found in landlocked Deadegg. At best, there was only the muddy smell that occasionally wafted up from the green-brown swamp water of the gully. Elara turned away from the balcony view to get a napkin to clean her hands with and realized that the queen of San Irie was in her bedroom.

She nearly dropped her mango.

"Oh! Your Majesty!" Elara went back inside and slid the balcony doors shut. As an afterthought, she also closed the curtains, though she doubted anyone could see them up here. "Um, Faron just left, but she'll be back in a—"

"I am not here for Faron."

Elara hadn't seen the queen since the night before, when she had agreed that Elara should leave behind all she'd ever known for the safety of everyone she'd ever cared about. Whether due to exhaustion or the emotional ordeal, Elara had slept through the medical summoning and then through most of the morning. When she'd woken up in the early afternoon, she and Signey had been discharged—and with the second day of the Summit canceled while the queen dealt with all of this, Elara had nothing else to do but pack.

She eyed the Queenshield lined up before the door as she stuffed her half-eaten mango back in the bag with the rest of them. The sight of so many soldiers made the fruit sour in her stomach.

"I will try to keep this fast." Aveline strode forward, her golden diadem catching the light. She spread her arms, and a glittering film, thin as the congealed surface of a bowl of porridge, began to spread across the floor, the ceiling, the walls. It muffled the sounds outside the room, until Elara could hear nothing but her own breathing. Despite this show of power, the queen's voice was a low whisper when she spoke. "I've placed a barrier around this room to be safe, but can they hear you?"

Elara began to say no, but the seriousness of the situation made her stop to actually check. Even without concentrating, she could feel Signey and Zephyra like extensions of her body. She knew at once that they had gone flying. She could feel the cool brush of the wind on her face and, when she closed her eyes, she could even see the ocean as a rippling blanket of blue between gaps in the clouds. But her thoughts and her feelings were definitely her own. She could hear nothing from them unless they were directly speaking to her, and it had stayed that way since Signey had put her mental walls up. It was a comforting thing, considering how many uncharitable thoughts she'd had about Signey in the last few hours.

"No," she answered. "They can't hear me unless I want them to, I think."

"I need to give you an assignment, if you are *certain* we can speak freely."

Elara reached out to Signey and Zephyra, screaming both of their names as loudly as she could without speaking. Neither of them gave any indication that they'd heard her, not even a flicker of annoyance to show she was being purposefully ignored.

"I'm certain," she said. "An assignment?"

Elara squashed the part of her that wanted to ask, again, if the queen meant to be saying this to Faron. Aveline had come to *her*. Aveline was looking at *her*. She didn't want to give her a reason to look away so soon.

"I know you likely think me cold for pushing you into the enemy's arms so easily. Or perhaps you hate me for breaking my promise to you that you could return to the army. But I believe that the Langlish are planning something, and, right now, you are at the center of that." Aveline said this as if it were an accepted fact and not something that made Elara's eyes widen. "You are going there at their invitation, bonded to one of their sacred creatures, and thus you will be privy to things only their so-called saints usually get to be privy to. I think you can likely tell where I am going with this."

"You ... want me to spy?"

"More or less. You are in the perfect position to be our eyes and ears in Langley, provided, of course, that your co-Rider really isn't listening in. And provided that you can even keep this from her when she's in your head." Aveline frowned. "Maybe this is a bad idea."

"No!" Elara blurted. She was no spy. She'd never worn deception well. She had wanted to be a *soldier*, something that seemed open and honorable compared to this kind of subterfuge. But she could never join the Sky Battalion now, and at least this would give her a chance to feel as if she were making a difference. "No, I can do it. I think I can do it. There might be some trial and error, but I'm willing."

Aveline's smile was small but warm. "You're very brave, Elara. Both you and your sister are incredible, brave, wonderful women, and it's been the best kind of honor to watch you grow."

Elara's heart thudded in her chest from the strange finality of the compliment. It was almost as if Aveline didn't actually expect her to come back, but she pushed that idea out of her head. It didn't matter whether the queen expected her to come back or not. *Faron* would expect her to come back—and, if Elara didn't, Faron would tear apart both countries looking for her.

But her heart beat hummingbird-fast, even so.

"It's been an honor to know you, too, Aveline," she said. "And I appreciate you trusting me with this mission. I won't let you down. But...what do you think the Langlish are planning? What am I supposed to be looking for?"

Aveline stepped past her toward the balcony doors. She was quiet for so long that Elara began to feel awkward about her question. Maybe she shouldn't have asked. She wasn't Faron. What right did she have to question the queen?

But the queen was not the queen right now. She had softened those sharp edges, that steel demeanor, something she only seemed to do around Elara. As if Elara were the sister she'd chosen.

"This situation feels wrong," said Aveline. "They arrive with more dragons than I expected, so I call in the Empyrean early. You, of all people, bond with one of the dragons they've brought, and we find out about the Fury for the first time. Now the Empyrean has to divert her attention to curing it for them because your life is at stake? Too much of this has worked out in Langley's favor for me not to believe at least some of it was planned. And it's much easier to go back to war if you don't lose control of your dragon midflight."

This time, Elara's heart stopped. "You think the Langlish Empire wants to start another war?"

"They've almost started three in as many days." Aveline turned around, looking older than Elara had ever seen her. "San Irie has only just recovered from the last war. We can't handle another."

"We have the drakes." The last thing Elara wanted for her island, for herself, and especially for Faron was another war. But she couldn't stand that look on the queen's face, as if she'd already been defeated before the first battle had been fought. "We have more drakes built than we ever had before! I think we'd be able to hold them off the island this time, if it comes to that. Maybe even take the fight to them."

"War takes more than drakes, Elara. Wars also require support, and I'm just not sure I would have that going into another one only five years after the end of the first. I am barely clinging to public support as it is. You were in the city. You saw the protesters. The position I am in is so precarious; anything could shatter it." Aveline rubbed her temples. "Even if I'm seeing plots where there aren't any, there's still the fact that if they decide to attack with the very dragon who you're bonded to, we can't fight back without hurting you as well. And that alone is a weapon we can't let them keep up their sleeve."

Aveline looked so hopeless. She had seemed like such an adult just a few years ago, when Elara had been thirteen and convinced that Aveline was the most beautiful girl she'd ever seen. But in this moment, Elara saw Aveline for what she really was: an orphaned woman barely out of her teens, thrust into a legacy she hadn't asked for but was giving everything she had to uphold.

"We'll help you avoid a war," Elara swore. "Faron's more focused on finding a cure for the bond than one for the Fury. I'll keep my eyes and ears open in Langley and alert you to any sign that they're preparing for another attack. Whatever they teach me about dragons' weaknesses and vulnerabilities, I'll report back to you, too. I won't let them use me against my own country. I refuse."

This time, Aveline's smile was wider. "Thank you." She adjusted her diadem over her head wrap. When her hands lowered, any trace of weakness had been wiped clean from her expression. The vulnerable woman had disappeared; the untouchable queen had returned. "I will come to you again to say goodbye before your flight. Right now, though, your family is outside, and I am sure they are eager to see you."

Elara winced, and, to her surprise, Aveline laughed. It was such a bright, rare sound. Elara couldn't remember the last time she'd heard it.

"Your fear is unwarranted," she said. "They do not know about your enlistment, and they will not hear about it from me." The queen winked, removing the barrier with a wave of her hand. "You and your sister are not the only ones who know how to lie."

As soon as Aveline was gone, Elara turned back to the balcony doors. Soon, her parents would enter, blissfully ignorant of her crimes as they saw her off. Soon, Faron and Reeve would return, and they would all get to say a proper goodbye. Soon, Signey and Zephyra would arrive to help her secure her bags to Zephyra's saddle for the long trip across the Ember Sea. This was the last time that she would be in the only home she had ever known before she stepped forward into an uncertain future—a future in which she would have to pretend to become everything she'd learned to fear. Worse, she had no idea how long it would be before she would come back. Or if she would even come back at all.

But she was ready for that. She had a mission. No matter how hard things got for her in the Langlish Empire, she would not fail.

Elara Vincent didn't need to be the Childe Empyrean to be a hero. And she was going to prove that to everyone. Her family. Her countrymen. And, most of all, herself.

CHAPTER THIRTEEN

FARON

ARON'S TIME WITH HER SISTER WAS RUNNING OUT, AND YET SHE stood planted like a new palm tree in the hallway outside Elara's chambers. She didn't want to say goodbye to Elara. She wanted to sweep into her room with a solution. But after last night's attack, the Port Sol Temple was so full of people praying that there had been a line for the sunroom—and a sunroom was the only place that Faron could speak to all three of the gods at once.

At the time, Faron had pictured the look of disappointment on Elara's face if she heard that Faron had thrown people out of the temple on her behalf. And summoning the gods one by one for answers would have only resulted in her sleeping through Elara's departure. Now, lingering in the hall, Faron wished that she *had* cleared the sunroom. What was the point of being the Empyrean if she couldn't use the title to help the people she cared about?

Stop being such a child. Go spend time with your family. With Elara. Before it's too—

Movement at the mouth of the corridor drew her attention. Two figures were passing by on their way to somewhere else. Reeve Warwick... and Commander Gavriel Warwick.

Of course. *Of course.*

Faron followed them. The Queenshield who lined the walls showed no reaction to them or to her, making her wonder how often Reeve had been openly meeting with his father. Did the queen know? Did *Elara* know? And should Faron even tell her when she was about to enter a den of snakes?

She slipped into an empty room just down the hall from the one the Warwicks had entered. Then she reached out for Mala and her powers of illusion. Faron felt the surge of divine magic spreading throughout her body, her senses more alert than they'd ever been, her body running hotter than usual. Mala settled within her, and the room came back into view. It was empty except for a gilded trunk and an ornate mirror. Her reflection in the latter told a story of a wild-eyed girl avoiding her problems.

Faron cloaked herself in Mala's power, using the energy of her soul to bend the light in the room until she couldn't even see herself. She was still solid and audible, but if she stayed quiet and out of the way, then the Warwicks would never know she was there.

They'd left the door open, which seemed like the height of arrogance before Faron realized the first problem with her plan. Commander Warwick was standing in front of the window, but he was speaking Langlish—and Faron could barely say her own name in that language. Reeve was leaning against the wall to the left, next to a half-stocked bookshelf. Just like last time, he was putting on a performance. The Reeve Warwick she knew was sarcastic and collected, arrogant and sanctimonious. Now, alone with his father, his shoulders were an insouciant line and there was a dangerous smile on his face.

It wasn't exactly like looking at a stranger, but it was...something.

The commander had been given a room no different from Elara's, except that his color scheme was sea blue and salt white, and he had a mahogany desk and cushioned chair by the bathroom. His bed had been made with military efficiency, and if he'd brought any belongings with him, then they were nowhere to be seen. He had no balcony, but he had a set of windows that overlooked the ocean. San Mala was a narrow strip of green in the distance, and he faced it with his hands folded behind his back.

"It's been five years, but I know you better than anyone here, Father," Reeve said in patois. "This is my home now, this is the language I speak, and these are the people I would do anything to protect. I trust it won't come to that."

Commander Warwick turned. There was a friendly smile on his face, but his eyes were so cold that Faron almost took a step back. Neither of them knew she was here, and yet there was a thick tension in the room. This didn't feel like a private reunion between father and son, and it certainly didn't feel like a relaxed meeting between spy and spymaster.

Something was wrong.

"From what I've observed," said Commander Warwick in his accented patois, "these people you'd do anything to protect wouldn't shed a tear if you died in front of them."

"The Langlish wouldn't shed one for you, either," Reeve said brightly. "That tends to happen after losing an easy war to a child."

"There is no such thing as an *easy* war."

"Then why is the Langlish Empire the laughingstock of the continent?"

"Ignorance." That single word was filled with so much loathing that even the commander's rictus smile couldn't make it seem polite.

Reeve just shrugged, as if this were nothing but a nice afternoon stroll in the park for him. But when he switched into Langlish, and Faron was no longer distracted by his words, she could see the way his hands were tucked into his pockets as if he were afraid they would give him away by shaking. His posture was loose and easy, but she knew him—she knew him whether she wanted to or not—and this verbal battle wasn't as effortless as he was making it seem. Both of them were smiling, casual and amused, but their eyes were searching for a weakness to fire into.

They hate each other, Mala mused. *You can just* feel *it.*

Faron could definitely feel it, and she didn't know what to do with it. For the last five years, she had believed that Reeve was a trap set by his father, and she had waited for the moment that trap would be activated. Part of her had even been eager to finally have her suspicions confirmed, to put an end to her conflicted feelings toward her sister's best friend and be vindicated once and for all. But Commander Warwick seemed as if he'd rather kill his son himself than wield him against anyone else.

It was something she would never have believed if she weren't seeing it for herself.

And if that was true...if Reeve had come here to threaten him even knowing that...

"I had hoped you would be more susceptible to reason after so many years, but I see you've chosen to be a disappointment," the commander said, switching back to patois. "You betrayed us. You ruined everything. Langlish blood is on your hands, while you debase yourself for people who will never care about you. Continue to waste your life on this island of rebels and thieves. It's no concern of mine."

Reeve pushed off the wall and strode across the room with a predatory grace. His gaze was sharp, his jaw set. The commander had clearly seen too much in his long life to be unnerved by a teenager, but Faron saw his hands clench just slightly at his sides. As if he were getting ready for a fight.

"You always think you shouldn't be concerned about me. That's your mistake to make," Reeve said in a low voice. "But I'll find out what you're planning, and I'll stop you. Just like I did last time. Just like I will *every* time."

Reeve turned to leave but stopped when the commander said something in Langlish that made a shadow pass over Reeve's face. "You can try," he replied darkly.

It took Faron a long time to dust off the old knowledge of lessons in the back of her mind and translate one word from the commander's statement as *mother*. By then, he was already sitting at his desk, clearly finished with this interaction. His first interaction with his only son in five years.

It didn't make any sense.

She studied the commander's back, half expecting him to turn with a smirk that would reveal he'd known she was there all along. But he was flipping through his papers, and Reeve was walking toward the door. The commander didn't pause, didn't even seem to be listening for the door to close. It was as if Reeve didn't matter at all.

Swallowing her confusion, Faron hurried behind Reeve and silently slipped past the door before it shut.

All the bravado Reeve had wrapped around himself dissolved into nothing in that hallway. His shoulders were slumped with fatigue, but his steps were quick with an eagerness to get away from that room. Faron had to jog to keep up with him, and even still, she had no idea what to say or what to feel. Everything she'd ever thought about Reeve—five years of assumptions—had gone up in smoke in the last twenty minutes. Where was she supposed to go from here?

Gods, did she have to *apologize* to him? Her tongue might fall out.

Reeve didn't slow down until he'd left the guest wing of the palace and was making his way toward Elara's room. Faron mumbled a goodbye to Mala before dismissing her, then stumbled a little from the emptiness that rushed in to replace the magic. Reeve caught her arm, erasing the distance between them in an instant. Once she could stand on her own, he seemed to realize what he'd done—or, rather, for whom—and let her go as if she were on fire.

"Did you know I was there?" Faron demanded instead of lingering on how nice his touch had felt. How she almost missed it.

"Where?" Reeve asked. "Following me? I don't know when you started, but you've been stumbling around loudly behind me for at least three hallways now."

She believed him. Irie help her, she believed him. And if he hadn't known—if *they* hadn't known—

"What did the commander say? When you were leaving that room, he said something in Langlish. What did he say?"

Reeve inhaled sharply and scanned her with too-wide eyes, as if he were trying to figure out exactly how much she'd heard. Then he dragged a hand over his face. "He said that my mother might have forgiven me for what I'd done, but *he* thought I was too old to excuse it with childhood innocence. And he said that if I ever set foot in the Langlish Empire again, he'll kill me himself."

You can try, Reeve had growled back.

Faron suppressed a shiver. Reeve's tone was matter-of-fact now, but the way he avoided looking at her spoke of a pain deeper than she'd ever taken the time to acknowledge. *I'm sorry* felt insufficient for something like this, especially coming from her. *That's so terrible* would sound sarcastic on her tongue. And *Are you okay?* seemed like a question she hadn't earned an honest answer to.

The silence stretched past the acceptable amount of time for her to come up with something. When Reeve finally looked at her, he'd reconstructed his mask with her on the outside where she belonged. Any trace of vulnerability was gone, replaced by a solemn determination.

"More important," he said, "we have the confirmation that he's definitely planning something, so we should tell the queen."

"Wait. We do?"

"You don't know my father like I do. He didn't say anything that would incriminate him to anyone else, but he still said a lot. Langley is a laughingstock because people don't know any better. San Irie is full of 'rebels and thieves' rather than people. Even the way he was looking at San Mala was..." Reeve straightened, as if something new had occurred to him. "Curing the Fury will only help him, but I think this goes deeper than that. His loss to San Irie was one of the most humiliating failed military campaigns of this century, and within days of coming back, he's excused a direct attack, talked the queen into letting Elara leave, and has you essentially working for him. He wants something. He's planning something. And it's big."

Faron didn't like the idea that things could get bigger than this. The threat of another war hung over her head like a blade, ready to cleave her in two. Part of her remembered the rage that seemed to spark at her fingertips as she was made to perform her power for the Novan dignitaries; they wouldn't be so entertained if they were facing her on the battlefield, forced to remember once more that San Irie and the Childe Empyrean were a force to be reckoned with. But that was a small part of her, drowned out by nightmares of fire and destruction, smoke and death.

War didn't prove one country was stronger than another. It just snuffed out lives from each nation until only mourners were left to make sense of it all.

She stopped in the center of the hallway, heart sinking. "What if there's no way to save Elara without playing right into his hands? What if, no matter what we do, the Langlish Empire is going to—"

"We're going to save Elara," Reeve said as if there were no room for doubt. "And we're going to stop whatever my father is planning. We stopped him when we were younger than this. It should be easier now that we're older and already united."

"Are we?" she couldn't help asking. "United?"

Reeve raised one shoulder in a small shrug. "The one thing we've always had in common is our love for Elara. I'm willing to put aside everything else to focus on helping her if you are."

The apology she wanted to give rattled around in her throat, trapped by her pride. Who said she had to apologize to him, anyway? The best apology was changed behavior, and here he was giving her an opportunity to change.

"All right," she said. "Truce."

Her hand reached out, hovering in the air between them. Reeve stared at it and then stared at her. She couldn't read his expression. Maybe one day she would ask him why he studied her all the time as if she were one of the books he was always reading. She never knew what he was looking for, only that he rarely found it.

Then his hand clasped hers in a firm grip that felt like its own kind of promise. "Truce."

Faron's palm felt hot as it fell back to her side. She resisted the urge to wipe it on her skirts. "Great. Fine. Now, let's go tell the queen."

A smile crossed Reeve's face, but he didn't say a word as they started walking again. Faron hid her own smile, picturing Elara's reaction when she found out they'd called a truce without her intervention. If they could do that, maybe their combined efforts would find a way to break the bond before the Summit was out. Maybe this was a problem too personal for the gods. Maybe it needed a human touch.

Because Reeve was right. The one thing they'd always had in common was their love for Elara, and it was their love for Elara that could save her.

If it couldn't... Well. There was nothing that Faron wouldn't do for her sister.

PART II

SCHOLAR

CHAPTER FOURTEEN

ELARA

FEAR CHILLED ELARA'S BLOOD AS THEY FLEW TOWARD HEARTHSTONE.
She had never left San Irie before, and she'd certainly never
seen a continent in person before. Deadegg was her world; San
Irie was her planet. War had done little to widen that scope. For
her family, she'd made her world small again, made her*self* small
again, until she had dreamed no larger than the boundaries of her
island. Langley spilled on and on and on, a patchwork of endless
greens that dammed the Ember Sea. Somewhere beyond, on the
rest of the Novan continent, lay Étolia and Joya del Mar, and Elara
couldn't imagine how large those empires were. How long would
it take to fly from one end of Nova to the other?

How many cultures had thrived on this massive land before the
empires snuffed them out?

Before, their victory against Langley had seemed inevitable. But
now, that victory seemed like a miracle. An anomaly. The queen
was right. They could not beat this colossus of a country again.

"*The Hestan Archipelago is a chain of islands situated in the middle
of Serpentia Bay, which feeds out to the Crown Sea,*" Zephyra informed

her as they flew. *"It's where Riders and dragons spend most of their time when they aren't in Beacon."*

"Beacon's the capital," Signey said before Elara could ask. *"We'll be spending our weekends there."*

Elara wanted to ask why, but even without seeing Signey's face, Elara felt the icy chill of her resentment. She chose to ignore it, if only because they were miles off the ground, and, even though they were both strapped to the dragon's saddle, she didn't trust that her co-Rider wouldn't shove her off.

Then Zephyra dipped through a break in the clouds, and Elara's gasp flew away on the wind.

Seven islands of various shapes stood out from the cobalt ocean. As Zephyra circled the northernmost island, titanic multi-colored forms emerged from the mist: soaring around the buildings, splashing in the water, slumbering on the sand of the nearest beach. Though it couldn't have been more than four, Elara hadn't seen so many dragons together since they'd swarmed San Irie. Zephyra was a pebble against these gem-colored mountains.

Elara's arms tightened around Signey's waist. As much as she hated to admit it, she was a Rider now—at least until she got the information the queen needed. She couldn't be afraid of other dragons just because they were bigger than her own.

Zephyra landed in a wide field with a *thump* that Elara felt throughout her body. As the dragon jogged to a complete stop, Elara noticed that the grass was flattened, as if it existed solely for the purpose of these arrivals. Behind them, a beach outlined the field, its sandy shoreline revealed and then swallowed by the waves. In front of them was a hill with a flat plateau, too steep to see the dragons who lay beyond.

Once Zephyra kneeled down to bring them closer to the ground, Elara undid her flight strap and slid eagerly from the saddle. She landed with none of the grace of her Firstrider, but her thighs burned from the hours-long flight. It was a wonder she could even still walk.

At least the pain shooting through her legs was a distraction from the heaviness in her chest. Her feet were on Langlish soil now, but the homesickness had set in before they'd even left San Irie. Every time she blinked, she saw her sister's tear-streaked face as they said a final goodbye on the Pearl Bay Airfield. If she concentrated, she could almost feel her parents holding her close, wrapping her in the twin scents of cooking oil and cocoa butter. And when the breeze whipped across her face, her eyes burned with phantom tears like the real ones she'd cried into Reeve's shoulder when he'd given her one last hug.

"We'll bring you home. Until then, don't let them diminish you," he'd told her. "They're good at that, and you're better than any of them."

Elara held the words close to her now as she watched Signey unstrap their bags from the base of Zephyra's saddle. She couldn't think of the past when she had to stay present, but she could at least draw strength from her loved ones until she had the chance to call them.

She hoisted one of her bags over her shoulder. "Tell me more about Hearthstone."

Signey had grabbed Elara's other bag, as well as her own, balancing both on her shoulders as if they weighed nothing. Her answering sigh was laced with annoyance. "Hearthstone Academy is here on Caledon, which is the largest island in the archipelago.

All Riders need to be certified here before they can join the Dragon Legion."

"Certified?"

"We get certified in the Five Fields: history, theology, politics, etiquette, and combat. And we need to pass them twice, once as a solo Rider and once with our co-Rider when we find them. Which means," Signey said, rolling her eyes, "that even though I've technically passed them all, I've got to do it *again* now."

It sounded to Elara as if Signey would have had to do that regardless, but she bit back her retort. Signey was actually giving her answers. Now was not the time to ruin it with a fight.

"How is that going to help me control—"

Signey groaned. "*Saints*, can we at least go inside before you plague me with primary-school questions? Everyone's waiting."

Elara tried not to look as if she'd rather swallow broken glass than follow Signey anywhere. Instead, she closed her eyes and counted backward from eighty, reminding herself that she could do this. She *had* to do this.

"Vincent! Let's go!"

Signey was already halfway up a nearby hill; Elara hurried to catch up. On the other side of the grassy knoll was a lush valley, and in the center of that field of green was a black stone castle. Her lips parted in surprise. No, it wasn't a castle. It was a *fortress*.

Hearthstone Academy was surrounded by an obsidian wall that was at least twenty feet high, with four towers reaching toward the sky in evenly spread points. Flags with the Langlish sunburst topped each one, though the fabric was in four different colors— red, yellow, blue, and green—as opposed to the regular Langlish black that usually surrounded the symbol. As Signey led her inside,

Elara saw that the first wall had just been the outermost defense. Within was a weather-washed gray stone keep, with thick walls lined with four more towers and a gatehouse entrance with a portcullis bearing dagger-sharp tips.

"Welcome to Hearthstone," said Signey as they walked through the gatehouse. "Close your mouth."

Elara did as she was told, but it was hard. She'd never been in a proper castle before. Even Pearl Bay Palace was just a three-story manor house, repurposed into the queen's home after the Joyan enslavers had been ejected from San Irie. These stone walls likely had a history that was no less bloody but that stretched much further back than before San Irie had even existed. Bright red tapestries with silhouettes of dragons hung from the ceiling. Glass lamps with lit candles behind them brightened their path. A blue carpet rolled out across the stone floor toward a wide staircase. Everything she saw suggested new opulence covering evidence of ancient warfare.

"How long has this been a school?" she asked, eyeing a suit of armor that clutched a sword with the point stabbing the ground.

"I wouldn't want to ruin your history class," said Signey, "before you have a chance to fail it."

Elara glared at her.

"Hearthstone has existed for at least a century," Zephyra cut in, her voice as gentle as Signey's had been cruel. *"It was a fortress at first, obviously, but once the archipelago was secured, the ruling family turned it into a school for training Riders."*

"Why? What are you training for?"

Signey scoffed. "Does the Iryan military collectively take a vacation during peacetime?"

Elara ignored that to commit the details of Hearthstone to memory as she followed Signey up the stairs. She could hear voices echoing down from the upper floors, conversations and laughter. The first floor had been empty, Zephyra explained, because the dormitories were on the second floor and the classrooms were mostly on the third. Elara had trouble wrapping her mind around the fact that she would be sleeping here for the foreseeable future, and fear settled in her stomach.

"Are we sharing a room?" she asked.

Signey glanced at her through narrowed eyes before she seemed to decide this question was worth a proper answer. "We'll be staying with our den the whole time you'll be here."

What's a den? Elara buried the question, figuring out from Signey's matter-of-fact tone that this would be another primary-school question. Her hands tightened around her bag, feeling the hard edge of the pocket that she'd wedged the queen's drake figurine into. She drew in a steadying breath.

"All right," she said, and this time her voice was even. "I'm ready."

Signey paused outside of a glossy wooden door with *206* engraved on a golden plaque. "I doubt that. Just try not to embarrass me."

"We're here," Signey called into the apartment-style space. "Jesper? Torrey? Where are you?"

A kitchenette was to the left, dishes piled high in the sink, and a table surrounded by four wooden chairs stood before it like a makeshift dining room. To the right was a recreational area, with a circular red rug beneath several couches and armchairs. Across from the door was a hallway that led to what Elara guessed was at least one bathroom and maybe separate bedrooms, because they weren't the only people in 206.

A rail-thin girl perhaps a year older than them was reading on the couch. She had shoulder-length wavy hair the color of cornmeal, rosy skin, and black lipstick that made as bold a statement as her kohl-lined eyes. She wore riding leathers, long boots, and a blazer with wine-red cuffs. A dragon-shaped silver cuff curled around the shell of her right ear, and her left hand had iron claw rings on each finger. Elara couldn't tell if they were relics, embedded with a piece—and thus the magic—of a deceased dragon, or if they were just decoration.

The girl surged to her feet as soon as she saw them, her smile blinding. "You've arrived! Oh, you must be Elara Vincent."

Before Elara could confirm, she was pulled into a hug. It was warm and welcoming but wildly overfamiliar. She blinked and then blinked again when the girl pulled away, before she could decide whether to hug her back.

"I'm Torrence Kelley, but you can call me Torrey. It's so exciting to meet you!" She hugged Signey next and then turned, a hurricane of energy that Elara could hardly keep up with. "Jes, they're here!"

From the mouth of the hallway, a boy strolled toward them. Tall and muscular, with copper skin a shade darker than Signey's and a large beauty mark on the right side of his jaw, he, too, was dressed in his riding leathers, except his boots only went halfway up his shins and his flameproof long-sleeved shirt was wine red. Fluffy dark brown hair bounced against his thick eyebrows as he walked.

"Finally," he said as he enveloped Signey in a hug. "It took you guys long enough."

"This is my brother, Jesper. Torrey is his Wingleader." Signey took Elara's arm and dragged her farther into the room like a dog on a leash. "Their dragon is Azeal, who you'll see later."

"It's nice to meet you," said Jesper. Unlike his Wingleader, he made no move to hug Elara, though he seemed no less friendly. "We've heard a lot about you."

"You have? From who?"

"The den can all hear one another and our dragons if we want to." Signey's hand was tense on her arm, and Elara felt Signey force herself to relax before her nails drew Elara's blood. "We're behind in your training, but things should move quickly now that we're at Hearthstone. She doesn't know a lot, so go easy on her."

"What's a den?" Elara finally asked.

Signey tensed again, and this time her fingers dug unpleasantly into Elara's skin. Elara pulled out of her grip and put some space between them.

"A den," Jesper explained, "is a group of dragons that were born from eggs that hatched at the same time at the Nest. All dragon eggs are laid in an area at the Beacon Dragon Preserve called the Nest, but not all dragon eggs hatch at the same time. When they do, those dragons tend to consider one another siblings, and their Riders become a family called a den."

Elara tucked the Beacon Dragon Preserve away as something to look up later. She could see now that every basic question she asked would reflect badly on Signey as her co-Rider, and she wasn't in the mood to find a spiteful satisfaction in that. Maybe with everyone else, she could use her ignorance to her advantage, but she wanted to get on the good side of the people who would have access to where she slept.

"Hey, I'm sorry," she sent awkwardly through their bond. Talking to someone in her head wasn't as easy as Signey made it look; she could feel her lips moving silently. *"I'm still just trying to get used to everything, and it feels as if there's so much I don't know. I thought it would be safe to ask your . . . your den."*

"There's nothing we can do about that now," Signey snapped back. Her lips weren't moving, Elara noted bitterly. *"Just stop talking before you make it worse."*

"Why do you always have to be so—"

"I'll show you to your room," Signey said. Elara realized that an embarrassing silence had fallen over the room while they'd been trading thoughts. Torrey was on the couch now, Jesper beside her with his chin hooked over her shoulder to read the book. From here, she couldn't see the title. Perhaps it was homework.

Elara followed Signey down the hallway, discovering that each bedroom was already labeled with a name on a golden plaque. At the very end of the corridor was a door that just had a piece of paper with her name taped to it.

"I don't know whether to be flattered or insulted," she said.

"Insulted, obviously," said Signey. "They don't think you'll be here very long."

Elara hoped that she wouldn't be, for reasons she was sure differed from Signey's, but she made herself ask the question anyway: "What happens to Riders who don't get certified?"

"I wouldn't know."

Signey pushed open the door, abandoning her in the hallway. Scowling, Elara stepped inside after her, kicked the door closed, and finally allowed herself to explode. "What is *wrong* with you?"

"Excuse me?"

"You've been talking down to me since we met! And I could handle it—sort of—when we were in San Irie. But I can't deal with this attitude when I'm in *your* country with all *your* friends." Elara barely managed to keep from shouting, and only because she didn't want Torrey and Jesper to overhear. "Do you think I want to be here? Do you think I *want* to be your co-Rider? I'm trying my best to deal with everything, and all you seem to be trying to do is drive me to commit a murder."

Signey's eyebrows lifted until they were almost one with her hairline. "*You're* trying your best to deal with everything? *You?* You've been staring open-mouthed, making absolutely no effort to learn anything that matters, and you're the one whose life is supposedly on the line! At this rate, you'll be the first person to learn *exactly* what happens to Riders who flunk out of Hearthstone."

Elara's entire face felt as if it were on fire. Her blood was a hot pulse beneath her skin. She could hear her heartbeat ringing in her ears. For a moment, she thought she was succumbing to the Fury again, but then she realized that she'd just never been this livid before in her life. It had bubbled up so suddenly, so strongly, that it overflowed into the bond, and Signey's equal ire met hers in the middle, meshing together, building upon each other until Elara couldn't tell whose wrath was whose. The air between them felt electric, sizzling with dark hostility.

It was terrifying. It was infuriating.

It was exhilarating.

"Get out of my room," Elara snapped before she did something she would regret. "*Now.*"

"Fine, you bloody child."

Once there was a locked door between her and Signey, Elara

pressed her forehead against it and *breathed*. She had never felt so out of control, and, though part of her liked it, the rest of her was crawling with adrenaline that had nowhere to go. The anger leaked from her body, replaced by a rising anxiety. She was in Langley, she was at Hearthstone Academy, and her co-Rider blatantly hated her.

Fine. This was fine. Everything would be fine.

She had a mission. She had a purpose. And, best of all, she had a sister who was working hard on a safe extraction. All Elara had to do was make sure she had what she needed before that happened, and all of this would be nothing but a bad memory she would laugh about one day.

Still.

Faron, she thought, her eyes clenched shut, her heart cracked open. *Please hurry and get me out of here.*

CHAPTER FIFTEEN

FARON

THE IRYAN TOWN OF SEAVIEW GLITTERED BEFORE THEM AS FARON and Reeve walked out of Nobility.

Renard Hall was at the top of a cliff cradled by the town. This estate had been in the Renard family for generations, and it boasted the oldest and most varied collection of books on the island. Faron and Reeve *could* have gone back to Deadegg with her parents, but, as Aveline had pointed out, Seaview provided them with the privacy and the resources they needed to make sure that, when they did go home, it was with Elara safely in tow. How the queen had managed to convince Faron's parents of that, Faron would never know, but they'd only hugged Faron slightly harder than usual when they'd separated. At least this time they *knew* Faron would be safe.

Though the capital of San Irie was officially Port Sol, it was Seaview that was their true treasure. The ancestral seat had once housed one of Aveline's mothers, Nerissa Renard, before she and her wife had been killed by dragonfire during the war, and Seaview Temple was one of the first ones ever built on the island.

She should have known the latter would be a problem.

Santi were the first people whom Faron saw as she stepped off the exit ramp, and that was mostly because they were crowded in front of the manor house in their white robes and gold belts. An ocean of bent brown heads lifted almost at once as everyone fought to catch a glimpse of the Childe Empyrean. Behind them, Renard Hall stood as tall and proud as an oak tree, so close and yet so worryingly far from where she was standing.

Faron took a step back and collided with Reeve. She'd forgotten he was here.

His hands curled loosely around her shoulders. "Was the temple supposed to know you were coming?"

"No. I mean. I don't know?" Faron caught sight of children in the crowd, children who weren't wearing robes or golden waistbands. It wasn't just santi before her. Townspeople were threaded through the gathered group, adding to the noise that hammered at her skull. Some of them held signs that begged her to intercede with the queen, to stop the Summit, to be the people's champion again. "Maybe we should wait a bit before we—"

Reeve led her back up the exit ramp, where, in the absence of drake mechanics, the pilots were running their own logistics on the drake to prepare for the flight back to Port Sol. A few quick orders later, three no-nonsense Queenshield soldiers escorted them through the mob. Reeve stayed close by her side, carrying both their bags with a commanding expression on his face, but he didn't need to. People cleared a path for the Queenshield, maintaining a respectful distance that Faron had never gotten before.

But to compensate for that distance, the clamor grew louder as people shouted over one another to catch her attention.

"Please—we came all this way just to see the Empyrean!"

"Stop the Summit! The Empyrean has the power!"

"At least take our offerings," said a woman with a wicker basket in her arms. Fat mangoes in vivid shades of green, crimson, and gold nestled together inside. "I've been growing these for months. They're the sweetest on the island!"

"Coconut water?" shouted another person near the back. "Would the Empyrean take some coconut water?"

"Irie curse your coconut water! The Empyrean needs to stop the Summit—"

By the time they broke through the other side of the swarm, she'd almost forgotten how Seaview had gotten its name. That changed when she saw the stunning expanse of ocean beyond Renard Hall, so bright that she had to cup a hand over her eyes like a visor to block most of the glare. Instead of taking the cleared path toward the front door, Faron walked around the house until she was a few feet away from the steep drop at the cliff's edge. Far below, a narrow line of white sand was littered with rocks, sharp and dangerous. The waves crashed against them violently, even on such a crisp, warm day.

"This way, Empyrean!"

Faron turned from the water to see one of the hall servants waving her back toward the house. Reluctantly, she moved away from the overlook, making a mental note to come back here later and just . . . *be*. Once she brought Elara back to Deadegg, she had no idea when she'd next have the chance to see the ocean, let alone sit by it.

The inside of Renard Hall was just as lavish as the outside. White marble floors were covered with soft aqua carpets, scented with some sort of floral powder. Tasteful seaside paintings decorated the walls, threaded in between wall etchings of suns in Irie's honor. By the time Faron made it to the second floor, where the bedrooms were located, she'd lost track of the details about her surroundings. It all blurred together into one message: *This is what money and royalty can get you.*

For a girl raised in a small village, it was as intimidating as the palace. And yet it would be her home until she figured out how to save Elara.

She felt woefully out of her depth.

Reeve had dropped her bags in front of a door that she assumed led to her room. Faron stood there staring at them until she got her heart rate to slow down and her skin to stop itching from the memory of the hundreds of stares. After five years, she should have been used to being stared at, but it still unnerved her when she wasn't expecting it.

"You threw Papa's dominoes in the gully on a dare," Elara had said once when Faron had complained about a group of worshippers that had passed through Deadegg just to see her at home. "How can you possibly hate attention?"

Faron hadn't known how to explain that negative attention was something she could deal with. She encouraged it, in fact. But these people looked at her as if they expected her to do something wonderful, and she didn't know how to navigate that.

"Do you need help unpacking, Empyrean?"

She jolted. A servant girl stood there in an ivory day dress, her hands folded behind her back.

"Sure," Faron said. "Where's Reeve's room?"

"Mister Warwick's room is around the corner, but he's in the library right now."

"Already?"

She found Reeve sitting in a high-backed chair in Renard Hall's library, a book open in his lap. The frescoed ceiling bore a fading map of San Irie, the main island, and the southern islets of San Mala and San Obie—all Aveline's queendom, surrounded by the Ember Sea. White-painted oak bookshelves flowed through the room in wavelike curves, designed to evoke the ocean. Each shelf was bursting with books, but Faron was more interested in the fireplace in front of Reeve's chair. It would be perfect for calling Elara after she'd spoken to the gods about her predicament.

And the new voice she still hadn't found an explanation for.

"Getting started already?" she asked as she approached Reeve. He tucked his finger into the book to hold his place, allowing her to see the title: *A Concentrated History of the Novan Empires.* "I don't think Elara will mind if we unpack first."

"Lenox said that he'd do it for me," said Reeve. "He also said that dinner is in an hour."

Assuming Lenox was a servant, Faron nodded and drifted over to one of the shelves. It was unlikely to her that the answer to breaking a bond between a dragon and a Rider could be found in any of these books, but Aveline had been right that some of these books were very old, maybe even older than the island itself. One was so ancient that its spine seemed to cave when Faron ran a finger over it. Maybe within these pages there was another person, lost to history, who had once spoken to the gods. Who had once heard voices without origin and had the answers she sought.

Elara and Reeve were the ones who reached for information when faced with a problem they couldn't solve. Faron liked to blunder around, making it worse until she made it better. But even if there was no simple, straightforward answer, maybe she might read something that would shake an idea loose.

She grabbed a book about the first two drakes at random and curled up with it on the carpet in front of the fireplace.

Three sentences in, her attention began to wander.

Faron rubbed her eyes, frustrated. She'd never been the best student, and, unlike Elara and Reeve, she didn't have the patience for books. She liked *hearing* about them, if she had to, but reading was not particularly her thing.

"Are you actually going to read that?" Reeve asked.

She made a face. "Apparently not. Thanks for having faith in me, though."

"We all have our strengths. Yours are elsewhere. There's nothing wrong with that."

Faron searched his expression for any sign that he was mocking her and found none. Uncomfortable, she closed the book and pushed herself onto her feet.

"I'll try the temple," she said without looking at him. "I didn't get to go before we left Port Sol, anyway."

"Good idea." Reeve disappeared behind his book again. "Make sure you're back for dinner. I got the impression from Lenox that the servants are so excited you're here that they've put a lot of effort into the meal."

"I'll come back when I feel like it," she snapped. A guilty groan escaped seconds later. "Sorry. Force of habit."

"Right."

"So, I'll just...go then."

"Okay."

Faron didn't run for the door, but it was a near thing.

To her relief, it was easier to get inside a sunroom at the Seaview Temple than it had been at the Port Sol Temple. Like all these hallowed buildings, the Seaview Temple was a palatial single-story structure with glass-covered sunrooms to the east and west. The outer walls were the bright yellow of an egg yolk, with a white wraparound veranda enclosed with ventilated windows. But, regardless of their architectural beauty, Faron generally didn't like temples.

Like the palace, they required her to stand on ceremony.

Everyone in this building was a pious worshipper of the gods. She used them to cheat in races. She talked back to them when they tried to chastise her. If she weren't the Childe Empyrean, she could never be a santi. There was a purity to their devotion that she lacked.

The High Santi met her at the top of the flared staircase, dressed in white robes cinched at the waist by a broad golden belt. His salt-and-pepper locs fell past his shoulders, the back half wrapped in a white crochet cap. Luckily, he seemed embarrassed by the display his novitiates had put on when she'd arrived. Instead of the usual fawning, he personally escorted her to the sunroom at her request, and she didn't see another person on the way.

The sunroom door was open and waiting for her, heat already leaking into the otherwise cool hallway. There were sunrooms in every temple, one where the sun rose and one where the sun set. People prayed in them, and santi grew plants like mint and thyme in them, but they were mostly meant to be living examples of Irie's power. The glass panes that made up the walls and ceiling amplified her sunrays, bringing life-giving heat to the herbs and drawing beads of sweat to the surface of her people's skin like a biological sacrifice in her honor.

The High Santi ducked his head respectfully and then left Faron there alone. But, within seconds, she wasn't anymore.

Obie appeared in his pure white suit, his hood drawn, as always. Next came Mala, her curls hovering like a cloud around her narrow face. And, finally, Irie shimmered into view, braids decorated by a golden crown.

"Hello, Empyrean," Mala said brightly, floating forward to pull Faron into her arms. Affectionate and bubbly, Mala was always the first to take advantage of the fact that the pious power of temple grounds allowed the gods a rare measure of corporeality. Faron only came up to her knees, but she never cared. "How may we help you?"

Irie stared icily through the glass walls of the sunroom. "I can feel them."

Even if Faron hadn't seen her expression, she would still know that Irie was talking about the Langlish miles away at Pearl Bay Palace. Irie had once explained that the gods had neither the interest nor the ability to intervene in every war of man, but Langley oppressed the island with tools that had escaped from the divine plane where all the gods of every religion resided. It was no longer one country's magic against another.

It was a problem that deities had created, and thus a problem the Iryan deities had to help solve.

"I need your help," Faron said. "And my sister needs your help. There was this voice... This dragon... And then—"

"Oh, Empyrean, hold your tears." Mala gave her one last squeeze before she rejoined the line of gods. "Tell us what happened."

The story spilled from Faron like water through the cracks in a dam, trickling at first and then pouring out in an unstoppable deluge. The Summit. The screams. The dragon attack. She shook as she described almost drowning her sister, how she *would have* drowned her sister and never noticed until it was too late. And then the voice, that stupid voice, talking her through taking command of the dragon's soul. Helping her end the attack without bloodshed.

In contrast, it took only a few seconds to summarize everything that Commander Warwick had said about the Fury and Elara's fate. By the time she finished speaking, Faron was ready to collapse from emotional exhaustion.

And none of the gods looked happy.

"The problem is that you are trying to break a bond without killing anyone involved," said Irie. "It is an impossible task, Empyrean. Dragons choose Riders whose souls are made of the same celestial material as their own, and the bond fuses that ethereal matter together to create a channel between them to share power, emotions, and thoughts. Your sister's soul is inextricable from that of her dragon and her co-Rider, because their souls are the same. That is the very basis of the dragon bond."

It took everything Faron had to keep from screaming. "My sister does *not* have the same soul as a *dragon*. That's impossible. She's Iryan. Why would you—How could you have allowed this?"

"We cannot affect the mortal realm except through proxies like you. Yes, we created your world, but we did not create the dragons, and they are now on a different plane than—"

"There has to be *something*. Please, give me *something*. That voice—" Three sets of faces closed off in an instant. Faron's heart stuttered. "You know who that voice belongs to."

Irie sighed. "Empyrean, you need to understand. If this voice belongs to the being we suspect it does, you and your world are in grave danger—"

"Who *is* he?" Faron demanded. "He's reached out to me twice now, and all he's done is help me." *And*, she thought but didn't say, *he made me feel powerful.*

"He was the one who taught the founders of the Langlish Empire how to bond with dragons and how to ride them," said Mala. "They may have forgotten his name, but they still worship him as a god, even though his regard for them is nonexistent."

Faron's eyes widened, though she couldn't truly say she was surprised. How else could that voice know so much about dragons? How else could he have helped her soothe one? Iryans knew as much about dragons as they knew about the clouds; there were scientific theories, but no one had ever gotten close enough outside of a drake to really know anything for sure.

"We have no proof of it," Mala continued, "but I suspect that his reappearance might be a symptom of the Fury that you speak of. He is the one who opened the door that brought dragons into your world, and it would be just like him to originate a problem with them and then put a hefty price on returning to fix it."

Which meant that it *could* be fixed. If this man had taught the Langlish how to bond with dragons, then surely he knew how to break that same bond. If this man had created the Fury, then surely he knew how to cure it. Her sister's life hung in the balance, and all Mala was doing was confirming that the answers Faron sought were in the hands of the same voice the gods were trying to warn her away from.

"*Is* he a god?" she asked. "Can I summon him the way I summon you? What's his name?"

"He would call himself a god, and in many ways his powers are equal to our own," Irie said. "But his name is irrelevant. He was born a man, and a duplicitous one at that. If he is talking to you, whatever he tells you will be a lie to get what he wants."

"But, unlike you, he can affect the mortal world? So doesn't that make him the more powerful god?"

Obie was a silent ghost behind Irie, but Mala looked stricken by Faron's words.

"Faron, dragons are creatures with cosmic power. They were never meant to be in this realm. The Fury is beyond anyone's ability to create or control at this point. We think, in fact, that this is a sign the creatures have overstayed their welcome." Mala said this as if she were trying to calm a toddler. "The way forward is clear. Once, we came to you to be the Childe Empyrean and save San Irie from the dragons. Now we must call on you to save the world from them."

It was a moment that Faron had always known, at the back of her mind, would come. The war was over, but the gods had never left. For all their complaints that she used their powers for trivial things, the gods were seemingly content to be at the beck and call of a teenager who had done her duty.

Why else would they have done that if there wasn't a larger duty waiting?

"How do I save everyone?" she asked. "Is there a way to break all the bonds at once?"

Obie reached up to lower his hood. His bushy eyebrows drew together over his pale eyes, lending him a more severe appearance than usual. "You have misunderstood us, child," he said. It was always a shock when he finally spoke, his rich timbre a rare gift.

"There is no way to break the bonds before you rid the world of dragons."

"But then...what about Elara?"

The gods exchanged glances. Finally, it was Mala who continued. "Eradicating the dragons will destroy the threat of the Fury, but it will also destroy their Riders along with them. Including your sister."

"I—What?" Faron stumbled back, nearly hitting the glass wall. "No. *No!* You're supposed to help me save her. You're—"

"This *will* save her, Empyrean," said Irie. "Her soul is tainted by her connection to that creature. Death is the only mercy that we can offer. There is no other way."

"There *has* to be. You're wrong! I'll find another way. Without *you.*"

Faron shoved out of the sunroom before they could say anything else, their words echoing unpleasantly in her head. *Death is the only mercy that we can offer. It will also destroy their Riders... Including your sister. You have misunderstood us.* As if it were a simple thing for her to accept, being responsible for the death of the sister she'd promised to save. She imagined telling Elara that the gods she and the rest of the island worshipped had casually suggested she must pay for her unwanted bond with her life, and had to choke back tears. Knowing Elara, she would obey the gods' will if she thought it would make the world safer. Her sister had always been the nobler of the two of them.

How could they sentence someone like that to death? What kind of world would she be creating, if good people like her sister had to be sacrificed to build it?

No. *No.*

Faron stumbled sightlessly through the hallways of the temple, rage curling in her chest. They had tried to keep secrets from her. They were using her to solve problems they had caused. Again and again, they used her, and when she was in need, they turned their backs on her. If she couldn't trust them with this, then how could she trust them at all?

And if she couldn't turn to the gods, who could she trust?

CHAPTER SIXTEEN

ELARA

As much as Elara wanted to avoid unpacking, she could not spend her time at Hearthstone living out of her two bags. After putting away her clothes, she sat on the edge of the bed with the drake figurine in hand, unearthed from beneath her dresses and shoes. Aveline had given this to her—a rendering of Justice based on the red color of the flank—to use for covert astral calls. Elara found the switch at the bottom that allowed harmless pea-size bursts of flame to erupt at regular intervals. She'd heard stories of these kind of figurines overheating and shattering in explosive blasts if used incorrectly, but Justice warmed her palms in a way that felt more comforting than hazardous.

Instinctively, she tried to draw upon her summoning, to feed an astral's power into the fire so that the call would find the exact person she was looking for.

Only a howling absence answered.

Her chest tightened, a pressure that built and built the more her attempts to summon someone, anyone, failed. The figurine remained a useless hunk of scalestone in her hands. The bedroom around her was lit by the electric lamps affixed to the walls, without the glow of a single astral to brighten it. She screamed her aunts' names again and again, but none of them appeared to her.

Alone. She was truly alone.

"*Not entirely*," said Zephyra, making her jump. "*My apologies, little one. You were calling too loudly for me to ignore—*"

"*I wasn't calling for you*," Elara sent back. "*I was trying to summon.*"

"*I see.*"

Something about the dragon's even tone made Elara's throat close up. She forced herself to breathe, to relax, even as she asked, "*Why can't I summon?*"

"*Your Iryan magic is incompatible with the bond.*" Though Zephyra was gentle, even apologetic, in her delivery, every word felt like a needle beneath Elara's nail beds. "*Think of our bond as . . . as a merging of fractured souls never meant to be separated in the first place. From what I can tell from your memories of schooling, the basis of summoning is to send one's soul outside the body as a beacon to attract ancestral souls. Once the astral accepts the call, the summoner can manipulate the added power of that second soul as they see fit. Is that not so?*"

"*I . . . Yes. But—*"

"*Because those souls are inherently different, inherently incompatible, prolonged exposure results in fever, fatigue, and even death. But what you weren't taught is that summoning is only made possible because the human soul is fractured by nature. It is but a broken piece of the divine spirit of creation, limited in its power and scope. With me and Signey, your soul is finally whole, your power and senses magnified by ours— and, as such, it is impossible for you to summon.*"

Elara's mind spun. She had never heard summoning—or dragon bonds—described like this, as if they were somehow interconnected. The bond was a mystery and a curse. She couldn't seem to accept that she had been chosen not because of an accident or a mistake, but because her very soul was somehow connected to a divine war beast and an angry Langlish soldier. If what Zephyra was saying was true, then it had always been her destiny to be a traitor to her country, to be wielded as a weapon against her sister.

The room rippled into swirls of color. Elara wiped at her eyes, but the tears kept coming until she couldn't see, couldn't breathe, could only sob into the empty bedroom with Justice's tail digging into her thigh like a warning. She didn't want this. Yes, she'd wanted to be chosen, to be special, to be remembered, but not like this. She'd thought she'd reached the depths of her grief for a future that would never be, lying in that infirmary bed as the queen told her that she couldn't join the military. But now she couldn't even summon.

She couldn't call her sister or Reeve, her parents or Aveline. She may never see her aunts, or any other deceased member of her family, ever again. She was alone. Alone, alone, alone.

"Little one—"

"Get out of my head!"

Zephyra retreated at once, behind that ever-present wall that Signey had erected, a wall that Elara had yet to learn to maintain but for which she was grateful. She pressed her face against the pillow and cried until her throat felt scraped raw, until her body stopped shaking and she no longer felt seconds away from screaming. Instead, she was hollow and exhausted, but that numbness was a relief. At least she could sleep.

"Hello? Elara? Hello?"

She sat up, scrambling for the drake figurine. The flame was now consistent, a deep red, and from its depths she heard her sister's voice, edged with annoyance.

"I swear to Irie, if you don't answer today, I'll take the next drake to—"

"I'm here! Faron, hello, I'm here." Tears gathered at the corners of Elara's eyes again. "I'm here. You have great timing."

"I've been calling every hour, but your figurine wasn't switched on, so I couldn't reach you. Why haven't *you* called yet?"

Elara swallowed back another bout of crying, explaining to her sister what she'd discovered about her ability to summon. Faron was silent for perhaps the first time in her life, but it was a horrified kind of quiet, as though she couldn't fathom a life without their magic. Elara wouldn't have been able to imagine it, either, if she hadn't been living it.

"All right," Faron finally said. "All right, well. I'll let Aveline know. And we can set up a designated time for us to call you, so—so, there's that. Do you think you could talk just after dinner every night?"

"Probably. I don't know what the curfew is yet, but I'm sure there is one."

"We have a plan, then. How are you otherwise? Are they keeping you in a dungeon? Are they feeding you? Did they go through your things?"

"Sort of. Yes. No." Even though she still felt too raw for laughter, Elara couldn't help smiling at her sister's antics. "Hearthstone Academy is a fortress on an archipelago, surrounded by Riders and dragons. Apparently, we're going to the Langlish capital this weekend, but my Firstrider hates me, so I don't know why."

"The Summit ends this weekend, so the commander will be back. Maybe you're going to see him?"

"I think I'd rather be in a dungeon."

Faron laughed. "I miss you. I wish I could tell you that I already know how to bring you back, but..."

"It's only been a few hours. I wasn't expecting anything."

"I have a lead. I just... Well."

As Faron explained what she had learned about the voice she'd heard at the Summit and the potential he had to solve their problems while creating many more, Elara stared at the cream bedsheet in concentration. She had never heard of a fourth god, and it wasn't for lack of research. There had been a time, many years ago, when she'd thought she might join the temple instead of the military, when her respect and awe for the gods who had kept her parents safe through the revolution had manifested in a religious fervor.

"Did you tell Reeve? He can see if there's anything in Aveline's books about this." There was a short pause. Elara rolled her eyes. "Faron, go and tell Reeve what the gods said."

"He's been reading since we got here. I don't think he's even breathed."

Elara's smile widened. "That's just one of his quirks. If you say his name enough times, he'll listen. You won't be able to help me if you don't work *together*. I shouldn't have to tell you that."

"Fine, *Mother*, I'll talk to the Warwick. Do you want me to get him now?"

Elara considered it and then said goodbye instead. Reeve would immediately be able to tell that she had been crying, and she wasn't ready to talk with him about her loss of summoning. He understood her, but he wouldn't be able to understand her connection with Iryan magic. And, right now, she didn't want him to try.

The flame retreated into the Justice figurine. She set it on her side table, tracing the jagged lines of its head with loving fingers. She wasn't alone. Not in any way that mattered. And everyone was counting on her to do more than lock herself away in her bedroom, weeping, even if she wasn't quite sure yet what she was looking for.

Checking one more time to make sure she couldn't feel so much as a whisper of Signey and Zephyra in her head, Elara got dressed. For now, there was at least one thing she could do.

At night, Hearthstone was a haunted place, full of lengthening shadows and mysterious sounds.

The same grit that had carried Elara to war carried her through the endless symmetrical hallways, lit only by moonlight. She could hear her own breathing, soft and swift, as she traced a path toward the headmaster's office. She could hear the rumble of the dragons that swarmed the archipelago on their own internal schedules. And she could hear a thousand reasons she should return to bed, reasons that pressed down on her shoulders with every step.

Reasons she had come too far to acknowledge.

It would be easier if she could *summon*. She missed the comforting heat of her ancestors' souls mixing with hers. She missed their raw power and the confidence with which she could direct it. Iryan magic felt like home, as easy as breathing, but this magic felt like an invader, a virus without a cure. Langley had carved her open, removed a part of who she was, and shoved something new and frightening within.

It was only fair that she take something back.

Her footsteps quickened. With Signey ignoring her, and Torrey and Jesper missing, Elara had spent the afternoon exploring Hearth-stone. She'd found a library near the back of the dormitory with a spiral staircase in the center of the room that led up and down to more floors of books. She'd discovered offices on the first floor that appeared to belong to professors, as well as a gymnasium the size of a drake hangar and a dining hall with several rows of tables. She'd even seen back stairs that led to a smelly area where they disposed of garbage and old food, as well as several paths that looped into a cluster of trees too small to be considered a forest.

All her earlier wandering had been to prepare for this. Now, on the first floor, she found the office farthest from the gymnasium, the one with LUXTON carved into a gold plaque, and contemplated the problem of the locked handle. Fearless Faron considered a locked door a challenge. It was just Elara's luck that the only person who could help her was an ocean away.

Elara gripped the handle, and it gave way easily. She swallowed.

"Hello, Headmaster, I just wanted to talk about—" She stopped when she realized the office was empty. The lights were off, as she'd seen from the hallway, and there was no one waiting inside. She paused in the threshold, trying to come up with a reasonable explanation for why the headmaster would leave his door unlocked beyond simple cultural differences. Perhaps Hearthstone was really that secure. Perhaps he kept nothing of interest in this office, rendering her presence irrelevant. Perhaps he'd simply forgotten, a fortunate coincidence.

None of the explanations felt quite right, and that put her even further on edge.

The office was vast, roughly the size of the communal area of 206. A large wooden desk was in the center, surrounded by several plants in cauldron-like pots. To her right was a door, also closed, that probably led to filing cabinets or a second office or maybe a small library. Rows of portraits of old white people, with Headmaster Luxton's own portrait near the top, filled the wall to the left.

Elara let the door fall shut behind her. Already she was running out of time.

The desk drawers were unlocked, but empty of anything useful. She found fountain pens and cream-colored letter-writing paper. Open envelopes with sunflower-yellow lining. An empty leather glasses case. One drawer held nothing at all, but Elara had absorbed one more lesson from Faron. She slid her hands over the wood until her fingers caught on a hidden hinge, allowing her to lift the false bottom. A treasure chest of documents stared up at her, some of them student files and some of them letters. Elara grabbed the letters first, hoping they were important. For now, she'd have to stuff them beneath her shirt until she could have Reeve translate them.

Then she realized she could read the letters as easily as she could read patois, more easily than she would have expected from nothing but half-forgotten school lessons. It baffled her for a moment before she remembered what Zephyra had said in the infirmary: *As long as we are connected, no form of language will be unknown to you.*

She paused to squash her bitterness that the same bond that had ruined her future was now proving helpful.

Keeping one eye on the door, Elara began to read. The letters were correspondence with Commander Gavriel Warwick, going back years at a quick glance. Many of them mentioned the Sotos, and Signey in particular: "an excellent student with a challenging personality," "the first member of the Soto Dynasty to take this long to be paired," "deeply affected by reminders of her father's incarceration."

Her father's incarceration.

Elara filed that away for later with wide eyes.

The final letter at the top of the stack was dated from the week before the Summit.

72 Harvest 1894

To O. Luxton,

There is a chance, however small, that we may soon have the answer to at least two of our problems....

Elara nearly spilled the papers across the floor. Someone was entering the office. She shoved the stack back into the drawer, replaced the false bottom, and dived beneath the desk with seconds to spare. Excuses for her presence flashed through her head, each more absurd than the last, and she covered her mouth in the hopes that not even her breathing would draw Headmaster Luxton's attention before she could sneak back out.

But it was not Headmaster Luxton who entered.

Instead, Signey Soto emerged from the side door on silent feet.

Elara's muffled gasp was loud in the quiet, and when Signey stopped inches away from the desk, she knew she was caught. Slowly, she emerged, her hands in the air to placate her Firstrider. Signey cycled through several expressions—surprise, anger, curiosity—before settling on resignation. Signey's fingers tightened around the papers in her own hand, papers she shoved behind her back when she caught Elara staring.

"What are you—"

"*Shh.*"

Signey ate up the space between them before she could blink. Her hand was surprisingly supple when it clamped over Elara's mouth—and then Elara realized that Signey was wearing a pair of dragonhide gloves, decorated with the diamond outline of scales across the back of her palm and knuckles. They were so close that Elara could count her freckles, as innumerable as stars in the night sky, so close that she could see each individual eyelash that curved, serpentine, around her earth-brown eyes, so close that she could feel Signey's breath like a silk-soft touch against her skin. Their proximity stole her words, her ability to even move.

Once Signey seemed sure Elara wouldn't make a sound, Signey removed her hand. She made it all the way to the door before she realized that Elara wasn't following her.

She rolled her eyes, and that was enough to remind Elara that this was not just any beautiful girl, but her Firstrider, who hated her, condescended to her, resented her. Whose hostility was like a third presence between them—a fourth, if one counted Zephyra.

Whose past Elara now knew a little too much about.

She followed Signey into the hallway, watched her spread her gloved fingers and summon a flame beneath the doorknob. The gloves must have been made of *real* dragonhide, turning them into a relic she could use to do magic. Seconds later, there came the *click* of heat-activated tumblers sliding back into place. Signey didn't speak again until they were safely back in the dormitory.

"What were you doing in the headmaster's office?" she hissed.

"What were *you* doing in the headmaster's office?" Elara hissed back.

Signey still clutched a sheaf of papers. Elara snatched them while she was distracted and sprinted toward the couch to read them.

Elara Vincent

Deadegg, San Irie

Eighteen Years Old

"Is this my student record?" she said, blinking. "What do you want with my record?"

"I needed to know how much they know about you," said Signey through clenched teeth. "How much they've always known about you."

"And you didn't think to just ask me?"

"Your appearance was too convenient, Vincent. I suspected that it might be—" Signey shook her head. "It hardly matters. That record is newly made. If they knew you existed before your arrival at Hearthstone, then you clearly didn't matter in the grand scheme of things."

For some reason, that stung. "Well, were you going to tell me you're part of the Soto *Dynasty*?"

"How do you—"

"I might not matter, but apparently you matter a lot. All the headmaster does is write letters to the commander about you."

Signey grew oddly still. "Letters saying what?"

"Just because you caught me doesn't mean I trust you."

This time, the silence of the Hearthstone night seemed less threatening and more like a cage that trapped the two of them in their own world. Signey was impossible to read, and Elara was too tired to try. But they now knew each other, knew sides of each other that could either form a bridge over their differences or launch them to new heights of animosity. Given Signey's behavior to this point, Elara expected at least one murder attempt before the night was through.

So she was completely surprised when Signey said, "I think we can help each other."

"Do you?"

"You're clearly terrible at this. Hiding underneath the desk, Vincent? The first place anyone would look?"

"Leaving the door unlocked, Soto?" Elara shot back. "The first place to raise suspicions?"

Signey surprised her again by smiling. It was not a wide smile, nor a particularly friendly one, but there was amusement there. "You make a compelling point. Listen, we have classes in the morning, and it's already late. I won't tell anyone I saw you if you don't tell anyone that you saw me. After dinner, we can talk. *Really* talk. Down by the boathouse with Zephyra, perhaps?"

"I still don't trust you."

"Good," Signey said simply, taking the student file back from Elara. "See you tomorrow."

Elara watched her until her bedroom door slipped closed and then sank down on the couch with her head in her hands. Her first night as a spy, and she'd already been caught. But why had Signey been in Headmaster Luxton's office, looking into Elara's records?

An oval wall clock hung above the fireplace, warning her that sunrise was in a few short hours. Rest. She needed rest. She needed to get through a full day of classes.

And then she would find out if Signey truly wanted to be allies in whatever she was doing or if she was going to become the biggest threat to Elara's mission.

CHAPTER SEVENTEEN

FARON

FARON KNEW THAT SHE WAS BEING ANNOYING, BUT SHE COULDN'T bring herself to stop.

She'd awoken with a restlessness that had followed her throughout the day, making her desperate for any kind of stimulation. Only the memory of the crowds from yesterday kept her from sneaking into the city while the sun was high in the sky. Instead, she tried to lure the servants into conversation, cleaned her own room, took a long walk down the beach, and then attempted to make bulla and cheese for lunch before being chased out of the kitchen by workers alarmed at the idea of the Empyrean making her own meals. She'd ended up near the library entirely by accident, but she'd decided to stay once she caught sight of Reeve.

She'd never met a boy who loved to read as much as Reeve did. In Deadegg, Faron had often found him passed out with his cheek pressed to a page in the most random of locations, as if he'd dragged himself somewhere private to avoid being disturbed.

However, Reeve was the only person in Renard Hall who didn't bow to her when he saw her coming. And though his presence here was because *he* was the one skilled at research, only one day into what felt like exile had Faron dangerously close to smashing one of the walls of the house just to have something to do.

"Find anything interesting?" she asked. Reeve was curled up in the same armchair with a giant tome in his lap and a lukewarm cup of peppermint tea at his feet. "Or even anything helpful?"

Reeve made a curious sound, slowly dragging his eyes away from the page. "What?"

"I'm bored."

"Of course you are." Reeve debated with himself for a moment before waving her closer. "It depends on your definition of 'interesting' but come and look at this."

Faron had been hoping to lure him from the library to entertain her, if anything, but she reluctantly did as she was told. The library was such an oppressive space, and books were so dry and boring. Her restlessness increased to a physical itch across her skin, begging her to go back outside and find something to *do*.

But she didn't leave.

Reeve's book was still open in his lap. She saw stylized pictures of dragons and shadows, of flames and blood. One page was half-covered by a paper and pen. Reeve had filled most of the paper with notes that she couldn't read even though they were written in patois. His spelling left a lot to be desired.

"This is one of the only books I've found so far about the first dragon Rider," Reeve said, turning back to the beginning of what she assumed was the chapter. "Sort of. It's a version of the Langlish legend about the Gray Saint, but almost everything you told me lines up with it."

He lifted the book so that Faron could examine the gilded portrait of a man who was wearing an iron helmet that obscured his face and holding a golden sword above him. The open maw of a dragon waited above, poised to descend over his head. Flames rose on either side of the mountain he stood on, but there was no hint of tension in his shoulders to suggest fear. Of course, it was just an illustration of an event that likely hadn't happened, but Faron still found it oddly inspiring. Humans had been overcoming dragons for centuries, in one way or another.

"'The First Dragon crawled free from the tip of a volcano long thought to be dormant,'" Reeve read. "'The people were scared, but the Gray Saint wasn't. With nothing but a golden sword and his own courage, he went to face the dragon to save his people.'"

Faron snorted. The words, she noticed, were written in Langlish, which at least explained the glowing terms they used to describe this Gray Saint. They worshipped him the way they worshipped their dragons, but this was her first time hearing that title.

"'Everyone thought he would die for his arrogance. A few people thought maybe he would manage to slay the beast. But instead, he returned home riding on the dragon's back as if he were a winged horse. Somehow, some way, he had not only tamed the dragon but befriended him. Through him, the dragon learned speech and empathy. Through the dragon, he learned strength and magic. And the Gray Saint and the First Dragon—now considered the original Langlish deities—passed the knowledge of bonding down to their people, so that every dragon that crawled free of their realm of fire and ash would have a Rider to protect it.'"

Reeve turned the page to another picture, which featured the same dragon and man from the previous page being swallowed by shadows. "But the Gray Saint and his mount were lost to history. No one knows quite what happened, but afterward every dragon began to choose two Riders instead of one. This book claims it's so they could share the burden of the loss of their dragon together."

Faron yawned, drawing it out even more when Reeve glared at her. "So what's interesting about that?"

"What's *interesting* is that your gods were right. The Gray Saint is the closest thing we have to a supreme being, venerated as the one who taught us to bond with dragons. It doesn't say anything about him opening any doors and freeing the First Dragon in the first place, admittedly, but if the Gray Saint and your voice *are* the same person then there are more books we can—" She yawned again. Reeve ran a hand over his face. "Never mind."

He returned to scribbling on his paper, his shoulders hunched in a way that suggested he wanted her to leave. Faron, of course, now wanted to spend all day in the library if it was going to bother him this much. The entire time he'd been talking—and even now, when he was adamantly ignoring her—she hadn't felt as if she were going to crawl out of her skin. Her issues with the gods, her inability to help her sister with all the power at her fingertips, seemed distant compared to her issues with Reeve. At least the latter was something that she could handle.

Faron sat on the floor next to his armchair and leaned her head against the wood. "You hate me, don't you?"

"What?" The scratch of Reeve's pen against the paper was loud in the hush of the library. "I don't *hate* you. I just don't like you sometimes."

"Right." Faron rolled her eyes. "Well, I know why I don't like *you*, but why don't *you* like me?"

He had a point, though. A few days ago, she would have been able to list a handful of reasons for why the sight of him made her furious. He was the face of the enemy, no matter which enemy she was rankled by that day. His blue eyes and pale skin marked him as of Langlish descent. His sharp jaw and the reddish tint to his dark brown hair marked him as a Warwick. And the dragon's-eye relic lying dormant beneath his shirts reminded her of the war beasts she'd fought. It had been impossible for her to separate him from the worst days of her life, and she hadn't trusted him at all.

Until she'd seen him talk to the father who wanted him dead just to protect her sister.

Now she didn't hate him. Not anymore. But she didn't like him, either. She could work with him, for Elara's sake, but she didn't have to like him.

Reeve closed his book. "Why do you care what I think of you?"

"I *don't* care. I'm just bored."

He pinched the bridge of his nose as if he were trying to ward off an incoming headache.

"I think," Reeve said, each word pointed and deliberate, "that you can be selfish and self-centered. I think that as much as you complain about being the Childe Empyrean, it's deluded you into thinking that everything revolves around you. Elara's in trouble, and you can't even open a book to help her. You haven't been to the temple to talk to the gods since yesterday. Faron, you're sitting on the floor, talking about how *bored* you are, instead of finding something useful to do when your *sister* is in *danger*."

Faron shot to her feet. It felt as if he'd punched her in the chest, and it *hurt*, and she wanted to hurt him so badly, it was like an animal instinct. "And reading myself into a coma, staying up until I'm incoherent, is supposed to help her? Don't act as if you're not clinging to your books because it's the only thing you know how to do, whether it's *useful* or not. What use is a mind with no relevant information?"

"At least I'm *trying*," said Reeve, and now he was on his feet, as well, his book abandoned on the seat cushion. "All I ever do is try, and all you ever do is judge, as if you could do better—"

"You're calling me judgmental when you're always looking down your nose at me, treating me like I'm inferior—"

"The way you treat me like a spy? A traitor? The big, bad nemesis in all your worst nightmares? I never say a single word about it, even though it's unfair, so you don't get to act as if *I'm* the bully here."

Reeve's eyes were livid, his breathing harsh. Faron had never seen him so angry before, and it thrilled her. *Finally.* Here was the monster behind the mask. Here was the boy she'd always known was there, a worthy adversary instead of some mild-mannered bookworm. She pressed even closer, so close that their noses were almost touching, baring her teeth to antagonize him more. And, for once, Reeve rose to her bait, not backing off or backing down, snarling right back.

Finally.

"The fact, Faron," he continued, "is that everyone talks about you as if you're a saint. Elara included, sometimes. But all I see is a spoiled, selfish child who wastes all her potential, blaming everyone else for her problems."

Faron's hands clenched into fists at her sides. "I take it back," she sneered. "I do hate you. I *hate* you."

"If you were the one in trouble," Reeve finished coldly, "Elara would never let herself have the *time* to be bored. Not for a second. Not until you were home. She would do *anything* for you. Clearly, you can't say the same."

The air inside the library was perfectly still, all perfectly quiet except their heavy breathing. Faron stepped away from him, swallowing hard. Reeve was six inches taller than she was, but right now she felt less than six inches tall. Those words cut deeper than anything else he had said, smothering the cold fire of her rage. Faron hadn't told Reeve that the gods wanted her to kill all the dragons—and Elara, along with their Riders—but that didn't matter.

He was right.

She *had* been sitting on the floor, distracting him from reading because she was *bored*, when her sister was in danger. Elara would never have done that. Elara would have done whatever it took to bring her home.

Faron *was* spoiled.

She *was* selfish.

He was right.

"Like I said, it shouldn't matter to you what I think of you," Reeve said, but there was a note of unease there now. His anger had retreated, and now he seemed almost apologetic. For some reason, that hurt even more. "Besides, you're not...you're not wrong. I *am* reading because it's all I know how to do. I'm taking these notes for your benefit, actually. I hope they're an easier read than the dense text."

It was an offering, but Faron was too dazed to accept it. Her legs didn't even feel as if they belonged to her as she floated toward the exit of the library. Reeve might have called her name, or he might have muttered something under his breath. All exterior noise had turned to static. She had no idea where she was going, except that she had to put as much space between herself and those sharp truths as possible.

This was how he felt about her when he *didn't* hate her? How could he not hate her? Gods, Faron hated *herself* after hearing that.

She slid out onto the back patio of the manor house. Stone tiles turned to steps at the base of the patio. A grassy path curved from there to the edge of the cliff. The ocean shimmered beneath the sunlight before her, but she could draw no comfort from that right now.

Even the gods thought she was selfish. They'd asked her to save the world from the Fury, and Faron had declined because her sister would be hurt in the process. *Everyone talks about you as if you're a saint*, Reeve had said. Faron closed her eyes. No one would worship the Childe Empyrean if they knew she had refused to be their savior the moment she had a personal stake in the fight.

And maybe they shouldn't. Faron had never asked to be worshipped. She'd only ever asked for one thing—her sister, safe and happy—and all the good she'd done had only given her pain. If doing the right thing meant losing everything, then Faron was done trying to do the right thing. She was done trying to be something, someone, other than herself.

If Reeve thought she was selfish—if Irie and Mala and Obie thought she was selfish—then let her be selfish. Forget the world. She wanted her sister to come home. And there was only one way to make that happen, only one thing that Faron *alone* could do. She was tired of sitting around waiting for books and gods to solve her problems. She was tired of other people telling her what to do or who to be. She was tired of being lied to and used and blamed and yelled at.

Gray Saint, she sent out into the void. *I'm here, and I'm ready to listen.*

A large ball of light, like a floating sun, appeared before her and coalesced into a translucent but corporeal boy around her age. He was ivory skinned and hazel eyed with high cheekbones and midnight hair that brushed his shoulders. His face was all architectural angles, but he was tall and his arms, legs, and chest were corded with muscle made obvious by his tight cotton shirt and fitted trousers. He was barefoot and faintly glowing, as if he were outlined by the same sunlight that had birthed him.

And he was beautiful, even if it was in the way a desert flower was beautiful until you tried to pick it and discovered a cactus beneath.

"Hello, Empyrean," he said in a hypnotically deep voice. "My name is Gael Soto."

"Your—what?" Faron's eyes narrowed. "I was summoning the Gray Saint. Who are you?"

"We are one and the same."

Gael Soto. The name was both familiar and not. She had never heard it in connection to him, but—*Soto? As in related to Signey Soto?* She bit back the question before it could leave the safety of her head. It was information, and she didn't know yet if she wanted Gael Soto to know his potential descendants were still alive.

"Okay...*Gael.* They say that you were the first dragon Rider," she said. "They say that you're a god, but they didn't say of what. I need to know about dragon bonds. How they're made and how to break them." She took a step forward, tipping her chin up to hold his gaze. "You showed me how to do the impossible. I'm asking you to do it again. Can you help me? *Will* you help me?"

Gael Soto, the Gray Saint, smiled as slow as nightfall, and all Faron saw was the abyss she was willingly stepping into.

"It would be my pleasure."

CHAPTER EIGHTEEN
ELARA

E LARA'S NEW BOOTS TRACED A CONFIDENT PATH DOWN THE STONE
trail that led to the boathouse. Waiting outside her room this
morning had been a package containing her Hearthstone uniform: fitted breeches lined with leather, a pine-green lace-trimmed
blouse with a standing collar, a rigid black blazer with pine-green
cuffs, and supple leather boots. All of it was fireproof.

There had been a small box of dragon relic jewelry in the package, as well—cuff earrings and claw rings, scale chain-mail collars
and horn headpieces—but that had felt like a step too far. The line
between fitting in and assimilating was narrow enough as it was
without wearing the tools of her enemies.

As she burst through the trees, she came upon the dock, a long
stretch of wooden planks that wound around the boathouse and
jutted out into the brownish-gray-and-algae-green water. She made
a face at the color; it had nothing on San Irie's crystal-blue seas,
cool and inviting.

"Hello, little one," said Zephyra, creeping into her mind. "Signey
waits for you inside."

Elara couldn't immediately see her dragon, but she didn't feel scared or powerless as she entered the boathouse. She may have lost her astral summoning, but she had something almost as dangerous: information. And until Signey knew exactly with whom she had shared it, Elara was worth more to her Firstrider alive.

The boathouse looked pared down only compared to the fortress that was Hearthstone. Wooden like the dock that surrounded it, the building was two stories tall. In the cavernous first floor were three more docks, without any visible boats, and a path that extended backward into a living area and walls of doors. One of those doors must have led to a flight of stairs, because she could see a deck above her head that overlooked Serpentia Bay. Unless she jumped into the water and swam beneath the overhang to freedom, the only exit was behind her.

And Zephyra floated, belly up, between two of the docks like a silent threat.

"Come upstairs!" Signey called.

With a last glance at Zephyra, Elara followed the sound of that voice to the door that led to the staircase. It opened into a great room with vaulted ceilings, where two open doors with inlaid glass and rippling curtains took her onto a massive sundeck. White X-style railings surrounded the space, which had three matching tables scattered across it.

Signey was sitting at the one on the left with her back to the bay and her blazer discarded to reveal the puffed sleeves of her pine-green shirt. A gold ring on the middle finger of her left hand bore a green dragon's-eye instead of a jewel, its slitted pupil watching Elara's approach. The sun brought out the honey undertones in Signey's cedar skin, turned her saddle-brown hair rose gold, shadowed her freckles until they looked like raindrops on dry earth. When she turned to look at Elara because she wasn't looking at the bay before, her eyes glowed with the light of the sun, a glorious, gorgeous amber.

She was beautiful. She was off-limits.

Elara reminded herself to breathe.

"Before we begin," said Signey, gesturing toward the empty seats, "I have certain conditions."

"So do I," said Elara, who did not think to prepare any. "But you can go first."

"My brother can never know about this. Torrey, either, because she'd tell him, but—" Signey didn't even blink as Elara sank into the chair across from her, as if breaking eye contact would prevent Elara from taking her seriously. Her arm was thrown over the back of her seat, but her casual pose was ruined by the tense line of her jaw. "My brother is not and cannot be involved."

"In exchange, I want you to teach me how to keep you and Zephyra out of my head," Elara countered. "I've been relying on your goodwill in keeping up the mental walls. *I've* been trusting *you*. If this is going to be a true partnership, then you need to trust me." "*Both of you*," she added in her mind. "*You cannot force me to accept this bond. I have to come to you by choice or not at all.*"

She felt an answering thread of remorse float from Zephyra and ignored it. No such thread came from Signey, but that was all right. She had kept up her walls, kept out of Elara's head. Whether she'd only done so to keep Elara from learning Signey's own secrets was irrelevant.

Signey shifted in her seat, as if Elara had become interesting for the first time. "Agreed. My second and final condition is that we can't be seen working together. If...if they're watching me as closely as you alluded to, it will only restrict both our movements."

"You just want an excuse to continue insulting me in public."

"If you've felt insulted by my mild behavior so far, you've led a rather easy life."

Elara snorted. "Fine. But I get to tell my sister anything and everything I think she needs to know. I'll lie to everyone else, but never to her."

"Fine."

"And Reeve."

"Fine."

Elara raised her eyebrows. "Fine?"

"I have no issue with Reeve Warwick." Signey held up a hand before Elara could argue. "You'll understand why in a moment. For now, I agree to your terms."

Below, the water churned like the ocean during a storm, but it was simply Zephyra twisting her lithe reptilian form out from the boathouse and into the wider bay. *I am going to swim with the others,* she reported. *I am merely a breath away if either of you needs me.* Signey watched her go with such a fond expression that Elara almost forgot they were here to negotiate.

"The Soto Dynasty," Signey explained, "began in Isalina."

Several puzzle pieces snapped into place, from Signey's clear discomfort in the presence of her own commander to the brown shade of her skin. Isalina was another island in the Ember Sea, roughly four hundred miles north of San Irie. Despite having been colonized by Joya del Mar, Isalina's people, the Linda, were long friends of the Iryans. The empire had forbidden all their colonies from getting involved in the war for Iryan independence, but several Lindan mercenaries had still provided naval support in secret, sinking Langlish supply ships.

"Enslavement has been abolished in Isalina, but Joya del Mar still chokes our resources. And although Joyan influence smothers every aspect of our culture, our people still dance and sing, eat and smoke, live and laugh beneath a sun that never seems to set on us. When the first of my ancestors left Isalina, we settled in a land that soon became part of the Langlish Empire. Somehow, we've always had a natural aptitude for dragon riding. There isn't a member of my bloodline, in any generation, who didn't form a bond." A wrinkle appeared between her eyebrows. "My brother and I were just the most recent. Only my father, who married in and took our name, avoided conscription. He became a military dracologist."

"Is...that why he was arrested?" Elara whispered, a subtle reminder of what she'd read in the letters that had led them here. A subtle reminder of the information she held. "Because he didn't bond with a dragon?"

The wrinkle deepened. "He was arrested for treason."

"*Treason?* What—"

"What indeed," Signey said in a clipped tone. It seemed to take a great deal of effort for her to corral her anger, but at least this time Elara knew that she wasn't the real cause. "As I said, I have no issue against Reeve Warwick. I don't disapprove of his actions during the war. I simply have a role to play until I can achieve my goals."

"Which are...?"

Signey gave her a look that plainly said *If you shut up long enough, you'll find out.* Elara, still processing that the girl she'd known until now was a phenomenal actress, couldn't even find the energy to be annoyed. "Commander Warwick has always taken a special interest in our education because of our status as one of the most important dragon-riding families. My mother pleaded for him to add classes to Hearthstone that gave the students more options for the future than the armed forces. And now that we're in peacetime, I'm hoping that being a part of the inaugural diplomacy track will help us solve more conflicts with conversation instead of combat. For the first time, the Dragon Legion doesn't have to be this... this ceaseless war machine. We finally have the opportunity to do some good if we join."

"If you believe that, then why were you in the headmaster's office?"

"Because the commander is planning something, and he is a warmonger. I suspect that we're somehow part of a scheme to retake your island."

Though it was exactly what the queen had said, Elara was still stunned to hear someone else legitimize the theory. Especially someone like Signey Soto, who had been, up to this point, the perfect little soldier. It was terrifying to think that the commander's motives were so transparent that even one of his own people could see through them.

Signey was clearly a good liar. But was she lying to Elara right now?

Elara closed her eyes. Took a deep breath. "I think so, too. I was looking for proof. Any kind of proof. Instead, I found those letters about you and your family, which just proves what you already knew. Whatever is going on, it's about both of us."

"I wasn't even meant to be at the Summit. None of us were, none except Commander Warwick and Irontooth. But two or three weeks before, the den was summoned to Luxton's office. The commander said that because of our high marks, he was presenting the opportunity to learn about international relations by attending the Summit. But then he kept me later than the others." Signey wrinkled her nose. "He told me there was a chance, however small, that we might find my Wingleader among one of the other Novan countries. After all, I'm descended from Lindans. It stood to reason that my co-Rider might be, too."

"But we didn't invite any Lindans to the Summit. We're already allied with them."

"Something he neglected to mention. If he didn't look as stunned as anyone else to find that you were my co-Rider, I would think he'd planned *everything*. But no one could have planned for someone like you."

What's that supposed to mean? Elara bit back the question. "So you were looking at my student record to see what, if anything, he knew about me that you didn't?"

"Exactly. I didn't find anything of interest, though, so we'll have to wait until we go to the capital to learn more. He's had all these years to mentor me as I passed all my other compulsory classes. But it's only now that you're here that we'll be spending our weekends with him? Something is going on, and the sooner we figure out what, the better."

"Are you sure Jesper shouldn't be—"

"*My brother cannot be involved.*" Signey got to her feet so quickly that Elara jumped. "My mother, my sister, and their dragon were all killed fighting in a war they didn't even believe in. A war *none* of us believed in. If I join my father in the Mausoleum, Jesper will be the only one of us left. I need him to stay clean. I need him to survive. Please, I—" Her voice cracked. "I can't lose him."

Elara's mouth snapped shut. She hadn't known that Signey had lost her mother and sister. There was a wildness in her eyes right now, a bottomless grief that was impossible to fake. It spoke to something inside Elara, the parts of her that had heard her mother through the walls crying over the loss of her sisters, the memories of crawling into bed with Faron so they could share each other's grief through the years. No one could lie this well. No one was this good an actress. Signey had lost and lost and lost, and still, she was trying to find a peaceful way forward.

Together, maybe they finally could.

"I understand. I swear, I understand that better than anyone." Now it was Elara's turn to stand, if only so that she could reach across the table, her palm upturned. "We'll investigate together. We'll find out what the commander is planning. We'll keep your brother out of it. You have my word."

Signey looked down at Elara's hand for a long time before gripping it with her own. Her palms were rough with calluses. Elara told herself that was the only reason a shiver ran down her spine. "You have my word, too."

They shook, and it felt like a powerful beginning.

Beacon was deceptively exquisite, a city that wore its long history in every structure and every street. The Langlish capital hoarded buildings that were a diverse collection of stone and wood, clock towers as tall as the clouds and tenements as squat as tree stumps.

But a miasmatic smog smudged the skyline, obscuring Elara's view from Zephyra's saddle, carrying the putrid scent of chamber pots and burning coal. The city was beautiful on the surface, but its filthy underbelly could stay hidden for only so long.

Commander Warwick had summoned them to something called the National Hall of Honor. It still looked like a castle, made of brick and stone and slate with mansard roofs and colonnades. Pearl white and taking up an entire section of the city all by itself, there was more than enough space in the back garden for Zephyra to land. Zephyra nudged her snout against Signey and then paused, her face turned toward Elara in question.

Elara smiled and pressed a hand against Zephyra's scales. It was the first time she had touched the dragon for anything other than travel since the night they had bonded, and she'd expected to hesitate, to feel reluctant. But as Zephyra pressed against her touch, loving and warm despite her bumpy granite skin, all she felt was... belonging.

"We'll be back," Elara sent tentatively across the bond. Though the dragon had no expressions to speak of, she could tell that Zephyra was smiling as she shuffled off to drink from a fountain in the center of the verdure.

Gavriel Warwick met them in the North Chamber, a long gallery lined with oil portraits and curtained windows, lit up by gas chandeliers with iron dragons wrapped around the bases. Their empty eyes seemed to be watching Elara as she and Signey came to a stop in front of the man who had ruined both their lives, a man who smiled like an old friend.

"Young diplomats, welcome to the National Hall," the commander said in a booming voice. This was a voice that rallied soldiers, that made speeches, that subjugated empires. "You'll be spending every weekend here with me, sitting in on meetings, shaking hands with politicians, and writing an eventual paper on your ideas for the future of this great nation. By the time you leave my mentorship, it is my goal that you will be fully prepared to go out into the world and represent Langley's interests on a global scale."

"Um," said Elara.

"Oh, of course this does not apply to you, Miss Vincent." The commander smiled wider. "It's a standard speech, you understand."

Elara glanced at Signey. Signey glanced at Elara.

"May I use the bathroom?" Signey asked.

The commander led them to the entrance of the gallery, then pointed Signey in one direction before leading Elara in another. According to her classes, Langley was an imperial republic with the commander as the head of state. The National Hall was home to the Conclave, formed by elected officials from each county and led largely in absentia by Director Mireya Warwick, the commander's wife. It was also home to the Judiciary, the highest court in the Langlish Empire, and the current research department headed by the dracologist general.

It felt as if they were *all* in attendance today, just from the endless conversations. But the doors that lined the hall were too thick for her to make anything out.

"Professor Smithers tells me you're doing particularly well in history," said Warwick, his arms behind his back as he paused in front of one of the doors. "What have you learned about the origin of dragon riding?"

Elara blinked. She'd learned far more about it from Faron astral calling her than she had from a week of classes, but she couldn't very well say that. Was he asking her because he wanted to know what she knew? Or was he asking because he wanted her to know that he'd been keeping tabs on her?

"I know that the Langlish worship their dragons," she began haltingly, "and that there's a divine figure called the Gray Saint who's venerated for being the first dragon Rider. I know that, according to legend, the Gray Saint's disappearance is what led to dragons choosing two Riders instead of one, but I'm not sure I understand why. It seems to go against what I've learned so far."

"We believe that the First Dragon emerged from the divine plane in the Cinder Circle."

Elara filed away that title for later and consulted her mental world map. The Cinder Circle was located above Isalina; it was a ring of islands that were uninhabitable because of the active volcanoes that had created them. Their ever-shifting landscapes were formed and reformed by the constant eruptions; if a dragon were going to explode into the mortal realm, that would definitely be the place for it.

"From there, the First Dragon flew to the lands that would eventually become the Langlish Empire and faced the Gray Saint. They bonded, and they passed that sacred knowledge on to our people. But the Gray Saint..." Warwick chuckled, though there was no humor in it. "They say that he went mad. A dragon's mind is so large, so alien, so *vast* compared to that of a single human that, rather than intertwining, one soul consumed the other. Instead of tempering the First Dragon's instincts, he embodied more and more of the dragon's savagery. He became a tyrant instead of a hero, more monster than man. From his failure, dragons learned that they had to find *two* souls that shared the celestial material of their own, because one alone is too weak for a true partnership. *That* is why there are two Riders for every dragon."

"Because the Fury affects the Rider instead of the dragon when there's only one."

Warwick made a thoughtful sound. "I hadn't thought of it that way, but I suppose you're right."

He opened the door into what looked like a laboratory, staffed with people who didn't look up when they entered. Long tables were weighed down with the massive remains of dragons: tails that were four feet long, teeth that were the size of her forearm, rib cages large enough to trap a person.

"Here, we have dracologists studying the residual magic that powers dragon relics and the foundations of the bond," said Warwick. "We're hopeful that an answer to the Fury might be found among this research, and, since we have the Empyrean's cooperation, I'll leave you here to poke around. It's not as though you'll need the diplomacy lessons."

Elara frowned, wary of leaving Signey alone with this man. But Warwick closed the door on her before she could say another word. The stench of cadavers hit her a second later, making her gag and lean against the wall. Her eyes teared up, but every time she blinked, the lab fell away and she was back on the battlefield. Soldiers scorched beyond recognition by dragonfire, pilots splattered across the pavement after falling from damaged drakes, people— *children*—screaming as they were trapped in burning houses. The scent of charred skin. The sour taste of her own vomit.

Pain lit up her cheek. She was back in the lab, breathing hard, black spots dancing in her vision. Before her, a dracologist studied her, their hand raised to slap her again. Elara's cheeks were wet, and her chest *hurt*. But she was in a lab. She was safe—or, rather, as safe as she could get right now.

The dracologist studied her a moment longer and then presented a set of dragonhide gloves. "Activate them to help with the smell and then follow me. We have a lot to show you."

Elara stared at the gloves, then at the dracologist, and then at the dissected pieces of dragons scattered throughout the giant space. Fighting the urge to gag again, she quickly slipped on the gloves. As soon as she thought of the putrid smell, she felt the hum of magic surrounding her hands, and it disappeared. Even after the hum settled, she could still *feel* the magic, different from Zephyra and the bond, but similar enough that it felt like blending two colors to make another.

It was as easy as summoning had been. Easier.

The smile dropped from her face. She clasped her hands behind her back where she wouldn't have to see the gloves, wouldn't have to acknowledge that thought. "All right, I'm ready. Show me what you have so far."

CHAPTER NINETEEN

FARON

FARON WATCHED THE SUN RISE OVER THE BEACH, SENDING RIPPLES of fiery red and wheat gold across the water's restless surface. Renard Hall slumbered on the cliffs, but she had been up for hours. Her stomach grumbled at the reminder, begging for the relief of fried dumplings and scrambled eggs or Mama's homemade flash out. All she had until the servants awoke was a bowl of guinep she'd found in the kitchen, and though the fruit was hardly the most filling breakfast, she steadily bit the peel, sucked at the sweet, jellylike pulp, and spat the inedible seed within back into the bowl. It was a mindless task perfect for her chaotic brain.

She hadn't seen Reeve in days.

Without consulting each other, they had begun astral calling Elara on alternating days, Reeve using the servants to make the call and Faron using the size of the manor house to avoid seeing him. It was almost funny, how in sync they were when they weren't speaking. No matter how often Faron told herself that this was exactly what she'd wanted, it was quiet. She hated quiet.

Footsteps crunched on the sand behind her. She didn't turn around.

"May I join you?" Reeve asked, and she hated that, too, the hesitant way he spoke. As if she were some scared puppy, waiting for any rise in his voice to run away. As if *he* were some scared puppy who'd bitten his owner and expected to be rehomed. "If you'd rather be alone—"

"Sit, Warwick." Faron patted the sand beside her, then began picking at the grains that immediately clung to the skin between her fingers. She'd forgotten how much sand loved to find the most inconvenient places on the human body to rest. "But if you've come to apologize, you can go and drown yourself instead."

Reeve sat. His mouth was twisted into a half smile. "I shouldn't have said those things."

"You told your version of the truth. It's all right."

When he didn't respond, she tried to watch him from her periphery. He wore a crumpled collared shirt and wilting suspenders, which were attached to khaki pants. Instead of walking shoes, he wore house slippers. His hair was a disaster. The shadows beneath his eyes were deep enough to have their own address. She'd never seen him so undone.

Her gaze snapped back to the ocean. "I liked that I could make you angry."

Reeve made a confused sound.

"You're always in control. And so smug about it. I wanted you to be angry. I wanted you to be honest, for once."

"*You* wanted honesty from *me*? I'd say between the two of us, I'm the one who is usually honest."

It's different, Faron wanted to say, but she couldn't even explain to herself why that was. And what did it matter if there was a wall between Reeve and other people? Between Reeve and herself?

"If you're going to be irritating, you can go back inside," she said instead. "I'm trying to enjoy the sunrise."

Reeve drew up his legs to his chest and wrapped his arms around them, which made him look younger than usual. His chin pressed against his knees and his eyebrows furrowed as he watched the water lap at the shore. The silence was almost comfortable, if not for her *awareness* of it, if not for the novelty of it, the two of them sitting in peaceful contemplation.

I summoned the Gray Saint, she wanted to say. *It was easy. Too easy. He says his real name is Gael Soto. He says he can help us.* She wanted to look into those pale-sky eyes and lift her chin and say, *I'm doing something. That's what you wanted, isn't it?*

Reeve's eyes slid shut. He turned his head toward her, pressing his cheek against his trousers with a soft, even breath. His skin was waxen in the dawning sunlight. His frenzied curls twisted in all directions. Small. He looked so small and young and tired. He was a year older than her, and yet he looked both immortal and infantile. He looked like a boy, and that made her feel like a girl, and their *aloneness* was suddenly impossible to ignore.

"Have you found anything new in your research?" Her voice seemed to ricochet across the empty vista. "Anything helpful?"

He cracked open an eye. "I'm trying to watch the sunrise."

"I'll drown you myself."

Reeve laughed. It was slightly delirious and muffled by the fabric of his trousers, but it was still a laugh. Faron had never made him laugh like that before. She had no idea what this was. What to do next. She wanted him to leave. She wanted to make him laugh again. She rubbed her slick palms against her skirts, staring out at the vivid horizon. His laughter echoed in her bones.

By the time Reeve finally stood up, the sun was a blinding lemon yellow, curtained by clouds. Somewhere across the world, Elara was probably watching this same sky. Somewhere across the world, Elara was spending another day surrounded by enemies and monsters, unsure when she would be able to come home. Faron didn't have to ask to know Reeve felt the clock ticking onward, amplifying the danger that Elara was in. She only hoped that she hadn't made him feel guilty for something as small as watching a sunrise.

Not that she cared. But he was hardly of any use to Elara if he was ashamed and exhausted.

"Breakfast is probably ready," Reeve said, stretching. "We should head back in."

"I'll be there soon. Tell them to leave mine on the table."

She handed him the half-eaten bowl of guinep, discarded peels and seeds still damp with her spit. Reeve made a face, but he didn't say anything. She watched him disappear up the stone steps carved into the cliffside, one suspender hanging off his shoulder and slapping against his thigh.

"Interesting," said Gael Soto, appearing at the strandline like an apparition.

Faron swore.

"Sorry," Gael continued with an amused smile. "Should I have started with hello?"

Faron climbed to her feet, dusting sand from the folds of her tiered day dress. She hadn't summoned him, but she felt oddly comforted by his arrival. It drew a sharp line between whatever warmth she'd just felt and the rest of her day. It made her heart beat fast from shock rather than... anything else. "It's fine. But if you're calling Reeve interesting, I assure you he's very boring."

"You seemed interested."

"I'm not."

"Hmm."

Faron glared at the gritty sand instead of at the god still strolling up the beach. "I didn't summon you. Surely you aren't just here to ask questions about my love life."

"I *wasn't* asking about your love life." Gael Soto stopped in front of her and tilted his head. His smirk was damnation incarnate. "Was I?"

"Do you have the information I need or not?" He was taller than her, but not as tall as the gods she was used to. If not for the translucent quality to his pearl-white skin, she would have thought that he was a normal boy. Maybe that was the real reason he'd trusted her with his name. Maybe he'd correctly guessed she'd never take him seriously as a deity. "My sister is in a precarious position."

"The magic you seek is ancient and dangerous," said Gael. The sunlight crowned his dark hair, eclipsed his earthy eyes. "The bond between a Rider and a dragon is a union of souls. To break it, you require absolute control over souls, dead and living, human and dragon."

"Like at the Summit." Faron remembered the feeling of chaining herself to that dragon's soul—the raw power that dwarfed her own—and shivered despite the heat. "Why do you know this and the gods don't? What are the risks?"

"Your astral magic is effective because the souls that your people channel no longer have a will of their own. They're impressions of the dead whose only desire is to taste life. Most summoners could not command a living soul, with its own wants and drives, without being consumed. It's only your practice with calling on the gods that makes me believe you are uniquely suited for this kind of magic. Though, to be fair, they are willing souls weakened by the travel between realms."

"*Weakened?*" Nothing about the power at her fingertips had ever felt weak.

"When you have limitless power in your own plane, the loss of some feels like nothing at all." Gael studied her from the top of her head to the toes of her shoes, frowning thoughtfully. "You asked the risks. The risk is that this may be beyond even your capabilities. The risk is that you will lose the person you think you are. The risk"—the smirk returned—"is that I am the only one who can teach you this power, and I require some convincing."

Faron had to bite back a smile, the last of her discomfort fading. She'd always been good at this part: bargaining, haggling, *lying*. Gael Soto was all confidence, all ageless radiance, but she was a little shit. He didn't intimidate her. "I don't suppose you accept rayes."

"You're asking for my help. In the future, I'll require yours—"

"I don't make blind deals," Faron said immediately. "And everyone I know has warned me against you. So here is the only bargain I will make: Prove to me that you really can help. Prove to me that your methods are effective, and that this magic actually exists. If you can do that, I'll listen."

Gael Soto raised a single eyebrow. "Only listen? After gaining so much?"

"I only want one thing: my sister's freedom. You could teach me everything in the world, and it would be useless to me if it doesn't help me with that. Prove yourself, and I'll listen. And if I agree to what you have to say, *then* you can show me how to use all I've learned to free Elara."

The waves crashed over the sand, then retreated in a ripple of white foam and colorful shells. Rhythmic and calming, it was the only sound for such a long time that Faron thought she'd asked for too much. That Gael Soto would disappear to find another pawn in whatever scheme he had concocted. That she would be stuck waiting for books to solve the problems that the gods could not.

"All right," he said. "I accept."

Faron tried not to show her relief. "Let's start now, then. How—"

Her stomach growled, so loudly that it even caught the young god's attention. He looked torn between bewilderment and delight, two expressions so *human* that she almost forgot, again, that he was dangerous.

"You should eat," Gael Soto said, beginning to fade at the edges. "There is no reason to rush, Empyrean. I will always come when you call."

"But I didn't—" she began, but it was too late. Once again, she was alone on the beach with more questions than answers.

"Please tell me you have found something," Aveline said from the fireplace. "Something. Anything."

"You'll get gray hairs before you're even twenty-five if you don't calm down," said Faron. She was curled up in Reeve's favorite armchair, her legs thrown over one side, her skirts an added cushion bunched beneath them. The chair sank under her, already accustomed to the weight of Reeve and the ten or more books he tried to read at once, all day, every day. Faron's decision to call Aveline was partially to get him out of the library. "Isn't the Summit over with?"

"Somehow word has spread that your sister is in Langley."

Faron sat up. "What?"

"It is impossible to know who could have leaked—"

"You had representatives from all our enemy countries in the palace, and you don't know who could have leaked it?"

"—but I suspected it might be someone with an interest in sowing civil unrest." Aveline sighed, and the flames flickered in response. "Protests in the capital are at an all-time high, and it is spreading to the surrounding towns. So I ask again: Please tell me you have found something that will allow us to bring Elara home."

"I wish I could. Really, I wish I could." Faron toyed with her skirts, feeling an uncommon flash of guilt. But she didn't think that telling Aveline of her deal with Gael Soto would do anything but worry her. Besides, she hadn't yet told Elara. "Reeve is still researching. The gods have given me no further guidance. I hate waiting as much as you do, but that's all we can do right now."

"Right. Okay."

But the call didn't end. Faron watched the flames dance, the wood crackle. Finally, the queen spoke. "I didn't think they would react this poorly."

Faron was surprised more by the vulnerability than she was by the words. Gone was Aveline's clipped, sanctimonious accent; instead, she sounded young. Too young.

"I expected some backlash, of course. We've received a number of complaints since the first Summit announcement and through-out the planning. But the protests. The signs. The anger. I just—did I do the right thing?" Faron couldn't see Aveline, but she was sure the queen was pacing the length of the room. Her voice sounded close and then far away, over and over again. "We cannot survive on trade with the other islands alone; our imports and exports are largely the same. The rest of the continents are too far away for meaningful engagement. We needed these trade agreements with Nova. Didn't we?"

The questions seemed rhetorical, but Faron answered anyway. "I think you're doing the best you can, and that's all anyone can ask of you, Your Majesty."

Aveline inhaled sharply. Faron had never called the queen by her title before, not unless under duress, not without being forced. But even on their worst days, when it felt as if Aveline blamed her for everything wrong with her life and ignored Faron's own struggles, Faron had never doubted one simple truth: Aveline loved her country. She wanted to do right by it. She wanted to exceed her mothers' legacies.

She was young, and she was imperfect. She'd lost her temper, and she'd made catastrophic mistakes—especially in that first year on the throne. Those were also truths. But she'd never once considered ignoring her lineage, running back to her farm, and maintaining the lies she'd been told her entire life. Her country had needed a queen, so a queen was what Aveline Renard Castell had become.

Faron would always respect her for that.

"Thank you for the update, Empyrean," Aveline said, her voice surprisingly thick. And then: "Have a good rest of your day, Faron."

The fire banked itself, leaving Faron to her thoughts. She hadn't believed they would be able to keep Elara's absence a secret for long, but she also hadn't thought anyone but she and her family would care. Then again, when people had already taken to the streets in protest, anything and everything could be another spark. Maybe they thought Elara was a hostage. Maybe they thought Elara was a traitor. Maybe they thought Elara was a victim of Aveline's incompetence.

No matter what, things would only get worse if Faron didn't break her bond. The gods already wanted her to kill Elara, to get rid of the dragons. She couldn't stand it if the Iryans wanted Elara dead, too.

"Aveline can handle this," Faron said to herself, pressing the backs of her hands against her eyes to stave off a headache. "She'll talk to them. She's good at that. They love her. They'll listen. Everything will be all right."

Hollow words, hollow comfort. But she clung to the gilded promise anyway because the alternative just might break her.

PART III

SINNER

CHAPTER TWENTY

ELARA

DURING HER FIRST MONTH IN LANGLEY, ELARA ABSORBED INFORmation like a dish sponge. Most of it was contextually interesting yet virtually useless, but she reported it all back to Aveline, regardless.

She learned that there were four breeds of dragon. Carmine dragons, the largest breed, came in different shades of red; medallion dragons, the second largest, came in shades of yellow; ultramarine dragons, blue-colored and more aquatic than all the other breeds combined, were the second smallest; and then there were sage dragons like Zephyra, small and green and scarily intelligent. Hearthstone uniforms were color coded, Elara's pine-green cuffs and shirt symbolizing to anyone and everyone that a sage was her mount.

She learned the differences between Firstriders like Signey and Jesper, and Wingleaders like her and Torrey. Firstriders led the dragons into battle and maintained an active offense. Wingleaders fought on the ground and provided a ranged defense. Humans didn't know which one they would be until they bonded with their dragon, and only dragons seemed to know what made a soul more likely to be one than the other.

She learned that her class schedule required her to take some courses with Signey, some courses alone, and even some courses with the den. Each one fell under the heading of one of the Five Fields—history, theology, politics, etiquette, and combat—and were divided among five professors whose sessions seemed to run long or short based on nothing but a whim.

She learned far too much about the biology of dragons every time she and Signey spent their weekends at the National Hall. Each weekend, they were separated until sunset, exchanging information on the flight back to Hearthstone before, tentatively, beginning to share the details of their days through the bond instead.

What she didn't learn in those first few weeks was how to deal with her classmates.

Signey's pointed, public barbs were one thing, but the rest of the students weren't satisfied unless Elara literally felt the piercing edges of their hatred. There were small wounds, like someone leaving a claw ring on her chair so it stabbed her when she sat down, or someone locking eyes with her as they spat in her soup. Then there were the larger attacks, like when she woke up in the middle of the night to someone holding a dagger to her throat and threatening to carve her open if she "tried anything," or when someone set fire to a tree while she was sitting under it. It got so bad that, after the first couple of weeks, her professors began escorting her from class to class.

It was clear from the first day that she was a museum exhibit to these students, who had rarely seen an Iryan on this side of the Ember Sea. Elara stood out in every conceivable way. She spoke what sounded to everyone like accented Langlish, thanks to Zephyra, but it was not an accent they were used to. She wore her hair in long dark brown braids that tumbled down her back, but her classmates' rainbow hair ranged from pin straight to curly and made the texture of hers a subject of whispered conversations.

Her skin was darker than that of any other Rider she'd come across, though the Langlish Empire spanned so many regions that there was no single skin tone to make her feel completely othered. Some students were pale, some had olive complexions, some had golden undertones, and some had the copper Lindan hue of Signey and Jesper. The gorgeous shades of brown from San Irie, a prism against which Elara's own umber skin would have blended, were just less represented.

"The Langlish Empire comprises almost fifty territories across the world," Professor Damon Smithers said in one history class. It had become her favorite class, admittedly because she'd done so well from the start that Professor Smithers had praised her to Commander Warwick. Her need for validation had won the battle with her dread. "Although different, these Langlish territories are all united by their people's freedom to maintain their individual cultures and to move freely throughout the empire for work or residency. Thanks to that, the Langlish people are a diverse group within the larger Langlish identity."

He said this as if it were supposed to be a good thing, but all Elara could think of were the "almost fifty territories" that hadn't yet been set free. How many of them actually *wanted* to be part of the empire? And what happened to the revolutions that, unlike San Irie's, had failed? During one class, she'd gotten brave enough to ask that question, and Professor Smithers had smiled. "Let's explore that," he'd said.

It had almost been worth the extra homework.

Soon, the only place where Elara truly felt at home was the three-floor Hearthstone library. It was also, she quickly discovered, the best and least suspicious way to get information. As far as she could tell, there was no topic forbidden for Hearthstone students to learn about. Her politics and theology classes alone required her to do so much reading to catch up that she could use the high stacks of books as a makeshift barrier between her and everyone else. No one could see what she was really studying, and, best of all, no one could throw anything at her.

And no one dared throw anything at her when Signey joined her, lending them the illusion of privacy. With their heads bent over their respective tomes, they were able to talk, *really* talk, and this seemed like the best time to reveal one thing that she had been holding back.

"*Gael Soto?*" Signey didn't look up at her, but Elara could feel her shock as if it were her own. "*The Gray Saint is my ancestor?*"

"*It could be a coincidence,*" Elara mused. "*But it would be a rather big one.*"

"*But are you sure he's the Gray Saint? A god? Or . . . can the Childe Empyrean summon Langlish ancestors?*"

Elara doodled at the bottom of her paper to look busy. "*Summoners can only call on their own ancestors for help. Faron's unique in that she can call on the gods, but she can't summon or see other people's astrals.*"

"*A vessel, then. The Gray Saint is using the likeness of my ancestor to manipulate us into trusting him.*"

"*Signey,*" Elara sent as gently as she could, "*the Gray Saint died centuries ago. No one would blame your family for his crimes if they knew—*"

"You don't know that." Signey slammed her book shut and stood. "I'm going to look for a different one. I'll be back."

She stalked off with the determination of someone who would not be right back. Elara let her go, sitting back in her chair with a sigh. It was possible that Gael Soto was just a projection the Gray

Saint was using to obscure his true motives. But it was equally possible that they were one and the same, another alias for the same man-turned-god who had started this mess. It made more sense to her, given what Signey had shared about her family history. How else could a Langlish dragon-riding dynasty have originated from Isalina, unless the line went so far back that neither country had existed?

But Signey was understandably sensitive about her family and their reputation.

"My race came to your world so long ago that few of us were alive to remember it. You were so small, so weak, that we took no notice of you as we laid claim to these lands. You rallied and began to hunt us in turn, leading to the Draconian Wars," Zephyra said. Elara felt the brief sensation of cool water over hot skin. Her dragon was swimming around the bay again, creating lazy circles as she told her bloody bedtime story. *"The fighting might have continued until both species were extinct if the boy that the Langlish refer to as the Gray Saint hadn't faced down the First Dragon and treated him with kindness rather than violence. But nowhere in the legends does it say that the First Dragon or the Gray Saint died."*

"Then what happ—"

A tower of her books clattered to the floor. She jolted back to the present.

"If it isn't our newest student," said a boy, standing over her with a small pack of friends. He was square jawed, peach skinned, and dark haired, with narrow sea-green eyes. His red shirt and collars marked him as a carmine Rider. "I thought that was you hiding back here."

"I'm not hiding," Elara replied, trying to keep her tone polite and nonthreatening. Sometimes, when she got angry and lashed out, her bullies would shout for a professor and accuse *her* of harassing *them*. Depending on the professor, she might actually get in trouble, and detention made it hard to keep up with the schoolwork. "Have we met?"

"I'm Marius Lynwood," said the boy. He pointed at another pale boy in the same uniform, with amber eyes and close-cropped brown hair. "That's my cousin and Wingleader, Nichol Thompson." Behind them was a third boy, blond haired, dark skinned, and wearing the sky-blue shirt of an ultramarine Rider, and the sole girl of the group, a copper-skinned redhead in the same blue, who introduced herself as his Wingleader.

Elara remained on her guard. Their smiles were bladed, and she didn't want to give them the opportunity to draw blood. "It's... nice to meet you?"

"Is it?" Marius put a hand on the back of her chair and leaned down so they were almost at eye level. "Because I can't say I'm especially happy to have an Iryan here spying on us."

Elara kept her expression mild. "I'm here because I'm a Rider—"

"A Rider? You're a grub who got lucky."

She was on her feet before she could stop herself. It was the first time she'd ever heard the slur for Iryan people before, though she'd heard *of* it. Her aunts had sometimes whispered about it before they'd gone off to war. It implied that Iryans were no better than insects, worker ants who had rebelled against the queen, and the unexpected and harsh sound of it was like a punch to the face.

"Fuck you," Elara said, shaking. "How *dare* you?"

"I'm just telling the truth," Marius said. "You know you don't belong here. And *I* know you're probably just looking for information to use against us in the next war."

"There isn't going to be a next war. Our countries are at *peace*."

"I love that you're still calling that union of provincial idiots a *country*. It's a social experiment that's basically failing."

Elara shoved him.

Immediately, she regretted it. Faron was the one who sometimes tussled with the other children in the schoolyard. Elara's fights were always spars arranged by both parties. But the petty satisfaction she got from watching Marius Lynwood stumble backward was undeniable. Punching him in his stupid square jaw would have been even better, but Elara hated facing an opponent she wasn't sure she could beat.

The poisonous look in his eyes was a warning sign that she may have already done so. "If you're going to be a child about it, then face me properly. I challenge you to an incendio."

She had no idea what that was, which gave him an advantage that she wasn't comfortable with. "I'd rather just fight you. Unless, of course, you don't think you could take me in a combat class."

It was the only other class that she was excelling in. Elara was pretty sure she was already Professor Petra Rowland's favorite student, if the harsh woman was the type to name favorites. Five minutes with Marius in a partner session, and she was sure she could make him cry.

"Combat," Marius snorted, "is for the battlefield. The incendio is for personal grievances—and, believe me, this is personal."

Before Elara could decline a second time, someone new joined the crowd. "She accepts."

Marius's friends parted to reveal Signey striding through with a book in her hand. Her wavy ponytail swished back and forth from the force of her steps as she marched up to Marius to jab a finger against his chest. Even though she had to glare up at him, her anger made her seem ten times taller than he was.

"Challenging my Wingleader to an incendio without me present, Lynwood?" she snarled. "I didn't take you for a coward."

"Those are brave words from the girl whose father is in *jail*."

Signey's face darkened. "Name the time, and we'll be there to turn your dignity to ashes."

"Midnight. Tonight."

"Done. You and your lackeys can go drown yourselves now."

Marius gave Elara one last ferocious smile, and then he and his group filed out. Elara sank back into her chair, the adrenaline from the confrontation draining so quickly that she felt light-headed.

"What in Irie's name is an incendio and why did you just sign me up for one?" she asked.

Signey returned to her own chair, setting the book down in front of her. "It's a battle to settle disputes between Riders. Marius is a remorseless bully. If you give in to him, you'll paint yourself as an easy target to everyone else."

"I'm already an easy target to everyone else!" Elara dropped her forehead against the wooden table, wishing she could rub the last few minutes from her mind. "And now I have to fight someone in something I know nothing about? Great. Just what I needed. Thanks."

"You'll be fine, Elara."

She opened her eyes to see Jesper and Torrey had arrived. Torrey had her blazer thrown over her right shoulder like a cape, revealing the line of dragonscale bracelets around her left wrist. Jesper placed a hand on the back of Elara's chair, but, unlike Marius, it felt more comforting than threatening. Especially paired with the concerned scowl he was wearing on a face that didn't seem built for anything but smiles.

"A newborn could take Marius in an incendio. He's all talk," Jesper continued. "And this will be a great experience for you."

"Zephyra told us what he said about San Irie. And," Torrey said, lowering her voice, "what he called you. None of that was okay. You *have* to knock him on his ass for that."

"I want to knock him around myself," said Jesper. When he stepped away, his hands were fisted in clear frustration. "He was smart to catch you alone, because the things I'd do to him..."

Elara wondered if she was in the middle of an extended dream sequence, one that had perhaps begun the night she'd snuck out of her parents' house. The way the den was staring at her, it was almost as if they supported her over their countryman. They had been nothing but nice to her all this time, but this was different. This was a line drawn in the sand. This was a deliberate choice. This was...this was unexpected.

"Is this a trick?" she had to ask. "Are you all pushing me into an 'incendio' so Marius Lynwood...I don't know, sets me on fire, and then Signey can get a better co-Rider?"

Torrey laughed. *"What?"*

Elara raised her eyebrows. She saw Torrey and Jesper exchange glances as if they couldn't decide who should answer her. Faintly, she remembered Signey revealing that they could all communicate with one another and their dragons. She hadn't learned to do that yet, hadn't particularly wanted to, and this was the first time it had ever frustrated her to be out of the loop.

"Look," Jesper responded. His voice had lowered to a whisper, his eyes darting around the mostly empty library. "Not everyone in Langley was in favor of the war. The fact that it happened, the tactics we employed, the continued propaganda against San Irie... *Some* of us see that for how horrible it is. Obviously, there are plenty of people like Marius at this school, who buy into Langlish superiority and all that, but you don't have to worry about that with us. It's weird that you're Iryan and a Rider, but we don't look down on you or your country."

Elara blinked slowly. Her gaze cut to Signey. *"Are you sure you don't want to tell him what we're doing?"*

"I will literally kill you." Outside their bond, Signey shrugged. "I don't hate you because you're Iryan. I hate you because you're incompetent."

"Good to know," Elara deadpanned in response to both.

Torrey grabbed a chair and flipped it around so she could sit on it backward. She folded her arms atop it, using them as a chin rest. "We're here for you, all right? We're den, no matter where we or our families come from. And we'll be there at the incendio to support you, too."

They were serious. She could see it. She could *feel* it.

And she was spying on them.

Elara was dangerously close to a hysterical laugh. She choked it back. "All right, I guess since you already volunteered me, then I'm doing it. Tell me exactly how this incendio works so I don't embarrass you."

And as her den began to talk over themselves to give her the history of the incendio, tell her about several they had witnessed, and recall in colorful detail ones they had participated in, Elara felt a rush of affection through the bond, wrapping around her like a mother's hug. She sent a smile back to Zephyra, ever-watchful Zephyra, who she now knew had called her den to encourage her without Elara even having to ask.

If this was what a bond was supposed to be like, maybe it wasn't so bad after all.

CHAPTER TWENTY-ONE

FARON

DESPITE HER DESPERATION, FARON WAS STILL A POOR STUDENT. A month of fruitless lessons passed, and, for once, it wasn't due to a lack of effort. Gael Soto had wanted to start with commanding dragon souls, something she had already done, but it seemed that energy and fear had more to do with her success that night at the Summit than capability. She thought about dragons during meals, as she fell asleep, when she took morning walks along the beach, and she was no closer to summoning the soul of one than she was to crowning herself queen.

"Are you sure they're not too *far away* to listen?" Faron asked in exasperation. Her vague memories of early summoning classes had focused on calling to the astral of the most recent relative who had died, not reaching generations into the past. It seemed ridiculous that she should be able to feel the souls of creatures that were an entire ocean away. "They all went back to Langley last month, you know."

They were on the patio where she'd first summoned him. Faron sat cross-legged in one of the three wicker chairs that were spread out across the tiles. Gael Soto was perched on the white-painted lattice fence that hemmed in the patio from the grass. It squeaked under his weight every time he shifted, but he seemed unconcerned. Faron, on the other hand, found it mildly concerning. Every time she saw him, he seemed to get more solid. She could no longer faintly see through his skin.

But right now, she needed him too badly to care.

"Distance doesn't matter," he said. "If your will is strong enough, you can reach them no matter where in the world they are."

"Or you could just stop the Fury yourself and save me the trouble."

A slow smirk spread across his face. "Could I?"

"Can't you?" she shot back. "I'm not naïve. You can't convince me it's a coincidence that there's a new dragon disease and you *happen* to be the only one who knows how to cure it."

"I'm hardly the only one who knows how to cure it. I know *a* cure, and you came to me for it." Gael raised a single eyebrow. "I think that says more about you than it does about me."

"That's your story? Really?"

"It seems like you've already heard one. Tell me"—and now his smile was as sharp as his cheekbones—"what else are the other gods saying about me these days?"

"If your name is Gael Soto," Faron asked instead, "then why do the Langlish call you the Gray Saint?"

"That's another story, and you still haven't told me one."

Anything she could say felt like a weapon she'd be adding to his arsenal. Her blood pumped with the same energy she felt during battle. The knowledge that she couldn't dare trust him even though she needed him turned their conversation into a dance at the edge of a rooftop. One wrong move, and she would plunge to her death. One small opening, and she could push him to his.

And both of them were feeling the other out to see who would fall.

"First, you tell me this," said Faron. "I've been talking to the gods for over five years without hearing from you. Why come to me now?"

"Because you needed me." Gael eased down from the fence, then glided across the tiles toward her with all the predatory grace of a boa. "Because I have knowledge that the gods never wanted you to know. The power that I am unlocking within you, the power to command living souls, has not been seen in this world since I was a part of it. Do you have any idea what you could do with magic like that?" His fingers captured her chin, as gentle as a lover's kiss. "You could rule this world. You could bring it to ruin. You—"

"I just want to rescue my sister," Faron interrupted, her heart thundering in her chest. The way he spoke, the beguiling cadence of his voice, was a trap. It was no wonder Langley still referred to him as a saint even though the commander admitted that the strain of his dragon bond drove him mad. He wore his charm like a cloak, and she refused to fall for it. "I want to learn to break the bond between a dragon and a Rider. I want to go home with my sister at my side, free to live her own life. I'm not interested in anything else from you."

He stared at her, stared *through* her. "Very well."

Gael stepped back, and her held breath shook loose from her chest.

"Again," he said. "Really try to reach out this time."

But before Faron could follow his instruction or demand more information, someone called her name.

"Class," Gael drawled, "dismissed."

He faded away, leaving her with her still-racing heart and the sense that she had won this interaction—barely. Faron climbed onto slightly shaky feet, searching for any hint that the god still remained, but his presence was gone. Only his impact lingered, raising goose bumps along her skin. Was he making her stronger, or was she making *him* stronger? Was she controlling him, or was he controlling her?

He made it so hard to think when he was around.

"Faron!"

With one last frown, she went inside.

Reeve brought Faron to the library, where the fireplace was lit and Elara—or, rather, Elara's voice—waited to share the latest information she'd gained. The bags under his eyes had gotten deeper, his skin paperlike beneath the gas lamps. His hair was limp. Ink stained one cheek, as if he'd fallen asleep atop his own notes. Even with the short breaks he'd begun to take between hours of research, it was clear that Reeve was falling apart. Breaking himself to piece her sister's life back together.

"Did you eat?" Elara asked from the fireplace once the two of them were settled. "You don't sound well."

"Later," said Reeve impatiently. "I'm glad you were around to take this call because this is important. I looked for more books about the Draconian Wars that Zephyra mentioned to you, and I think I've found something interesting."

Faron was sitting in the armchair she had come to think of as his, watching him pace back and forth in front of the fireplace. Concern threatened to overtake her mild interest in these Draconian

Wars they'd clearly discussed without her. Elara couldn't even see Reeve, couldn't see the way he paused to rub at his eyes, the way he ran his hands through his hair as if he wanted to pull it out. Seeing his agitation made Faron want to take care of him...and that was an impulse she needed to squash before she was forced to examine why.

"I've finally read all the books in the library about the Gray Saint, the First Dragon, and the Draconian Wars. After he ended the war, the Gray Saint became a despot. The first four people who he taught to bond with dragons became his generals, helping him bring the rest of the world to heel. Some sources say that the Four Generals betrayed him, and others say that the people rose against them all. But either way, he and the First Dragon disappeared from history."

"Okay," Faron said to Reeve. "And...how does that help us, exactly?"

"Because that's *all* these books say." Reeve stared at her as if this should mean something. "Every single one of them just says he disappeared from history."

"That's not what Zephyra told me," Elara added, following his train of thought in a way that Faron could not. "She said that nowhere in the legends does it claim that they *died*, but if they disappeared—"

"That's the thing. Langley has multiple legends about what happened, but it's not that they died *or* disappeared. In fact, one version of the legend claims that the Gray Saint and the First Dragon went into stasis somewhere and will return one day once certain conditions are met. It's the most famous version."

"And it's not in any of the Seaview books?"

"*Not a single one.* Seaview was occupied during the war, until your army reclaimed it, and now all the books left here are missing the most famous legend about the Gray Saint? What if Langley didn't *want* us to have record of it? What if raising the First Dragon has been the plan all along?"

Faron swallowed as Reeve paused triumphantly in front of the fireplace. Part of her wanted to feel excluded by how easily they fell into step with each other even with an ocean between them, but the rest of her had turned to stone. An alarm was going off in her head, drowning out every other thought. "You think the First Dragon is...what, here? Somewhere in San Irie? And that's why your father won't leave us alone?"

"I don't know about that, but I *do* think the First Dragon was the most powerful dragon in history. A perfect weapon against San Irie. Against the world. My father said that ignorance was the reason Langley was a laughingstock. He's destroyed any record of this legend, leaving the library intact so we wouldn't notice. This has to be it. This has to be his plan. And I think he's close to seeing it through."

Faron realized she was shaking her head, but she couldn't stop. "How close?"

It was Elara who answered the question, her tone slow and thoughtful. "Signey told me that the commander brought her to San Irie under false pretenses, claiming that she might find her co-Rider among fictional delegates from Isalina. And in the letters I told you about, he mentioned solving two problems with one action. What if...what if he figured out that the final Rider had to be from another country, and he used the Summit to test three countries at once? What if every dragon having a Rider is one of the conditions to awaken the First Dragon?"

"Because the First Dragon brought them all here from the divine plane, taught them how to bond with humans. Or the Gray Saint did, according to Faron," Reeve breathed. "But maybe that's why the Gray Saint spoke to Faron the same night Zephyra bonded with you. We woke him first. Which would mean he's the next step, somehow."

Elara swore. "Signey's already upset that she might be related to the Gray Saint. She's not going to like that the bond she's dreamed of might have led to all this."

"We don't know that it has," Reeve reassured her. "These are just theories."

Faron's fingers tightened around the fabric of her dress, her mind on Gael's promise to teach her how to command living souls. Would it actually help free her sister? Or had summoning him only given him more power? He'd come to her of his own volition a month ago, and he was looking more and more solid every day....

The Gray Saint was getting closer and closer to full strength.

Because of her.

Because she'd jumped in without waiting for information. As always.

Guilt clenched her stomach. She hadn't told Reeve or Elara about her connection with the Gray Saint, let alone about their lessons in the past month. She'd assumed they would chastise her, talk her out of it, and she'd wanted to surprise them with her success. Now she felt like the worst kind of fool.

"I can talk to the gods again," she mumbled, not looking at Reeve or the fire. "I'll bring them our theories and see if I can press them for more facts."

"And you haven't heard from the Gray Saint since that first

night, right, Faron?" Elara asked. "Have you tried, I don't know, calling him the way you do the gods?"

"No." Faron toyed with a thread at the seam of her dress. "Should I?"

"Let's try your gods first," said Reeve. "At least until we know more. Acknowledging him might speed up the process."

Faron tugged the thread loose. The seam widened into a hole, revealing a peek of sweaty brown skin. "All right. I'll fire call the queen later. Maybe she has more books at the palace that she can send you."

Reeve and Elara began to say their goodbyes to each other, peppered with promises to talk again soon, and Faron added her own hollow farewells. Her heart felt leaden in her chest from the lies she'd wrapped herself in, from the trap that she had walked into and now needed to destroy before it was too late.

But it wasn't too late. Not yet. She would just tread even more lightly around Gael when he came to her again. If he was helping Commander Warwick raise the First Dragon, she would not be a pawn in that plan.

Gael Soto would learn the hard way that Faron was so much more than a plaything of the gods.

She was much worse than he had ever prepared for.

CHAPTER TWENTY-TWO

ELARA

ELARA AND THE DEN SNUCK OUT FOR THE INCENDIO TEN MINUTES before midnight. She kept to the back of the group, watching Signey's ponytail swing left and right and worrying how badly her Firstrider would take the theories she'd formed with Reeve and Faron. Signey was already uncomfortable with the idea that the commander had been paying her close attention. She refused to accept that her ancestor could be the Gray Saint. Their bond being the key to the commander's scheme might be the thing that shattered her.

Compared to all that, the incendio seemed like the least of Elara's problems. But here she was.

It was a full moon, so bright it turned the sand pearlescent. The bay was a trembling black line on the horizon, kissed by silver. The other den was already waiting for them. Like Elara, Marius Lynwood had traded in his uniform for his riding leathers. Like her den, his gang was still in their uniforms. It felt like combat class, but far more serious. Worse, Marius's arrogance made him seem more threatening under the apathetic stars. Elara took a shaky breath.

"*You'll be fine,*" Zephyra reassured her. She was standing with Marius's dragon, Goldeye, near the path that twisted away from the beach. It led toward the bridge that connected Caledon Island to Margon Island, the next in the archipelago's chain. "*I am confident in your abilities.*"

"*I'm glad one of us is,*" Elara sent.

"*Two of us,*" Signey added. Elara almost tripped over a twig. Her Firstrider rolled her eyes at her clumsiness, but even that couldn't erase the warmth her words left behind. "*Don't worry. I haven't been reading your mind.*"

"*I know that,*" said Elara, her cheeks burning. Better for Signey to think it was surprise that had made her heart skip a beat. It was already hard enough to ignore her attraction to her co-Rider.

Nichol pulled a dragoon from his pocket, the ivory Langlish coin standing out against the night. "Challenger's choice. Fangs or scales?"

"Fangs," said Marius.

The coin tumbled through the air and landed with the snarling dragon insignia in the sand and the scale-textured back facing upward.

"Looks like it's your call, grub. Sky trial or soil trial?"

Though her choice had been settled by an afternoon-long debate with the den, Elara took a moment to reconsider her options. The sky trial was a race between their dragons, as much a test of their bond as it was of her skills. After just a month of Hearthstone classes, her skills were lacking. The soil trial, however, was a straightforward fight, channeling the magic and strength they drew from their dragons. As Marius's slur dug into her skin, Elara wanted nothing more than to slam her fist into his face.

But she reminded herself that she didn't know how he fought, and the beach was too dim for her to properly study his movements. She might lose to him then, and she couldn't stand that.

"Sky trial," she said. "If you think you can keep up."

Marius marched over to his dragon. Though Goldeye was a carmine, by nature bright red and enormous, he looked even larger perched next to Zephyra. The largest dragon breed versus the smallest dragon breed should have meant that Elara had a natural advantage in this race, but that was far from guaranteed.

"Sages are aerodynamic, but carmines have superior wingspan, so they cover more ground," Jesper had said. "Besides, Marius is a seasoned Rider, so he and his dragon can work in tandem much better than you and Zephyra. It'll be a close race."

Marius scaled Goldeye's back and settled in the saddle attached to the middle of Goldeye's spine. Even though Riders had perfect balance on their mounts as part of the bond, Elara turned away to make sure she was securely strapped into her own saddle, her gloved fingers trembling. As they rose, their dens blended into a single crowd of spectators, the distance making it impossible to tell friend from foe. Elara took a steadying breath as she allowed Zephyra and Signey to ease into her mind. Zephyra flared out her wings behind them, and if she could have smirked at that moment, Elara sensed she would have.

She would win this. *They* would win this. Zephyra hated Goldeye as much as Elara hated Marius, and she was eager for the chance to make a fool of him.

"*Remember the most important rules of the incendio,*" Signey said to them both, a smile in her voice. "*Have fun and make them cry.*"

Zephyra roared her version of a laugh. Elara grinned.

A ball of fire shot into the air and exploded overhead.

The sky trial had begun.

Five minutes into the race around the archipelago, Goldeye was a dark speck ahead, every flap of his wings helping him cover three times the distance that they could in that time. Zephyra coasted along the wind currents, conserving her energy and giving Elara plenty of time to think.

And strategize.

The first dragon to return to the island of Caledon would be the victor. Goldeye had started strong, but not the kind of strong that burned through the reserves of energy stored in his bulky form. He flew in a way that was neither fast nor fancy, the dragon equivalent of a brisk walk. Elara didn't think his mass allowed him to fly any faster than that, and the bull-like horns—a feature unique to Goldeye—that jutted from his triangular head slowed him down further. The horns would be even more of a liability when he had to turn, changing his trajectory and making him easy to overtake if they caught up in time.

In combat class, Professor Rowland spent a lot of time drilling into them the need to study the wind currents in various countries because they affected a dragon's effectiveness in battle. Thanks to the homework assignments she'd been acing, Elara was intimately familiar with the breezes that Serpentia Bay was famous for. And there was a particularly famous swell around the edge of the archipelago.

"Hold steady," she told Zephyra. *"We'll catch them at the next island, so there's no need to waste our energy now."*

Zephyra made an approving sound. *"I have raced Goldeye many times before. He tries to put as much distance as he can between us at the start because his weight makes it hard for him to make sharp turns and build speed. The last time we raced, he banked so awkwardly that he went spiraling into a tree."*

Elara snickered, imagining Marius hanging upside down from a branch, his face bright red and his pants tearing open. *"Why were you racing?"*

"Signey challenged Marius to an incendio for insulting her father. He chose a sky trial, likely because he knew she would love the opportunity to make him eat sand."

Marius's earlier barb echoed in her head: *Those are brave words from the girl whose father is in jail.*

Elara's grip tightened on the straps of the saddle as the final island, Avilion, reared up before them. Goldeye was swooping around the tip in a broad circle, wings spread wide and Marius no more than a black spot in a sea of brown between two ivory back spikes. In seconds, they would turn back toward Caledon.

"Now," said Elara. *"Take the northwestern winds first."*

Zephyra shot forward, cresting the island so easily that Elara almost missed the turn. They spun over and over, adding an extra burst of speed to Zephyra's flight pattern, and flapped their way past the chain of islands between them and Caledon. Wind roared in Elara's ears, buoying Zephyra's agile body as her northwestern trajectory carried her along every current that would increase her speed. Elara realized that she was laughing, and then she couldn't stop. Until now, flying had ranged from a terrifying experience to a reminder of how far she was from the person she had wanted to be.

But now that she was in control, it was actually *fun*.

Goldeye roared behind them, and Elara didn't need to understand him to know that he was furious. Zephyra released a roar of her own, loud and joyous, and Elara added her laughter to the symphony.

"Want to have a little fun?" Zephyra asked.

"Always," Elara replied.

She heard a rumble of laughter, and then Zephyra took them up and up and up, through the thin line of clouds that cupped the moon. Elara threw a look behind them, but Goldeye was still near the northern tip of Ealdon. Zephyra hurtled back toward the black water, pulling up just in time to fly parallel to the waves. Her wings dipped beneath the water with every flap, throwing crystal droplets overhead. Elara leaned over just far enough to trail her hands through the frigid bay, giddy with excitement.

"Careful," Signey sent.

Goldeye had caught up. In fact, he and Marius had flown past them and were closing in on the victory.

"Zephyra!"

"A little trust would be nice, ladies," said Zephyra, still zigzagging across the surface of the bay. *"I know what I'm doing."*

Elara didn't need to see Signey to know she was rolling her eyes. *"Showing off?"*

"You did say to have fun."

"She's not wrong. You did say that," Elara pointed out.

Signey sighed across the bond like a mother with a brood of unruly children. Elara grinned and tightened her thighs around Zephyra. *"Let's win this thing."*

"As you wish, little one."

Zephyra picked up speed again, pulling away from the water and spiraling upward until the clouds covered them. Elara could see Caledon between the gaps in the clouds, could see that Goldeye was only yards away. And yet she wasn't worried because Zephyra wasn't worried. She trusted Zephyra just as Zephyra had trusted her. They could win this. And they would win this.

Together.

As if that was all she'd been waiting for, Zephyra zipped in a diagonal arc toward the island. Applause and cheers erupted from Caledon, both dens screaming the names of their preferred Riders. But somewhere in those voices was Signey, silent and observant, confident and proud, and Zephyra's focus had narrowed to her. Elara allowed her focus to narrow to Signey as well, allowed Signey's confidence to become her confidence. The ground rushed up to meet them—

And Zephyra landed hard on the beach, scattering sand everywhere, seconds before Goldeye touched down.

Marius's den abruptly fell silent.

Before Elara had even finished sliding out of the saddle, Jesper and Torrey were surrounding her in a cacophony of cheers and delight.

"You were so good!" Torrey cried, throwing her arms around Elara. "The two of you worked like a perfect team—"

"I thought for sure he had you," shouted Jesper, thumping her on the back and nearly making her lose her balance. "Zephyra, you had me convinced you'd gotten distracted by the water—"

"Thank you," Elara said, searching the crowd for one person in particular.

Signey had apparently skirted the den entirely. She was resting a hand on Zephyra's hide and whispering quietly to her, but she looked up when Elara approached. Then she smiled, wide and genuine. A single dimple appeared in her left cheek, and her eyes caught the light from the moon overhead, sparkling like tiny stars. Her teeth were adorably uneven, her pronounced canines ruining the straight line of her wide smile, but it didn't make her any less beautiful.

Oh no.

"Hey," Signey said warmly. "Congratulations."

"Thank you," Elara whispered, feeling like she'd been struck. *Oh no.*

Her mouth had forgotten how to form other words, but there were too many people around for it to be noticed. Jesper wasted no time in getting between them, dragging his flailing sister into a bear hug.

"Congratulations to *you* for having such an amazing Wing-leader." His knuckles rubbed against her head, messing up her ponytail. "I've never been prouder of you."

"Why are you such a bloody child?" Signey grumbled, shoving at him. Jesper caught her hands, and an impromptu wrestling match broke out. Watching them made Elara miss Faron with a sudden ferocity, even though they had just spoken before the race. Would Faron congratulate her on having won? Or would she be worried that Elara was getting along too well with the enemy?

Signey finally managed to win the match by kicking her brother so hard in the shin that he cursed. Elara's smile fizzled out when she noticed that Marius and his den were halfway up the hill. No acknowledgment. No congratulations. No *Nice race*. Nothing.

She broke into a run, catching up to Marius at the top of the hill. The smarmy expression on his face was so at odds with what had just happened that it took some of the magnitude out of her victory. He didn't respect her any more than he had before the sky trial. He would probably tell people that her victory had been a fluke to save face. In his eyes, she would never be worthy of respect.

Elara expected the conclusion to hurt, but she realized that she didn't care. She didn't care what Marius Lynwood thought of her or San Irie. She had proven him wrong, not to gain his respect but to remind herself that she could. To remind herself that people like him were the ones who were nothing, because they only had as much influence as she chose to give them. He might have been Langlish born, privileged and powerful and surrounded by people only too happy to tell him that this made him better than her, but her very existence in his world was proof that his position couldn't change the facts.

She had come to Hearthstone Academy.

She had beaten him in the sky trial of an incendio.

She was everything that he had been taught to fear: an Iryan with the intelligence, strength, and confidence to turn his own skills against him.

So, in the face of that arrogance, she smirked, a sharp and scathing thing that felt like a weapon on her lips. "Hey, Lynwood? Fuck. You."

And then she walked away to celebrate with her den.

CHAPTER TWENTY-THREE

FARON

T HAT NIGHT, GAEL SOTO CAME TO FARON IN HER DREAMS.

He stood unmoving in the center of Deadegg's town square. Even though the sun was high in the sky, Deadegg was quiet and still. There was no wailing from babies bouncing on their mothers' hips or screaming from children too young for compulsory education, begging their fathers for the money to buy a cherry drink. There was no bleating of goats clogging the narrow roads or barking of stray dogs in search of scraps. Even the storefronts appeared to be empty, wooden shutters drawn closed, awnings lowered and doors chained up.

There was just her and Gael and the city of Deadegg around them, as silent as fog.

"You lied to me," Faron said instead of wasting time trying to determine if any of this was real. "You're trying to raise the First Dragon."

Gael tilted his head, his hair sliding against his smooth cheek like rivers of ink. "I have never lied to you, Empyrean. I told you that I wanted something from you in exchange for my help."

"You didn't tell me the whole truth, then," said Faron, well versed in the many forms a lie could take. "You made me think that you needed me. But that's not quite true, is it? You only need me if Commander Warwick doesn't give you what you want first."

"It sounds as if you think you have me all figured out. So why don't *you* tell *me*?"

"I'm sick of your games, *Gray Saint*. I want the truth, or I swear to Irie I will never summon you again."

Gael studied her in silence, his hazel eyes sliding over her face with so much intensity that she could almost feel it. Faron didn't blink. In a battle of wills, she had few peers. He would meet her as an equal or not at all.

A faint smile bloomed on his face. "All right, then. The truth."

"What do you want from me?" Faron demanded. The question seemed to echo around the empty town, louder and louder until it were as if she had screamed it.

What do you want from me?

What do you want from me?

What do you want?

"I want the same thing you want, Faron Vincent," Gael said, cutting through the clamor. "Freedom."

"From?"

Gael moved then, and, at first, Faron thought that he was going to approach her. Her mind flashed back to the feeling of his fingers on her face before she pushed the memory away. But he was only stepping closer to the wall that surrounded the dragon egg before them, staring up at it the way so many Deadegg children had done in the past.

"They say I went mad a long time ago," he said. "But what does that word even mean? I made certain choices that led to my downfall, yes, but that could be said of any leader throughout history. As punishment, I was imprisoned in a place they call the Empty. There, I slept, unable to age, unable to think, unable to leave. Until, against all odds, I was awoken." Gael looked at her over his shoulder, his eyes as deep as an endless field. "Do I seem mad to *you*, Empyrean?"

The gods had never told her about the Empty. Reeve's books had never mentioned it. *One version of the legend claims that the Gray Saint and the First Dragon went into stasis somewhere and will return one day once certain conditions are met.* Well, at least she could confirm for Reeve that the legend was true, if not the conditions.

"Who woke you?" she asked.

"Gavriel Warwick."

"How?"

"I'm uncertain. But I was weak then. Weaker than I am now." His hands flexed. "I am still weak."

"But you've gotten stronger," said Faron, gesturing around them. "You can come even if I haven't called. You can speak to me even in my dreams. You grow more solid every time I see you. What happens when you regain full strength? What has the commander asked you to do?"

Gael turned to face her fully now, and there was a guilelessness to him that she had never seen before. "The First Dragon was a threat to this world. It was he, not I, who brought dragons into it, and he thought that giving humans such a gift meant that he should rule them. In the divine plane, dragons are considered animals by the gods. In the mortal plane, he wanted them to be worshipped like the gods. But while other dragons genuinely came to care for their Riders, the First Dragon only cared about destruction. So he was locked away, and, because we were bonded, I was locked away with him. His story became my own."

"And you think I can help you rewrite that story?" Faron considered this. "You're great with words, but you keep missing something important."

"What's that?"

"You're lying to the best," she whispered, as if they were sharing secrets in the dark. "I know the rhythm of deceit. I always recognize a tell. I can craft a lie so subtle and sweet that it will dissolve in your mind and make you question what you thought you always knew to be true." She smirked. "You want to turn me against the gods. You want me to believe you're this misunderstood innocent. But I am the queen of dishonesty, and you are *full of shit*."

When he approached her this time, she met his gaze straight on. Her eyebrows rose, daring him, taunting him, *inviting* him. His face was a stone mask, but his eyes blazed with emotion. Anger. She was getting to him.

"I am *telling you the truth*, Empyrean. I'm the only one who ever has."

"You want me to believe you?" She lifted her chin. "Tell me what the commander wants from you. No more secrets. No more lies."

"You're the most arrogant, frustrating, stubborn woman I've ever met." Gael sighed. "The commander wants to raise the First Dragon. In exchange, he wants the power to conquer the rest of the world under Langley's banner. But instead of unleashing the First Dragon, he woke me." Gael didn't seem to notice the lack of space between them, and it made what he was saying feel intimate somehow. "Faron, that dragon...is a dangerous creature. This is the first time in centuries my mind has been my own, and the honest truth is that locking him away was the best thing for this world. The commander cannot be allowed to succeed in his plan. No one can control that beast. I tried and, well. You've heard what happened."

"How can we stop the commander if he's already freed you?" Faron reached out then pressed a hand against his pale skin. Even here, he felt solid. Real. "And why do you even want to stop him from freeing the First Dragon? We've read about you. Together, the two of you were an unstoppable power. In my experience, men who have tasted power are loath to give it up."

"*He* tasted power. The Gray Saint. But it wasn't his power. He was nothing more than a symbol, chained to the will of a creature that was always hungry for more. The Gray Saint is the story they tell about me, the villain that the First Dragon made me, the worst parts of myself. But I told you my name, my *real* name, when you summoned me. Because all I want is to be that man again. I was a good man, once. A hero."

Faron hesitated, searching his face for signs of deceit. Instead, Gael looked pained. Perhaps even a little desperate for a way out of this. She recognized that kind of desperation. It was the same emotion she'd been feeling since Elara had bonded with a dragon.

"I am awake in the Empty. But he is not. Not yet. If you can master the art of commanding living souls before Warwick succeeds in unleashing him, you can bring the First Dragon to heel. You can *free me* from him. Please." Gael placed his hand over hers, his fingers gentle around her own. "I never wanted to be the villain of this story. I only ever wanted to protect my people."

And she believed him. Damn it, she believed him.

Or, at least, she wanted to. After all, she knew better than most what it was like to have other people write your story for you. To have people who had never spoken to you decide that they knew everything about you. To have your entire life forever changed by one simple act—and to be trapped in the consequences of it.

Maybe he was lying to her, but *everyone* lied. People and gods alike. He was still one of the few willing to help her and Elara, and for that alone she would trust him.

"All right," she said. "All right. If this will save Elara...if this will stop the commander, then all right. But if you're lying—"

"Trust is a fragile gift, Faron. It's only right that you refuse to give it away. But I'll prove myself to you, I swear it." Gael's eyes darted upward before returning to her face. "I think you're going to wake up now."

Faron jolted upward in bed, trying to wrap her mind around the sudden change in scenery. A tray was on her side table; the scent of roasted breadfruit and scrambled eggs wafted from beneath its cover.

The temple, she reminded herself as she bit into a slice of breadfruit. She would go back to the temple today. She had to talk to the gods. She had to ask them about the Gray Saint and the Empty. She had to confirm Gael's story before she shared it with Reeve and Elara.

Eradicating the dragons will destroy the threat of the Fury, but it will also destroy their Riders along with them.

Including your sister.

Faron swallowed hard, the food turning to paste on her tongue. Maybe she would bring Reeve with her to Seaview Temple. She didn't think she could make it through this line of questioning without some support, and, unfortunately, he was the only one available.

Reeve stopped at the opening of the wall that surrounded the grassy yard of the temple, a tight expression on his face. "I'll wait here."

Faron considered pressing the subject. There was no point in bringing him along for support if he wasn't even going to come inside the building. But at the same time, she understood his hesitancy. Reeve generally approached the Iryan faith with a mixture of scientific curiosity and polite deference. One memorable summer, Faron had caught him reading a stack of books the height of her arm about Iryan summoning magic and ancestral spirits. Just because he couldn't perform it, he'd said, didn't mean he shouldn't research and respect it.

But Reeve's father had also given the order to burn several of San Irie's temples to the ground. A Warwick stepping inside one even now would feel like a crime.

"Okay," Faron said at last. *Be careful* caught on her tongue. Elara had told her about finding Reeve in Port Sol, about the shopkeeper who had spat in his face. The people of Seaview hadn't experienced the visceral horror that those in Port Sol had, so it seemed unlikely that Reeve would be hassled in these streets. But unlikely wasn't impossible. Faron couldn't decide if she wanted to care or not.

"Are you actually going or...?" Reeve drawled, resting his elbows against the stone wall with an amused smirk.

Faron decided she definitely didn't care.

"Empyrean," said Irie as soon as the sunroom door closed. "It's been a long while since you've summoned us—"

"We *missed* you," Mala interrupted. She stood between Irie and

Obie, the curly-maned, big-eyed emotional heart to their divine detachment. "Are you all right?"

"Reeve's been doing research," Faron said, focusing on a point over Mala's head so she wouldn't be distracted from business. "He told me that in one story the Gray Saint never died. That he's imprisoned somewhere called the Empty. Is it true?"

Silence followed her question, a silence that said as much as any words would have.

Faron took a deep breath to control her temper. "What would have been the harm in just telling me that?"

"The reappearance of the Gray Saint, as well as your interest in him, worries us," Irie responded. "Your situation has made the right thing to do...a complicated matter for you. We knew what he was likely to want, and we knew you couldn't be coaxed into giving it to him if you didn't know anything about it. Or about him."

Faron's cheeks burned. The fact that she'd spent the last month in Gael Soto's company, under his tutelage, didn't matter as much as the realization that the gods were still treating her like a child incapable of making her own decisions. When they hid things from her, they narrowed her choices and undermined her ability to make informed ones. She should not have learned about the Empty from Gael, whom she had no reason to trust.

And after all she'd done, she should not have been learning now that the gods didn't trust *her*.

"Well, the Langlish might be planning to break the First Dragon out of there before I can be 'coaxed' into it," Faron said with only a hint of the anger that coursed through her body like poison. "Elara thinks the commander has already begun the process with her bond and the Gray Saint's reappearance. Tell me where the Empty is, so I can protect it."

"I don't think that's a good idea, Empyrean."

"But the commander—"

"Hasn't found it yet and can't be led there by you accidentally if you don't know where it is. The best protection is for its location to be lost to time."

"We don't even know where it is," Mala added. "Truly. We know where it *was*, but the world has grown and changed and shifted so much since then."

"But you could find it, right? If I summoned you, you could—"

"Empyrean." Irie narrowed those unfathomable eyes. "Your stubbornness betrays you. Why do you really want to know?"

The fact that she even had to ask made Faron's temper flare hot once more. She couldn't tell if they were being honest with her. She couldn't tell if they *would* be honest with her. And they had the nerve to stare at *her* with suspicion, as if her problems were a mystery to them. As if they'd hardly thought of her since she'd seen them last.

She was their chosen champion. She was their connection to the mortal plane. She was the weapon they had pointed at the Langlish Empire and their beasts of fire, and what had she ever gotten in return?

A past, present, and future defined by blood and flame.

"What if," she asked, "the Gray Saint has the power to break the bond between my sister and her dragon? What if he could teach me, and I could use that power on the First Dragon—"

Obie turned his head away as if he couldn't bear to look at her. Irie's expression was exasperated. And Mala was the worst of all, wavering between betrayal and pity. Faron's mouth snapped shut, tears prickling at her eyes. She wasn't sure if it was humiliation or rage that clogged her throat, but she swallowed down everything she wanted to say next. She was afraid of what would come out if she kept going.

"It simply isn't worth the risk," Irie said into the silence. "The Gray Saint and the First Dragon are so much more dangerous than you realize, and now that one has awakened, the continued existence of these dragons will likely only make them stronger. The time has come for you to meet your destiny, Empyrean. You must exterminate them before it's too late."

"What about Gael? Does he deserve to be exterminated, too?"

Another thick silence followed her words. A thick silence during which the last thread of doubt over Gael's intentions shrank to nothing. He *had* told her his real name. The gods *did* refuse to see him as anything but the Gray Saint, perpetually tied to the First Dragon. And they all agreed that the First Dragon was too large a threat to the world to be freed.

Which meant that he had told the truth about this power being the way to break Elara's bond.

While the gods continued to keep her in the dark.

Irie frowned. "How do you know that name? Empyrean, have you—"

"If you guys would just *talk* to me, I wouldn't have to"—Faron withered slightly under Irie's harsh gaze, the golden flame of Irie's pupilless eyes communicating her anger better than any words— "research all this. My sister's in danger, and you won't help me. So I'm trying to help myself. Is that so wrong?"

"This *will* help you," said Mala. "Don't you see what dragons have done to this world? Their power is so vast that only some-one with equal divine magic can actually end them. Only you. We gave you our magic for exactly this, and some sacrifices need to be made—"

Anger won out in Faron's vortex of emotion, spiking through her. "My *sister* is a Rider. You keep asking me to kill my sister for you. Because it's what *you* want. What about what *I* want?"

"Empyrean—"

"No! All you ever do, all any of you ever do, is take and take and take from me, and the one time I ask you for something—"

"Besides the incredible divine power that you waste on childish races," said Irie.

"—you refuse to help me and then ask me to give you *more*? Elara is more than just my sister. She's the best person I know. She's my hero. *She's* the saint. Any time I've ever needed her, she's been there for me. She gave up her *dreams* for me. And I can't—" Faron realized, to her horror, that she had started to cry. "I—I need to do this for her. What's the point of all this power if I can't help the one person who needs it the most?"

"*You* prayed to us to help San Irie win the war. Your prayer was the first we heard when we entered this plane, and your strength enabled you to channel our magic," Mala said. "We are gods, Empyrean, and the Iryans are our people. Because of us, they are suffering, and they will only continue to suffer until the dragons are gone. Unlike you, we don't have the luxury of prioritizing one person over all the rest."

"If I'm only the Empyrean because you heard me *first*, pick a new one," Faron snapped. "Because I won't kill my sister to save *anyone.*"

Irie looked even more tired. "We've seen this level of arrogance only once before. It is tragic, how much you sound like the Gray Saint."

How is it arrogance to want to save my family? Faron wanted to scream. *What else are you keeping from me?*

But the room was a blurry swirl of greenery through the curtain of her tears, and she couldn't *breathe* in here anymore.

"You don't stop being the chosen one just because the war is over," said Obie, and the rare sound of his voice ensured that those blunt words chased her from the room. "The sooner you accept that, the sooner we can move past this."

CHAPTER TWENTY-FOUR

ELARA

"WHAT IF I TRIED SPEAKING TO HIM?" SIGNEY ASKED AS THEY walked through the market.

It was almost the weekend, almost time for their next meeting with the commander, and Signey had caught Elara after class with an invitation to see the open-air market on Margon Island. *We need to properly celebrate your incendio win*, Signey had said, unaware of the goose bumps left behind by her touch and the fluttering in Elara's chest incited by her words.

Signey made her feel as if she'd never seen a girl before, let alone dated one, but she refused to act on her infatuation. There were many beautiful girls in the world. Signey was not special in that regard. If Elara had feelings for her, it had to be a result of the bond, a result of the potential to know each other better than anyone else could. She remembered her breakup with Cherry, the awkwardness it had added to their friendship for a few months afterward. She couldn't imagine how much worse that would be with their bond, feeling each other's heartbreak when it slipped past their walls.

It wasn't worth it. This wasn't why she was here.

At least she had the comfort of the market to distract her. Like the ones in San Irie, the market was stuffed with vendors behind their stalls, shopkeepers in front of their doors, and sellers balancing baskets on their heads, all yelling at people to come buy. Unlike the ones in San Irie, this one was vast and chaotic. Instead of being restricted to a single square, it spilled down every alleyway and side street. Children raced through the crowds with light feet and sticky hands. Instead of bananas and guinep, there were roasted chestnuts and hazelnuts, cod and herring, cherries and parsnips.

"I'm talking about Gael," Signey continued, pulling Elara back to the present. "Maybe he'll be honest with a member of the family."

Elara had underestimated her co-Rider's emotional state. Signey had patiently listened to Elara's theories without emotion and then proposed that Faron *should* reach out to Gael for more information. Her opinion had only gotten stronger after Elara had related the news of Faron's disastrous meeting with the gods, and, though Elara wasn't *happy* that Faron was communicating with a former tyrant, she supposed she did the same every weekend when they went to see the commander. Faron would be careful—and Reeve was there if she forgot to be. She had to trust them both.

Elara paused to stare at a small pyramid of cherries, wondering if they tasted different from the ones back home. "Well, if Gael Soto is anything like you, he won't be honest at all."

Beside her, Signey rolled her eyes. Her hair was loose today, softly curled beneath a dragon horn hairpiece. "Is this about Jesper again?"

"He's your older brother," Elara said, "and he deserves the chance to look out for you."

"Spoken like an eldest sibling."

Elara shrugged. "That doesn't mean I'm wrong."

"It *does* mean you're biased." Signey grabbed her arm as she was about to walk away. Her Firstrider took a coin purse out of the pocket of her breeches and counted out enough money for a bag of cherries. She handed the bag to Elara and kept walking. "It's egotistical to assume I need his protection because I'm younger."

But Elara wasn't listening. Her eyes were on the bag of cherries, a red so dark they were almost black, the bag that she wouldn't have been able to buy because she'd realized a second too late that she didn't have any Langlish money. And Signey had bought it for her, casually, without a word exchanged between them.

Signey realized that Elara wasn't behind her and pushed back through the crowd to her side. "Are you all right? I didn't upend your entire worldview, did I?"

"No. No, I—no." Elara blinked. Swallowed. "We'll just have to disagree on this subject. And I don't believe you can do anything with the Gray Saint that Faron isn't already trying."

Signey grabbed a cherry and popped it into her mouth. The pit was spat on the cobblestones. Red cherry juice stained the corner of her lips. Elara swallowed again. "Well, we have to try *something*." Signey wiped at the juice and missed half of it. "I wish my dad were here. He could help. He loved this kind of thing."

"Espionage?"

Signey snorted. "No. Family. Growing up, he made sure that Jesper and I could speak Lindan, that we enjoyed Lindan food and music, that we knew Lindan history and culture. Although he was a dracologist, one of his proudest research projects was only *tangentially* related to dragons: the Soto-Zayas family tree." She made another valiant swipe for the cherry juice, leaving a single smear right at the seam of her mouth. "I wish I'd paid more attention. Gael's name was probably on it."

It was a long time before Elara could think of anything else. Since they were treading onto sensitive information, she sent her next statement through the bond. *"Well, we still have our own resources here. We go to the National Hall tomorrow, right? Maybe it's time to try breaking into the commander's office, see how far along he is in raising the First Dragon."*

"I've already been in the commander's office. He keeps nothing of note there. If he's hiding anything, let alone a list of next steps, it would be at Rosetree Manor."

Elara bit into a cherry and followed Signey down the street. Rosetree Manor was the private residence of Gavriel and Mireya Warwick, Reeve's home before the Warwick family had moved to San Irie to occupy Pearl Bay Palace. She could think of no pretense under which they could infiltrate the commander's home without being caught, but they had learned as much as they could from the National Hall—which was nothing. She could probably build a dragon from scratch if she had to, bones, muscle, and all, but the connection between their magic and the bond eluded her and the dracologists. Signey could likely name every member of the Conclave and Judiciary, but she'd learned more about the commander's plans from Elara than from the man himself.

In fact, every time they went to the National Hall, Elara felt as if they were giving more than they were getting. There was a gleam in the commander's eyes when he greeted them that made her nervous.

He had once come to check on her in the laboratory, where she had been watching a dracologist test how long a dragon had to be dead for the magic in their relic to weaken. The carcass of the dragon in question—Skythrall—had been dead for five years. The other—Raisel—had been dead for fifteen.

Elara had asked if it was necessary to know the dragons' names when carving up and experimenting on their corpses, and the dracologist had replied, "Dragons are divine creatures, their chosen Riders worshipped as saints. We honor our dragons in war and in peacetime, in life and in death. When a dragon falls, we learn what we can from their bodies and then craft their remains into relics through which their magic can temporarily live on. And when our people create rings from claws, necklaces from scales, bracelets from fangs, it's to venerate those who have lent us their protection and their power. So, yes, Miss Vincent, it's necessary to know the names of the creatures we're honoring."

Her cheeks had burned in response, and that was when the commander had found her. He'd been dressed in a navy-blue suit, his tie a deep green that almost matched her uniform, and he'd been smiling in that strange way he had, as if she'd given him a gift that he hadn't been expecting.

"Raisel was ridden by twins Kenya and Sebastian Edwards, who perished helping free San Irie from the clutches of Joya del Mar," he'd said. "Skythrall, well. Skythrall was the mount of Eugenia and Celyn Soto." He'd nodded in the face of Elara's shock. "Signey and Jesper's mother and sister."

Immediately, Elara had reinforced the wall between herself and Signey, making sure that her Firstrider wouldn't pluck the image of her dead family's dragon cut open on a laboratory table.

"Skythrall was killed during the war by an Iryan drake. Many of the relics that the Soto siblings wear were created from him." The commander had placed a hand on the table, inches away from a silver tray that contained a pile of Skythrall's blue scales. "Has your co-Rider told you about the history of her family?"

"I'd rather hear it from her," Elara had said. "Sir."

The commander had smiled, and it had been an unfriendly one. "The Hylands, the Sotos, the Warwicks, and the Lynwoods are all dragon-riding dynasties, but the Sotos stand above them all. Imagine what one could do with so much power."

Before she could think of a response, the commander had drifted toward the door. "It's been illuminating to have you here, Miss Vincent. You and I have far more in common than I think you know."

Those words had kept Elara up long after she had finished speaking with Faron and Reeve. They still haunted her now, weeks later, when she knew that he had made contact with Gael Soto at least once before and planned to inflict the First Dragon on the world again. It felt as if she, Signey, Faron, and Reeve were trying to chip away at a mountain with nothing but a toothpick.

"*Elara.*"

She blinked out of the memory. From the urgency in Signey's voice, this wasn't the first time she had called Elara's name. "*What?*"

Her Firstrider stood in the middle of the street, an unmoving crowd around her. Everyone was staring upward in various states of horror. Elara turned to see what they were looking at, and her stomach dropped. A dragon tore through the sky flame-first, its wings flapping hard as it shot over Margon Island. Even when the fire faded, it was followed by a roar that made the earth shake beneath her feet, the bellow of a dragon who was absolutely livid.

"That's Nizsa," said Signey aloud. "Professor Smithers's dragon. He and his husband must be up there."

"The Fury," Elara continued, following her train of thought. "We have to help."

She was the one to grab Signey's arm now, dragging her back toward the bridge to Caledon. Signey not only kept pace with her, elbowing their way past everyone running to safety, but also called Zephyra to fetch her saddle and meet them there. *We finally have the opportunity to do some good,"* Signey had said the day they'd called their truce. It wasn't that Elara hadn't believed her until now, but it was the first time they'd been united in exactly what that meant.

For the first time, the three of them were going to do some good.

They caught up with Nizsa near the southern tip of Nova, where Langley curled around the Hestan Archipelago and pointed west toward San Irie. Professor Smithers and his husband, Rupert Lewis, sat unmoving in the saddle, ignoring all cries of their names. Elara still had only patchwork memories of her own time gripped by the Fury, but she remembered the desire to hurt, to maim, to kill. There hadn't been enemies and friends, but targets, and the howling rage coursing through her had made her eager, even desperate, to strike.

But as Zephyra closed the distance between them and Nizsa, Elara realized something about the Fury that should have been obvious to her before now: Everyone wore their anger differently. She, Signey, and Zephyra might have been apoplectic with rage, but Smithers, Lewis, and Nizsa's fury was seething and methodical. They didn't simply want to strike anyone or anything. They wanted to raze. To annihilate.

To conquer.

"How do you want to do this?" Signey sent when they were so close that Elara could see the gleaming silver of Professor Smithers's hair over Signey's shoulder.

Elara assessed the situation. Nizsa was another sage dragon, swift and smart, and they had no idea where she was flying to. In a few minutes, she would be outside the boundaries of the continent, which would take her away from civilization but risk the lives of her Riders if Elara and Signey brought her down in the open ocean.

"Fly over them," she told Signey and Zephyra. *"I'll try to bring the professor around. You make sure Nizsa doesn't fly out any farther."*

"I'm not sure I care for this plan," said Zephyra.

"You could get hurt," Signey added. *"They're not themselves right now, Elara."*

"A little trust would be nice, ladies."

Zephyra snorted at the echo of her words from the incendio. Signey sighed—so deeply that Elara could feel it through the bond—before she twisted around in Elara's hold. She detangled her horned hairpiece from her fraying curls and held it out. *"At least take this. You might need its magic."*

Elara, who still refused to wear dragon relics in her everyday life, smiled as she affixed the hairpiece around her braids, the horns curving just above her ears. *Many of the relics that the Soto siblings wear were created from Skythrall,* the commander had said. Now here was Signey, trusting her with a piece of her mother and sister. A part of her ancestors, given for Elara's protection. Maybe it meant something different in Langley than such a thing would mean in San Irie, but...

"*Thank you,*" she sent, touched. "*I'll definitely need it.*"

Was it her imagination or were Signey's cheeks pink? "*Thank me by being careful.*"

Zephyra pulled up into the air over Nizsa as Elara untied herself from the saddle, sending her gratitude to Irie that even without the added security measures, she, as a Wingleader, had perfect balance. Because it was only her clenched thighs and her arms around Signey's waist that otherwise kept her from tumbling off her dragon's back.

"*Be careful,*" Signey said one last time.

"*Always am,*" Elara replied.

Zephyra arced sideways, aligning directly above Nizsa, and Elara leaped into the air, leaving her stomach behind. Wind rushed around her, a moment of pure stillness. Then the fall began to register and a scream tore from her throat, lost in the frigid air.

Elara hit the saddle, pain shooting up her thighs. Nizsa didn't so much as dip, but Lewis turned to watch her cling to the edge of the leather. Nizsa's scales scraped against her clothes, dug into her stomach, and her arms strained to pull herself farther away from the dragon's spiked tail. She watched Lewis lift a hand, watched a ball of flame spark above his palm. She could almost feel the heat of it, the way it would scorch her skin.

And then Nizsa hissed and drew up short.

Lewis jolted in the saddle. The flame went out. Elara dragged herself up behind him, relieved when she saw straps dangling from either side of Nizsa's body. They'd succumbed to the Fury so quickly that they hadn't bothered to tie themselves in, relying solely on their Rider magic to maintain their balance, and that worked for her. She'd barely managed to strap herself in when Nizsa spiraled away from Zephyra. Apparently, perfect balance didn't apply if she rode any dragon besides her own.

Lewis and Smithers were moving seamlessly with every twitch of Nizsa's body, but Elara felt as if she were riding a wild horse and only her wits would keep her from ending up in an infirmary. Signey and Zephyra were doing their part, corralling Nizsa back toward the Langlish borders, and now she had to do hers.

Elara reached for the magic in the dragon horns. Once again, it was as easy as a breath, as easy as a thought. The hum of magic replaced the whistle of the wind, waiting for her direction, eager to help. And as Lewis moved again to attempt to dislodge her, Elara aimed the cloud of magic at him and the professor, commanding it to put them to sleep. He raised a hand as if to block or counter, but she was faster. It took seconds for Rupert Lewis to slump against his husband's bent back. Professor Smithers snored lightly, his forehead almost low enough to touch the saddle.

She held tightly as Nizsa hovered in midair, visibly confused. The Fury was a relentless wave of feral rage, but it also built on the minds consumed by it. Without Lewis and Smithers to add to Nizsa's viciousness, she was left to tend to the single ember of her own anger. Elara opened her mouth to tell the dragon to fly back to Hearthstone and screamed instead.

Because Nizsa was falling from the sky, fast asleep like her Riders.

Her lithe body dropped so quickly that Elara was partially lifted from the saddle, only the straps keeping her from spinning away. She gripped the back of Lewis's shirt, still screaming, her eyes burning from the sharp air and the sudden knowledge that she had miscalculated, that she was going to die, that she would never again see her sister or her family or her home or Reeve, that she would never summon again, never return to school, never stop the commander—

She slammed against the saddle like a bird against a window. The faded ache from earlier pulsed through her a second time, in not just her thighs but her ribs and chest, as well. A shadow had blocked out the sun, and Elara looked up to see that it was Zephyra. The talons of her arms were gripping Nizsa's, keeping the slumbering dragon aloft. Zephyra's leg talons gripped Nizsa's as well, carrying her, carrying *them.*

"Are you all right?" Signey and Zephyra asked together.

Tears soaked Elara's cheeks, but this time they weren't from fear. *"I'm fine. We're all fine."*

She felt their relief, as powerful as her own, and closed her eyes to sink into that wave of affection. Her Firstrider. Her dragon. Once enemies, once punishments, and now her saviors, her protectors. Her friends. Elara still wanted to go home—perhaps even more so now that her final thoughts had been only of the people she'd left behind—but she would miss this, too. She would miss them.

And she didn't know what to do with that realization.

CHAPTER TWENTY-FIVE

FARON

I N HINDSIGHT, IT WAS A WONDER THAT IT HAD TAKEN FARON THIS long to try sneaking out of Renard Hall.

The longer she stayed in this admittedly grand house, the more restless she got. Gael had visited her every day since her dream, but they had made no further headway on unlocking her power to command dragons. He never seemed impatient or annoyed with her lack of progress, but Faron wanted to scream. Her sister had been trapped among the enemy for almost two months now. Faron couldn't suffer through a dry text like Reeve could, so the least she could do was use her magic to bring Elara home. Gael was supposed to be the key to that.

And yet she continued to make no improvements.

"You were in a state of desperation the first time," Gael suggested one day, when Faron kicked over one of the wicker chairs on the patio just to feel some satisfaction. "Maybe you need to be in that state again."

"I *am* desperate," snapped Faron. "I keep talking to you, don't I?"

A smile as slow as honey dripped over his face. "I don't think that has to do with desperation. I think you like talking to me."

"I think *you* like talking to *me*."

"Have I denied it?" he asked, eyes dancing. "This is the most like myself I've felt in centuries."

Faron hadn't known what to do with that, so she'd decided to ignore it. Several deep breaths later, she'd tried again only to fail *again*.

At this point, she caught herself fantasizing about setting fire to one of the servants' shirts just to see what excitement might result, and that was when she figured it was about time she got herself out of here. Just for a few hours, at least. Just to see what else Seaview had to offer besides the ocean and a house too large for any one person to be anything but alone in.

Of course, as soon as she climbed down her balcony and landed soundlessly in the grass far below, a hand darted out of the night to grab her wrist.

"You're so predictable," Reeve said before she could call on the powers of the gods. "I knew that look in your eye today meant trouble."

"Ugh," Faron replied. "I'm not even doing anything."

He raised his eyebrows at her, then gazed pointedly from where she'd just climbed down, then looked back at her.

Faron folded her arms. "What about *you*? How long have you been lurking around outside my window, you creep?"

"I wasn't 'lurking around' outside your window," said Reeve, rolling his eyes. "I was sitting on the patio, trying to figure out if your lessons with the Gray Saint are playing into my father's hands, *like you asked*, when I heard you clambering down the side of the house like a crocodile on wheels."

"His name is Gael," Faron muttered. "And I *was not*—" She

stopped herself, but only barely. She didn't *want* to knock him out and leave him here, but she would if he tried to stop her. She took a deep breath for the patience to try diplomacy first. "I just need a break from the studying and the pacing and the worrying. There's a whole town at the base of this cliff. Don't you want to see what goes on there besides the temple?"

"It doesn't matter if I do or not. *You're* going, so I'm going."

"Oh, please. You want to see it as much as I do. Don't pretend you have some noble reason for it."

Reeve gestured for her to lead the way. Faron held her head high and did just that.

Seaview was a completely different experience at night. The first things that Faron saw were the lights. The town glowed against the starry night sky, and she could hear calypso music luring them in, drowning out the sound of the ocean. She had put on a navy head wrap to cover her hair and wore nondescript clothes in the hopes that few people out here would recognize the Empyrean. Maybe finding a dance hall would be the best way to keep her identity under wraps. People drinking and dancing under dim lights weren't likely to look too closely at whom they were dancing with, and she wouldn't mind attending a party right now.

She wouldn't mind having a moment of joy in the middle of so much frustration.

"Are you hungry?" Reeve asked, nodding his chin toward a grill surrounded by savory smoke. There were already a couple of customers milling by it, drinking and exchanging gossip. It wasn't that Faron had tired of the elaborate meals that the servants prepared for them every day, but there was something irreplaceable about fried street foods. Maybe it was the slightly burned taste from spending too long on the grill, or the rowdy company and conversation, or the echoing smacks of people trying to stop a mosquito from stealing their blood.

Maybe it was all the above. That was the *real* San Irie, the San Irie that Faron knew when she wasn't busy being taken from one gilded cage to another.

"I'd love some," she said, shivering a little at the cold. That was another thing the grill would help with. "I hope that means you're paying."

Faron and Reeve found a table near the back that seemed to be out of the blast zone for most of the smoke. He got them two sliced-up pieces of jerk chicken as well as a paper bowl filled with festival. Faron began attacking those curved fried dumplings while he showered his chicken in hot sauce.

"I can't believe the queen let them come back here," said a portly man at the bar, taking a long drag of his beer bottle. "It's disgraceful, is what it is."

"I'm not too mad about it," said his companion, a tall man with locs drawn up into a knitted cap. "I understand the urge to show those Novan pigs how far we've come since they thought they could claim us."

"We didn't fight for our independence so we could roll out the welcome mat for them the second they decided to recognize it!"

"It's been two months, mon."

"I don't care if it's been two years. It never should have happened!"

Faron looked at the men more closely. The first was dressed in a white collared shirt and black trousers, but there was a medal glinting on his breast pocket that caught her eye. She recognized it from some of Elara's posters; it indicated that he had fought in the San Irie Revolution in one of the branches of the army. She only knew it wasn't the Sky Battalion because she knew *that* symbol intimately, thanks to Elara. The other man had no such decoration, but looking closer revealed that half his face was twisted and scarred from burns. It didn't take much of a leap to guess he'd fallen victim to a dragon attack.

That was one of life's most tragic secrets: War never actually ended. It survived in the lives destroyed by things large and small. The soldiers whose nightmares haunted them even with their eyes open, whose reflexes were forever set on *kill*, whose adjustments to peacetime came with the sobering knowledge that they were forever out of sync with a world that was desperate to move on from what they couldn't. The families whose loved ones were the soldiers who never made it home, whose lives had been bisected into the before and after of having them around. The civilians who had lost mobility, lost property, lost sanity, or lost sleep to the shadow of a beast that announced itself with a roar before the roaring fire—if you were lucky.

War survived in the buildings now built to withstand fires, as well as hurricanes and floods; in the redrawn town lines; in the landmarks turned to ruin. And it survived in the hearts now filled with a hatred, suspicion, and paranoia that hadn't existed before they were forced to grapple with all the ways humans could hurt one another.

Faron understood the pain rotting away inside the first man, bleeding out now that he'd had a few beers. She'd felt it herself. But she still thought it very bold of both of them to be talking about the queen like this in full view of her ancestral home, even if they knew she wasn't there.

"What would you have her do, then?" the man with the locs asked.

"Show them that we fought our way out from under their thumbs and they can't shove us back there."

"And risk another war?"

"I've always been ready for another war." The first man finished his beer and slammed the bottle on the bar so hard that Faron thought she heard it crack. "When a country's used to having everything, it doesn't let anything walk away. I've heard the rumors."

"What rumors?"

Reeve started to say something. Faron hushed him and tipped sideways in her chair a bit, straining to hear the conversation.

"—were looking for something here, and they used the whole thing as a distraction to get it."

"Don't be ridiculous," Locs scoffed. "What could they possibly want? I mean, besides the scalestone, and they know the Queen-shield have that under guard."

"I'm just telling you what I've heard. I've *also* heard that they've got the Childe Empyrean's sister."

"Got her? What do you mean, got her?"

"They took her to Langley in secret."

"I think we'd have heard about that."

"Not if the queen was keeping it quiet to avoid a panic." Beer Man's chest puffed out. "I have a cousin who knows a girl who works at the palace, and she said there was a huge commotion on the first night that the queen covered up."

"We'd know if the Empyrean's sister was missing, Roger! You're drunk, mon."

"So what? It doesn't mean I'm wrong."

Faron frowned, adjusting her head wrap so that it hid more of her hair. The half-finished meal in front of her no longer looked appetizing. She turned her face away from it, and from the men, hoping they would leave before she did.

"Hey," whispered Reeve, touching her wrist for attention. "What's wrong?"

"Rumors are traveling farther across the island than the queen might have wanted," Faron whispered back before summarizing everything she'd just overheard. "We have to let the queen know that she has to address this. Nationally, rather than locally. Otherwise..."

Instead of dying down in the wake of the Summit, things seemed to be getting worse. And if the unrest had spread across the island rather than being limited to the capital, that was dangerous. The last thing that San Irie needed was to fall into a civil war with Langley circling like a vulture, trying to awaken the First Dragon and Rider.

This whole night had been a mistake.

"Listen, maybe we should go back to the—"

"I hear music," Reeve said suddenly, wrapping up the bones of his chicken and tossing them into the nearby wastebasket. "Want to dance?"

"*Now?*" Faron asked. Though she'd barely touched her own food, she couldn't deny the excited thump of her heart at the idea of one more distraction. "Here? Don't we have more important things to—"

"Yes, now," Reeve interrupted. His hand touched her wrist again and then, when she didn't pull away, wrapped around it. Faron glanced down at the point of contact and then up at him, confused and strangely warm. He didn't blink, and neither did she.

"Listen, I'm not ready to go back to that house yet. So let's just stay out a little while longer. Okay?"

This was so out of character for him that Faron knew without asking that he was doing this for her. She just didn't know why he would do it, and her heart was pounding too loudly for her to gather her thoughts. She looked back down at their hands, and her gaze stayed there. "Okay."

The closer they got to the thumping call of the music, the more the beat seemed to slide through Faron's body, energizing her legs, her hips, her heart. The anxiety of what she'd overheard fell away, replaced by simple joy. Her hand was in Reeve's, and she refused to waste time questioning why she didn't mind. Under the cover of darkness, wrapped in the blanket of melody, nothing mattered. Nothing but this.

An open field appeared at the end of the block, and a crowd was milling across the grass, drinking beer and listening to a live band set up in the center of it all. A woman strummed a cuatro, the small guitar keeping perfect time with the vibrating thump of her companion's steel drum. Another two musicians played an abeng horn and a tambourine, respectively, and the final one sang a bright, unknown song in the heavy patois common in the countryside. Faron saw adults dancing, laughing, talking as the makeshift party brought the community of Seaview together beneath the half-moon.

Reeve grinned at her and Faron grinned back as she tugged him into the fray. Once she found a clear patch of grass, she whirled around to face Reeve, feeling strangely shy. With the moon lining his face in silver and shadows, he looked like a different person, unknowable and strange.

But then he smiled and he was Reeve, frustratingly familiar. Comfortingly constant.

"Ready to watch me make a fool of myself?" he asked, squeezing her hand.

Faron squeezed back. "You *always* make a fool of yourself."

They danced. Neither of them was any good, but that just made things more interesting. More fun. Between her obligation to the queen, her obligation to the country, her obligation to her family, and her obligation to the gods, Faron rarely had time for something so simple and wholesome. To just be a girl, holding hands with a boy, bouncing up and down as if that were dancing.

Her cheeks hurt from laughing so hard, and, when Reeve tried to spin her, she nearly swiveled right off her feet and into the grass. He danced like a chicken with his head cut off, all flailing limbs and wide-open mouth, winking when she bent over cackling. Her cheeks hurt, her ribs hurt, but her chest was light, full of nothing but the music and the starlight and the surprisingly bright presence of this stupid, stupid boy.

Impulsively, she threw her arms around his waist between songs, pressing her cheek against his chest. "Thanks for this. I'm having a good time."

Reeve froze for a moment, clearly shocked, but then he hugged her back. "I'm glad. I could tell that you needed it. You looked . . ." He cleared his throat. "I don't like to see you look like that, is all."

She didn't have the words for how badly she had needed this, so she pressed even closer for as long as she dared before letting go. He was a good hugger, she told herself, and it had been ages since she'd gotten one. That was all. She gestured toward a nearby bag juice cart and Reeve nodded, wandering closer to the band while she went to get them some drinks. There was a line at the cart now that the set had paused, and Faron joined it with a small sigh.

She tipped her head back to look at the stars and watched them twinkle uncaringly up above. She hoped that they were watching over Elara, too. She hoped that Elara was safely looking up at these same stars and maybe thinking of her. She was so happy in this moment that all she wanted was to share some of that joy with her sister. Faron smiled at the thought of how Elara would have nagged at her for sneaking out of the queen's house just to go to some party, barely disguised and unnecessarily reckless. How she would have chided Reeve for going with her. How she would have gotten dragged along anyway and ended up having more fun than she'd be willing to admit.

Gods, she wanted her sister back.

Faron was somber by the time she collected the bag juices. Reeve took his with a grateful smile that fell when he looked at her face. "What's wrong?"

"I miss Elara," she confessed.

"I miss her, too," Reeve replied. "Even though no one has ever broken a bond between a dragon and a Rider before, I thought for sure we'd have found something that would allow her to come back by now. Over there ... she's not safe."

Faron bit a hole into her bag juice, let the cool, fruity flavor moisten her tongue. "You lived there for almost thirteen years, but you talk about Langley like an Iryan. Is it really so dangerous?"

Instead of answering right away, Reeve watched the band with a furrow in his brow. The musicians were mingling with the crowd, taking requests, laughing as they prepared for the next set, but Faron knew that Reeve didn't really see them. What she didn't know was if he would actually share what was on his mind, even on this night when the tentative companionship between them felt fragile but real.

"Langley is my home. Even without..." He gestured into the distance, to encompass the pain the Iryan people still felt from the war. The wounds that Langley had caused. "It was all I knew for a very long time. But because it was my home, I know that it could *be* better than it is. I see its flaws, its corruption." His fingers tightened around his bag juice. "After the war, I looked up the names of the soldiers who had died in the final battle. I looked up their faces, their families. I see it all every time I close my eyes. I wonder if I did the right thing, if there had been a different way to do the right thing, if those deaths were worth everything that came after. If my country can truly be good, or if it will only find new ways to be cruel. If San Irie will ever feel like home. If I'll ever be allowed to find a home here. If I even deserve it."

Faron's hand was on his arm before she'd made the conscious decision to move. Reeve's smile was fleeting.

"I don't mean to complain. I just... Elara is not seeing Langley at its best, and I don't know how much worse it's gotten since I left. That's why I worry. She's too good for a place like that."

"You're not complaining," Faron said softly. "I asked. And you never... You've never told me any of this."

"You're the Childe Empyrean. If we stack our burdens against each other's, you'll win every time."

"That doesn't mean we're not both carrying them."

Reeve looked at her then, and Faron could no longer feel the chill of the bag juice in her hands. His eyes were bright, and for once it didn't feel alien and alarming, that soft blue shade. Those were Reeve's eyes, the same boy who had forgone sleep to help her sister; the same boy who had dragged her to this party because he could tell she needed it; the same boy who had taken the time to learn her, despite her barbed words and poisonous glances. This was her sister's best friend, the Langlish traitor, the smug intellectual, the silent guardian.

Faron had seen Reeve Warwick almost every day for the last five years, but this was the first time she had ever *really* seen him. The first time she had ever liked what she saw.

The band launched into another song, a fast-paced version of the Iryan national anthem. Reeve laughed and held out a free hand.

"Shall we dance?" he asked, azure eyes eclipsing every bright star in the sky.

Faron cleared her throat. Took his hand. Heard the pounding of her heart, louder than the steel drum. "Okay."

CHAPTER TWENTY-SIX

ELARA

COMMANDER WARWICK HAD ARRIVED AT HEARTHSTONE, AND Elara, Signey, and Zephyra had no one to blame but themselves. When they had returned with Nizsa and her Riders safely slumbering after their recovery from the Fury, Headmaster Luxton had insisted on contacting the commander to give them some sort of commendation. Their protests had been waved off, their reputations elevated to heroic status. Warwick had brought his dragon, Irontooth, and his wife, the director, with him to convey the depths of their gratitude to Signey and Elara.

They'd been awarded small gold medals of valor over breakfast, welded into the shape of dragon wings, and classes had been canceled so that everyone could shop and prepare for a celebration ball after dinner. A ball that had rushed up more quickly than Elara had anticipated, too quick for her to find something Langlish. Besides, no amount of sophisticated fashion would disguise the fact that Elara didn't belong here. She'd gone in the opposite direction and drawn attention to it.

From her closet, Elara had pulled out a dress she'd been saving, a strapless black maxi that cinched at the waist and billowed around her legs. Over that, she'd paired a beaded necklace shaped like a gorget, the beads in the green, blue, and gold of the Iryan flag—a statement none could ignore.

She heard a quiet knock seconds before she sensed Signey's presence on the other side of the door. She crossed the room to let her in and nearly swallowed her own tongue.

Once again, Signey had pulled back her wavy hair into a tight, high ponytail that fell down her back like rippling water. She wore a midnight-blue dress, snug in all the right places, with white boning on the sides. Her feet were tucked into a pair of midnight-blue flats, and dark blue fingerless lace gloves covered her hands, the lace sewn to imitate dragon scales. Would it kill her Firstrider to try looking repulsive for once?

"You look beautiful," Signey said with a hesitant smile. Elara realized for the first time that Signey was carrying a box in her hands. "Can I come in?"

Elara shook herself out of her appreciative stupor and stepped aside.

Almost two months at Hearthstone, and Elara hadn't done much to make her room feel like home. Her clothes had migrated from her bags to the wardrobe, her shoes were tucked in a neat line poking out from beneath her bed, and her drake figurine perched proudly on the nightstand unless Elara was using it for astral calls. Aside from that, the room was mostly unchanged, except for the rumpled sheets that proved she'd made use of the bed, and the few personal items she'd unpacked. It wasn't sterile, but it wasn't cozy, either. Elara had never quite committed to the idea of staying here.

If Signey noticed, she decided not to mention it in favor of setting down her box on the nightstand. Elara realized that it wasn't white boning that decorated her dress. It was backless, Signey's modesty protected by a golden spine with curved ivory ribs that framed her sides. Real dragon bone, a type of relic Elara had never seen before, making Signey look both powerful and dangerous.

Striking.

Attainable.

Elara wanted to scream.

Signey opened the box—a peach container inlaid with mother-of-pearl—to reveal several compartments full of dragon jewelry. She had sterling silver claw rings in different colors. She had more earring cuffs designed to look as if a tiny dragon were crawling over the lobe. She had a necklace that appeared to have a dragon's-eye inlaid in gold as the pendant, and another necklace that looked like scales cascading down to one's collarbone. All the kinds of things only a country that worshipped dragons could think of as fashion.

Even after they had twice helped her, Elara still found it a bit creepy, wearing the bones of dead animals. "Um," she said. "I don't—"

"It's traditional," Signey said, ushering Elara closer to the box with both hands on her shoulders. "And expected, for a function like this."

The shiver that raced through Elara's body had many sources, and she didn't want to examine any of them. Her attraction to her co-Rider was like an itch she couldn't scratch. Without irritation to temper it, it snuck up on Elara at the most inopportune moments, and it was at times like this that Elara worried Signey could feel it through the bond. But surely she would have said something?

Signey lifted the necklace of scales from the box and held it in her palm in front of Elara's face. "This seems very you. And it would probably go a lot better with your dress than that beaded thing. Unless, of course, you want to borrow something of mine—"

"No." Elara slipped out from between Signey's warm body and the nightstand, her heart beating unevenly in her chest. "This is an Iryan dress and an Iryan beaded necklace, handmade by a woman in Deadegg named Miss Elmiyra Johnson. She has nine children and still found time to give this to me for my last birthday." Her fingers reached up to trace over the beads, which clacked rhythmically together. "*This* is me."

Signey was still clutching the necklace as she dragged her eyes from Elara's head to her sandals and slowly back up again. Elara felt as if her whole head had been set aflame, even more so when Signey's gaze seemed to snag at her hips. Signey's lips curved upward, and Elara noticed for the first time that she had painted them rose-petal pink.

"Fair enough," she said with a smile that simply hinted at the dimple Elara had only seen once before. "The claw rings, then? Maybe you'll get lucky, and Marius Lynwood will pick a fight."

Elara's laugh was a bit strangled, but Signey didn't comment as she helped her affix a ring to each finger on her right hand. Signey's hands were callused but gentle, the scratch of the lace against Elara's skin making goose bumps rise everywhere they touched. She shouldn't be feeling like this. She needed to get over this. What was wrong with her?

And yet Signey continued to hold her hand even after she was done, her head bent low so Elara couldn't see her expression. "Can...you do me a favor?"

"I...Sure?"

"Don't..." The words seemed to struggle free from Signey's

mouth. "Don't leave me alone with the director. Or the commander, for that matter, but especially the director. Torrey will be looking out for Jesper, but I...It would be nice if you could look out for me."

Elara's eyebrows knitted together. "Yes, of course. Is it because of your father?"

"Becoming a Rider was always the plan, to honor my mother and sister. But if I pass my final exam and land a government job, then I might get to see my father. If I play the patriotic soldier well enough, I might even get to request a pardon. My family could be whole again." Signey released Elara's hand to wrap her arms around her own stomach. She was not, Elara realized, a girl accustomed to intimacy. "But until then...Every time I see the director—I just—I remember that he's trapped at the Mausoleum for something I know he didn't do, and I—"

Elara pulled Signey into a hug. She resisted for so long that Elara began to let her go and apologize. But then she melted against Elara's chest, locking her arms around Elara's waist, and Elara pulled her trembling body closer. She had been struggling with homesickness after being away from her family for almost two months, even with daily calls to her loved ones. Signey hadn't seen her father in over five years. Her mother and sister in even longer.

"I'll make sure you're never alone," she promised, feeling Zephyra sending comfort and approval across the bond to soothe them both. "We're a team. You and me and Zephyra."

"You and me and Zephyra," Signey repeated like a promise of her own. "Okay."

The Hearthstone ballroom was lavish and crowded. Three chandeliers lit the long room, which was lined with framed portraits of white people who Elara didn't recognize. The only furniture in the room was against one of the wood-paneled walls, a line of tables filled with finger foods and bowls of punch. The students and professors seemed to be serving themselves, as, unlike at Pearl Bay Palace, Elara could see no servants walking around with trays. In fact, the only people she saw who she didn't recognize from one class or another were the musicians on the raised dais across from the food tables.

Near the back of the room, the doors had been thrown open to reveal a stone patio. Beyond, in the early winter darkness, Elara could see dragons huddled close to enjoy the festivities. Even though they couldn't fit through the opening, they could hear the music, feel their Riders' joy, and cuddle with one another on the lawn. She could sense Zephyra among them, an easy and comforting presence at the boundary of her mind, and sent her a greeting. Her dragon trilled in response.

"It's a shame you're so eager to go," Signey said as they joined the throng. Eyes ran over her appreciatively, but Signey didn't seem to notice the attention. Or maybe she didn't care. "I haven't seen Zephyra this happy in her whole life."

"How old were you when she hatched?"

"Four or five. My mother and sister were already paired. Jesper's egg had hatched a few days before, but it would be a while before he found Torrey." They made it to the tables. Signey grabbed two small plates and began to fill them with food, dinner rolls with sweet cream butter and cucumber sandwiches, rose-petal drop scones and almond shortbread cookies. "All dragons from the

Beacon Dragon Preserve are born colorless. She was snow-white, with the gentlest eyes. I wanted her to choose me so badly I was sick with yearning."

Elara swallowed, reminded of her attempt to join the Sky Battalion. "I know that feeling. And," she added softly, "I'm not eager to go. Sure, I don't want to be a Rider and I don't want to live here. But I wouldn't say that I'm eager to say goodbye to y—to all this. Everything's not as straightforward as I thought."

"Did you ever figure it out?" Signey asked, handing her a plate. "If you enlisted for the wrong reasons?"

"I did. I definitely did." Elara nibbled at a dinner roll, swallowing before she continued. "I'm the Childe Empyrean's sister. I joined the Sky Battalion because I wanted to do more. To be more. But that's not a good reason. That's not the *right* reason."

Signey was watching her with an unreadable expression. "I think you're more than just the Childe Empyrean's sister. Much more."

Elara ducked her head, even though her skin was too dark to show her blush. It should have meant nothing, but it meant everything. The first time they'd met, Signey had questioned Elara's right to be in the room. Now her Firstrider looked at her as though Elara were the only person in this one.

"Miss Vincent. Miss Soto."

Professor Smithers approached in a steel-gray suit with a forest-green pocket square. Behind him, Mr. Lewis wore a forest-green suit and a steel-gray pocket square. Elara smiled at how, even here, the two men moved in sync.

"We just wanted to give you our thanks," the professor continued, "for your help the other day. Who knows what might have happened if... Well. I suppose the two of you know well enough."

"You don't have to thank us," said Signey. "I don't think any of us wanted an...incident."

Mr. Lewis slid his hand into his husband's. Though he was not a Hearthstone professor, he lived in the castle with Professor Smithers during the school year. Elara had heard rumors that he was a historian, which essentially meant he could work from wherever he pleased, and it clearly pleased him to be at his husband's side. "We've gone a year without suffering from the Fury, and we were hardly prepared for it now. These old bones don't have the resistance that they used to."

Elara laughed. Both men were in their late fifties, hardly what she would call old. "Are you feeling all right? Has Nizsa recovered well?"

"Yes, thank you." Professor Smithers grinned, his mustache crinkling. "You are a remarkable young woman, Miss Vincent. A remarkable Iryan, as well as a remarkable person in your own right."

Elara swallowed back a sudden wave of emotion, wondering if she would ever grow out of her need for adult approval. She nodded, afraid that if she spoke her voice would crack.

When they were gone, Signey snorted. "I can't believe you've been here less than two months and you're already a professor's favorite. Disgusting."

"Jealousy looks so ugly on you, Firstrider."

"Nothing looks ugly on me."

Elara couldn't argue with that. Especially when it gave her an excuse to give Signey a slow once-over. "I didn't say this earlier, but you look...Well, you *always* look...But tonight, you really, really look—"

"The director and the commander are leaving the party," Zephyra reported, saving Elara from herself. *"I think they are heading to the waterfront so I cannot hear what they discuss."*

Elara and Signey abandoned their plates on the table and crossed the room leisurely. Though they were looking at the ballroom around them, Zephyra sent her view of the darkened grounds and the Warwicks disappearing down the path toward the boathouse. Jesper caught sight of them from near the dais, then tapped Torrey's shoulder and pointed them out, but Elara shook her head before they could cut through the crowd. Signey didn't want her brother involved, and she respected that.

By the time they made it to the patio, the Warwicks were gone, the woods hiding any trace of the couple. Signey led the way, as silent as she'd been that night in Luxton's office, while Elara watched their backs. None of the dragons milling about took notice of them as they passed, none except Zephyra, and it was only their bond that told Elara she was the sole focus of the tranquil dragon's attention. Zephyra would let them know if anyone came looking.

The boathouse seemed deserted when Signey activated her dragon relic and lifted them off their feet. They touched down on the same sundeck where they had first called a truce, the golden wood turned silver in the moonlight, the curtains behind the slightly open doors swaying like ghosts in the dark. Signey shoved her against the wall beside the entrance, pressing in close, and Elara froze, light-headed from shock and excitement.

"Shit," Signey sent, oblivious as ever to the effect her actions had on Elara. *"They're right there. I thought they'd be downstairs."*

"Do they look like they're coming outside?"

If she noticed the long pause before Elara asked the question,

Signey ignored that, too. She pressed closer, trying to squint through the inlaid glass without being seen. She smelled delicate yet spicy, like honeysuckle and cloves. *"No. No, I think we'll be fine as long as we're quiet."*

Elara tipped her head back until it hit the wall and closed her eyes, pretending to concentrate.

"...fourth time this year," the commander said, his voice soft but clear from this close. "It's getting worse. We need to accelerate the plan."

Director Mireya Warwick sounded exhausted. "At this point, things will fall where they may or fall apart entirely. We've done all we can."

"If it hadn't been for Reeve—"

"Do *not* start—"

"He ruined everything five years ago, Mireya. We were so close. We were poised to find it. We would have found it if we hadn't—"

"I said, don't start." The director's voice was as sharp as the crack of a whip. "He is our son. We're in this predicament because we loved him, and that means loving *all* of him. Even the parts we don't agree with."

Elara could feel Signey's eyes on her face, but she didn't open her own. Her mind was racing, trying to piece together this new information. What did Reeve have to do with the commander's plan to raise the First Dragon?

We were so close. We were poised to find it.

If *it* was the Empty, how had Reeve stopped them from finding it during the war? He had never even heard of it until researching with Faron...right?

She shook her head. She trusted Reeve, more than almost

everyone. He would never lie to her. Whatever his parents had planned or were planning, he wasn't involved.

"Perhaps we should pay Barret a visit. He was useful before. He should prove useful again."

"The Mausoleum hasn't been kind to him. I don't think he's the man he once was."

The commander sighed. "He's lucky that we need him alive."

It was only when Signey began to tremble against her that Elara realized Barret must be her father. Before she could do anything, her Firstrider was already on the move, shoving open the doors so hard that the glass in them almost shattered against the inside wall. Elara cursed and hurried after her. Commander Warwick looked surprised, but, beside him, Director Mireya Warwick was a blank slate.

This was the first time that Elara had seen Reeve's mother up close, and she could immediately see the resemblance between them. The director was a pale-skinned woman, her dark hair in loose curls that framed her face. Her eyes were mahogany, her eyebrows thin and expertly arched. She was tall, like Reeve, with a swanlike neck, and she wore a black leather wristband with an emerald dragon's-eye.

"Let me talk to him, sir," Signey said. She sounded so confident, so fearless, that even Elara almost believed she'd come here with a purpose. But she could feel Signey's nerves across the bond, and she sent as much silent encouragement back as she could. It was too late to do anything but commit to this course of action. "If he'll come back to his old self for anyone, you know it will be me."

Commander Warwick stared at her, clearly trying to figure out how much she had overheard. Elara stepped closer to her Firstrider, ready to fight their way out if they had to. At the back of her mind, she felt Zephyra shift, concerned.

But Signey lifted her chin. "I don't know what's happening, sir, but I am one of the top students at Hearthstone. I managed the dragon bond by myself for over a decade before I found my Wingleader, and I'm one of the youngest recipients of the medal of valor in history. I'm a scion of the Soto Dynasty and, above all, I'm Barret Soto's youngest and only surviving daughter. If you need information from my father, I'm the person to send, whether you trust me with the full details of this mission or not. Consider it my final exam."

It was so quiet that the distant sounds of the party, clinking glasses and classical music, drifted across the grounds. Elara could hear her own heart beating loudly in her chest, hear Signey's racing across the bond as the Warwicks weighed the consequences of her offer.

Finally, Mireya Warwick said, "All right. I'll get you clearance for a visit to the Mausoleum. I'll allow you to see your father. But in return, the information you seek must not be shared with anyone aside from us and our dragons. Your den included. Believe me, Miss Soto"—her eyes were like gaping pits in the dark—"Gavriel, Irontooth, and I will know if you cross us."

"We won't," said Signey.

"We won't," Elara echoed, uneasy over how quickly the Warwicks had given in to this demand. Either Barret Soto had information they needed very badly...or they didn't expect Elara and Signey to come back.

The commander slid a hand around his wife's waist. She leaned into him, and he smiled at them in a way that was both amused and deeply ominous. "Let's return to the party, then. After all, you're the guests of honor."

CHAPTER TWENTY-SEVEN

FARON

SWEAT COOLED ON FARON'S SKIN AS SHE AND REEVE LEFT THE dance to make their way back to Renard Hall. She still felt light as air even now, as if she were flying down the street, as if the rhythm of the bass had pressed itself into her very soul. Her body felt warm everywhere that he'd touched her: her hands, her back, her sides, her wrist. Their hug replayed behind her eyes despite her best efforts to shut it out. It had been a good night. One of the best she'd had in months.

"I don't think I've seen you this happy in a while," Reeve said, pulling her gently back down to earth. "I'm glad."

"Thanks for coming."

"Your sister told me to keep an eye on you."

"Yes, but that doesn't mean you had to drag yourself down here with me."

Reeve hummed thoughtfully, scanning the street as though memorizing Seaview for his personal records. "I had my own reasons for being out tonight."

"You could've gone alone." The chill of the night began to creep back in, the sweat on her skin more uncomfortable than satisfying.

Years. She'd hated him for years. And what did tonight change? Nothing. Not really. "I know you don't like me."

Faron didn't quite keep the resentfulness out of her voice, so she wasn't surprised when Reeve stopped walking. She stopped, too, stomach churning. They'd been having such a good time that she thought she'd buried her feelings about that particular argument in the library. But maybe there was no burying anything that deep. Maybe she could only ignore her problems until they found a new way to ruin her.

"Faron," he began and then stopped. Soft conversation wafted from the buildings. The nearby ocean waves hissed against the shore. Somewhere in Seaview, the music was still playing, inviting them back to the party. Reeve's sigh was louder than all that, and he couldn't meet her eyes. "I'm *sorry*. For what I said to you. I really am."

Faron's pulse jumped. "Like I said, it's how you feel. That's fine. I've definitely said worse to you in the past."

And she'd never apologized for any of it, she remembered with a wince.

"You *have* said some awful things." Reeve's acknowledgment was matter-of-fact, almost dismissive. "But I understand why. I'm a Warwick. Someone should pay for the crimes of my family."

"Reeve, that's not fair to—"

"But you have to know," he said, and now his gaze seemed to be boring into her. "Faron, you *have* to know. Every awful thing I said about you . . . Everything I told you is everything I have to tell *myself*. To keep myself from wanting the impossible."

Faron's heart stopped entirely as she stared at him. Like friends, romance was a sacrifice she'd made to be the Childe Empyrean. It hadn't mattered much to her until now, because Faron had figured out long ago that she didn't feel attraction the way other people did. She had never looked at a random person and *wanted* them. She had never seen the beauty of others as anything other than an objective observation. She had never pictured herself kissing anyone the way she'd seen her sister kiss Cherry McKay.

But she pictured it now. She'd felt *something* for a while, something like a silent yearning for Reeve Warwick's touch, and in this moment, it screamed too loudly for her to ignore. Was this how romances began? Did Reeve want to start one with her? Maybe he'd felt what she'd felt in that field. He *had* witnessed all the messy, dark, and selfish parts of her, all her bratty stubbornness, all her trembling social anxieties, and he was still here. Maybe he had stood on the wrong end of her sharp edges and still found her worthy.

Her heartbeat kicked into a gallop. Her eyelids began to slide shut.

And then he said, "Being friends with you felt impossible."

Her entire face went up in flames. *"What?"*

"To me, you're Faron. To you, I'm a nuisance," Reeve continued, oblivious to the humiliation she was drowning in. "But to the rest of the island, you're the Childe Empyrean and I'm Langlish and a Warwick. If we were friends, they'd think the same thing that you did: that I'm manipulating you for my father. They'd think I was evil and you were naïve. It would put a target on both our backs. It felt impossible before now. That's why I told myself I didn't really want to be friends with you, anyway. You and Elara are so different, and you seemed...you were..."

His words escaped him, and it was that more than anything

that jolted Faron out of her embarrassed spiral. She'd rarely seen Reeve Warwick at a loss for words before. He always seemed to know exactly how his sentences would end before he started them, but now his hands were twitching at his sides.

"I'm the Childe Empyrean," Faron said into the quiet. "There's a target on my back no matter what. What makes it bearable is having people around me that I can trust. And...I trust you."

Somehow, that felt more dangerous than *I like you* could ever be. She didn't have to like him to trust him, but a betrayal of her trust would hit worse than a betrayal of her affections. Faron remembered her determination to never fall into the same trap as her sister, to never trust Reeve Warwick, Langlish spy. Almost two months in relative isolation, and here they were.

She wished Elara were also here to see this.

"I trust you, too," said Reeve, a small smile on his face as he started walking again. It took Faron a second to trot after him.

In that time, two shadows slipped from the bushes to block the path ahead of them: Roger and Locs from the grill. Roger swayed a little as he came closer, visibly drunk, but Locs seemed scarily sober as his dark eyes dragged between them.

"I thought I recognized you, but I didn't want to make assumptions," he said. "You're really the Warwick whelp. Eating our food, walking our streets, *breathing our air* as if you have *any* right."

Roger sneered. "Your father set my entire company aflame with a single, silent command. Ninety soldiers—ninety *people*—gone. While you squatted in the queen's palace."

Reeve flinched as if they had shot him. He said nothing in his own defense because he never said anything in his own defense. Faron knew that whatever violence was in their eyes, Reeve would stand there and take it as penance for people who weren't even sorry.

She slipped between him and the two men, dragging off her head wrap. Her braids tumbled over her shoulders and back as she stood as tall as she could in the face of their obvious confusion. "I'm the Childe Empyrean, and he's with me."

Roger scanned her face, and then his glazed eyes went wide. "So it's true. Langley did manipulate you."

"What? No, I—"

"You son of a whore," he said, knocking Faron aside like an empty bottle on the edge of a table. She barely managed to stay standing over the sounds of grunts and bone hitting flesh. When she whirled around, it was to see that Roger had Reeve pinned to the floor, his bloodied fist drawn back to deliver another strike. "When will enough be enough for you Langlish? *How much blood and land will satisfy you vultures?*"

"Stop it!" Faron screamed, but a hand yanked her back before she could run over to them. It was Locs, twisting her arms behind her back until it was impossible for her to get free without breaking her wrist. *"Let me go!* He's hurting him! He could *kill* him!"

"I'm sorry, Empyrean," said Locs, tightening his hold even more. Her range of movement was reduced to twitching from side to side like a lizard in a child's fist. "I don't know what magic he's performed on you, but we'll take you to the temple once we deal with him."

"I'm not under any magic! He's my—He's my *friend!*" The only response was Reeve's cry of pain. Blood flashed through the air, splattering against the ground beneath his head. Roger's swings were wild but forceful; Faron could hear every crushing blow, every sickening crack. "Stop it!" she begged, her voice thick with tears. "Stop it! STOP IT! *STOP IT!*"

"Hold her still, Jarell," Roger huffed, swiping his free hand over his sweaty forehead. "This will be over soon."

Reeve wasn't moving. Reeve wasn't moving, lying there on the ground like a corpse. Faron saw his unmoving body, and then she saw so many more, scattered around her on a battlefield. She felt heat on her face, saw the flash of fires overhead. She drowned in the shadows of drakes and dragons trying to blast one another out of the sky. She saw a sword buried in the gut of an Iryan soldier, watched them collapse as their viscera escaped through the fingers they clutched against the wound. She saw bodies in the dirt, bodies roasting under the unforgiving sun, bodies reduced to stumps and exposed bones and ashes.

Reeve wasn't moving, and she was trapped here, facing down another life she couldn't save. What was the *point* of being the Childe Empyrean if she couldn't save the people she loved? What was the point of being good in a world where the best night of her life could turn so quickly into a nightmare?

Faron heard herself screaming as if from a distance, her words, if she had formed any, unintelligible. She had surged beyond her body, and all she saw were swirls of light. Souls, she realized. She was seeing them not as men, but as souls. Living souls.

Living souls that she could manipulate.

She reached out to Roger first, pressing her will into the very fabric of him. *Stop this*, she wrote into his inner being. *Leave us alone. Go home and forget that you ever saw us.*

Drunk and furious as he was, his will was nothing compared to hers. It was like giving orders to a toddler. His strikes slowed to a stop as Faron curved away from him. Jarell still caged her, his fingertips pressing bruises into her arms, and, as she skimmed the essence of his soul, she saw nothing but weary resentment there. Visions of medical summoners and infirmary stays, lost opportunities and permanent pain. Everything that Langley had taken away, laid bare on the surface of his soul. It was a wound he always carried with him, a wound he couldn't look into a reflective surface without being reminded of.

Let me go, Faron told him. *Leave us alone. Go home and forget that you ever saw us.*

He wasn't as drunk as Roger, but he was *tired*. His hands loosened around her, her instructions burrowing so deep within him that he would think it was his idea. Faron's soul slipped back into her own body, disoriented but ecstatic. After so much failure, she had done it. She had *done it.*

She had commanded a living soul. A human soul.

Roger was standing up, his expression alarmingly blank. Faron massaged the hinge of her shoulders as Jarell moved to join him. There wasn't a flicker of light behind their eyes or a twitch of life across their faces. They shuffled as one unit down the path until it merged into a sidewalk lined with storefronts and bars. Only once she could no longer see them did Faron rush to Reeve's side and kneel next to him.

His blood soaked into the fabric of her pants. "Please don't be dead."

His lip was split. Both eyes were swollen, his skin darkening to varying shades of purple. Roger must have been wearing a ring, because there was a jagged cut across Reeve's cheek that spilled red down the side of his face. His hair was smeared with dirt and grime, but, as he turned his head to look at her, something in her settled. He wasn't dead. She'd saved him, and she hadn't needed the powers of the gods to do it.

"You need a medical summoner," she said. "You look even uglier than usual."

Reeve gave a wet laugh that ended in a cough. Blood bubbled up, along with a tooth. Faron made a face as she plucked it off his shirt, tucking it into her pocket for the medical summoner to fix later.

"You did well," said Gael Soto, appearing over them with a wrinkle between his eyebrows as he gazed down at Reeve. By now, his sudden arrivals had stopped surprising her. "Better late than never, I suppose."

"I need to get him back to Renard Hall," Faron said, her brief flush of pleasure at the compliment snuffed out by a wave of fear. There was so much blood everywhere, on Reeve's clothes and on her hands and—and she had forgotten how much she hated that tangy, coppery scent that had only ever meant death. It was an effort to gather her scattered thoughts back together. "I need help. Will you help me?"

Gael kneeled down beside her. "What would you like me to do?"

Her lips parted, but nothing came out. She had no idea anymore. The stress of the night slammed into her, and her fingers were sticking together as Reeve's blood dried between them. Control of the situation was rapidly slipping away. If Elara were here . . . If only Elara were here . . .

A hand covered her shoulder. Gael's amber-flecked eyes were all that she could see, holding her gaze with a steady calm. "If I possess him, then he'll be able to walk without aggravating his injuries. All you have to do is lead the way. Can you do that?"

"Yeah," she whispered.

"I'm happy to help." Gael gave her shoulder a squeeze before letting go. "Everything will be all right, Empyrean."

It had been so long since anyone had said those words to her instead of the other way around. Faron fought back tears.

She stood, giving Gael room to lean over Reeve's prone form so he could, she assumed, ask him for permission to borrow his body. Light enveloped them both, and then Gael disappeared. Reeve sat up unsteadily, his eyes glowing as Gael figured out how to work this new shape. They weren't too different, Faron mused as Reeve stood. Reeve was shorter than Gael, his hair lighter, his eyes bluer, but they were both boys she had conflicted feelings about.

And when Gael smiled at her with Reeve's face, she was unsure which one of them was making her heart race. Unsure if it was fear or relief that made her pulse stutter. Or something else.

"It's just up this way," she said. "Follow me."

"Anywhere and always," Gael said with Reeve's voice.

Faron hesitated for only a moment more before leading them back to Renard Hall, hoping that Reeve wouldn't hate her for what she'd done to save him.

It took two days for Reeve to be back on his feet. The damage ran deeper than Faron had thought.

A medical summoner had diagnosed him with a broken nose as well as three broken ribs. It was a miracle, she said, that Faron had managed to get him back to Renard Hall without doing further damage. *It was Gael*, Faron had wanted to say, but he remained one of the biggest secrets that she was keeping. Gael had not appeared since he'd positioned Reeve in bed and vanished in another flash of light, and Faron craved his presence. Without him and without Reeve, there was no escape from her doubts and questions.

Had she done the right thing?

She closed her eyes and saw the inhumanly blank expressions on those strangers' faces as they'd acted on her orders. Her initial pride at mastering Gael's magic felt sickening now. She was meant to use these powers against dragons, to save her sister, to save Gael. Instead, she had wielded them against her own people.

It had been in self-defense. They'd been about to kill Reeve. She'd saved his life. Those words felt like excuses, like *lies*. She'd loved the power. She'd reveled in it. And she had no idea what that said about her.

"Is he going to be okay?" Elara had asked during their astral call last night. Even through her own exhaustion and fear, Faron could tell that her sister was tired. The kind of tired that weighed on the mind rather than the body. But both times Faron had asked if she was all right, Elara had insisted she was just busy. She hadn't specified with what. "Maybe if you use his dragon relic—"

"Maybe if I *what?*" Faron had responded, baffled. "Why would I touch that disgusting thing when the medical summoner is already hard at work?"

Elara had been quiet for a moment before clearing her throat. "You're right. Sorry. I just...It kills me that there's nothing we can do."

"You can stay safe. When he wakes up—and he *will*—he'll want to know that you're okay."

There had been another pause, interrupted only by the crackle of burning wood. Then Elara had sighed. "I miss you."

"I miss you more." Faron's loneliness had felt like a snake, coiling around her heart and squeezing. "I'm sorry it's taking so long. I'm sorry I can't get more out of Gael or the gods. I'm sorry I can't—"

"You don't need to apologize for anything," Elara had said firmly. "You're doing your best, and so am I. That's all we can do: stay safe, do our best, and hope that we see each other again."

With Reeve injured, her magic tainted, and Elara an ocean away, Faron had felt short on hope then. But, as always, talking to her sister made her feel at least a little better.

Now she made sure to pay the medical summoner handsomely with the rayes that the queen had given her. Because Reeve wasn't just awake. He was, in fact, standing in front of his wardrobe and trading his bloody shirt for a new one when Faron slipped into his room. She watched him in silence, appreciating the way it was impossible to tell that he'd ever been hurt, from the color back in his cheeks to the toned line of his stomach to the rippling muscles in his back to the soft curve of his jaw and the swell of his arms....

"Say something. This is starting to get creepy," Reeve said, tugging on a light blue cotton shirt. All those muscles disappeared, forcing Faron to realize that she'd been intently focused on his biceps.

Her face burned. "I just—came to make sure you were alive."

"I'm alive." Reeve's smile had a shy edge as he rubbed the back of his neck, where his chestnut hair had grown long enough to curl over his fingers. "What happened?"

"You, um. You don't remember?"

Reeve crossed the room to pull the sweaty sheets he'd been wrapped in off the bed. He paused with his fingers curled into the fabric. "It's funny. I used to spend so much time in bed when I was a kid. I had no resistance to anything. If the wind blew, I got sick. My parents sent me to every medic, but everyone was convinced I'd die before I turned twenty." She saw him attempt another smile, but there was no joy in this smile. It was as empty as his eyes as he tumbled into his memories, memories he was finally sharing with her. "Because I was always so sick, they sheltered me. You know I had no idea there was even a war going on when we moved here? That's how ignorant I was."

"You were just a kid. We were all just kids back then," Faron said, taking two uncertain steps forward. She was unsure of her welcome, so she didn't get too close, but she wanted him to know that she was here. "Reeve, you can't blame yourself for—"

"I've done everything I can to make up for that ignorance," he continued as if she hadn't spoken. "I read everything I can get my hands on—newspapers, books, journals. I try to stay informed and mind the harm I'm causing, intentionally or otherwise. But since we've been in Seaview, it feels as if I've been losing myself a little. And I have no idea what happened last night. I've never seen *anything* like that before." Reeve dragged the sheets off the bed at last, rolling them up in his hands without looking at her. "Faron, what did you *do*?"

Her hands twisted together as she tried to figure out what to say. How to explain. "They were going to kill you. I just—I wanted to help."

Reeve tossed the sheets into the basket by his wardrobe. "That wasn't Empyrean magic."

"No. . . ."

"Is that what the Gray Saint has been teaching you?"

"You know his name is Gael. I—I haven't just been using him for information. He's been teaching me a different kind of magic, the kind of magic that will help me save Elara. And I didn't know that I could use it on humans until I did it, and I'm not sorry, because they could have *killed* you. I couldn't let that happen! What would *you* have done?"

In the silence that followed, Faron realized she was breathing hard. She couldn't read the expression on Reeve's face. It was that stupid, assessing look she had always hated, as if he were studying her soul, but his conclusions were for him alone. Faron had always assumed that he was finding her lacking, but now... Now she had no idea.

"What would you have done?" she repeated weakly.

Reeve glanced off to the side, a thoughtful furrow appearing between his eyebrows. "I've always believed that what we know isn't as important as how we choose to act on it. You've done so much good for the world, Faron. *So much*. You've also made a lot of mistakes. If you're asking me which one last night was..."

Faron leaned forward slightly, hanging on his words, hungry for his opinion. With her crimes laid bare next to her virtues, Reeve was the only one who could cast judgment right now, and she was surprised to find that she actually cared what he thought.

But all he did was shrug. "I can't answer that for you. I'm sorry, but I can't. And I'm hungry. Do you know what time it is?"

Faron was rooted to the spot as he moved past her to the door, still waiting for something that would clearly never come. By the time she got her heavy tongue to move, he was gone, and she was left alone in a room that smelled of blood and sea salt.

CHAPTER TWENTY-EIGHT

ELARA

E LARA'S PALMS WERE SLICK AS DIRECTOR MIREYA WARWICK LED her and Signey through the Mausoleum. The building was large enough to occupy half a small island off the coast of Beacon, surrounded by hemlock trees and windowless brick walls. Soldiers were everywhere, but there were no dragons; Irontooth was in Beacon with the commander, and even Zephyra had been unwilling to linger on the island after dropping them off. *"This place reeks of sadness, of death,"* she'd sent faintly. *"It sickens me to think of Barret living here."*

Signey's face was placid, but her emotions were so tumultuous that she was failing to keep them from leaking through the bond. It was killing her to be here, killing her to keep this from Jesper, killing her to see her father only to benefit the very people who had put him here. Elara tried to keep a dam between Signey and her own concern, because this was not about her. She was only here because being alone with the director was a prospect just as daunting for Signey as seeing her imprisoned father again.

Director Warwick stopped before an iron door with a closed

peephole. "Barret Soto is inside. I will be standing right here. What is your objective?"

"To find out how to communicate with the Gray Saint," Signey said without inflection.

"And yours?" The director asked, turning her intense gaze on Elara.

"To contribute my knowledge of Iryan magic inasmuch as it relates back to the original objective," she said carefully.

"Now that we're here, I would like to make one thing clear," the director said with eerie calm. "Your presence here is a last resort. The stakes are just high enough to justify your involvement, but I trust you even less than you trust me. If you don't get the information I seek, you won't graduate, Miss Soto, Miss Vincent. No one outside of this prison will ever see you alive again. Do I make myself clear?"

She summoned flame to her palm and held it under the doorknob as if she hadn't just threatened two children. The added layer of security was something Elara had learned was common across Langley; fire locks were spelled to open only when the metal reached a specific temperature, and any deviation from that temperature alerted the person who had spelled it. She focused on the flame to distract from her racing heart, from how far they were from the mainland, from how hard it would be for Zephyra to come for them. She focused on the flame to ignore the pulse of fear she could feel from Signey through the bond; unlike Elara, her co-Rider had obviously never considered that the Mausoleum might be her grave.

Not like this, anyway.

Elara followed Signey inside, trying not to flinch when the door slammed shut behind them. The cell was large but sparsely furnished. A single window was high up on the wall, with bars set too close to fit a finger through. A putrid chamber pot was in the front corner, as if Mausoleum prisoners didn't even deserve the internal plumbing that many other buildings in Langley enjoyed. A bed with thin sheets and a single pillow was in the back, near a desk with a rickety chair. A man was slowly rising from that chair, haggard but smiling. Tears lined his eyes.

Barret Zayas Soto.

"Signey?" His voice was hoarse from disuse. He stepped forward, rail thin and blinking rapidly. "Signey, is that you?"

"Father," she breathed, rushing into his arms.

Elara lingered by the door, allowing the Sotos to have their reunion. It was hard for her not to cry, too, even though she had never met Signey's father. Five years. Signey had kept her head up while her father rotted away here for five years, and still, she had never lost her sense of justice. Even seeing him for the first time like this, she could tell that Jesper had his father's chin, Signey his hair, Jesper his nose, and Signey his sharply intelligent gaze. Even with their executioner waiting on the other side of the door, it was heartwarming to witness the first steps of a family healing.

Barret caught sight of her over his daughter's head and blinked. "Who is this?"

"Oh. *Oh*," said Signey, drawing back just enough to gesture in Elara's direction. "I found my Wingleader. This is Elara Vincent."

"Vincent?" Barret's brows furrowed.

"Her sister is the Childe Empyrean."

Barret's arms fell to his sides. He muttered something, pacing back toward his desk before returning to Signey. He ran his hand through his thinning hair, then left it there, as if he'd forgotten what he was doing. The furrow between his brows deepened.

"'But though his grave is nowhere to be found, all know the Gray Saint slumbers underground,'" he said. "'When the earth splits open, and the fool outsmarts the wise, when all dragons have their Riders, then our champion will rise.'"

Now Signey looked confused. "Why are you quoting nursery rhymes?"

"It's not a nursery rhyme," Barret said grimly. "It's a prophecy, and it's about to come true."

Elara stepped forward to join her baffled Firstrider, the two of them standing united against Signey's father's rambling. "I was the last Rider," she said. "All the dragons have both now. But who's the fool and who's the wise? And when did the earth split open?"

Barret's eyes flicked to the door, and he lowered his voice. "The Gray Saint told us all this years ago. He told us how to raise him. How to raise the First Dragon. He—"

"The Gray Saint is my ancestor." Signey wrapped her arms around herself, as if this were yet another thing she wanted to protect herself from. "Gael Soto. Do you know about him, from your research into the family? Anything that you haven't told the Warwicks?"

Barret blinked owlishly. He muttered something else. This time, when he walked back to his empty desk, he stayed there, his fingers splayed across the wood. "Years ago, the director's son was sick. Very sick. He seemed marked for death, even after they moved him to Pearl Bay Palace. The sun and the island air, they hoped, would help. The war would be over with soon. Their son would be well.

"He was not well. And since they had exhausted all known Langlish methods, the commander turned to gods he did not believe in. He offered, four times, to end the war if your queen agreed to give him the Empyrean. He wanted her to use her divine magic to heal his son. When the queen refused, he burned the temple in the capital and held the High Santi captive. When the High Santi failed, the commander killed him and combined the santi's remains with a dragon relic. Desperation makes monsters of us all. He was mad with it. But instead of the gods...someone else answered."

"The Gray Saint," Elara said.

"He'd been imprisoned. Slumbering," Barret continued. "Something about the combination of two magics was enough to awaken him. But the Gray Saint was still imprisoned. The relic was like the narrow gap between two prison bars." He pointed above him to demonstrate, though the window was several paces to his left. "He was no stronger than a toddler, hardly capable of affecting this world. He wanted his freedom. His power. In return, he promised to grant power. Control. Wealth beyond the pale."

Elara swallowed. "But Reeve stole the battle plans. He helped us stop his father from burning San Irie to the ground."

"The door to the Gray Saint's cage would be easier to find among the ash than among the trees. And the Empyrean would be easier to capture if broken by the loss of all she held dear. A perfect plan, so neat, so tidy. But it didn't work. And here I am."

Tears were sliding down Signey's face. Her hand lifted, as though she wanted to reach for her father, but then hovered there, uncertain. "Why are you here? What does any of that have to do with you?"

"I am the one who crafted the relic," said Barret. He turned, tracing a circle around his heart as though something hung there. "Too useful to kill, but too informed to be set free."

Elara stared at his hands, another piece of the puzzle locking into place. "The dragon's-eye necklace that Reeve wears around his neck. That's the relic you crafted. That's the Gray Saint's tie to this world. Every time Reeve uses it—"

"The closer it is, the more it's used, the stronger the Saint grows."

Elara's heart felt like a steel drum, rapid and loud. "He doesn't use it that often. The Gray Saint can't be—can't be very strong right now. Not strong enough to break free. The commander wouldn't still be scheming if he were."

"Father," Signey begged, drawing Barret's attention back to her. "You have to tell us how to summon the Gray Saint again. The Warwicks need to speak with him. If you don't tell me, they'll have us killed."

"You were dead the moment you stepped inside this place," said Barret indifferently. "And we'll all die, anyway, if the First Dragon is freed."

"Please," Signey repeated, her voice cracking. "Please. I need you. Jesper needs you. *Please*—"

"Oh, Signey." Barret came to stand in front of his daughter, his hands gripping her damp cheeks. There was a light in his eyes that hadn't been there this entire time, as if her pleas had returned some of his clarity. "You look so much like your mother. And bonded to an Iryan! She and Celyn would be so proud of you."

A sob caught in Signey's throat.

Elara touched her wrist, almost unsurprised when Signey

caught her hand and squeezed it so tightly that it hurt. "I have a name, sir. And it's not 'an Iryan.'"

"Of course, of course. My apologies, Elara Vincent." Barret was still gazing at his daughter, unblinking. "The commander believes that the First Dragon is his key to power. He thinks he is the fool who is outsmarting the wise, the lowly human who toys with gods. But he's wrong, do you hear me? He's wrong. And because of him, this world will burn."

"Then tell us how to summon the Gray Saint," Signey tried once more. "Not for them, but for us. If we can get to him before the commander does, maybe—"

Barret's expression crumpled. He turned his back on his daughter.

Behind them, the door slid open. "Useless," the director's voice snapped. "I should have known you'd be *useless*. Vincent, consider yourself lucky that I can't kill you yet. Let's go. Now."

Signey was crying openly, still gripping Elara's aching hand, and Elara's head was thick with a fog of horror at how big this all was, how far back it all went, and how little they'd been able to change things, even though they'd won the war. If anything, they had only delayed a tragedy that now seemed inescapable.

"Because of hubris, this world will burn," Barret Soto said as the director pulled them out of the cell. "And I'm beginning to think that we should let it."

The flight back to Hearthstone was silent, with Elara, Signey, and Zephyra each lost in her own maudlin thoughts. Irontooth was a dark shadow above them as the commander and the director personally escorted them, a soundless threat. Elara didn't have the energy to sift through the feelings she could sense from either side of the bond, especially when the director's "yet" still echoed in her ears. Why did they need her alive? And until when? She felt as numb as she had the day she'd woken up and been told that Langley was her future, that her dreams would come second to this bond she had never asked for. She felt as if her world were in tatters, and there was no hope of weaving it back into something that made sense.

Once, Reeve had been dying. His parents had been desperate enough to commit atrocities to keep him alive. Before they could pay their debts, he'd betrayed them—and in doing so had only postponed their plans. The war wasn't over. The war would never be over. The Gray Saint was so close to victory that Elara could see no way to stop him, and she couldn't tell Faron, Reeve, or Aveline anything she knew without risking their lives, too.

And that was if they even made it back to Hearthstone. Iron-tooth was still above, perfectly poised to kill them the second the commander gave the word.

It was too much. For the first time in a long time, Elara felt eighteen years old. A child with too much weight on her shoulders, playing at adulthood. This was so much bigger than she was, and, no matter which path she chose, someone would lose.

"I think...you were right," Signey said, the wind muffling her already soft voice. "We should have told my brother everything. Before."

Elara's arms tightened around her. "So he could die with us?"

"Maybe it would have been better for the entire Soto line to be wiped out. Look at where we are." She couldn't see Signey's face, but she could tell from the bond that the girl was on the verge of tears again. "You didn't know him before. My father was such a shy, studious man. We were everything to him. The Mausoleum has stripped him of all that. He's as much a prisoner in his mind as he is in that place, stuck on the past, callous toward the future. I didn't want to lose him, Elara. I didn't want to lose anyone else. But, thanks to my own ancestor, I already have."

"We aren't dead yet," said Zephyra. *"We could—"*

For a moment, it felt as if the open channel of the bond were a candle that had been snuffed out. Elara began to ask what was going on when the candle was relit…with dragonfire. Beneath her, Zephyra's body began to shudder.

"Shit, shit, shit," Signey shouted. "It's happening again."

"What?" Elara asked before her eyes went wide. *"What?* No! It's been two months, and we haven't—"

Zephyra snarled so loudly that it drowned out Elara's words. Fire licked at her arms, not on the outside but on the inside, boiling her blood, swallowing her calm. She realized too late that her mouth was open and she was screaming, screaming, *screaming.…*

No, she thought, one final cry for help.

And then she thought nothing at all.

CHAPTER TWENTY-NINE

FARON

Y OU SEEM TROUBLED," GAEL OBSERVED MIDWAY THROUGH THEIR training session. "Are you well?"

Reeve was awake, which meant that Reeve was in the library. Unable to face him after her confession, Faron had summoned Gael Soto to make sure her newfound powers weren't a fluke. Gael circled her on the patio, and, for once, his eyes on her weren't making her skin crawl. It was easy, now, for her to sink into a state of concentration and feel every living soul moving through the surrounding area. If she wanted to, she knew she would be able to take control of them just as she'd taken control of those men. But she was no closer to helping Elara than she had been before she'd mastered this technique, and all she could see was Reeve's unfathomable expression as he kept his conclusions to himself.

Had Gael already led her down a path away from the gods? Was she fooling herself into thinking she was using him instead of the other way around? Was she a monster or a saint?

"Those men," she said. "The ones I...Are they all right?"

Gael stopped in front of her, tilting his head. "You ordered them to leave you alone. You'll never see either of them again. What does it matter if they're all right?"

Faron gaped at him, but that only seemed to confuse him more. He came to her as a teenage boy, thoughtful and charismatic, so it was easy to forget that he was a god...or close to it. As much as Irie, Obie, and Mala hated him, it didn't change their obvious similarities, their obvious lack of empathy for human affairs. She was asking them to care about disputes between crabs, between fish, between dolphins.

The difference, as far as Faron could tell, was that Gael seemed willing to try.

"I don't agree with the way they're processing their grief, but I can't blame them for it, either," Faron said. "Reeve is okay now. I want them to be okay, too."

Gael resumed walking. Faron let him sit with that and slid back into her mind, searching for the souls of Roger and Jarell, to see for herself if they were healthy after what she had done to them. She stopped only when a hand covered her cheek, pulling her attention back to Gael. He was fully solid when he came to her now, no longer translucent as a ghost, no longer limned with divine light. Maybe that should have unsettled her, but instead she found herself relaxing into his touch. She had given him a piece of his life back, in this way. She'd done at least one good thing.

Besides, like Reeve, he had seen her at her worst. Unlike Reeve, he could not judge her. His reputation was far worse than anything she had done to this point, and she found that comforting today. They were both monsters. Maybe that was why they would save each other.

"The men are well," he said softly. "Your kind heart is a credit to you, but you've wasted enough of your energy on them. Shall we keep working?"

Faron opened her mouth to respond to his question and gasped instead. A soul both vast and celestial was close, and she recognized the impossible force of it from that night in the Victory Garden. It was a dragon's soul, hurtling toward her island, and she could feel its rage as surely as she could feel her own heartbeat. She'd never felt it so strongly before and never from so far away. Mastering Gael's teachings had enhanced her awareness...and clearly not a moment too soon.

"Empyrean!"

She was already heading for the door seconds before a servant burst through it. "I know. Take me."

Faron found her shoes and dashed through the manor. Reeve was already waiting in the front yard, where Nobility was parked, its door slowly lowering into the grass. Clearly, Aveline had sent for her. The sun reflected off Nobility's silver gears, nearly blinding Faron, but she couldn't concentrate on anything but the pounding of her heart.

This was it. This was her chance to prove that all her training with Gael had not been in vain. That she had done the right thing learning from the one god who knew his way around dragons. That this power was *good* because she would use it for good.

Everyone would expect her to summon the gods, but Faron would instead wield her new magic. Gods, she wished she'd had more time to practice.

A man appeared at the top of the exit ramp, his smile at odds with the urgency of the situation.

"Oh good, you're together," said the head pilot, whose name

Faron could not remember. He dipped his head in a polite bow and then gestured for them to hurry aboard. "Her Majesty was very clear that we not leave *that one* alone in her mothers' house."

If Reeve was offended by being referred to as "that one," he didn't show it as he led the way. Faron tried to absorb some of his innate confidence as she followed, but her heart still felt close to giving out.

Nobility took off as soon as the door was closed. While Reeve retreated to one of the upper suites, Faron remained in the open room around the center cockpit, watching the clouds pass. Her skin was clammy as she reached out to check the status of the dragon speeding toward the island like a massive ball of ire. She had barely taken down the dragon at Pearl Bay Palace. Who was to say that she could even do it again?

You can, Gael assured her without actually appearing. *You're stronger than they've ever led you to believe.*

I'm the Childe Empyrean, she told him. *No one is stronger than me.*

His voice was amused. Perhaps even fond. *So you are. And yet you're also so much more than just that.*

Faron moved to the windows, the same windows that she had stared through what felt like a lifetime ago, and watched the clouds bob outside as she considered her next move. The drake would get her close enough to the dragon that distance would no longer be a barrier to her powers—if that weakness even still held now that she had gotten stronger—and then what?

She pressed her hands to the window and rested her forehead against the backs of them, letting her eyes slide closed. Her soul slipped beyond the boundaries of her body, but, instead of calling the gods, she reached out to that otherworldly soul.

Calm down.

It was easier this time. Tethering herself to the dragon's soul was still like leashing herself to a comet, but she knew that she was stronger than any of them now. She *knew* her will was stronger than theirs; she just had to make sure they knew it, too. As she shoved her way in deeper, submerging herself in this light and this power to control the dragon completely, she realized that she recognized this particular soul. The dragon bending to her orders was the same one from the Victory Garden. It was Elara's dragon. If Faron pressed hard enough, she could feel the flicker of her sister's soul bonded to this one.

Once she felt the fires of the dragon's anger dim to embers, she was able to open her eyes to stare dizzily through the glass. Her soul dropped back into her body like a boulder, begging her to rest, but the sight before her was more effective at keeping her awake than the strongest Iryan coffee. She recognized this mud-brown farmland, these squat buildings, that recognizable hunk of scales that acted as a town landmark. Nobility was hovering over Deadegg.

She was home.

"They were headed here," Gael said. His reflection appeared in the glass next to hers, but while she could see that she was worn down, bags under her eyes that hadn't been there before she'd left Seaview, he looked lively and bright-eyed. "Of course. I should have seen it before. The universe can never resist this kind of symmetry."

"What are you talking about?" Faron asked around a yawn. "What kind of symmetry?"

"There's a reason the dragon was drawn here. It's the same reason that I appeared in San Irie in the first place. The entrance to the Empty is in Deadegg. It seems our connection runs far deeper than I imagined."

A chill raced down Faron's spine. She pushed herself away from the window, swaying only slightly. Gael was still staring out the window with covetous eyes, but her sudden silence soon drew his attention. Except, this time, she saw his innocent confusion for the sinister act that it was.

"Is all this happening *because of you*?" she asked, voice trembling with anger. "Did you lie to me again?"

"I haven't lied to you. I'm not lying to you now," said Gael. "Don't you see? All this is happening because the door between realms has been closed for too long. The Empty is a realm between the divine plane and the mortal one. With the door closed, dragons are cut off from the divinity that created and sustains them, and they're starting to feel the effects of that. Opening the door means curing them."

"But that's where the First Dragon is. Right? I'm not strong enough to—"

"You are." He took a step toward her, lifting a hand and then dropping it when she backed away from him. "Faron, you are so much more than they have ever allowed you to be. You have become stronger still under my guidance. The First Dragon is beyond that door, but so am I. And you are now the only person in the world who can destroy him. The only person who can save me."

Faron turned away from his sharply beautiful face so she could think. The gods had told her the same thing, she realized. The Fury was the result of dragons overstaying their welcome in the mortal world. Their solution had been to eradicate the dragons. Gael's was to cure them. Could there be a middle ground where she cured them of the Fury, freed her sister and Gael, and *then* sent the creatures back to their world?

"How do I open the door?" she asked, still staring at the walls partially lit by the pulsing glow from the center cockpit. "Assuming I can even find it, that is. Deadegg is small, but it's not *that* small."

"The door to the Empty can be opened only by the same thing that sealed it in the first place: the magic of the gods. A power only the Childe Empyrean can wield." Gael had moved silently closer, his breath warm on the back of her neck, his voice low and hypnotic. "The commander never knew that you were the key to his plan. The key to everything. He's still trying to figure out why the First Dragon has not yet risen. If you open the door first, you can save the world and your sister at once. What you do after that is up to you . . . but I hope you choose to help me, too."

Faron closed her eyes, fighting to ignore him. He made it sound so simple, so easy. But nothing was ever that easy, and, if he wasn't the person who she thought he was, then what he did after his release would be on her head, too.

She thought of Elara. The soul of her dragon was almost too distant to reach out to now, but Faron remembered the feel of their connection. Gael was right. She was stronger now. She felt stronger—certainly strong enough take down any dragon. The First Dragon was the danger. Not Gael. And if Gael *was* a problem, she was the solution. She was the Childe Empyrean. There was *nothing* she couldn't do.

And she was Faron Vincent. There was nothing she wouldn't do for her sister.

It was time she stopped letting people dictate the kind of saint she was. She would prove to her gods, to her island, and to herself that she could *still* save the world—whether she remained the child they remembered or not.

CHAPTER THIRTY

ELARA

W HEN ELARA WOKE UP IN AN UNFAMILIAR BED, SHE WANTED TO rage. Not because of the Fury, the memory of which came back to her in fits and starts like the world's worst stage show, but because she knew that she had once again played right into the commander's hands. What better catalyst for war than a dragon attack on San Irie, perpetrated by the mount of the only Iryan Rider in history? What better scapegoat for the necessity of such a war than the Iryan everyone already assumed was a spy?

She climbed out of the bed and nearly tripped over a package on the floor. It was one of her bags, fully packed and transported from Hearthstone. The other was half-hidden under the mattress, equally full. Elara's stomach dropped as she headed for the door. There were soldiers in the hallway, dressed in black and carrying swords. They began to draw them as soon as they caught sight of her, and Elara quickly retreated into her room.

Before she could close her door, the one across the hall opened. Signey stepped out, ignoring the soldiers, and backed Elara into her own bedroom. She kicked the door shut behind them, but a soldier reopened it and stepped inside to watch them. "Are you all right?"

"Where are we and how did we get here?" Elara asked.

"I saw Irontooth in the garden when I woke up, so I assume he forced us here after we flew back that day. This is Rosetree Manor, the home of the commander and the director," said Signey. "Something about this place, it's blocking my connection to the den. Zephyra is right outside, and I can't even hear her."

Elara's eyes widened. "But how?"

"Dragon relics. Their magic can be directed to influence the natural world and neutralize the unnatural magic of the creatures they come from. If the commander built this manor with the remains of dragons, he could conceivably keep his own den from spying on him. It's rare, dangerous, impossible magic, and it's not in any of the books about this place."

Elara eyed the soldier's impassive face, biting back her idea for a possible solution. Instead, she silently searched through her bag and then cursed again. Her drake figurine was there, but she couldn't summon and thus couldn't use it anyway, making it useless to contact anyone. But depending on how long they'd been unconscious after the flight from San Irie to Langley, she might have missed Faron and Reeve's last call. They might be looking for her.

Unless they were too busy preparing for war.

"Are we allowed to wander around?" she asked, trying not to sound defeated.

"With an escort, yes. I've found the soldiers only get stabby when I approach the front door. Would you like to take a walk?"

Elara raised her eyebrows. "Now?"

"Yes, now."

"I have no idea why your queen sent you here," Signey added through their bond. That, at least, was still intact. *"You make a terrible spy."*

Rosetree Manor was excessive, far too excessive to have been home to only three people. It was situated behind a large fishpond, ringed by thick trees and buffeted by an expansive back garden that was divided into sections. Zephyra waited for them by the fishpond, surrounded by her own ring of escorts; they carried swords and what looked like net launchers, likely so they could ground her if she tried to take flight. As soon as Elara got close to her dragon, she could once again feel the subtle tide of Zephyra's emotions from her side of the bond. Whatever magic the commander had erected, their proximity to each other was enough to temporarily sidestep it.

After nuzzling them both with her snout, Zephyra reported that Irontooth and the director had left a few hours ago—and that, even out here, she could not reach the rest of the den to call for help.

"All the doors are guarded or locked or both," Signey told Elara. *"They wouldn't let me see you until you woke up, probably so they could eavesdrop. It seems like we have to play along for now. At least until the director or the commander arrives."*

"The war could have started by then," Elara sent back. *"He could be saying anything about us."*

"I know." Signey sighed. *"I know."*

Instead of going back inside, they joined Zephyra by the pond. She curled her body into a crescent, and they sat against her flank with their legs touching, protected by a line of soldiers from the occasional sunlight that broke through the otherwise gray clouds.

The fresh air should have done wonders for Elara's anxiety, but not today. Not with Barret Soto's revelations running through her head. Not with the dread of a second war hanging over everything. Not with her sole means of contacting her family taken away.

She watched the soldiers watch her, swallowing. *"Do you think the den is all right? Or would the commander have people watching them, too?"*

"The latter seems most likely, but honestly, I don't know." Signey picked up a blade of grass and began to pick it apart. Then another. Then another. *"If they're in danger, it's my fault."*

Elara reached over to take her hands, rubbing bits of greenery off her skin. *"Jesper, Torrey, and Azeal are made of stronger stuff than you're giving them credit for."*

Signey's lips quirked upward in a faint smile. *"Wow, it's almost like you care for them."*

"I do. I care about all of you."

And she did. Even with the wall up, Elara could feel the traces of Zephyra's affections, the whispers of Signey's respect. The den had somehow become her friends when she wasn't paying attention, and Langley was not the land of nightmares that she had imagined it to be. It was a country like any other, where the people in power devoured others whole just to gain more, while the people underneath them lived and worked and laughed and loved.

"I never asked you," Elara said, lacing their fingers together when Signey didn't pull away, *"but you're Langlish and a member of the Dragon Legion. Even after everything, even with your family on the line, you keep working against the Warwicks. How do you know that you're doing the right thing?"*

"I guess it depends on what you mean by 'the right thing,'" Signey replied, her gaze lowered. *"Before he was arrested, my father always used to say that it's our job as Riders not just to defend the rights of the empire but also to make sure that the empire is kept on the right side of history. Even before I met you, I knew there had always been something*

off about our interactions with other countries. And now ... Now San Irie is collateral damage in something that was never about it to begin with. That's not right. Mama and Celyn wouldn't stand for it, and neither should Jesper and I."

Do not kiss her, Elara told herself sternly.

"*As I said many suns ago*," Zephyra said with so much amusement that Elara worried her stray thought had, in fact, been overheard, "*the two of you have the same soul. You both want to fight for something that you truly believe in. You're both capable of such great things. You're both an inspiration to everyone around you.*"

"*Stop*," Signey groaned as if Zephyra were a parent determined to embarrass her.

Elara laughed because she knew the feeling—but her laugh cut off abruptly once a sword was shoved in her face.

"While you're on the manor grounds, you will speak aloud," said a nearby soldier. The sword shifted until it was pointed at Zephyra. "Or we've been given permission to start collecting dragon relics from now on."

"All right," Signey snapped. Only Elara knew her well enough to hear the tremor in her voice. "We're talking out loud."

The soldier gave them one more hard look before sheathing the sword. Elara swallowed, looking out at the fishpond with nothing to say. Her pulse pounded in her chest when she noticed that there were even more guards there; had they arrived while the three of them had been talking? Those soldiers were murmuring among one another, assuming that the two girls were paying them little attention. Elara might have started another conversation to distract herself from her stress if she hadn't heard one of them utter the word *queen*.

"*Zephyra*," she sent before saying aloud, "Do you want to tell me how your classes went before I came?"

Signey caught on to the plan immediately, launching into a spiel that Elara could easily tune out. Meanwhile, Zephyra allowed Elara to use her ears, to hear all that she could hear. The world was so much louder to a dragon, but Zephyra was so used to picking voices out of the din that everything hushed except for the single soldier speaking. "...coming to the National Hall for peace talks. I hear that she's desperate."

"Not desperate enough," said a second. "I can't believe we have to babysit instead of being in Beacon."

"Well, if you hadn't—"

Elara dropped back to her own senses, anxiety pulsing across her skin all over again. Aveline was on her way here because of her. Aveline had no idea what the commander had done, what Elara knew, and this couldn't be good. If anything happened to their queen, it would be her fault. It would be all her fault.

Signey's hand covered hers in the grass. Her lips were still moving, but her gaze was steady as she sent across the bond, *"We need to get you home. Maybe the peace talks will go well, but in case they don't, you can't be here. You could be used as a hostage or—or worse."*

I'm already a hostage, Elara almost said, but that was hardly a productive thought. Signey had risked her education, her family, and now her own life to do the right thing every day since Elara had caught her in Luxton's office. It had seemed as if they had time, to wait and to scheme, but that time was rapidly running out. When the queen arrived, it might be too late.

"*Okay.*" Elara forced herself to breathe, a slow in and out, before she met Signey's determined brown eyes. *"What's the plan?"*

CHAPTER THIRTY-ONE

FARON

AVELINE'S FACE WAS AN ALARMING SHADE OF RED WHEN FARON and Reeve entered the audience chamber.

Nobility had flown them to Pearl Bay Palace after the dragon had retreated and Gael had disappeared. Afterward, they were rushed through the hallways to meet the queen like handbags being passed off from owner to owner. Faron would have found it hilarious if she hadn't been so drained from summoning the dragon's soul. She leaned against Reeve, watching Aveline through half-lidded eyes. Reeve's arm was locked around her upper back, the only thing keeping her standing as she bore the queen's obvious anger and the stone-faced Queenshield who surrounded them as if they were common criminals.

"Can I rest before you yell at me?" she asked around a yawn. "I know I make it look easy, but Empyrean work is very draining."

Aveline's cheeks deepened to purple, but Faron was too tired to be satisfied. "I do not think you understand how serious the situation is, Empyrean. People are already calling the appearance of that dragon an unprovoked attack that spits in the face of the Summit and needs to be answered with a declaration of war."

"Isn't it?" Faron asked to be contrary, though Aveline's words sent her heart racing.

"San Irie cannot handle a second war," said Aveline, her tone icy. "Though we have the support, we do not have the resources. They have ten fully bonded dragons; we have five drakes—four, if mine is excluded. They have an army and a navy that can draft additional soldiers from over fifty territories with an approximately combined four hundred million people. We have an island of just over one million people, only a portion of which is able-bodied and of age for drafting into the army, and a navy largely comprised of raiders, pirates, and volunteer soldiers from the other islands. If there is another war, *we will lose.*" Her black eyes were as cold as obsidian. "You and I will be captured and executed. Our island will be colonized. Our people will be enslaved again to send a message to the rest of the empire. Do you understand the severity now?"

Faron's smile faded. "Yes, Your Majesty."

"Good." Aveline continued to stare at her for a long moment before she finally moved on. "I will be taking Nobility to Beacon for an emergency peace talk with Commander Warwick. In the meantime, I need you to stay here and protect San Irie if anything should happen."

"Um." Faron exchanged a glance with Reeve, who looked similarly mystified. "Your Majesty, I'm seventeen years old."

"And you were twelve years old when you went to war. Age is not a factor here. If these peace talks break down, if I am kidnapped or worse, I need to know the island is in capable hands. Your ability to summon the gods may be the only shield San Irie has against however the Langlish plan to raise the First Dragon."

Faron tried not to wince. Aveline had no idea how long it had been since she'd summoned the gods. The queen would probably agree with the gods that the dragons needed to be eradicated, regardless of whether Elara could be rescued first. She would probably condemn Faron for what she'd done to save Reeve's life. And confessing to Aveline about being in touch with the Gray Saint, let alone learning magic from him? Faron might as well lock herself up and save the time.

But Aveline was right that the Childe Empyrean was the only thing the Langlish truly feared. Faron couldn't shake the queen's faith in her now, not with everything going on. Now, more than ever, they needed to stand united.

"We can handle things here," she assured Aveline. "Just let me get some sleep before you leave, and there's nothing to worry about."

Aveline nodded, and for once there was something in her eyes that might have been respect instead of resentment. It was hard to tell, because it was so unexpected, so new, but the potential of it made Faron smile, anyway. As much as the thought of another war made her body grow cold, she had forgotten how a common enemy had been the only thing that kept her and Aveline from being at each other's throats. They'd won the war together. And together was how they would win again now.

"Your rooms are still open for you," said Aveline. Her eyebrows were drawn together beneath her diadem, her mind clearly thousands of miles across the Ember Sea. "Welcome back to Port Sol, Empyrean, and thank you for your service."

Nearly a full day had passed by the time Faron finally woke up.

Nobility was still parked on the airfield, alongside two other drakes that had newly arrived, and she padded down the hallways until she found Aveline in her room with her hair in a loose Afro and a leather-bound book in her hands. Candlelight brightened her room, rather than the lamps, and the flickering flames brought out the golden undertones in her light brown skin.

She looked up as Faron stepped past her outer guard, gold illuminating her umber eyes. "In another hour, I was going to send a servant to make sure you were alive."

"You can't get rid of me that easily."

Aveline's answering smile was a little off, but Faron ignored it to come closer. Everything seemed new to her after the last two months, like the light gold color of the walls that shone like trapped sunlight and the bay window that overlooked the queen's private beach. Even Aveline looked new to her, more like the girl she'd once admired and less like the woman who took every opportunity to slight her.

"My mothers left this journal for me at Renard Hall," Aveline said, opening the book and smoothing down the pages. "I found it there when I visited after the war, addressed to me. Explanations for why they left me on the farm instead of raising me themselves. A personal treatise on ruling the island—in case they didn't make it to teach me. 'To be queen,'" she read, "'is to live on borrowed time. It's to train your daughter for a job she will have only when you are dead, to be but one runner in a marathon that will have a bloody end. To be queen is the most complicated, unfair, frustrating, rewarding, enriching, and humbling experience one can ever have, and it's the result of a simple accident of birth. We are all born to die, but by chance you are born to lead.'"

She slammed the book shut so hard that Faron jumped. "But it wasn't by chance, was it? I was perfectly happy with my adopted family. I was perfectly happy with the farm. You brought me into this, and now we're both trapped."

And there it was, Aveline's simmering resentment laid bare between them. Raised as Ava Stone far from the palace while her mothers fought for independence, unknowingly orphaned in a single dragon attack, and brought to the throne by a twelve-year-old Faron on a mission from the gods. And once the war was over, she became the teen queen of San Irie, fumbling around on an international stage, while the Childe Empyrean retired home to Deadegg to rest.

Faron had always known precisely why Aveline hated her so much, but it still stung to have it thrown in her face right now.

"Your *mothers* brought you into this when they had you. Don't blame me for what's always been in your blood," she snapped. "And the gods are the ones who handed you a queendom for you to build. If you're unhappy with how you've built it, that's your own problem. Tell *them* you'd rather have lived on your stupid farm until it *went up in flames.*"

"I guess we're both masters at dodging responsibility for our actions," said Aveline in an acidic tone. "Or were you not the one who prayed to the gods for their help in the first place?"

Loads of people prayed to the gods during the war, Faron wanted to shout. *It's not my fault they decided to answer* me. They'd admitted that hers was the first prayer they'd heard, but she had been a twelve-year-old girl. A twelve-year-old brat, if she were being honest. They should have waited for another prayer. Elara would have been the better choice, or maybe even Aveline herself.

But it was Faron's prayer that had been answered, and now they were all trapped.

"Maybe I did pray to them," she said. "But you're not the only one who didn't know what they were signing up for back then. I just wanted the fighting to stop."

Something softened in Aveline's expression—not much, but enough for the tension to bleed out of the room.

"So do I, Empyrean. So do I." Aveline set the book atop her desk with gentle hands. She crossed the room to her vanity mirror and began rubbing oil into her tangled curls. "Let's hope my trip proves successful. I'll see you when I return."

Recognizing a dismissal when she heard one, Faron stepped toward the door. She felt as if there were more that she should say, but her mind was empty. Maybe they would never truly get along. Maybe they would never stop resenting each other for how their lives had turned out. Maybe the only thing they would ever have in common was wanting the fighting to end. But if this was the last time she saw Queen Aveline Renard Castell, she was at least glad it was on these terms.

A temporary cease-fire. An unbroken trust.

As she slipped into the hallway, Faron knew the latter was something she barely deserved. There was always a chance that Aveline's trip would prove successful and they would avoid a second war, but it was just as likely that they wouldn't. And Elara was still bound to a dragon in the enemy country, just as trapped as Aveline and Faron were. Months had passed since Faron had promised to save her, but time had officially run out. It was now or never.

And after all those months, Faron had only uncovered one sure-fire way to keep her promise.

Reeve was standing outside of her room when she returned to

it, his puzzled expression melting into relief when he caught sight of her. "Hey. I was wondering where you went. We all thought you were dead."

"Hey," she replied. "I need you to be both a researcher and a liar."

"Am I going to like this?"

"Not even a little bit."

Reeve studied her in silence for a moment, searching for answers that she knew he wouldn't find. There was nothing left inside her but determined resignation, the intense focus that only came when you knew that your options were limited and there was only a very small window for victory. She could do this without Reeve Warwick. But after everything they'd been through, after everything he'd witnessed, she wanted him by her side for this.

"All right," Reeve finally said. "Tell me what you need me to do."

PART IV

SACRIFICE

CHAPTER THIRTY-TWO

FARON

As soon as Faron stepped out of her room, the number of Queenshield who looked her way made it obvious that Aveline had warned her private guards to be on the alert for any of her shenanigans. Thankfully, they didn't follow her around as she planned exactly that, though *shenanigans* seemed like too light a word for what she wanted to do. Aveline would not support her leaving Pearl Bay Palace, let alone releasing a trapped god for at least long enough to save Elara. But Reeve hadn't tried to talk her out of it, and, even if he was blinded by his own love for Elara, how bad an idea could it be if a notorious killjoy was willing to lend a hand?

In Nobility's absence, drakes Valor and Liberty had taken up residence in the airfield. Reeve looked them both up in the library to help with her scheme. Liberty, emerald green and the first drake ever built, had all four pilots replaced a few years ago, their names listed in the royal records. Valor, butter yellow and the last drake ever built, had just gained its pilots in the last few months, after the library book had been printed.

"I have a better chance with Valor," Faron told Reeve when he brought this to her. "They're new, which means they're young, which means they're stupid, eager to please, and probably won't recognize you."

Reeve's eyebrows lowered judgmentally. "I think they'll still recognize me."

"I guess you'll have to be *really* commanding, then."

A fluffy curtain of clouds had covered the sun when they set off down the hill to the landing strip, inviting the breeze from the nearby ocean to cool their skin. Faron couldn't bear to strap herself back into the Empyrean chain-mail dress from the Summit, so she'd selected a salt-white day dress that billowed around her legs as they approached the sole pilot by the drake. It was a girl who couldn't have been more than two years older than Faron, her thick hair in two large braids on either side of her head. She appeared to be setting up a game of dominoes on an overturned wooden chicken crate.

Reeve strode with confidence across the airfield. The girl caught sight of him immediately, but she made no move to get up.

"Well, if it isn't the Warwick whelp," she sneered until she caught sight of Faron. "Childe Empyrean! What an honor."

Faron nodded in acknowledgment but didn't say anything.

"The Empyrean needs to return home to Deadegg," Reeve said as if he hadn't been insulted. "The queen has given permission for her to visit her parents before being brought back here to the palace. I'm told you can make that round trip in less than a day?"

"Of course we can. But we'll have to check with the queen before we can just—"

"This really can't wait," Reeve replied. "It's supposed to be a quick trip."

"Can you fly this thing or not?" Faron added impatiently.

The girl looked between them, biting her lip. "Oh, this isn't my drake, Empyrean. But we can definitely take you in Liberty if we have the proper clearance—"

"Soleil, did you say 'Empyrean'?" said a familiar male voice from the top of Valor's exit ramp. "Faron fucking Vincent, I should have known you'd try to pull something like this."

Faron groaned. Jogging down the ramp was none other than Jordan Simmons, and, even after two months, little had changed about the boy whose rayes she'd stolen in a footrace. His curly locs had maybe gotten longer, inching down over his broad forehead, and he'd recently touched up his fade. Instead of his public school uniform, he was dressed in the green-and-gold military jacket and pants of the Sky Battalion. But though his name tag identified him as Flank Pilot Simmons, he still looked like an arrogant bully to her.

An arrogant bully who would mess up her whole plan.

"I'm not pulling anything," Faron said through gritted teeth. "Valor chose *you* as a pilot? You're too young to enlist!"

"I just turned eighteen, thank you very much. You really haven't been back in Deadegg for a while, huh?" he asked, as condescending as ever. "Valor is being called the Deadegg Drake because every pilot it chose came from Deadegg."

As if summoned, two more people came down the exit ramp. The first was a girl with burgundy braids spilling out from her golden knitted cap, long-lashed brown eyes, and deep brown skin freckled with dark spots across the tops of her cheeks. The second was a handsome boy with curly black hair tied into a messy top bun.

His teeth were bright against his dark skin when he smiled at Reeve. "Hey, mon. Long time no see."

"Wayne, Aisha, hey!"

Wayne Pryor dragged Reeve into a hug interrupted by the freckled girl, Aisha Harlow, who jumped onto the boy's back in an effort to join in. Reeve laughed, trying to adjust his grip to hug them both. His cheeks dimpled as he smiled wider than Faron had ever seen him smile before. He caught her watching and turned, his eyes the hazy blue of the Argent Mountains in the morning fog, and Faron's breath hitched in her throat.

"You're so predictable sometimes, Vincent," said Jordan, smirking. "The Empyrean and a Warwick? I don't think even you could pull that off."

"Again, I'm not trying to pull anything." Faron slid her hands behind her back so he wouldn't see the way they twitched. "Can you guys just take me to Deadegg for the day?"

"Anything for Elara's kid sister," Wayne responded before Jordan could. "As long as we get Valor back by sundown, I don't think it will be a problem."

Jordan's black eyes narrowed at Faron. "I agree with Soleil. We should have the queen sign off on this. If these two claim she has, it's definitely a lie."

"Who would you two rather piss off?" Aisha asked, stretching languorously. "The throne or the gods?"

Jordan scowled but accepted that he was outnumbered. The pilots headed back up the exit ramp to prepare Valor for takeoff, and Soleil packed up her makeshift table so it wouldn't be blown away. As Soleil headed back toward the castle, hopefully not to sound the alarm with Liberty's pilots, Faron realized, abruptly, that she and Reeve were now alone on the landing strip. Her pulse skipped as she turned to face him, but she tried to shake it off.

"I'll be back in a couple of hours," she said over the rush of blood in her ears. "And, hopefully, Elara will be free by then, too."

"I'll be right here," said Reeve, and it sounded like a promise. "Do whatever you need to, and then come back safely. Elara won't care that she's free if you had to get hurt in the process." Before Faron could muster a reply to that, he added, "And I'd hate if you got hurt, too."

Her face felt hot. Her lips parted, but she had no idea what to say that wouldn't sound like...like...

Like she cared for him. Like she wanted him. Like the truth.

"Vincent!" Jordan Simmons was at the top of the exit ramp again, his scowl even deeper than before. "How long does it take to say goodbye? *Move it.*"

"I'm coming!" Faron snarled back at him.

Before she could lose her nerve, she darted forward and kissed Reeve's cheek. After that, she intended to escape. To do what she did best and outrun the consequences of her own actions. To hide from whatever his response would be to her sudden burst of impulsivity.

She made it two steps before Reeve grabbed her wrist.

Faron's lips parted—for an insult or an excuse, she had no idea which—but Reeve kissed any potential words out of her mouth. One hand settled on her lower back, pulling her against the firm line of his body, and the other cupped the side of her face tenderly. In both cases, his touch was light, easy for her to break, if that was what she wanted. But it wasn't. What she wanted was this.

Him.

Faron had always thought—well, not *always*, but always—that

Reeve would kiss the same as he read: careful, focused, thorough. Instead, he *devoured* her with an all-consuming passion he could barely restrain. She didn't know where to put her hands so that they wouldn't be in the way. They settled on his shirt, fingers digging in as if that would give her some measure of control. But Reeve just kissed her harder, and her thoughts splintered in a thousand directions until she was nothing but a single nerve awash in sensations. His soft hair. His gasping breaths. His hot mouth. The smell of him, ink and spice and sweat.

Her toes curled in her shoes. She rocked upward to slide her arms around his neck, and he said her name in a way he'd never said it before, and she exhaled a sound that made his arms tighten around her and—

"Vincent!"

Faron ripped herself away from Reeve with a gasp. Jordan Simmons glowered at them as if they were lizards in his kitchen and he couldn't decide which one of them to kill first.

"Get," he snapped, "in the godsdamned drake."

Her heart was racing as she hurried up the ramp, and her lips seemed to tingle with the phantom touch of Reeve's fiery kiss. Jordan's glower meant nothing to her in the face of her sudden fear of Reeve's reaction. Every part of her wanted to forget her mission and kiss him again, but it had been her first kiss. She'd been clumsy and unpracticed, and what if he'd hated it?

When she did finally turn, Reeve was watching her with those storm cloud eyes, a thin line of vivid blue around wide, dark pupils, his mouth so very, very red. And she'd done that to him. That look was for *her*. Pride twined with the heat in her blood as the ramp lifted until she could no longer see him. Only once the door had sealed with a hiss did Faron finally stop smiling—and only then because she was sure she looked like a fool.

Before she'd taken more than two steps toward the deck, however, Jordan grabbed her arm to stop her. "You may have them fooled, but I *know* you're up to something. You're always up to something," he hissed.

Faron beamed. "Want to play dominoes and see if you can win your rayes back?"

Jordan considered this. Then he let her go. "Deal."

Valor landed on the abandoned farmland that surrounded the road out of Deadegg, long cleared as a makeshift landing strip by the queen.

"We need to be in the air after no more than three hours," Wayne told her as he lowered the exit ramp. "We'll run maintenance on Valor until you get back."

"*Three hours*," Jordan shouted from his cockpit. "Don't make me come get you."

Faron ignored him and stepped out onto the road. Deadegg slumbered before her like a lazy cat in the sun, a huddle of mismatched, multicolored buildings made of weatherworn concrete and aging wood, and she lost track of the time before she was crossing the town line.

As she walked through the familiar streets of her hometown, she was suddenly reminded of her race against Jordan. That had been an entire lifetime ago, and yet she was tracing the same path. The dull gray scales of the dragon egg in the center of the town still rose above everything like a lonely guard, drawing the eye.

Everything had changed and yet nothing had changed.

Okay, Gael, Faron reached out. *Where are you?*

He appeared to her easily, still inhumanly beautiful. "Empyrean."

"It's the egg, isn't it?" Her gaze was drawn to it again, to the way the sunlight glanced off it in rainbow prisms that hurt her eyes to look at directly. "It's the only thing that makes sense, the only thing we wouldn't get near—or, if we did, the only thing we wouldn't be able to move or destroy. The egg is the entrance to the Empty." Her gaze slid back to him. "Isn't it?"

"There's only one way to find out," Gael said, that familiar charm wrapped around his words like chocolate dripping slowly down a bowl. He stepped closer to her, close enough that she could almost feel his warmth, close enough that her world narrowed down to her and him and the dark bargain she was poised to fulfill her end of. "Are you sure about this?"

Her shoulders tensed. "You don't think I can do it?"

"I know you can." Gael's fingers tipped her chin up. His smile was a drawn weapon. "I've always known you can."

She moved away from his touch, artificial and manipulative where Reeve's had been right and real. His influence was harder to detangle herself from, but she just had to stick to her plan, and everything would be okay. "Swear to me you are who you say you are. Swear it."

"I swear." Gael sounded amused. "Good luck, Empyrean."

And then he disappeared, leaving her with a straight shot toward the dragon egg that had always been in the center of the town square.

It was midday in Deadegg, when Irie's sun burned the brightest, roasting the air until it rippled. On a normal day, Faron would be in the school building, or maybe loitering around the yard buying a bag juice or a freeze pop to compensate for the overwhelming heat. Instead, she wandered through the anemic crowd gathered in the square. The road curved to the left and right of the dragon egg, but everyone was giving it a wide berth, anyway. It was only the children who were ever stupid enough to touch the wall or climb the egg.

Faron couldn't seem to drag her eyes away the closer she got to the mottled silver shell. It felt as if the egg had a presence of its own and were calling to her, asking her to come closer, daring her to climb it like she had so many times before. She resisted the urge, studying it critically. What was the best way to crack it open? Did she even crack it open, or did she try to lift it?

"*Break it,*" she heard Gael's seductive voice whisper in her ear.

Yes, she would break it. She would crack a hole in the egg, and she would defeat whatever dared to crawl out of it. And, once she did, Elara would be free, and Faron would sleep for days. Maybe even at her own house, for the first time in months.

She was so close now.

A deep breath and she was reaching for the gods, for Obie in particular. She couldn't handle Irie's wrath nor Mala's pity. Not right now. Not today. When Obie appeared before her with his hood drawn and his eyes hidden, she shoved any indication of her plans as far down as she could. His soul merged with hers, flooding her body with the power of night and shadows, and, for once, the sudden feeling of being infinite made her laugh instead of overwhelming her. This close, *so close*, nothing could drag her down.

As soon as her vision cleared, she fed their magic into the shadow of the egg, lifting it from the pavement. With a wave of her hand, it separated into a thousand midnight daggers, all pointed at the shell.

Empyrean, said Obie. *What are you doing?*

She clenched her fist in answer. The daggers struck the egg from all sides, burying themselves so deeply that she heard the shell splinter to pieces even before the first crack began to show. The egg cleaved in two, the massive sides of its thick shell falling apart and tipping dangerously toward the stone barrier that protected the town.

Empyrean.

Faron breathed hard as she tried to hold on to Obie's defiant soul. Magma bubbled up from the center of the egg now, gushing but never falling, painting the pieces of the shell in bubbling red goop. She heard laughter, deep yet musical and very familiar.

A pearl-white dragon she had never seen before pulled itself free of the magma that continued to steam from the egg and rose up to stand in the sun. Behind it, the last of the eggshell crumbled, falling to the ground as a pile of ash. The earth made a gurgling sound like a drain, and then the magma and the heat faded, leaving nothing but the dragon. It was twice the size the egg had been, its eyes spring green, its teeth like swords the size of her arm.

A giant beast faced her down, malice radiating off it in waves almost powerful enough to touch.

The First Dragon.

Screaming. Everyone was screaming. Faron's body jerked left and right as people shoved past her to get away from the monster she had unleashed. Their screams. Their cries. Their confusion. Their despair. Each one struck her like a stone as the dragon roared so loudly that the ground shook beneath her.

Faron, Obie whispered inside her head. *What have you done?*

Faron lifted her hands. *Calm down*, she told the First Dragon. Asserting her will. Grazing the edges of a soul far larger and more ancient than any she had touched before.

And then, impossibly, the soul reached back. Trapping her. Claiming her.

The dragon spread its endless wings and rose into the air.

And, with another roar, it flew directly toward her.

CHAPTER THIRTY-THREE

ELARA

WITH SIGNEY'S TRAINING ALLOWING HER TO TALK ALOUD AND across the bond at the same time, they were able to cobble together a plan without alerting the guards who never took their eyes off them. Elara had barely looked at her room all day, and she didn't study it now. Instead, she studied the clock on the wall as it ticked closer and closer to midnight. If they succeeded, she could reach San Irie after dawn. If they failed...

She looked at her Justice figurine, waiting innocently on the side table, and she prayed. *Irie, please. Please help me save my island. Please help us get free of this place. You heard us once, and now I beg you to hear me. San Irie cannot handle another war. We need you. I need you.*

No one answered. Midnight arrived. Elara inhaled deeply—and an explosion rocked the manor, toppling her off the side of the bed. Zephyra had managed to fly directly into the house, causing one of the building's wings to collapse. At least, Elara *hoped* she'd managed her part of the plan.

She scrambled to find her bags even though her ears were ringing. Outside, footsteps pounded, and orders were shouted. But just as she grabbed the handle, her door swung open. Soldiers swarmed in, so many that she was forced back against the far wall, trapped between them and the side table that now dug into her hip.

"The prisoners have been secured," said one into his dragon relic, a claw ring that swirled with magic, probably allowing him to report to his commander.

Elara had been stripped of her dragon relics, but she had been practicing for half her life to become a soldier. Her fist shot out, punching the closest one in the throat, and she yanked his sword free as he stumbled back. She only had one blade in contrast to the wall of them before her, but she had to get to Zephyra before the soldiers outside captured her in their nets.

She reached out a free hand to grab her figurine, switched on its flames, and threw it like a bomb.

Justice shattered, sending flaming metal everywhere. Although their uniforms were clearly fireproof, the shards cut deep enough to distract the soldiers. Elara began to fight her way through using the element of surprise more than any skill. They were army trained with their weapons, and she was not. The minute they were out of range of those sharp pieces of drake figurine, they would over-whelm her in a second.

Signey appeared in the doorway, a ball of flame conjured between her hands. She said something that Elara couldn't hear over the din of battle and threw the fire in an arc that jumped from sword to sword, making them too hot to hold. Elara saw the soldiers closest to her sliding on what she assumed were fireproof gloves and swung her sword at them. She wasn't aiming to kill. She didn't necessarily want to kill. But the blood that spilled across the floor screamed *fatal*.

She knew all too well how much blood a human could lose and still survive.

It was much less than this.

She didn't realize she'd been frozen over their bodies until Signey grabbed her and yanked her out of the room. A single bloodied arm reached accusingly out of Signey's room before the hallway dissolved into a blur of colors as they ran. Zephyra had chosen the wing on the opposite side of the building from theirs, ensuring the soldiers were spread too thin, but reinforcements would arrive within five minutes. They had already wasted four.

Signey and Elara burst outside, where Zephyra was still midbattle. Her wings flapped hard as no less than ten soldiers tried to drag her out of the air. They weren't using net launchers, Elara realized now, but grappling hooks. Each one clung to some part of Zephyra's body while the soldiers pulled her close enough for the rest of their squad to carve her open. Elara hurtled over the grass, her bags slapping against her back. Everything was lit silver and crimson from the stars and the fire Zephyra belched at any soldier who came near. The fumes chased Elara through the night. She brought up an arm to cover her nose and mouth, hoping, despite herself, that the fire didn't spread and such a lovely house didn't actually burn down.

Or maybe Barret Soto was right. Maybe it all deserved to burn.

Signey threw herself at the first soldier, her fire ineffectual at breaking the rope. Elara cut Zephyra free with the sword she still wielded, ignoring the blood that stained the edges. Signey had not been called one of the best students at Hearthstone for nothing. Every time Elara caught sight of her in the fray, she was taking down a grown man with dangerous focus and steely precision. Signey left a circle of the dead behind her and climbed up Zephyra's back as Elara cut the final rope.

Elara threw her bags up to the saddle for Signey to tie down, and then she scaled the dragon's flank in seconds. She felt shakier than usual as she did so, but she chalked it up to fear. More soldiers were streaming out of the house to stop them. Distantly, she could hear the roar of dragons approaching. They'd run out of time.

Zephyra took a step, and Elara fell off the side.

Signey grabbed her wrist. Elara hit Zephyra's hard scales, crying out as they scratched her skin and sent pain ricocheting up her rib cage. The dragon took to the skies, and Elara kept dangling as Signey slowly pulled her up, asking questions the whole time.

The problem was that Elara didn't understand a single one of them.

Faron did it. She broke the bond.

Tears welled in Elara's eyes. She was free. She could summon again. She could go home—

Faron did it.

She . . . broke the bond.

And Elara was on the back of a dragon she could no longer understand, with more dragons closing in.

Signey dragged Elara into the saddle in front of her and said something that sounded like a curse when Elara almost fell a second time. In the grand scheme of things, she'd forgotten that it was part of a Rider's magic to be able to fly on dragonback without tipping one way or another. Signey wrapped her arms around Elara's waist, Elara's back pressed against Signey's chest. The soft feel of her would have distracted Elara if she didn't think she would probably die before they landed again.

"You need to speak patois," she said desperately in her native tongue. "The bond, it's been broken."

Signey's patois was accented and formal, not unlike Reeve's after he'd had a few lessons. Elara had almost forgotten the sound of it; the Summit felt as if it had been two lifetimes ago rather than only two months. "What do you mean it has been *broken*?"

"My sister makes a regular habit of doing the impossible."

"I see," Signey murmured before falling silent. Elara, who had no idea what more to say, fell silent, too, hating how bereft she felt. She was happy. Wasn't she?

Her stomach swooped as Zephyra swerved upward, through the cover of clouds. Below her dangling feet, Elara could see the faint outline of dragons heading for Rosetree, where they would find a broken house, dead soldiers, and missing prisoners. Even if she and Signey got away, Jesper and Torrey were still at Hearthstone. Barret Soto was still in the Mausoleum. What would happen to them? To Azeal?

If they made it back to San Irie, could they really leave everyone to pay for their crimes? The farther they flew, the more Elara became convinced that they were doing the wrong thing. That she was doing the wrong thing leaving people who wanted to fight the commander in his clutches. She didn't want to be a hostage, but she couldn't leave them behind to become hostages in her place.

Once, Signey had told her there was more than one way to help people. Elara hadn't known what she wanted then, but she did now. To help people across two nations, or more, if it came to that. To help people who thought they had no voice, no power, no chance. To help people who wanted to make a better world.

"We can't go to San Irie," Elara finally said, turning her head as much as she dared to look at her Firstrider. Her former Firstrider. "The den shouldn't have to pay for what we did—"

Signey cursed in Langlish.

"What?"

"*Saints*, Elara, could you stop being so—you? For even five min-utes?" Signey complained. "Your island is in danger, *you're* in dan-ger, and, even now, you're thinking of other people. Of *my* people." She sounded like she was in pain, and Elara's heart skipped. She wanted to turn around completely, but she didn't dare. "No matter what happens now, I need you to know that...you were every-thing I could have wanted in a co-Rider and more. You're an inspi-ration to me as a person. And you're one of the most beautiful people I've ever met, inside and out. Right or wrong, I would fol-low you anywhere."

Elara's face was burning by the time Signey finished. Now she was *glad* she couldn't turn, because her heart was rioting in her chest and she was sure that it was obvious on her face. She liked this girl. She really, *really* liked this girl. She hadn't come to the Langlish Empire for love, but somehow she'd found it. Her lips trembled, parted, ready to speak her truth.

"The First Dragon is freed," Signey said suddenly. "The War-wicks...they've won."

Elara twisted in Signey's arms. Just as she feared, the action would have sent her tumbling off the dragon if not for Signey's superior strength. "How do you—?"

"Zephyra can feel him now," Signey continued as if Elara hadn't spoken. "He's in San Irie. By the time we get back there, there might be nothing left."

"We have to warn them—"

"I'm sure they've noticed. From what Zephyra is telling me, the First Dragon is not small."

"We have to warn the queen, too. And the den."

"I've already reached out to them. But we'll need to fly all the way to Beacon to notify your queen, if those soldiers were to be believed."

In that moment, Elara remembered that the broken bond meant she could summon astrals again. Which meant that she could astral call again. Which meant that things didn't have to be as hopeless as they seemed. Not yet.

"Tell Zephyra to give me some flame. I'll try to call Aveline through it," she said. "But we need to get to Beacon as quickly as possible. She can't *be* here if San Irie is in trouble."

She'd never forgive herself, Elara thought but didn't say. *And neither would I.*

CHAPTER THIRTY-FOUR

FARON

THE FIRST DRAGON GRIPPED FARON IN HIS FRONT TALONS AND sailed easily over Deadegg with four powerful flaps of his wings.

It slammed the breath out of her, and, for a moment, Faron thought that she was dying. She expected to look down and see that one of those claws had speared her stomach and the shock was preventing her from noticing that she was bleeding out. But when she did look down, she saw her body tucked tightly between two ivory blades half the size of her body, her legs swinging loosely in the air above her town, her fingers scrambling for purchase on the scales of the dragon's paw. Still alive, and yet she felt exhausted, drained, *empty*, as if something inside her had died.

Then she realized she was alone. Truly alone.

Obie was no longer within her.

Gasping, Faron reached out for the gods, but her call fizzled instantly, her soul sucked back inside her body before she could even see a single astral. It felt as if she'd lost a sense that she'd taken for granted; the world looked different, smelled and sounded different, and not just because she was dangling over it.

Obie? Mala? Irie? Can anyone hear me?

"I can," said Gael Soto, and he sounded amused. This was not the open, fond amusement from his earlier quips. There was something deep and dark in his voice as it echoed through her head. *"Though I would advise we continue this conversation when you climb up here."*

Faron tipped her head back and squinted at the muscled form of the dragon. The wind made her eyes water, but she could just make out the black comma of a human form clinging to the sleek line of the dragon's neck. Gael lifted a hand and waved, and the First Dragon's grip on Faron simultaneously loosened. Her stomach dropped faster than her body did, and she scrambled up his leg before she fell to her death.

Gael grabbed her as soon as she was close enough, helping her settle behind him. Whether it was magic or physics, the moment she was sitting down, she felt perfectly balanced and strangely confident that she wouldn't fall. Gael's body was solid as she slid her arms around his waist for lack of anything else to hold on to. He smelled like earth and morning rain, with an underlying smoky scent that Faron assumed was from the dragon.

The farther they flew from Deadegg, the more she wanted to scream. Why couldn't she summon? What had the First Dragon done to her? What was going *on?*

"Where are you taking me?" she shouted over the roaring wind. "What about our plan? My sister?"

"I'm taking you to pick up something I left in the capital," Gael responded. "And a bargain is a bargain, Faron. I broke your sister's bond the moment Lightbringer was freed."

"Lightbringer?"

Gael pressed a hand against the white dragon, his smile fond. "This is Lightbringer. The First Dragon. An imperial dragon, in fact, and the only one of his kind."

Before she could ask another question, the dragon named Lightbringer shrieked in pain beneath her. The smell of smoke had gotten stronger, and heat flared up her spine in contrast to the frigid sky air. She looked over her shoulder to see Lightbringer's tail shaking off the embers of a flame that flickered with too many colors to be natural. Closing the distance behind them was Valor, its bright yellow color making it look as if the drake had been sent on behalf of Irie herself.

Gael stroked the dragon's neck in a soothing motion. "Well, that was unkind. They've made him angry."

Faron's heart cracked. "Gael, this isn't you. He's controlling you. He's in your head. You have to remember—"

But Lightbringer was already darting straight up, dodging a second blast from Valor with ease. Faron's fingers turned to talons of her own, digging into Gael's stomach as if that would stop the dragon, but he pried her grip loose with one hand. *Do you want to die before you can reunite with your sister?*

"Don't," she begged, struggling to get free of his hold. *"Please don't—"*

Fire gushed from Lightbringer's mouth, consuming the drake below. Drakes were made of scalestone, impervious to dragon-fire, but the force of the blast still caused Valor to dip in the air. The pilots couldn't see Lightbringer's spiked tail coming down like a hammer until it was too late. It slapped the drake like a fly-swatter, sending it careening to the ground far below. The trail of flame left in its wake turned to smoke the farther it fell. The scalestone shook off the attack. Thank the gods, the pilots could see again. Now they could pull the drake up before—

Valor exploded on impact.

Faron screamed.

Somewhere in that burning wreckage were the bodies of Elara's friends, her classmates, her townspeople. Dead, all of them dead. Because of her.

"A necessary sacrifice," said Gael, and he no longer sounded like himself. He no longer sounded like the boy she had thought she was getting to know. Or had the sinister edge to his voice always been there? Was he consumed by Lightbringer, or had he lied to her? Faron no longer trusted herself to tell. *"We have more important things to do."*

Faron screamed until her voice failed her. Then she began to cry.

By the time they landed outside of Pearl Bay Palace in Port Sol, Faron was numb.

Every time she blinked, she saw Wayne Pryor's smile and Aisha Harlow's burgundy hair. She heard Jordan Simmons's snide comments, his feet pounding across the Deadegg streets. Three lives snuffed out in an instant because she had freed Lightbringer from the Empty when the gods had told her not to go near it. Faron's throat hurt from screaming, and her eyes itched from crying, but she couldn't feel the magnitude of those three deaths. Her ability to grieve had hit a certain threshold during the war, and the three Valor pilots had simply slotted themselves into the emotional graveyard with the rest of the corpses of those she'd failed to save.

Lightbringer lay down on Pearl Bay Airfield, allowing Faron and Gael to slide off his back before he stood again. Part of her expected the dragon to begin setting fire to the buildings that had just been newly rebuilt after the war. But all Lightbringer did was eye the rest of the landing strip, where Liberty was still parked against the backdrop of the afternoon sky. Faron's breath caught, but the drake didn't move to intercept the beast. Its pilots must have been in town, unaware of how close they were to death.

Gael was striding toward the castle. Faron hurried after him, trying again and again to call upon the gods.

"That won't work anymore," he said once she caught up to him, startling her out of her own head. He was smiling the indulgent way one might smile at a child who had prepared a mud pie for dinner. "Didn't you feel it? Haven't you noticed us speaking through it? You're bonded to me and Lightbringer now. You're our co-Rider."

Faron almost tripped over nothing. "I'm—what? That's impossible."

As impossible as him hearing her thoughts when she hadn't sent them to him.

"It's the way it was always meant to be. I told you I had knowledge that the gods never wanted you to know, didn't I? Now that we're bonded, you can do so much more than they ever allowed you to do. You can become so much more than they would ever let you be." He stopped within view of the palace doors, gazing down at her with those perilous hazel eyes. "You're not their Childe Empyrean anymore, Faron. Our souls are the same. Before I was the Gray Saint, before I went mad, I had adopted a different name. Iya. A name worthy of a god bonded to the most powerful dragon

341

in existence. Now *we* are gods. *We* are Iya. And, together, we will rule this world."

"Gael, I—"

"Faron!"

For the second time that day, her heart stopped.

Reeve.

Reeve was coming toward them, his eyebrows drawn together in confusion as he saw Gael—Iya—for the first time. He took them in, read her body language, lifted his hand toward his chest where she knew his dragon relic was hidden beneath his shirt. She imagined loyal, intelligent, and stupidly noble Reeve going up in flames as Valor had, and her blood went cold in her veins.

"Reeve, go back inside!" she shouted. "Please, just go!"

"Cute," said Iya. "But I couldn't harm him even if I wanted to. He has something that belongs to me."

Reeve stood in front of them now. Faron saw him shift so that he was standing slightly between her and Iya, as if he were ready to jump in front of a blow for her if he needed to, and she reached out to cling to the fabric of his shirt. He wouldn't—*shouldn't*—protect her like this if he knew what she had done.

"What's going on, Faron?" he asked, casting Iya a suspicious glare. "Is this the Gray Saint?"

"You don't recognize me?" There was a malicious glee in Iya's eyes, in Iya's voice, that made goose bumps rise on Faron's arms. "I'm almost offended. But there's really no point in being insulted by you when you only live because of me."

"What is that supposed to mean?" Reeve asked, his voice coming out much stronger than his wavering expression would imply. "Start making sense."

"Reeve Warwick," Iya said like he was savoring the words, "you were dying of some human disease or other when you were a child. Your desperate parents used that very dragon relic around your neck to make contact with me, weak and trapped though I was. They promised me freedom in exchange for your life restored and their power returned. For the chance to rule this world beneath us.

"You were supposed to be my vessel, a human form I could use to move through the world, allowing me to find the Empty and release myself. But you forced me to make other arrangements. I didn't realize how much free will would be left in you. I didn't realize I would be too weak to do more than linger in your form like a droplet of rain in an ocean. But that's all right. Everything worked out as it was always meant to." His eyes flicked over to Faron with a satisfied smile. "Though he didn't know it, the boy standing in front of me right now is still an incarnation of will, meant to protect my only connection to this realm and to push the Childe Empyrean toward her destiny. Toward this moment. Toward *my* freedom. And now that I have my power back, you have served your purpose."

"What—?"

Iya disappeared in a flash before Reeve could finish the sentence. Faron began to say something—though she wasn't sure what could explain *any* of this—but Reeve grunted as if he had been shot. He stumbled back as his limbs splayed out like a pinned butterfly's, his eyes glowing gold. His skin had always been pale, but now it was translucent, shimmering, *gleaming*. It looked as if Reeve were holding the sun inside of him and now it was fighting to get out by any means necessary.

And then it was over.

Reeve dropped onto his knees. Heart pounding, Faron searched the surrounding area, but she could see no sign of Iya at all. She quickly kneeled by Reeve's side, sliding an arm around his back. "Are you okay? Please be okay. Tell me you're okay."

"I'm better than I've been in centuries." The same cruel slash of a smile that had seemed so at home on Iya's face now stretched across Reeve's. He shook off her grip and stood, flexing his fingers and cracking his neck. Then he laughed. "My form, my true form, long decomposed in that prison. How I appeared to you all this time was little more than a memory made flesh by the proximity of my relic." He gripped that relic now and laughed again. "Thanks to you freeing me, I now have the power to make Reeve Warwick a true vessel. I have all I need."

Somewhere behind them, Lightbringer roared.

What did any of this mean? Reeve was...what? Dead? Devoured? Erased from a borrowed existence? Though she had heard Iya's words and seen them merge into one, Faron couldn't believe that the boy she had come to know had been overwritten by the monster that had manipulated her.

Reeve Warwick, who had distracted her with international gossip to calm her down during the Summit. Reeve Warwick, who had called the Queenshield to get her through the crowd of santi at Renard Hall when she was hobbled by her social anxiety. Reeve Warwick, who had kissed her as if the world might end if they ever stopped. Eyes the color of the ocean she rarely got to see, and soft-looking hair the color of chocolate.

I loved him, she realized as her eyes burned with a fresh wave of tears. *Gods, I never even told him.*

A hand appeared in her blurry line of sight. Faron sniffled as she looked up to see Reeve bent over her. No, not Reeve. Just Iya, in the vessel that Reeve's parents had promised him. She remembered, suddenly, when he had offered to possess an injured Reeve to get him back to Renard Hall, how she'd thought he had bent over Reeve to ask permission to share his body. In light of what she knew now, he'd probably never asked. He'd probably just been glad to have the opportunity to test out his new form under the guise of a favor to her.

For all she'd claimed to be the queen of lies, she'd never seen this one coming. He'd played her like a tambourine while she'd convinced herself she was in control.

"You—*look what you've done*," Faron managed around the anger that was slowly taking the place of her pain. She clung to it tightly, because anger was active, anger would keep her from falling into the open grave in her chest. "What do you *want*?"

Iya's eyes darkened. "I want *everything*. I want all that I was denied when they locked me in that timeless, endless pit, everything that was mine before your gods and my own generals betrayed me." He leaned closer, so close that for a moment she feared he would try to kiss her with Reeve's lips. It took everything she had not to flinch. "When I am done, Faron, you will be the saint of nothing more than ashes, and I will be god of all that remains."

CHAPTER THIRTY-FIVE

ELARA

Before Elara and Signey made it to the National Hall, they were attacked by dragons.

The soldiers must have contacted the commander the instant they'd left Rosetree, because the Dragon Legion was treating them like approaching enemies. And Elara was rattling around like a marble in a tin can, clinging to Zephyra's back for dear life.

"I hope you're always this easy to read," Signey said, arms tightening around her. "Let Zephyra do what she does best. You try to figure out where your queen might be."

"It's not like I have a map of the National Hall burned into my memory," Elara snapped before realizing that she kind of did. One of the books in the Hearthstone library had given her a history of the place, and she'd gotten an extensive look at most of the halls and rooms during her and Signey's visits. Even without the bond, Elara could tell that Signey was laughing at her for having forgotten that. The one good thing about their weekends in Beacon, the one thing they'd learned, was the layout of the building.

"Try the North Chamber," Elara said. "Where we first arrived."

Zephyra dropped like a stone, so suddenly that Elara began

screaming. Signey laughed again, but her arms remained steady around Elara's waist. Despite the fact that it seemed as if she'd left her stomach in the clouds, Elara felt safe.

They landed outside a line of high-set arched windows that looked down into the great hall. From this angle, Elara could see the commander, the director, *and* the queen inside. Aveline was dwarfed by them both, but she carried herself like someone who eclipsed them in style, if not in stature.

"Go," Signey said, releasing Elara. "We'll lose the dragons."

Elara slid down the side of Zephyra's flank, tumbling onto her butt in the grass. Zephyra took off seconds later, chased by fireballs she dodged more easily now that she'd dropped the weight. Elara's chest ached as she watched them, but she had to trust them to do their job the way they trusted her to do hers. She had to reach the queen.

If, of course, she could get past these soldiers.

Fighting a smile, Elara studied the approaching officers: the way they carried themselves, the swords they had drawn. She took a deep breath and sank into the astral plane, and it was like coming home, like the first breath after emerging from the waves, like light and love and joy all at once. She laughed, pure delight shooting through as her aunts surrounded her, glowing and beautiful, when she had worried that she would never see them again. Two months had made her less wary of Langlish magic, but this? Summoning? She felt whole again. She never wanted to lose this.

She reached for Aunt Gabourey, the strongest of them all, and blended their souls together, trembling only slightly as they became one. She felt Gabourey's bloodlust as if it were her own. And maybe it was.

The officers raised their swords.

Elara smirked.

She left a small pile of unconscious bodies by the door and ran deeper into the National Hall. Her hands still glowed with unchecked power as she found the staircase that would lead her to the North Chamber. The guards she ran into on her way never saw her coming, and sheer adrenaline kept her from feeling the few strikes that grazed her skin. She could summon an astral and heal herself later. Thank Irie, she could heal herself again.

Elara laughed. *Finally.*

When she burst into the North Chamber, she was breathing hard. The commander, the director, and the queen were right where she'd seen them through the window, nothing changed except that the Warwicks now stood together. Aveline's eyebrows lifted.

"Elara?" the queen said. "What in Irie's name do you think you are doing? Were you the source of all that noise?"

"San Irie is under attack," Elara gasped.

"I know that," Aveline said impatiently. "That is why I am here. Why are *you* here?"

"No, I mean . . . Not the . . . San Irie is under attack *while* you're here. Right now."

The queen's eyes flashed. "Explain."

Elara told her everything that had happened, from the conversation she'd overheard at Hearthstone to the rising of the Gray Saint, from the imprisonment at Rosetree to the broken dragon bond. The more she spoke, the angrier the queen's expression got. But the Warwicks made no effort to refute or interrupt her story. They didn't even look concerned. That worried Elara enough for her voice to drift off.

And then she realized the truth. "You...you never cared if Faron cured the Fury or not. You just wanted her isolated. You wanted her *desperate*. You knew she'd turn to him."

Gavriel Warwick chuckled. "I had no way of knowing what your sister would do, but I suspected that her desire to save you might work in my favor if I kept you here long enough. This situation has been out of my control for some time, but I've always been skilled at improvisation."

"You never planned to let us return to Hearthstone. You were just waiting until the Fury took root," Elara accused. "You wanted us—me—to be the one to start the war. We did everything you wanted, and I'm your scapegoat."

"You assign yourself far too much importance, Miss Vincent. A long time ago, we made a bargain with the Gray Saint and failed to uphold our end. He could seep through the cracks of his cage, but his power was minuscule. The Fury, that rage? It's the First Dragon rattling the cage of the Empty, calling his creatures to him. We cracked the lock, but he wanted it shattered," he said. "All the dragons needed their Riders in order for the Empty to open, and I hoped that Miss Soto would find hers among the dignitaries. I even hoped, prayed really, that it might be the Empyrean herself. Wouldn't that have been magnificent? Defeating the Iryans with the very hero of their revolution? But, instead, it was you. The Empyrean's sister. Useless."

She didn't care what a man like Gavriel Warwick thought of her. She didn't. And yet it stung, anyway, to have him throw her worst fears back at her.

"But in war, one must use all the resources at one's disposal. I simply had to figure out your use. That's why I brought you to the capital, and it was there that I figured it out. You were clearly communicating with the Empyrean. She would do anything to bring you home. *Anything.* Even open the Empty for us. And so you see"—he tilted his head, unbearably smug—"the Empyrean's failure to cure the Fury is my scapegoat. The pressure of your own people to return to war after your attack is my scapegoat. You? You were never more than a hostage."

"How *dare* you?" said Aveline, stepping between the commander and Elara as though she weren't the queen of a nation in peril. "What about your people? What about your country? How could you condemn them to more endless warfare? How could you risk them based only on the dark promises of an imprisoned god?"

"The Gray Saint is more powerful and dangerous than you can imagine," said the director, and, instead of smug, she sounded almost sad. "If you fight him, you will lose."

"I am leaving," Aveline snapped, "and I am taking Elara with me."

A ball of flame appeared in the air above Director Warwick's palm. It cast an infernal light over her sharp features. "We must insist you stay with us for now. At least until our god safely returns to Langley."

Aveline lifted her hands and the windows behind them shattered. Elara jumped, but the glass just shot into the air like a hundred tiny knives all pointed at the Warwicks. "I am the queen of San Irie, and no power in this world can hold me somewhere I do not want to be."

The director's fireball launched, but Elara was quick. Her own hands lifted, a translucent shield appearing that absorbed the blow. She curved the magic into an even larger ball and threw it back, aiming for the commander. He dodged it with ease, but his gaze was severe. Assessing her as a threat.

Good.

Burn it down, niece, Gabourey told her, her bloodlust rising and mingling with Elara's own desire for justice. *Burn them all down.*

Gladly, Elara replied. She sent a wave of magic toward the wall and watched it crumble as if she'd flown a drake through it. The stone and wood disintegrated into a misshapen heap, revealing the hall to the open air. Part of her considered collapsing this roof on top of the Warwicks' heads, but then she remembered there were innocent people in the building. None of them deserved to suffer for what Gavriel and Mireya Warwick had done. Not again.

"We'll be leaving now," Aveline said. A line of glass daggers embedded itself in the ground before the Warwicks as an added threat.

Commander Warwick tilted his head. Then he laughed. "You can try, but you won't get very far."

No sooner had he finished speaking than the sky beyond them filled with dragons. Elara saw an ocean-blue ultramarine, a bloodred carmine, a golden medallion, and at least three forest-green sages flying toward them, none of which she recognized without her easy access to the wealth of Zephyra's knowledge. She froze, even as Aunt Gabourey encouraged her to get ready for the fight, promising that even if they couldn't take all the dragons, then they would certainly go down trying.

The queen held the remaining glass shards suspended over the Warwicks' heads. "Elara, can you handle that?"

Could she? It seemed like the worst kind of hubris to say yes. She was not her sister, the Childe Empyrean, able to channel the power of the gods to pull whole dragons from the sky. Even if they weren't under the commander's control, the Dragon Legion was still loyal to him.

But Faron wasn't here, and Elara was. Elara *had* to handle this, or San Irie would fall.

And Elara would never let that happen. *Never.*

Orbs of pure magical energy sizzled into being around her hands. "Yes, Your Majesty. I can handle this."

Before she could throw one at the nearest dragon, a deep roar split the air. Irontooth, the Warwicks' carmine dragon, appeared as a long shadow before his crimson body sailed into view. His teeth were bared in a snarl. He would fight the hardest of them all; Elara would have to take him down first before she fought the rest.

Irontooth's shriek of pain surprised Elara so much that one of her orbs disappeared. He swerved away from a sudden burst of incoming flame, but the ultramarine dragon swung its spiked tail at Irontooth and knocked him off course. Behind him, mouth still smoking, was Azeal, and Elara could make out Jesper and Torrey clinging to their carmine dragon's back. Combat professor Petra Rowland and her daughter, Hanne Gifford, were on their ultramarine dragon, which must have been Alzina. Together, they dragged Irontooth out of view in a collision of fire and fang.

Signey appeared then, clinging to the top of Zephyra's head. The sun haloed her dark waves, making her look like a saint. "Sorry, Commander, Director, but these dragons aren't here for you. We called them here to help *Elara.*"

"We'll be escorting Elara and the queen back to San Irie," said none other than history professor Damon Smithers, sitting side by side with his husband, Rupert Lewis, on the back of their sage dragon, Nizsa. "We'll submit ourselves for disciplinary action when we return."

Elara tipped back her head in an effort to keep tears from falling. Signey had already surprised her by showing up for her. So had the den. But the professors whose classes she'd aced, the handful of students who didn't bully her in the hallways—she would never have expected *anyone's* help, and yet here they were.

A tear slid free. She would do everything she could to avoid a second war—not just for her island, her sister, and her queen, but for all the Langlish people and dragons she had met who were unafraid to question their empire's actions. For all the Riders who had showed up for her, and the other citizens across the empire who had been and would become collateral damage, thanks to the commander's bad decisions. For the peace and progression they could all achieve together if the empire stopped for a second to realize that land was not to be owned and cultures were not to be assimilated.

Elara turned to the Warwicks, pleased to see that their smugness had cracked right down the middle, pleased to see the wariness in their eyes and the frowns on their faces. She smirked in return.

"Thank you for your hospitality," said Aveline with a polite smile. "But we will be leaving now."

She released the glass and calmly strode toward the wreckage that had once been the manor wall. Elara tried not to laugh as she followed.

CHAPTER THIRTY-SIX

FARON

I N JUST A FEW SHORT HOURS, IYA HAD CONQUERED PORT SOL. IT HAD
taken Lightbringer only one flight around the capital to cow
everyone into submission. Liberty had survived, but only because
its pilots had been killed before they could reach it. The other two
drakes had yet to arrive, which was for the best. Lightbringer was
resting on the roof of the palace, large enough to burn all of them
at once if they came without a plan.

Now inside, Faron followed the trail of bodies strewn throughout the hallways of Pearl Bay Palace to find Iya. The Queenshield
had tried to fight and been torched for their efforts. Their corpses
were unrecognizable, their scalestone swords either separated from
their hands or their hands separated from their arms entirely. The
pungent scent of burning flesh hung thick in the hallway, and Faron
had to cover her nose and avert her eyes just to keep from screaming.

It was all familiar. So familiar.

Except, this time, Faron was a prisoner in the palace instead of
a soldier come to liberate it.

Except, this time, Faron had invited the enemy here instead of
being the savior who could drive them out.

Except, this time, everybody she passed, every life that had been snuffed out, every bit of suffering that her people were facing, was all her fault.

She made it to the war room in a daze, half expecting the walls to be painted red with blood or the lights to be replaced with inky shadows. Instead, she found Iya standing over a table with an open map of the world.

Faron noticed for the first time that he was dressed in a black military uniform that he must have used his dragon relic to conjure. It was identical to the ones Langlish soldiers wore, if outdated in some ways. Instead of the midnight double-breasted coat with the Langlish sunburst on the arms, his was adorned with golden buttons, the Langlish sunburst on his right breast and a white dragon stitched on his left arm. His trousers had a golden line down the sides that disappeared into his black boots. On his back was an image of two curved white swords crossing each other, with KNIGHT OF THE EMPIRE written in gold thread beneath them.

As he turned to look at her, Reeve's face set in a solemn expression that almost looked normal, Faron's heartbeat sped up. She was in a room with an experienced soldier, who had trained for wars like the one she'd stumbled into.

"There you are," he said. "What kept you?"

"The dead people in the hallway. They're...they're a little distracting."

Iya was confused. She could feel his emotions whispering beneath her own, the bond turning him into an open book. She was reminded of when he'd asked her why she cared what had happened to the men whose wills she'd stolen; it was as if he'd been imprisoned for so long that empathy was a foreign concept. Or maybe he'd never felt it before.

Maybe Gael Soto had never really existed. Maybe Iya was all there ever was.

"I'll have the remaining servants move them, then," he finally said. "Come here."

Warily, Faron joined him at the table. There was a small clay figure of a crown on top of San Irie, a fist-shaped island above the islets of San Mala and San Obie. The other Ember Sea islands sat unsuspectingly within a day or two's boat ride of the area he'd already conquered. Hanging beside them like a storm cloud was the continent of Nova, divided into Joya del Mar, Étolia, and Langley.

Iya had placed another clay crown atop Beacon, the capital of Langley. Her eyes were back on his profile—Reeve's profile—so serious and distant. Reeve's face was made for expression, his mouth crafted for smirks and snide remarks, for happiness and history facts. She remembered the first time she'd truly relaxed in his presence, when he'd found her at the Summit and told her stupid things about all the international dignitaries. That felt like years ago, but Faron couldn't let go of that moment. It had changed something between them before she'd been willing to let it.

She couldn't believe that Reeve was gone. He had to be in there. Maybe *he* was now the one lingering inside Iya like a droplet of rain in the ocean. She had to know for sure.

Faron reached for one of the remaining crowns and placed it over Étolia's capital of Ciel. "Remember when Tournament Guienne Lumiére came to the Summit?"

"Tournesol," Iya corrected idly. "The heirs to the throne of

Étolia are called tournesols or tournesolas, and Guienne is third in line after his sisters."

He sounded more like Reeve than he had since Iya took over his body—and that was all the proof she needed. Faron made an interested noise as her soul slinked out toward him, searching for his. Searching for Reeve's. But when she made contact with him, his soul flared into a luminous, shifting cloud. She saw Reeve, she saw Gael Soto, she saw Lightbringer, she saw all three at once, and then no one at all as the light morphed again and again. The further she tried to push inside, the more she felt nothing but static, as if too many things were happening at once for her to glean anything but chaos. Faron tried to pull back but discovered that she was stuck like a fly on sticky paper.

And then, as Reeve's body gazed down at the map, she saw Iya's soul rise from within him in the shape of a dragon. It turned to look at her with eye sockets empty but for the flame that burned inside them.

"Stupid child, I am older than you can ever conceive. I am older than this world that birthed you. Your attempts to use a fraction of my own power against me are akin to throwing a pebble at a giant." Lightbringer's voice was like the feeling of a thousand needles pricking her skin. "Make no mistake: You live only because he cares for you. You are no longer the Empyrean, and you are no longer of use to me. If it were my choice alone, I would have slaughtered you the moment I was freed. Do not make me regret that I didn't."

Iya's soul slithered back inside him. Faron reared back from the table with a gasp, her vision flickering in and out as if she'd been channeling a god for hours. Iya turned to her, and all she could see was the dragon that had crawled deep inside his psyche.

"We have guests approaching," he said. "We should see what they want."

He slid past her and through the door. Faron waited until her hands stopped shaking to go after him. Reeve was in there, but Gael was in there, too. And Lightbringer was too strong—too ancient, too powerful—for her to overwhelm him with her new-found skill. He knew all her tricks because he had taught them to her through Gael, and his malevolence ran so deep that she worried he would kill what remained of both boys just to teach her a lesson.

She joined Iya on the balcony that overlooked the queen's private beach. What she saw on the horizon made her freeze for a different reason. Nobility hurtled toward the island, faster than she had ever seen the drake fly. Trailing it were six dragons of various colors and sizes, flying just as quickly in a pyramid formation.

"They're attacking the island," she said, hoping that Iya would care. That he would *stop* them. "Why are they attacking the island? I thought Langley was on your side."

"I thought so, too," he replied. "Look closer, Faron. Use your power."

Faron reached out toward the dragons' souls. One of the green dragons pulled up alongside Nobility almost like a shield, and she realized that she recognized it. This soul belonged to Elara's dragon, and that was Elara leading the pack. Faron could feel her determination, her courage, her fierce protectiveness just from skimming the light of her soul.

These dragons hadn't come to attack the island.

They'd come to save it.

"Adorable, isn't it?" Iya confirmed. "Oh, well."

Lightbringer took to the air with a roar that shook the world, and Faron could feel the pulse of magic—the pulse of rage—seconds before the line of dragons began to break, their pyramid formation cracking into chaos.

Iya had told her the truth. He hadn't created the Fury.

Lightbringer had.

And now he was using it against his fellow dragons.

CHAPTER THIRTY-SEVEN

ELARA

SAN IRIE WAS IN SIGHT WHEN EVERYTHING FELL APART.
Zephyra's body jolted beneath her as if she'd been shocked. Unlike last time, Elara couldn't ask her what was happening as she dived out of formation, speeding toward a stretch of beach several yards ahead. The whole way, she shook and trembled and snapped her head from side to side, as if she were having a seizure.

"What's going on?" Elara shouted.

"The Fury; it's the Fury," Signey shouted back, her arms tightening around Elara's waist. "We need to—You need to—"

Gloved fingers gripped Elara's chin and turned her head to the side. Signey slammed their mouths together in a kiss so fierce it felt almost like an attack, followed by a second, gentler glide of lips like a whispered apology. An immediate sense of warmth and rightness filled Elara, a sense that went beyond the taste of tea and sugar. Signey's hands cupped her cheeks and pulled her closer, and Elara tilted her head so that their lips slid together more smoothly. It was a kiss that felt like coming home.

Even with Zephyra's body roiling beneath them, Elara felt safe. Held in place by Signey's kind hands.

They smiled into each other's mouths, and Elara hadn't felt this level of comfort from a first kiss in her life. She buried her fingers in Signey's wavy hair and slid her tongue between Signey's parted lips and let the sounds that Signey made settle in her chest right next to her heart.

A place that Signey had already been for longer than Elara was willing to admit.

Signey's face was flushed when they parted, her eyes wide, her expression young and open.

And then Elara was free-falling through the air as Signey flung her off the side of Zephyra's back.

Elara's scream was swallowed by the frigid ocean that slapped her body with a splash. Cold water filled her eyes, her ears, her mouth, salty and glacial and yet blistering. She'd been mere feet away, but it still felt as if she'd been hit by a rock, and it took her too long to figure out which way to swim so she wouldn't drown. She emerged into the open air with a gasp, coughing water out of her lungs, rubbing at her burning eyes so that she could see. Her ears slowly popped, and the sound of roaring rushed in above the waves. The Fury had consumed all the dragons they'd brought with them. They raced toward San Irie, already spitting fire in anticipation of the buildings they hoped to set ablaze.

Elara blew out a breath, spraying saltwater everywhere, and then reached for an astral. As soon as Aunt Mahalet's soul settled in with hers, she made use of her aunt's athletic skills to swim to shore without tiring. Then she drew on that same magic to run faster than she ever had before.

Her surroundings blurred around her as the magic propelled her forward, faster than a dragon, faster than a drake. Port Sol appeared in only a few steps, and Pearl Bay Palace a few steps after that. But as she slowed, her muscles burning from the exertion and her clothes dry from the wind, she realized that she was still too late.

Zephyra was raining fire down on the boats in the harbor, their masts cracking in half and tipping into the sea. Azeal had landed in the middle of Port Sol's square, and Elara could hear people screaming as they tried to escape whatever destruction he had wrought. And hovering in the air above the palace was a dragon larger than any Elara had seen before, colorless but for its emerald-green eyes.

The First Dragon.

Oh, Faron. What have you done?

Elara had known her sister for seventeen years. She had watched Faron take her first steps, say her first words, drink her first sip of rum. She didn't need enhanced senses to know where she was. She *knew* Faron, all the way down to her soul, and she knew that there was only one place she had to be right now.

She ran for Pearl Bay Palace.

Only a few yards separated her from the front steps when she saw the first body. A charred husk was strewn across the path like a warning, and several more followed when she gave that one a wide berth. Elara's stomach dropped further and further with every corpse until she stopped running toward what would clearly be her death and instead redirected the energy of her aunt's soul into two swords made of pure light. She kept one wary eye on the dragon, but if the First Dragon had noticed her, then he clearly didn't consider her a threat.

That would be his mistake.

Elara jumped as the palace doors slammed open, but there was no enemy. It was Faron; *it was Faron*, racing down the stairs toward her. She barely had time to dismiss the swords before her sister was in her arms, clinging to Elara as tightly as Elara held on to her.

"I'm sorry, I'm so sorry," Faron cried into her neck. "I'm so, so sorry, I messed up, I'm sorry."

"It's okay, I'm here, it's okay," Elara murmured back, squeezing Faron that much tighter. "It wasn't your fault. You didn't know. You didn't know."

Faron sobbed out her version of the events, from training with Gael Soto to cracking open the door to the Empty, from the First Dragon—Lightbringer—destroying Valor to the Queenshields' deaths, from losing her connection to the gods to losing Reeve.

Reeve was . . . gone? Disappeared? *Reeve?*

No.

Not Reeve.

They didn't have time to deal with any of that. Carefully, she extracted herself from Faron's arms and reached up to brush the tears from her sister's cheeks. She gave Faron a quick recap of everything that had happened since the night in the boathouse: every secret she'd kept, every mistake she'd made, every treacherous word out of the Warwicks' mouths, until her sister's tears had stopped flowing and her face was reddening with anger instead.

"We can fix this, okay?" Elara promised. "But right now, dragons are attacking the island, and the queen is heading this way on Nobility. We need to clear a safe path for her to land."

"I can do that," said Faron. "I can at least do that."

Faron closed her eyes and took a deep breath, then let it out slowly. When her eyes reopened, they were glowing a strange amber color. Elara opened her mouth to ask what she was doing, but Faron lifted a hand toward the bay where Zephyra was still setting fire to boats, and Zephyra froze. Her flames sputtered to a stop, her body hovering in midair. Her head twisted from side to side, and then she flew toward them. Elara drew her conjured swords just in case, but Zephyra landed a few feet away without trying to attack. She lowered her body so Signey could slide down and then lowered it even farther until she was lying on the ground, as docile as a pet.

"Elara!" Signey said, checking her over for injury as soon as she was close enough to touch. "Are you all right? I'm sorry we—"

"Am *I* all right?" asked Elara. "Are *you* all right?"

"I'm fine. What just happened?"

"The power that Gael taught me isn't all bad." Though they were no longer bonded, Elara and Signey turned as one to face Faron. Her sister's smile was small, there and gone in an instant. "More important, I can control it now. I'm not sure if I can do it for all of them, but I...I owe it to everyone to try."

"I have no idea what you're talking about," said Signey, "but it's an honor to meet you, Empyrean. Uh, Miss Vincent."

Faron gave Signey an odd look before gripping Elara's shoulders. "Listen, I can't fix this mess. But *you* can. You need to go to the Port Sol Temple before they burn it down. You need to see if you can reach the gods now that you can summon again. Their power was the only thing that could open Lightbringer's cage, and I think they're the only ones who can still end this."

Elara hesitated. "I can't leave you here alone."

"I'll stay with her," said Signey. "Zephyra will, too. If we start to slip back into the Fury, she can pull us out. And my combat scores were just below yours, so she's in good hands."

There were a number of dead bodies at Rosetree Manor to

prove her point, so Elara didn't argue even though Faron was eyeing Signey suspiciously. Elara pressed a kiss to Signey's cheek, and it warmed under her lips. She tried not to linger on how cute that was, turning to face her sister's shock head-on.

"Take care of each other, okay?" Elara said. "I want this girl to live long enough for me to take her on a date."

"Right," Faron said.

"And my sister is the most important thing in the world to me," she told Signey, "so if anything happens to her, that date is canceled."

"Understood," Signey said, though she couldn't quite tamp down her shy smile.

Elara lingered, trying to memorize their faces. Faron's swinging braids and dark eyes and stained day dress. Signey's arched eyebrows and pointed nose and smooth skin. Even Zephyra's forest-green scales, massive gold eyes, and sharp talons. Three of the beings she loved most in the world, uniting in her honor. She wouldn't let them down.

With a final nod, she called on her aunt's power one last time to get her to Port Sol Temple.

CHAPTER THIRTY-EIGHT

FARON

So," Faron said. "How long have you and my sister been...?"

"I think there are more important things going on right now," said Signey Soto, her face darker than usual as she avoided Faron's eyes. Her accented patois was very formal, without a hint of slang, but somehow hers didn't sound as arrogant as Aveline's did. Maybe it was her shyness or her clear affection for Elara. Maybe Faron was feeling regret over the years she'd wasted resenting Reeve or the mistakes she'd made that led to this point. Either way, she found it hard to hate this girl. She'd brought her sister home safely when Faron hadn't been able to, after all.

"It's just a little weird," Faron continued, "that your ancestor is attacking my island, and you're...kissing my sister. I don't disapprove, mind you. It's just strange."

"Where *is* he?" Signey asked, glancing back toward Pearl Bay Palace. "Gael, I mean. I haven't...Is he...?"

Whatever Signey wanted to ask was drowned out by the sounds of battle. Over the water, Nobility's purple flank spun like a top as the drake rolled out of the way of multiple gusts of fire. Two dragons were doing their best to destroy it, and, while it was intact so far, Faron didn't like Aveline's odds. The other dragons were occupied with Mercy and Justice, the final two drakes that had arrived at last. All thoughts of Signey's personal crisis dissolved from her mind as Faron tried to figure out a plan. She couldn't fly Liberty alone, but the drakes needed help. . . .

"Zephyra and I need to get up there," Signey said. "But we'll do more harm than good if the Fury takes us again."

And that was when Faron realized what she had to do. There was a purpose to this power that she'd learned from a god who had used her as a pawn. A reason for the careless way she'd wielded it in Seaview.

"Let me help you," Faron said. "I have the power to command living souls. If you guys fly up there, I can send my soul with you. If you start to go feral again, I can order you to be calm. If—" Her throat closed as she thought of Roger and Jarell, the souls she'd controlled to save Reeve. "If you'll trust me, that is. It's a new power, and I'm still learning all the . . . the boundaries. I can't promise it will be as smooth as all that, but I *am* very familiar with your souls by now. And maybe that will make all the difference."

Signey stared at her. Then she said, "Elara trusts you, so I trust you. Do your best, and so will I."

Do your best. Faron held those words close as Signey strode back over to her dragon. Elara was the only person who had ever expected her to simply do her best. Everyone else expected her to succeed. To excel. To be the Childe Empyrean. But she had confessed her weakness to Signey, and her only request was that Faron *try.* There was a freedom in that trust that made Faron able to breathe again. No matter what happened, she could do that much. She could try her best.

Signey and Zephyra took off toward the fray. As soon as they flew past Lightbringer's line of sight, Faron felt the bright red edges of the Fury—of *his* Fury, she realized—trying to take over their minds.

Stay calm, she pressed into their souls. *Focus.*

They flew on, steady and in control. Zephyra attacked the red dragon that was attempting to set fire to Nobility's left wing, her teeth and claws aiming to hurt but not kill. These were still her friends, after all, and it wasn't their fault that Faron didn't have the time or the energy to help them, too. Faron tethered herself to Zephyra's soul, looking for any signs of violent danger, but her eyes followed Nobility as the drake tried to outfly the blue, yellow, and green dragons that remained behind it. *Come on, come on, come on.*

The three dragons went spiraling upward as one of the drakes shot blast after blast at their stomachs to knock them off course. Nobility flew onward, toward Pearl Bay Airfield. With Zephyra helping break the line of dragons, the other drake appeared to distract Lightbringer before he could knock the queen out of the sky. Still, Faron did not relax until Nobility sank out of view for a safe landing.

Winged war beasts filled the air, two drakes and Zephyra against four dragons and Lightbringer. The odds were abysmal, but they had survived worse odds before. Faron needed to believe that they would survive this, too.

"Empyrean."

Faron drew her soul back into her body just in time to see a furious Aveline marching toward her, trailed by Nobility's armed pilots. Her dress was a heavy golden brocade fabric that fell to her knees, matched by a gold head wrap and diadem. She was Irie's wrath made flesh, and Faron almost shivered at the sight of her.

"I'm sorry—"

"Shut up," said the queen. "I am so sick of people coming in and thinking they can take the island of my ancestors away from me. I am so sick of being looked at as a child playing at ruler, as weak or incompetent or nothing more than an accessory to you. I am *so sick* of *war* and of being unable to protect my people. It ends today. It ends *now*."

Power swirled around her, whipping the loose fabric of her head wrap. When Aveline drew on the power of her astrals, she drew on the power of Iryan queens. Faron had never asked if she got to see her mothers, to talk to them, when she was summoning, but Aveline was holding so much power that her dark eyes seemed to glow with tiny stars as she stormed past Faron and toward the castle. This was far more magic than she'd wielded the night of the Summit, far more magic than she'd wielded in the five years since the war. This was a warrior queen hungry for blood.

"GET OUT OF MY PALACE!" Aveline screamed.

Her magic lifted her into the air in a trail of sparks. Up and up and up, she went, until she collided with Lightbringer so hard that the dragon actually tumbled backward. Aveline's protective rage, her love for her island and her people, was more powerful than any Fury he could create. She threw her fist forward, and a golden dagger sank into the dragon's body. When Lightbringer cried out in pain, Faron could almost imagine the violent smile on Aveline's face.

In that instant, she felt like she understood the queen better than she ever had. She, too, was so sick of war, of being unable to protect the people who she cared about. And maybe that had led her down the wrong path, but it wasn't too late to make things right.

With Lightbringer distracted and the drakes handling the fight in the sky, Faron made her way back into the castle where the last remaining obstacle still hid.

CHAPTER THIRTY-NINE

ELARA

Port Sol Temple was under lockdown when Elara arrived. Santi streamed around the grounds like white-clad ghosts, channeling astral magic into a protective shield around the temple. One of the dragons, Alzina, was still stomping around the center of Port Sol, but the temple was a gorgeous landmark on the far side of the city, and it wouldn't be long before it caught her attention. Elara would have to get through to the gods before then.

If, of course, she could get inside.

A santi barred her way. She was a tall woman with a shaved head and a weary frown. "The temple is closed. Please evacuate the city. There are carts and coaches at—"

"My name is Elara Vincent," Elara said, "and I'm here on behalf of my sister, the Childe Empyrean. I need to pray to the gods now, or we're all doomed."

It was dramatic but effective. The woman not only moved out of her way but made it her personal mission to usher Elara to the nearest sunroom. Apparently, she had a painting of the Childe Empyrean in her room here at the temple. Elara tried to consider this sweet, even though the reminder that her sister was worshipped across the island never quite stopped being strange.

The sunroom was something she recognized in theory but hadn't seen for a very long time. This one was growing tomatoes and sweet peppers, the tiled floor replaced with tilled earth that held rows and rows of planted fruit. Sun shone through the glass panels, trapping Elara in a thick cloud of heat that made her sweat. She ignored the discomfort and closed her eyes, hoping that the gods were actually around to hear her.

Irie, Obie, Mala. San Irie needs you like we've never needed you before. My sister needs you, too. I'm praying to you for salvation. If you can hear me, please help me save my home. I'll do anything. Just—

"We've heard these words before," said a smoky female voice, "and we've since discovered that the person who said them didn't truly mean 'anything.'"

Elara opened her eyes with a gasp. A beautiful twelve-foot woman stood before her, more majestic than any mural or statue had been able to capture. Instead of the golden ball gown she was usually depicted in, Irie wore a high-necked white dress under a hoodless robe. Her skin was smooth, her lips painted a deep gold, her pupilless eyes a deeper gold to match. Her braids were decorated by a golden crown.

Elara dropped to her knees, pressing her forehead against the warm soil. "Irie. Blessed be!"

Warm hands touched her cheeks and tipped her head up until Elara had nowhere to look but at that divine face. Her eyes filled with tears. Irie. She couldn't believe it. Irie was *here*.

"Hello, Elara," said the sun goddess. "I am able to reach you because you share blood with the Empyrean. Thanks to Iya, she is lost to us, but we can still talk to you."

"We?"

To the left and to the right, two more giant figures appeared that Elara recognized from theology classes. Obie was a dark-skinned man in a milk-white suit with trousers that were embroidered with the phases of the moon. Over his shoulders was a matching robe, the hood pulled over his head so that only his jaw was visible. And Mala, wearing a pink ball gown with a ruffled skirt, had midnight curls loose around her head, crowned by a glowing halo of silver stars that twinkled as Elara stared at them. She was slightly shorter than both Obie and Irie, and she seemed younger somehow, but her presence was undeniable.

Somehow, Faron gazed upon this sight every day and didn't maintain her piety. Elara had been in front of them for less than a minute and she already wanted to cry.

"I," she managed. "I—Thank you. For coming. San Irie needs your help. If, in your infinite wisdom, you believe that this is the way our world should end, then I will try to accept that. But if you can share with me some way for us to win"—she lowered her gaze respectfully—"I'm here and I'm listening."

The gods were silent for so long that Elara risked looking up again. All three were considering her as if they had never seen a human before. A small smile was on Irie's face, though there was a melancholy to it that prevented Elara from smiling back.

"Before we can answer your plea, there is something you should know," Irie said. Her hands urged Elara back onto her feet. One remained on her cheek, brushing away the single tear that had fallen. "The divine realm is our home. It's home to the astrals.

But it's also home to godsbeasts. We, as gods, are the only ones who can survive the trip across realms for long periods of time without getting corrupted. Astrals must bond with summoners to maintain their form, let alone their minds. But godsbeasts...once they leave the divine realm, they become tainted. Feral." Irie let out a sigh that seemed to make the world tremble. "The dragon Lightbringer was the first godsbeast to travel across realms, and we sent the first Empyrean, who you now know as Iya, to banish him back. But Lightbringer thought to emulate the astrals by melding their souls together, creating the first bond between man and dragon. He twisted Iya's mind, and with all the power of the gods and a godsbeast, they were unstoppable. He and his followers, the generals who would band together to become the Langlish Empire, would have razed the earth if we hadn't sealed him away."

"How did you do that?" Elara asked with wide eyes. "If he was the Empyrean, how did you lock him in the Empty?"

"He was defeated the same way every tyrant is defeated: His own thirst for power exceeded his ability to cling to it," said Obie.

"His Four Generals tired of living under his thumb and sought to overthrow him," Mala said. "When Iya realized that he had been betrayed, he tried to relieve the generals of their dragons by opening a door between realms—to the Empty—to lock them into; instead, they joined forces to trap *him* there. And once he was no longer in the mortal realm, we were able to seal the door for what we thought would be forever."

"Until your sister set him free to save you," Irie finished. "We tell you this now, Elara Vincent, because the threat that Iya poses to this world cannot be overstated. All dragons were brought here by Lightbringer, the bond was created by Gael Soto, and thus all dragons and Riders answer to them, to Iya, whether they want to or not. Only an Empyrean can lock them back in the Empty." Her mouth twisted in sympathy. "Your sister has bonded with them, and so they have some control over her, too. She is lost to us. If we lend you our power, you *must* succeed where Faron has failed. You must defeat Lightbringer. You must imprison Iya. And, if necessary, you must kill your sister."

Elara tried to arrange these words into an order that made sense, an order that didn't mean she would have her sister's blood on her hands. But they hung between her and the gods like a death knell.

"No," Elara said when she could speak again. "*No.* How can you even ask that of me? If being the Empyrean means *killing my sister*, then I don't want to be the Empyrean!"

Irie made a frustrated sound. "You truly are related to her. The fate of the world is at stake, and all you can think about is each other?"

Elara reared back in horror. Suddenly, the gods no longer looked divine and majestic. Instead, they were all-powerful giants who could end her without a second thought. "Did you try to get her to kill *me*?"

"You are both powerful. You have both been touched by gods. Iya could take control of either one of you—he did, in fact, take control of one of you. This isn't about you or your relationship. The world will end if you don't—"

"I'm not hurting her," Elara said. "I won't *ever* hurt my sister. There has to be another way."

Silence followed her declaration, but Elara refused to be cowed into submission. Not about this. Faron was trapped in the palace now, hurting and terrified, trusting Elara to do what she was no longer able to. They had both made a mess of things, but neither of them deserved to die for that.

And neither of them deserved to be the one to bring about that death.

They were stronger together. They would save this world together. And if the gods refused to see that, then Elara suddenly understood how they'd lost not one, but *two* Empyreans.

"All right," Irie said. "All right, I...understand. Iya is a problem that has been plaguing us for longer than you have been alive. We're determined that his next defeat be his final one, no matter the cost. But we must respect that, for you, the cost is too high."

"The cost would be too high for *anyone*. Being the Empyrean sounds like a losing game," Elara pointed out. "You named Faron your Empyrean, and she went to war for you. Now you want her dead. Your first Empyrean was corrupted by a creature that you sent him to battle against. Then you locked him up for centuries. I'm sorry, but that's...that's *awful*. That's not the Irie I was raised to worship."

Irie's lips thinned. "The goddess you worship is a sanitized version of me, invented by devotees who need to believe in ultimate good and ultimate evil. There are gray areas."

"Doesn't that mean that Iya should have a gray area, too? If yours is *murder*."

"His gray area," Mala said, "is his love for your sister."

For the second time, Elara froze. "His...his what?"

"His incarnation, Reeve Warwick, is in love with your sister. Even though Iya wears his face now, he still feels that love because their souls are now intertwined," Mala explained. "He's keeping her from us in the hopes that he can turn her to his side. That is why we said you might have to kill her."

Elara frowned. "Faron would never join up with him."

"They are connected," Irie said, holding up her hands in a placating gesture. "That's all we're trying to say. Whether she realizes it or not, whether you accept it or not, they were able to bond because their souls are made of the same celestial material. At this point, she will either save him or he will damn her. And it's too soon to tell which it will be."

"Faron," Elara repeated. "Would. Never."

Elara knew her sister better than anyone—even the goddess who had created her world. Irie didn't know Faron. She didn't know Faron's *heart*. But Elara did.

"Make me your next Empyrean," she said. "I won't kill her, but I know I can help her. I'll save her if I have to. If what you say is true, I'm the only one who can."

Irie said nothing, but her gaze turned thoughtful. "The decision to become the Empyrean is not one to be made lightly. Your sister was very young when she made the choice, and she has resented us for it ever since. It is not, as she thought, a one and done. If your world is threatened again, you must rise to meet it."

"I'm eighteen years old. That makes me an adult on my island. I'm doing this first and foremost for my sister, but...it was my dream to join the Sky Battalion. To defend San Irie whenever war came to our shores. That wasn't a decision I made lightly, and neither is this."

A pleased expression flashed across the goddess's face, but then it melted into a more wistful one. "You sound so much like she did back then. The two of you..." Irie placed a warm hand on Elara's shoulder and squeezed gently. "Words cannot express how sorry I am."

Sorry about what? Elara wanted to ask, but found she couldn't speak. Irie's hand had gone from warm to blazing hot, the fire cutting through Elara's body until she couldn't do anything but scream. Her throat ached by the time the pain faded. She was still in the sunroom, Irie, Mala, and Obie standing in a line before her. All three of them were smiling as Elara fought to catch her breath.

"Hello, Childe Empyrean," Mala said, sticking out a hand.

Elara took it, her entire body shaking. "No. My sister was the Childe Empyrean. She's no longer a child, and neither am I."

"Maiden?" Irie suggested.

"The Maiden Empyrean," Elara echoed, loving the feel of the words on her tongue. The sound of her new title seemed to quell her trembles, her strength returning all at once. She felt determination pulsing through her blood as she smiled at the gods. "Thank you. Now, please...Lend me your power, and let me show you what I can do."

CHAPTER FORTY

FARON

F ARON FOUND IYA IN THE THRONE ROOM THIS TIME, SITTING IN THE queen's chair.

It was carved to look as if he were cradled by fire, scarlet and gold wound together into arcs of flame that stretched toward the sky. But Iya sat on the throne as if it were nothing more than a fancy stool rather than the symbol of a nation. He had one leg thrown over an arm, his chin propped up on one hand so he could watch her lazily as she approached. At some point, he had partially shed his military jacket. A white button-down was revealed while the jacket sat across his shoulders like a cape of shadows.

"I remember it, you know," he said idly. "The time when I was like you. Chosen. Gifted. Beloved. I was a Knight of the Empire, yes, but I prayed for the power to stop the dragon terrorizing my home. And, like you, the gods answered my prayers. I became the first Empyrean."

Faron stopped in the middle of the room. "What?"

Iya's mouth tipped into a cruel smile, but the words continued to flow as if he needed someone, needed her, to hear them. "Did they not mention that, either? I was not merely the first dragon

Rider, and you were never their first champion. That was me. All I wanted was to protect my home. But Lightbringer showed me the truth the gods had kept hidden from me. I didn't have to listen to them. They wanted to use me as a tool while keeping me from reaching my true power. Together, Lightbringer and I became Iya. Together, I tasted that power, if only for a while. And now that I'm free, I am so very loath to give it up."

"Gael," she said, hoping what was left of that boy could hear her. "Gael, you were a Knight of the Empire. That means you wanted to help people, right? But look at you now. All you've ever done with your incredible power is subjugate others. Power like this . . . It should be used to make the world better."

"Oh?" Iya shifted in the chair so that both feet were on the floor. "And how have you made the world better since the war ended, Faron?"

"That's not—" Faron began before the words caught in her throat.

Everyone talks about you like you're a saint . . . but all I see is a spoiled, selfish child who wastes all her potential, blaming everyone else for her problems.

We've seen this level of arrogance only once before. It is tragic, how much you sound like the Gray Saint.

You brought me into this, and now we're both trapped.

Her lips trembled. "At least I can admit my mistakes. At least I've tried to do good. *You've* only done wrong. You've become a monster like the one you were sent to stop, Gael, and now you're the one who needs to be stopped."

Iya sat back as if she had disappointed him. "Take your pointless moralizing to someone who wants to listen to it."

"Reeve would listen," she whispered, ascending the dais on which the throne was kept. "He loved to know things. He—"

"He's *dead*. Why do you keep bringing him up?"

"Because he's *not* dead. I felt him there, inside you." Faron reached out, her hand covering his heart. She felt the hard mound of Reeve's dragon relic hanging there. Even now, after taking his body and changing his clothes, Iya hadn't gotten rid of it. "I felt his soul, mixed with yours. He's not dead. He's just trapped. Lost, like you. You're both lost, but I can still see you. Stop all this and let me help you. *Please*."

Iya reached up, and wrapped his fingers gently around her wrist. Reeve's eyes gazed up at her, the blue of the water that she loved so much, and she wondered how she hadn't seen it before. Her fondness for him pressed against her rib cage, as if her heart longed to jump from her chest to his for safekeeping. With her free hand, she traced the curve of his cheek, trying to will him to take control of his body again. *"I know you're in there,"* she sent across the bond. *"I know you're fighting. Come back to me. Come back to us."*

He leaned into her touch, and Faron could almost pretend that she had been heard.

Then Iya's fingers tightened around her wrist hard enough to bruise. "Reeve Warwick is weak. Gael Soto is weaker. Whatever you hope to achieve, you will fail. And this world *will* fall to me."

He shoved her backward. Faron barely managed to catch herself before she fell down the stairs, her heart racing and breaking all at once. She'd been *so close*, but Iya's face was cold again as he swept down the stairs.

"This ends now," she heard as his boots thumped across the throne room floor. Even his voice was icy and dismissive, as if he had reached the limits of his patience with her. "Stay here unless you want to die with them."

The doors slammed shut behind him with a harsh finality that sounded like another warning. But Faron had never met trouble that she didn't want to get into. She waited exactly one minute before running after him.

Aveline Renard Castell, the blessed queen of San Irie, was a golden streak across the sky, colliding with Lightbringer again and again.

She had driven the imperial dragon away from Pearl Bay Palace and over the open ocean, and she was doing more to hurt him than the drakes were. Even Signey and Zephyra had joined in, Faron noticed, zipping around Lightbringer's body in a blur of green, scratching, biting, and blasting flames into his open wounds. Lightbringer was no longer pure white; he was streaked with scorch marks and blood trails.

He was losing.

Iya's shoulders were a tense line as he strode through the Victory Garden. The dragons had stopped fighting the drakes and were now helping them put out the fires and attack Lightbringer. Port Sol was covered in smoke rather than lit by flames, and Port Sol Temple stood unharmed over it all, glowing with protection magic. Elara had yet to reappear, but the tide of the battle had definitely turned.

Faron threw herself at Iya before he could take another step.

They hit the grass in a tangle of limbs. Iya was a trained soldier, but Faron had caught him by surprise. She also had a lifetime of schoolyard tussles under her belt. She dug her knee into his back, dragging one of his arms around until she heard his shoulder pop. "Do you remember when we met here?" she leaned down to whisper in his ear. "You told me to *take control*." Her knee pressed farther into his spine. "You said you were my salvation, but I think the truth is that I'm *yours*."

"This is your idea of salvation?" Iya grunted, though he made no move to break her hold. She felt the shiver that ran through his body and reveled in it.

"Lightbringer is going to die if this continues. You don't have to die with him. Let Reeve go, and I'll help you."

"We'll *both* die with him."

"I have a feeling you'll take that harder than I will. Let. Reeve. Go."

Iya turned his head just enough to glare at her. "I told you—"

"You've told me a lot of things. Not all of them were true." Faron leaned so close now that her lips brushed his ear with every word. "Listen to what I'm telling you: This world isn't yours to rule. Do you want to spend the rest of the days of your freedom fighting to retain it, or do you want to taste what freedom really is?"

Faron's back hit the ground as soon as the last word was out. She hadn't even seen Iya move, but suddenly he was pinning her down, straddling her legs so she couldn't kick him off. One hand pinned her arms above her head, tight as shackles. The other gripped her throat but didn't press. Not yet. "*What do you know of freedom? You live under the thumb of your parents, your gods, your queen, your country. You have never been free, Faron. Not until you met me.*"

His words whispered through her mind, settling into her blood. His eyes were dark pools as they stared into hers, his face hovering mere inches away.

"You are nothing without me," he said aloud.

"You'd be nothing without *me*," Faron snapped back, light sparking at the corner of her eyes. "And you may be stronger than me, but I still have powers you never will."

Iya chuckled, his thumb digging against her throat, making it hard to breathe. "Every power you had is one I perfected before you were ever born. Every power you still have is one I taught you. I am everything you could be, Faron, and you are nothing more than the heart I can't seem to destroy." Faron choked as the rest of his fingers tightened. "Do not fool yourself into thinking I won't try."

"Try this," said Elara, blasting Iya across the garden with a wave of divine magic.

Faron sucked air back into her lungs with a gasp, rolling onto her feet and stumbling over to her sister. Elara was glowing lightly, her fraying braids waving in a breeze only she could feel, and Faron knew without having to ask that she was channeling a god. She would have recognized that light anywhere, even if she couldn't tell which god in particular had given Elara's skin that unnatural glow. She reached up to rub her throat, where she could feel bruises in the shape of Iya's fingertips already forming, and scanned the garden for any sign of him.

She saw fire before she saw Iya.

He burned through a line of falling trees. Elara and Faron leaped in different directions to avoid them. Faron stopped short as Iya appeared in front of her. Fire danced between his fingers, curved around his hands and up his forearm.

"You were a distraction," he growled. "How clever."

"Fuck off," said Faron, throwing a punch.

He blocked her easily, but she threw another and another. His flames didn't burn her. Instead, they enclosed her wrists, as well, like a string that tied them together. He caught her fist and yanked her up against his chest before whirling her to face her sister and hooking an arm around her neck.

"I know you won't hurt her," he called across the garden. "So how about we settle this like civilized people?"

"You mean like cowards?" Elara asked, landing before them. Her Langlish clothing must have been fireproof, because Faron couldn't see so much as a scorch mark on her. Faron coughed, choking on the smoke that covered the garden as the fires spread. But no matter how hard she struggled, Iya's arms were like steel, and she couldn't break free. "Let her go and release her from her bond with you. Or I'll lock you up in the Empty where you belong."

"You'd lock Reeve up in the Empty? Your sister?" Iya scoffed. "Somehow, I don't believe you."

Elara stretched out a hand. Her eyes glowed. Faron felt something brush against her feet, but she couldn't look down to see what it was. Iya's curse was the only warning she got before they sank inches into the ground. Somewhere above, she heard a dragon screech, a guttural sound that went deeper than pain.

It was fear.

"Let her go now," Elara repeated, and her voice sounded like it was coming from all sides. "I am the Maiden Empyrean. I walk with the power and the blessings of the gods. I can save my sister and Reeve from the Empty and leave you there. Don't fool yourself into thinking I can't."

"Please," he said, and he sounded so much like Reeve again that Faron stopped struggling against him. "Don't lock me in there with him. Don't trap me in that place again. *Please.*"

Elara faltered, too. Whatever was dragging them down into the earth stopped, and the glow in Elara's eyes started to fade. For all her threats, Faron knew her sister. The last thing she wanted was to lock away Faron and Reeve just to stop Iya. It would save San Irie, but it would break her. Faron couldn't let her make that choice.

She'd ruined so much. She'd hurt so many people, even the one she'd wanted to save. She didn't want to be that person anymore.

"Leave her alone," Faron begged. "I know what you're doing, and you need to stop. I'll do anything."

"Anything?" Iya's word caressed her ear. "Come with me, then."

Before she could ask where, a strong gust of wind threw Elara off her feet. Iya and Faron were unaffected, so she wasn't surprised to look up and see Lightbringer hovering over them. The god who was once a boy released her and jumped, higher than any normal person could, landing easily on the back of his dragon. Then Lightbringer lowered his body just enough for Faron to see that Iya was reaching out a hand for her.

"Come with me."

Faron's heart clenched. She didn't hear Iya, the god of a dying world, in those words. She heard Gael Soto, the knight of the realm whose mind had been broken by the creature he'd tried to kill. She heard Reeve Warwick, the boy who had turned his back on his country to save her own. She heard two teens whose lives had been ruined by power they should never have wielded, and she felt so sad for them that she couldn't even speak.

"Faron!" Elara was back on her feet and racing toward her. "Faron, get out of the way!"

"Faron." Above her, Iya's upturned palm beckoned. "It's time to go."

She stood paralyzed, crying softly as Elara ran across the garden. Crying because Elara would not reach them in time. Crying because they would be separated again, and this time, it was her choice.

But San Irie had a new saint, a better saint. Faron had done nothing but cause everyone pain, and now two lives were in her hands. Despite everything that had happened, she and Iya had a bond, and not just the bond between them and Lightbringer. She understood him, and he trusted her. There was only one way to stop an enemy who wore the face of a friend, and locking him away was not the answer.

She looked at that face, at Reeve's face, and saw the potential of what could have been if she hadn't been so stubborn, if she'd been more self-aware, if the timing had been right. But she looked in those eyes, Gael's eyes, and saw a boy who had doomed the world trying to do the right thing. Perhaps he was the only person in the world who understood what she was going through. If she could save them both, maybe she could redeem herself. Lightbringer had to have a weakness. Faron could find it, trick it out.

She'd been a liar longer than she'd been a saint, after all.

Faron jumped, Iya's hand catching hers before she could fall. He swung her onto the dragon behind him, and then they took off. She made the mistake of finding her sister in the sea of grass and flowers, hoping that Elara would understand why she was doing this. Hoping that Elara would trust her, even though she hadn't earned it lately.

Instead, all Faron saw on Elara's face was open heartbreak before the clouds swallowed them up.

ACKNOWLEDGMENTS

First, I want to thank my best friend, Lauren. You were the first person to read my writing and encourage me to keep at it, and you stuck with me through so many unfinished projects to get to the publication of this book. I am living my dream because of you, and I don't care how hard you deny it.

Second, I'd like to thank my agent, Emily Forney. Your unwavering belief in this story is nothing compared to your unwavering belief in me as a writer, and I have leveled up so much with your guidance and support. I could write a whole book on how much I love you, but lucky for you, I have other people to thank.

Thank you to my LBYR team: Alexandra Hightower and Crystal Castro for your phenomenal editorial insight; Lindsay Walter-Greaney and Brandy Colbert for copyedits that showed a keen understanding of and respect for my story; Tara Rayers for being the kindest proofreader I could have ever hoped to have; Taj Francis and Jenny Kimura for the cover of my *dreams*; Patricia Alvarado (Production), Bill Grace and Andie Divelbiss (Marketing), Savannah Kennelly (Digital Marketing), Cassie Malmo and Hannah Klein (Publicity), and Victoria Stapleton and Christie Michel (School & Library). It takes a village, and I'm so grateful for mine.

Thank you to my support system: my cat, Sora; my little sister, Dashá; my cousin, Abigail; my uncle Aaron; the rest of my family; and my best friends Brittany Pittman, Chelsea Abdullah, Tashie

Bhuiyan, Suzanne Samin, Emma Lord, Jen Carnelian, and Zachary Longstreet. Thank you to my unofficial marketing team and occasional book club: Ebony LaDelle, Jane Lee, and Tyler Breitfeller. Jane, I know this isn't a paragraph, but I hope you'll forgive me if you get a solo one in the next book.

Thank you to my group chats: the BBLU (Joelle Thérèse, Ysabelle Suarez, Mel Karibian, Maddie Martinez, and Chelsea Abdullah again, because you are my light) for lifting me up and talking me off the ledge; the Finer Things Club (ended but never forgotten; thank you for the character name T-shirt that I still wear all the time!); and Writers Against Imperialism (Alaa Al-Barkawi, Arzu Bayraktar, Ryan Ram, Amani Salahudeen, Ale Massenbürg, Audris Candra, Nadirah Ashim, Marwa Sarraj, and our honorary members, Mr. Meow and Baby Ale).

Thank you to the people who were kind to me along the way: Tiffany Shelton for helping me with my #PitMad tweets; Victoria Marini and Jennifer Azantian for believing in me before anyone else did; Bethany C. Morrow for the agent-decision call of a lifetime; Terry J. Benton-Walker and Lauren Blackwood for the instant camaraderie and hopefully lifelong friendship; Namina Forna, Deborah Falaye, and Ayana Gray for your compassion and good vibes; Chloe Gong and Christina Li for always roasting me when I cancel plans; Sophie Kim, Nadia Noor, E. M. Anderson, Kelly Andrew, Ashia Monet, Grace Varley, Safa Ahmed, Victoria Alexis, Pascale Lacelle, Lexi, Betty Hawk, M. J. Kuhn, and David Valdes— you all make me believe in writing again.

Thank you to Law Roach and Zendaya for the Joan of Arc outfit from the 2018 Met Gala that inspired this story.

Thank you to anyone whose name I forgot. I'm sorry, I suck, forgive me.

Thank you to myself for finishing this one. It took you long enough.

Finally, thank you, Reader, for picking up a copy of my book. I'm only able to do what I do because of you, and I appreciate every second you spent between these pages.

Lauren Banner

KAMILAH COLE

is a Jamaican American author who answers only to her evil overlord, a cat named Sora. *So Let Them Burn* is her debut novel. She invites you to connect with her at kamilah-cole.com or @wordsiren on Twitter.